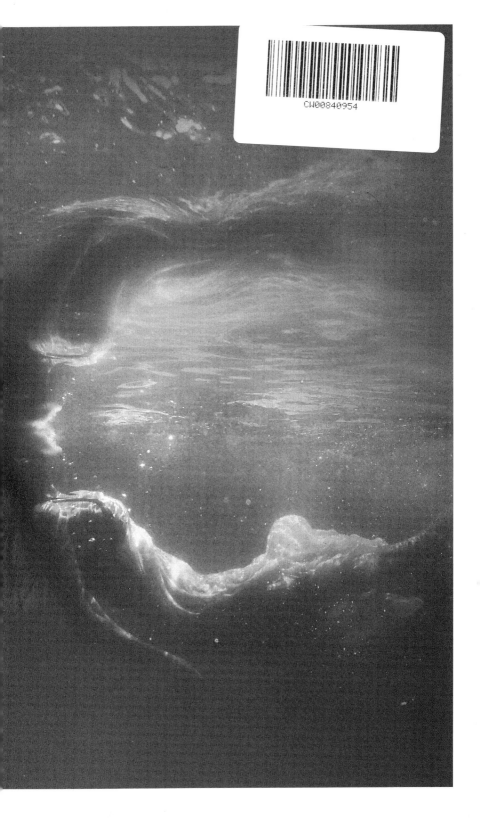

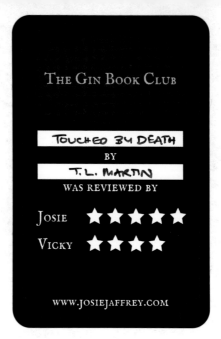

THE GIN BOOK CLUB

TOUCHED BY DEATH
BY
T. L. MARTIN
WAS REVIEWED BY

JOSIE ★★★★★
VICKY ★★★★

WWW.JOSIEJAFFREY.COM

TOUCHED BY DEATH
Published by DeLarm Press
Copyright © 2017 by T. L. Martin
officialtlmartin.com

This is a work of fiction. Names, characters, places and incidents are either the product of the author's imagination or are used fictitiously, and any resemblance to actual persons, living or dead, business establishments, events or locales is entirely coincidental.

Manufactured in the United States of America
10 9 8 7 6 5 4 3 2 1

Cover Design and Interior Format

© KILLION GROUP, INC.

TOUCHED BY
DEATH

T.L. MARTIN

Chapter One

ROMEO AND JULIET THEMSELVES COULDN'T have cast Mom and Dad better if they tried. In fact, if they'd ever had the chance to meet, my parents as a young couple splayed out on their high school stage would have been pretty tight-knit with Shakespeare's tragic duo. I can envision their first conversation perfectly:

Talli and Steve: Ah, yes. Poison, you say?
Romeo and Juliet: Poison, yes, yes. And a dagger, too, if you can spare one?
Talli and Steve: In the name of love? Of course!
Romeo and Juliet: So kind, thank you. Perhaps the two of you might consider playing us on stage in the twentieth century?
Talli and Steve: Why, we'd be honored! Even better, we may just try to outdo you two in our time!
Romeo and Juliet: Hahaha, how swell!

I shake my head, knuckles whitening as my grip tightens on the picture. The pair of them had set the stage all right, Mom and Dad. Even in a decades-old photograph, their love bleeds through as they lay tangled in each other's arms.

"Dammit, Lou," Bobby barks, snapping me from my thoughts. My gaze trails to the weathered porch where he's locking up the front door for me. I can hear it in his voice, the way his frustration is getting the better of him. Originally from Fort Worth, Texas, Bobby already has a heavy southern accent, but when he's irritated it comes out extra thick. "You can't keep ignorin' me. Won't you just stop and be rational about this for a second?"

I don't pause to look back at him as I carefully slide the picture into my back pocket. I grab the final duffel bag from beside my feet, then cram it into the bed of my packed Toyota Tacoma before fitting a blue tarp from one end to the other.

"I'm not doing this again, Bobby." I can't have this conversation right now, not while I'm such an emotional wreck.

God. Just being at the house, seeing Grams's small vegetable garden and getting a distant glimpse of the park I used to walk her to every morning . . . A fresh, deep ache settles in my chest, cozying up in a way that tells me it'll be there for a while. There's a lot more to see in Los Angeles than a beaten down park, but that didn't stop it from being one of Grams's favorite spots.

I suppress a groan at the memories bombarding me. Doesn't Bobby know how hard this is already? How I've almost talked myself out of it time and time again? Six whole months since I broke things off with him, and today of all days is when he decides he wants to talk?

"Lou . . ." The porch steps creak as he trudges down them. With a reluctant sigh, I finally look at him. It isn't until then, as I watch him drag his feet along the concrete driveway, his eyes cast downward and arms dangling hopelessly at his sides, that I begin to realize just how hard this move might be hitting him.

It doesn't matter that it's not his house I'm leaving, that he never could convince me to leave Grams behind and move in with him. To Bobby, seeing me walk away from this place is more of a goodbye than when I'd walked away from our relationship.

It's not that Bobby is a bad guy. In fact, he's one of the good ones underneath it all. When we first got together, he was the star of the basketball team, on his way to a full scholarship before he blew out a knee senior year. I couldn't care less about the basketball thing, it wasn't the game that drew me to him. We'd slipped into an easy friendship the same week he'd moved here, and eventually one thing led to another. What can I say? He was new and friendless, and the loner inside of me was drawn to it. Of course, the charming, goofy side of him didn't hurt, either.

But five years is a long time. Things, like people, change. We aren't in high school anymore, and I waited long enough for him to stop staring down the bottom of a beer bottle or at the TV screen.

He approaches me, his hat a little too snug above the newly formed creases between his eyebrows. "She left you the house for a reason, Lou. Maybe your grams wanted—" I cut him off with a warning glare, and he quickly changes tactic. "Look. I just . . . I don't know when—*if* I'm ever gonna see you again. And I have some things I need to say before you go." He scratches the unshaven scruff on his chin with his thumb.

I know it isn't easy for him, trying to open up like this.

What I want more than anything is to crank the engine and slam on the gas pedal, but instead, I'm patient. Leaning my left hip against the vehicle, hands tucked into the front pockets of my jeans, I listen.

"I get it, all right? I wasn't the best boyfriend in the world toward the end there." I cock an eyebrow. *Come on, Bobby. You can do better than that.* "I fucked up, didn't always treat you like I should've. But sometimes . . . well, sometimes it takes losing someone to appreciate what you really had"—I snort. He ignores it—"I'm nothin' without you. I should've begged you to come back to me then, the second you walked away, but I'm here now. And I . . . shit,

I need you, Lou."

There it is. *He's* nothing without me. *He* needs me. What about what *I* need?

"This move isn't about you, Bobby," I mutter. He's so far out of the story he's clear across the library, as far as I'm concerned. My right sandal taps on the concrete, revealing the irritation I'm struggling to hide from my voice. "I just—I have to get out of here. This house . . ." I swallow, the pain swelling behind my eyes again. "I can't stay."

"So you move to Ventura. Santa Monica. Whatever. I'd understand that. But not clear across the damn country."

"I never said I was going across the country. I—I don't know—"

"Exactly. You don't even know what you want," he interrupts, kicking his voice up a notch. He starts pacing, lingering around my truck. I can smell the cheap beer on him now; it seeps off his skin, mixing with cigarette smoke, the habit he must have picked back up again since the last time I saw him.

"I know what I want," I say. And it's true. Kind of. I bounce my hip off the truck and maneuver my way to the driver's seat, yanking the door open and climbing inside without a second thought.

My throat is thick, the nostalgia heavy in my chest. Grams is gone; her home is all I have left, and even though I know I have to leave, it isn't easy.

"No," Bobby says, his voice muffled by the cracked window. "What you're doin' is runnin' away."

Trying to save face, I roll my eyes and start the engine.

"So what?" I exclaim. I hate that tears are forming, threatening to spill over my bottom lashes. I just want to stay angry. Anger is so much easier than grief. "What's so wrong with running away? Grams is dead. Mom's *been* dead. And Dad made sure he wasn't too far behind her." The engine's low hum is already beginning to soothe me, a subtle reminder of how close I am to getting away from my cursed life. "I'm so over it."

Things are never as simple as we make them out to be. An uneasy, cold feeling snakes up my skin at knowing my entire life is packed neatly into the back of my truck. Here I am, leaving behind the only home I've known, about to come face to face with the unknown, and every second that passes only expands the vulnerability building inside me.

I brush the back of my hand under my eye, catching a tear before it falls, and shoot a final glance at Bobby. His hands are shoved into the pockets of his worn jeans, shoulders hunched forward, eyes still pleading with me. The truth is, it's not just me who's dodging a bullet here. We both are. One day, he's going to get himself cleaned up. One day, he'll remember who he used to be. And that guy, he deserves to be with someone whose whole heart burns for him. Unfortunately, that person isn't me.

"Goodbye, Bobby."

Bobby says nothing as he watches me shift the pickup into reverse and back out of the driveway. His frame is still fixed in my rearview mirror as I drive farther and farther away, but it isn't him I'm looking at. It's the faded blue shutters, the rectangular window beside the porch I'll always remember looking out of, and, lastly, the 'For Sale' sign propped up in the front yard.

Home.

From the corner of my eye, I watch the faded white house until it's small enough to fit into my pocket, and still as it shrinks into a tiny speck behind darkening grey clouds and dim streetlamps. I watch it until it disappears completely, imagining the shutters bright and blue, with Grams sitting at the breakfast nook at the other end of that window, waving me farewell with one wrinkled hand and sipping the cup of tea in the other.

I hardly notice the tears as they slide down my cheeks, though I taste the saltiness between my lips.

"Goodbye, Grams," I whisper.

ONE HOTEL STAY AND WAY too much caffeine later, heavy rain pelts my windshield, giving my worn wipers hardly a fighting chance. I narrow my eyes at the dark skies. Of course I've driven straight into a storm. How poetic. My thumb taps the steering wheel as my mind races. I still haven't fully convinced myself I'm really doing this. A single destination looms in the back of my mind, and I know nothing of the place except that it's the town Grams was born and raised in. Mom was born there too, but she was still a young girl when Grams uprooted their lives to LA.

I keep my foot on the gas and my vehicle heading east.

I know Bobby's right. I am running away. I'm also being irrational and spontaneous—two words I'd never have associated myself with just two weeks ago. Is it really so wrong of me, though?

I have no ties.

No family.

No goals.

Hmph. I give my head a shake.

I never thought I'd wind up like this, twenty-two years old and still no concept of what I'm doing with my life. All my friends have gone off to college, pursued a career in the industry, or gotten married and started families of their own. Even Jamie—my free-spirited, party-till-you-drop, I'm-never-settling-down-for-anyone lifelong friend—just had baby number two last spring. She still refuses to get legally married because, in her words, no piece of paper is going to tell people how much she loves Daniel, but they're as good as hitched.

Bobby and I never even talked about marriage. He brought it up once while completely wasted on his twentieth birthday, but it's easy to brush something like that off when you know he won't even remember it the next day. Fine by me—just because my legs are a little longer now and he can finally grow a full beard doesn't mean we aren't still kids, underneath it all.

Besides, I always had Grams to take care of. Cooking her meals, taking her out daily to stretch her joints, helping her bathe and dress. My kind of life is the simple kind—or it was—but I didn't mind. Not when she sacrificed so much to raise me on her own. It felt good to return the favor, being the one to look after her for a change. Even if she did argue with me about it and insist I deserved more, that was just Grams, always thinking of everyone else.

A burst of lightning reflects in my side mirror before striking the ground loud enough to make my fingers dig into the steering wheel. Pools of water flood the long, narrow bridge I've just veered onto, and I let off the gas to prevent hydroplaning.

The permeating sounds are nothing new to me; Grams and I sat beneath plenty of storms while relaxing to old movies and sipping hot cocoa by the fireplace. I swallow, my lungs tightening as seeds of doubt seep into my mind. I don't have a clue what I'm doing. Bobby may be Bobby, but at least he was safe. Familiar. I wasn't alone. Right now, with the howling winds tugging against the body of my truck and the cackling thunder only growing with each turn of my tires, I have never felt so aware of how alone and lost I really am in this vast, empty shell of a world.

I barely recognize it when it strikes—white and blue streaks of lightning shoot down from the sky, hitting an enormous tree at the opposite end of the bridge. The ear-splitting *crack* reverberates throughout my head. Eyes squeezing shut from the pain, my foot slams on the brake and my left hand reaches up to block one ear.

That's all it takes for the truck to spin out.

My eyes snap toward the window, breath hitching in my chest as my surroundings blur into obscure clouds of darkness.

A collision against the parapet slams my head back into the seat. With a *smash* and a *crack*, the windshield shatters. Pain shoots through my left shoulder; the vague sensation of warm blood trickles down my skin. My stomach burns as the seatbelt tightens around me, pulling all of my focus to the truck's sudden halt. I'm frozen, vehicle midair, staring straight at the sky with my back pressed against the seat. As the truck teeters in place, a terrifying creak filling my eardrums, I know.

I'm halfway off the bridge.

Hair whips around my face as the whirling wind pours into the broken window. Rain smacks against my skin. *Dammit, Lou. Think!* My phone, I need to call for help. Ever so slowly, I unbuckle my seatbelt. I know the rules of the situation I'm in. Seen it enough in the movies: move, vehicle slips, fall to your death. Inhaling a shaky breath, I turn toward the passenger seat. The phone's silver casing glints against the leather. *Just . . . a little . . . further . . .*

CREAK.

Freeze. *Shit. Shit, shit, shit.* There's some kind of lake below; I'd glimpsed enough of it earlier to know it's enormous. A fresh sliver of terror slides up my spine, climbing into my throat and squeezing my insides as I try to stop shaking enough to form a cohesive thought.

Then I drop.

A scream escapes my throat, disappearing in the harsh wind. I lean my upper body out of the shattered window just before my skin slaps against the chilling waters. The storm has the lake in a howling frenzy, and my truck is yanked away from me.

I choke back another wave of terror, kicking hard and throwing my head back to keep my mouth above the surface.

The water's push and pull is stronger than I'd anticipated, too strong, sucking me down and sending my body every direction but up. Lungs closing, I force my mouth open for air, but only icy water fills my throat. I swing my arms and push my legs to get my head back to the surface. Just a foot or so away from my face now, I can see it—even skimming the fresh air with the tips of my fingers a few times. *Air.* I need air. The ache in my lungs is stretching into a fiery burn.

The thunder drifts, distancing itself as I sink farther and farther, watching the bubbles from my last breath rise. My body convulses, each constriction of my lungs mocking me.

The burning dissolves, and soon all feeling abandons my body. I plummet into a world of darkness.

Chapter Two

DARK EYES. DARK HAIR.
It's a shadow. No, a man. An angel?

It's coming closer, floating, steadily closing the gap of blue-black water between us. The silhouette becomes clearer, revealing the definite form of a man. The edges of his large frame are blurred, almost convincing enough to be a dream. Still, I know the truth.

I'm dying . . . if I'm not already dead.

I can feel my life wasting away with each second, disconnecting me from my frozen heart. Something's tugging at me, calling my name. A magnetic force trying to yank me away from my body.

The closer he gets, the stronger the pull.

I don't know why I fight it—after everything I've lost, everyone who's already left and won't be waiting for me to come back. Still, I tug, twist, and writhe, struggling to free myself from the mental hold he has over me.

He's too strong; I'm a tiny puff of smoke going up against a wall of stone. Though hardness masks the man himself, there's a vibrating warmth in his pull. The invisible thread roping me toward him may as well be made of sunlight. It's a sweet, sugary sensation, reminding me of the comforting caress I used to feel as a child, when Grams would tuck me in and stroke my hair.

I want to be wrapped up inside it and coddled, lulled into a blissful sleep.

He's here, right in front of me, heat radiating from his body to mine. His eyes—cloudy pools of grey and black—finally meet mine. I don't care that the irises are cold, empty. There's something enchanting on the outskirts that beckons me.

And I know I will follow him anywhere.

Until out of nowhere, something shifts; I can feel it in his withering hold on me. I can see it in his eyes, tinges of green sparking behind the grey, and he pulls back, away from me. It's only an inch or two, but it hurts. I need to be close to him, whoever he is. I'm supposed to go with him.

Why does he pull away?

He snaps his gaze from mine and gives his head a small shake. His approach halts. I'm hanging at the tip of his invisible thread, desperate for the wall he's putting up to shatter so I can climb over and join him. It's inexplicable, this sudden force drawing me to him, yet I can't fight it. Don't want to fight it.

Finally, he brings his gaze back to mine, and I notice the green in his eyes has almost overtaken the grey. My stare is fixed, nothing can make me look away. He's closing the space between us again, parts of him as hazy as a distant dream while other parts are vivid. When his lips touch mine, they're surprisingly soft and warm. He's sealed my mouth with his, a kiss and yet not a kiss at all; cool air pours into me, traveling down my throat and filling my lungs. With a sharp inhale, I'm soaking up as much of it as I can get, devouring all that he gives me until I start to tingle.

His pull wavers, the invisible thread loosening its grip on me. A strong beat plays in my chest, and a flutter runs down my spine. My body is reclaiming me. With every new sensation, every spark of an awaking muscle, the man before my eyes fades into a distant memory. Thick strands of dark, almost black hair blend in with the lake's deep blue, creating a swirl of inky colors around him, within him. He's less real now, like a trick of the light, and I wonder . . . if I was to reach out and touch him, this man, this angel, would my hand run right through?

I T'S SO BRIGHT. WHITE AND yellow lights make my dry eyes water, and I squeeze them shut.

Where the hell am I?

I force my eyelids open and brave the brightness. I'm squinting, trying to shield them, and it helps.

There's a white ceiling above me. My eyes shift to the right, and I see a plain, large window, the source of the penetrating sunshine. There's a coffee-colored sofa along the wall, just below the window, and directly beside me is a small bedside table. It isn't until I turn my head to the left that I see the monitors. I follow a bundle of white cords down to my upturned arm and count one, two, three of them, piggybacking together on the tube piercing my skin.

Soft footsteps tap outside the door, coming closer, and a woman enters, dressed in a pair of turquoise scrubs. She rubs her eyes, stifling a yawn as she strolls over to the monitor. Eventually, her gaze lands on me, and her eyes widen.

"Oh! You're up." She smiles, a warm curve of her lips that makes my shoulders relax slightly against the stiff bed. "I know you must have so many questions, but don't you worry, hun. Everything is all right."

I'm sore, muscles throbbing from head to toe. I hardly feel like speaking, so I nod.

She retrieves a tablet affixed to the wall and returns to the monitor. Her fingernails tap against glass as she makes some notes, bobbing her head from the monitor to the tablet and back again.

"Can you tell me your name? First and last, please."

"Lo—" My voice croaks, and I clear my throat. "Lou

Adaire."

Her fingers stop tapping as she tilts her head toward me questioningly. "Legal name?"

"Right," I mutter. "Tallulah Adaire." Tallulah is a family name, but Grams was always Tallulah. Mom was Talli. I'm Lou.

Her expression softens, and I wonder how she already obtained that information. "Very good, hun. And how are you feeling?" she asks, stepping closer. She sets the tablet on a table beside me and gently readjusts the IVs. My left arm rests limply in her hand.

"I'm okay, I think. Just a little soreness."

"Mhmm. A little soreness and an angel on your side, I'd say." She nods as she walks away, disappearing behind the front door for a second before rolling in a vitals machine.

Something sparks in my mind at the mention of an angel, and it takes me a minute to place it. Oh my god. I wasn't alone in the lake. There was someone else. A man. No, no, that can't be right. *Come on now, Lou, don't go losing your mind just because you nearly died.* If anything, it was a dream. A remarkably realistic dream, but a trick of the mind all the same.

The woman stops at my bedside, grabs a thermometer, and sticks it in my ear. "Now, do you remember what happened?" When she blows a few strands of blonde hair out of her face, they fly up to skim grey roots.

I pause and mull it over as she withdraws the instrument from my ear. The bridge, the cold water filling my lungs, the man. Yeah, better leave that last one out of it. "I think so. There was a storm. My truck—I went off a bridge?"

She closes her eyes and gives a sympathetic nod. "You did, poor thing, straight into Tuttle Creek Lake. Dr. Perry says it's a miracle you're even alive." Her hand is resting over my own now, giving a small squeeze, but I hardly feel it.

A miracle.

Miracles don't happen to someone like me, and when it looks like they do, it's only a sign of something worse to come. Grams used to say I was a miracle for making it through the day I was born. But I'll never forget that my mother sacrificed her own life for that to happen. I thought I was lucky to at least still have my dad, but he could only take it for so long—life without his other half. I close my eyes before the image of his lifeless body on the bathroom floor can fully develop. I'd prefer never again having to see so much red.

"Oh, cheer up now, pretty girl." My eyes open, the concerned sound of the woman's voice wiping away my darkening thoughts. Her face looms over me, eyebrows puckered. "It's not every day we get to witness miracles like this one around here, I'll tell you that much."

"Um, where am I exactly?"

"Oh, of course. You're in Salina."

I stare at the woman.

"Salina, Kansas," she clarifies.

My brows crease. "Do you happen to know how far Ashwick is from here?"

"Oh, sure. A good half an hour's drive."

A light, fluttering sensation swells in my stomach as I absorb the fact that I'm so close. I'm almost there. In Grams's hometown. Mom's hometown.

"Now, hun, do you have anyone you'd like to call? Anyone who might be looking for you?"

"How long have I been here?"

"Just since last night."

I close my eyes, my head suddenly feeling heavy against the pillow as her original question echoes in my mind, taunting me. Jamie's determined brown eyes pop into my brain, but there's no way I'm going to freak her out over this. Finally, I manage to whisper, "No. There's no one."

She goes quiet again, and I can feel her still standing beside me. I must be making her uncomfortable, but I don't have the energy to do anything about it.

"Honey, how are you feeling . . . emotionally? You've been through something incredible, and you know, there are people you can talk to about it, if you'd like."

I know what she's asking, if I'm mentally stable. The answer is somewhere in between *hell if I know* and *far from it*, but I don't want to talk to anyone about Grams, about Bobby, about the accident. Or about *him*. The impossible angel my subconscious wants me to hold onto—a sick and twisted subconscious who gets off on showing me a world where not even the other side wants me.

Seriously, not that I'm complaining, but who gets rejected by death?

Some things are better left unsaid, so I stick with a safe, "I'm fine."

"Look," she says softly, "you won't be due for release for another twenty-four hours. Your vitals are looking good. Great, in fact. But I can see about pulling a few strings to get you additional nights if you need. Mind you, I make no guarantees, but—"

I'm already shaking my head. "That won't be necessary." I slowly open my eyes and turn my neck a fraction toward her. She oozes sympathy as she stares down at me. "Really, I appreciate it, but I'll be fine."

She raises her eyebrows. "All right. If you say so. Well, you're headed to Ashwick? Have you got a place to stay there?"

I chew the inside of my cheek, already regretting not planning this move better. Or at all. "Not yet."

"They've got the old inn. Can I at least get you their info? I've got a baggie with the clothes you were wearing at the time—they've dried by now, of course—and your wallet's mostly intact."

I let out a breath of relief and offer a small smile. My wallet, my ID; that must be how she already knew my name. "That would be great. Thank you."

Maybe I'm being stupid and should accept her generosity. It's not like things aren't tight financially. All I've got is my personal savings stash to lean on. Working as the front desk administrator for a chiropractor only paid so much.

Still, I don't want special treatment, and more than that, I don't want to be under a microscope or made to talk one-on-one about my feelings. As Grams could have attested, I'll run a 12K marathon before wasting hours discussing my feelings and what they might mean. In other words: not going to happen.

She nods. "Okay then. Dr. Perry will be right in to check on you, then we'll discuss your stitches and—"

Stitches? A frown tugs at my lips.

"Oh, not to worry." She pats my arm. "It was just for a cut on your shoulder blade, nothing major." It's then that I remember the windshield breaking. Warm blood on my skin. "Now, there's also an officer wanting to talk to you about the accident. Whenever you're up for it, of course."

I mutter some kind of acknowledgement, which seems to satisfy her because she turns to exit. The door clicks behind her, and silence fills the air. My mind isn't right yet, still foggy and drained. The monitor's beeping beside me, and there's something oddly comforting about the sound. Soft, steady, hypnotic.

Reassuring.

I keep my eyes open, staring straight ahead and taking slow, deep breaths.

I'm alive.

I should be happy. I should be experiencing more relief than I am, but all I can focus on are the many missing pieces of my heart. The thing is, I didn't just lose my grandmother on Sunday morning, but my entire family. She was my mother, my father, my sister, my best friend. The only person in my life who never left and always loved. The single constant in the ever-changing sea around me.

And now, as I lie in this bright room, the beat of the

monitor echoing in my ears, a blanket of haze and uncertainty rushes over me. When I think about my future, my life, my mind goes blank. It's not an illuminating, white slate either, full of warm lights and promises.

It's dark and lonely, and all I feel is cold. I'm alone, in a world filled with strangers and steel walls.

Chapter Three

ASHWICK INN IS A LARGE, Victorian style building. I can hear its age with each creaking step I take down the wooden hall floor. When I shove the bronze key into my room's keyhole, it jerks and sticks before I can turn the knob and push the door open. The room is oversized, bigger than any back home, and fits an enormous bed along the far-left wall, a worn loveseat pressed up against its foot, and floor-to-ceiling bookcases stocked with dusty material. There's a fireplace to my right, built into the base of the only red bricked wall in the room, and above it sits an older TV. The large, round rug laid out before it holds a single rocking chair.

I wonder if Grams has been here before. Clearly it's been around for a while.

Would she have ever needed to stay at an inn? Could she have walked down that very hall, on the top floor? As open and talkative as Grams was, her past was a solid door that remained shut. It didn't matter how many times I used to ask about her life before LA, about the grandfather I'd never known, my questions were never met with answers.

She would have loved this place, though: the natural scent of wood filling my nose, the comfortable, folksy feel that she filled our own home with, and the way the fresh coldness from outside wafts through the air. For those very same reasons, Bobby would hate it. Ashwick Inn lacks a certain ambience he tends to go for these days—the kind with smoky casinos and full-service bars.

I glance down at the new, stiff duffel bag in my hand, the price tag still poking out. A quick detour to the tiny town's only shopping strip allowed me to stock up with some basics before heading here. My wallet and clothes are the only visible ties to my life in LA now. I never thought I'd feel so bare without any of my own clothes, photographs, and other belongings, but now I can't shake the feeling a part of my identity was left at the bottom of Tuttle Creek Lake.

At least one of the shops carried cute postcards. I take a minute to write a little note for Jamie, letting her know I've made it and I'm doing okay. I may have conveniently left out a few of the darker details, but Jamie's the kind of bestie who'd drop everything and come cursing and banging down my door to make sure I'm all right. She has enough people to take care of under her own roof as it is. Setting the card aside for now, I cross the room.

The bathroom's small, cozy. A standalone, oval tub sits in one corner. No shower. That's fine with me; at least it's clean. I start the water, turning the knob to as hot as I can stand, then close the door to let the steam surround me as I undress.

The water is almost too hot when I lower myself down. Relaxation washes over me. After turning the faucet off, my eyes close as the soothing sound of water settling takes over. It's hypnotic, the smallest waves caressing me, and my body melts into it like butter. And somehow, it's familiar—the warmth, the syrupy sensation tugging at me, the tingling.

It's so quiet, I can hear my own inhales and exhales. Each breath a soft pull and whoosh, a smooth and steady stream of air. Until it's not, and I hear a different rhythm. It's quieter, but there's a roughness to it. It's deep and controlled, and it doesn't match the rise and fall of my chest. In fact, it doesn't seem like me at all.

My eyes snap open. Steam clouds the small bathroom, but I can see there's no one here but me. Still, I feel it. I feel a presence, a warmth on my skin, and I hear it in the air like a painter's brush stroking its canvas. I try to quiet my breathing, forcing each exhale to be long and slow, so I can hear the sounds better. It's clearer now, heavy, coming and going in strong, steady patterns. Breaths.

A cold sliver of unease sneaks up on me, mostly because the logical part of my brain tells me I should be panicking. That's the natural reaction, after all. Somehow, my body and my mind are on completely different planets. I know it can't be real, whatever this is. Yet I feel it, a gentle pull. A warm hum calling to me. Even if it is my subconscious tricking me again, manifesting some way for me to over-come Grams's death and the accident, it's hard to care when such a soothing cloud of calm surrounds me. No sense of malice, no threat in the air. Something about the presence comforts me, easing the ache of loneliness, and it's drawing me in.

For reasons I can't understand, I don't want to lose the feeling, the sound. The presence. Not yet. And right now, I'm choosing to feed it.

On a shaky breath, I close my eyes again, my breaths falling into pattern with the soft breaths behind me. When I hear the inhale, I fill my lungs. When I hear the exhale, I release. Soon, we're in sync with one another.

An entire minute goes by like this, with me continuing the slow and steady breathing and listening to them—it? him?—follow. I'm in a trance—a romanticized state devised by the newly unstable half of me, and it's the first true sense of peace I've felt since Grams's passing.

It's fading now, drifting away. I don't want it to leave me yet; I'm not ready to be alone again. But what can I do?

It's dwindling, the warm presence around me diminishing and leaving my skin cold, until the sounds are barely even an echo anymore. Once they're gone completely, my eyes slowly open and I look around once more.

The room is just as empty as it was before, but somehow I feel even lonelier.

CRACK.
  CRACK.
  CRACK.

A desperate, shaky scream climbs up my throat, but it's not mine. Boyish and small, the unfamiliar voice pours out on its own.

My arms, small and skinny, hang over the side of the bed. Jeans pulled down to my ankles, each draft of wind seeping through the open window sends a fresh wave of pain through my raw backside.

What's happening to me? This isn't me, my body, my voice. And yet the pain, the fear, the anger, it's real enough that it may as well be.

A long shadow stretches over the bed before me, warning me of what's to come.

CRACK.

This lash is harder than the last, tearing my flesh open as pain ripples to my core. "Please, Pops! No more!" I have no control over the words I cry, nor over this child body I don't recognize.

"Don't you fuckin' talk back to me, boy." Hatred burns through each word, and the giant looming over me inches forward. He doesn't stop until his tobacco and whiskey-stenched breath is close enough to touch the nape of my neck. He lowers his voice to a menacing whisper. "Unless you want little Tommy over there to take the rest of your beating for you, of course."

I feel my head involuntarily jerk toward the right-hand corner of the bedroom, where a boy lays in a heap on the carpet. I'm unsure how I know this, but the boy is six years old. One of his eyes is swollen shut, while the other looks up at me pleadingly. His nose is caked with dried blood.

On its own, my jaw snaps shut, teeth grinding together.

"That what you want, boy?" taunts the man, leaning closer still. "Your little brother to take what you ain't man enough to handle?"

My eyes narrow, and the voice that isn't mine grits out, "No, sir."

"Yeah, that's what I thought." He backs away, but my relief is short-lived as the shadow before me raises its arm. I know it's coming, the burn, the blood, but I keep my eyes locked on little Tommy. I will not close them for this bastard. I will not cower, not while the tiniest spark of hope still gleams in my little brother's single, unharmed eye.

When that next CRACK comes slamming down on my tender skin, searing through every inch of me and blistering me raw, I keep my eyes centered on Tommy.

And just like that, he knows.

He knows not to let go of his last shred of hope.

He knows I'll get him out of this shithole.

And I know, one day, I will make this sick, twisted monster pay for what he's done to us.

∙ ⁓ ∙

GASPING FOR AIR, I BOLT upright in bed, my hands clutching the comforter. *Thump, thump, thump,* my heart tries to claw its way out of my chest. My eyes flick around my surroundings. Fireplace. Brick wall. Rocking chair. Large window revealing a dark, midnight sky.

I'm in my room at the inn.

I release a loud exhale, my hands loosening their grip on the comforter as each muscle in my body relaxes, little by little.

It was just a dream.

A nightmare.

It wasn't real.

Instinctively, I reach beneath me and rub a hand over my backside, the same spot that was whipped. Over and over again. Except it wasn't me at all, was it? Of course, there's no sign now of the blood-curdling pain I could have sworn I just experienced. No sign of the deadly rage boiling inside me. No sign of the little brother I could have sworn I loved like my own flesh and blood, who, in that moment, I would have given my own life for.

Breathe, I tell myself.

It's over.

IT'S DAY TWO IN ASHWICK, and I haven't left the Inn at all. Forget the Inn, I haven't left the bed except to pee. The mattress is lumpy and my back cramped, but I can't get up. I'm tired. So tired, and the soreness from the accident still has my bones aching. I could barely sleep after the nightmare. Images of the little boy slumped in the corner of the room etched themselves into my brain, popping up every time I closed my eyes.

I know it wasn't real, but telling myself that doesn't make it feel any less so.

I keep the blanket over my face like a tent, taking comfort in the heavy solitude of darkness. The blanket is my wall, my shield. I don't know what I'm trying to shield myself from more: another nightmare or the new, empty reality that is my life. My eyes squeeze tighter as I clutch the edge of the blanket firmer, trying to will myself back into a dreamless, numb sleep.

I know I'm being ridiculous and dramatic, refusing to face the world on my own when there are some people who've never had anyone to begin with. Some who've had to do this thing alone since they were little, maybe even since they were born. I'm grateful to have known what it's like to be loved, to be cared for. And although the love between my parents may have ended in tragedy, in some ways I'm lucky to have witnessed what they had shared. The kind of love most people never get to see outside of romance novels.

Then again, the more I think of it, the more I wonder if maybe it was more of a curse than luck. Seeing the relentless passion between Mom and Dad—even if it was just through photographs, videos, and Dad's stories—set ridiculously high expectations for me. Perhaps that's part of the reason things didn't work out between me and Bobby; I never could settle for anything less than what they had.

Almost an hour later, I'm still awake, unable to fall back into any sort of blissful ignorance. It's torture. There's a grandfather clock ticking away somewhere, each second droning on and echoing in my eardrums. I kick the blanket off and stumble into the bathroom to brush my teeth. I rinse my mouth and set the toothbrush down, then splash cold water on my face.

My reflection reveals deep circles beneath dark brown eyes, making them seem more sunken than usual, and my hair is a tangled mess. I hardly even recognize myself right now. Hardly even know how to feel. Should I still be grieving? *Am* I still grieving? How is a grieving person supposed to act? Honestly, I have no clue, but something tells me selling the house of the deceased and running off to the middle of nowhere isn't the best start.

What am I even doing?

I don't know if Grams is watching, but right now, I actually hope she's not. It would pain her to see me like this, such a wreck. The thought of her reaction makes me close my eyes in guilt. Grams always had it together, a woman of routine and purpose, and there was hardly a day that either of us stayed in bed like this.

"Get it together, Lou." It's time to be a mature adult.

It's just a pair of fitted jeans with a white knit sweater, but it feels good, pretending I have something to get ready for again. In a way, I do have something to look forward to, getting to see the shops Grams saw, walk the streets she walked on. Mom, too, even if she wasn't here for long.

I brush the tangles out of my hair until the light brown strands are smooth and straight, falling to the middle of my back. I finish off by slipping on my new pair of winter boots and tucking Jamie's postcard into my pocket, along with my wallet and room key, then look back at the room in longing. The bed and nightstand are almost buried in day-old snacks—crackers, Cup Noodles, potato chips—and the rest of the place isn't much better.

Yet I'm finding it difficult to leave.

Muffled voices from the hall seep into my room, mixed with footsteps trailing down the stairwell. People. Civilization. Strangers. I curl my fingers around the doorknob. I can fool them for a few moments; act like my world has not fallen apart, like I didn't come back from the dead a few short days ago, like I'm not having vivid nightmares, like I'm not mentally unstable.

Hopefully.

Chapter Four

I TWIST THE KNOB AND STEP into the hall, wishing the place had an elevator as I slowly make my way down the stairs. I amble past the front desk and am just about to shove the inn's front door open when a soft voice calls out, "Oh, Miss Adaire!"

Turning, I see a petite girl standing behind the front desk. The same girl who checked me in when I arrived. She looks to be maybe nineteen or twenty, a couple years younger than me. Her smile is big and bright, her hair a sunny blonde, and I automatically know she's one of those people who are always happy. Like she eats rainbows for breakfast and spends her evenings cuddling with puppies.

"Yes?"

"I have a new key for you."

"A key . . ."

"Yes, ma'am, a replacement key. You got stuck with the one that gets jammed, right?"

"Oh, yeah." I cross the room and pull the key from my pocket before sliding it across the counter to her.

"Thanks," she says sweetly, grabbing it and pulling a desk drawer open. "I had it made the day you got here, but I hadn't seen you come out till now. Did I say that right? It's Miss Adaire?"

"Just Lou is fine, but yeah."

"Lou, great." Keys chink together as she shuffles through the drawer. "I'm Claire." She withdraws another bronze key and hands it to me. "Here you go. Should work better than the last, but if there's a problem, feel free to let me know."

I slip it into my pocket and smile back. "Thanks."

"Absolutely!"

She's looking at me with kind, wide eyes, eager to continue talking, and it's sweet, really. Just like the nurse at the hospital and like everyone else in this town seems to be so far. But I don't yet have the energy to keep up with such enthusiasm, so I thank her, wave goodbye, and head back toward the front door.

A crisp breeze hits the bare skin on my hands and neck when I step outside. It wafts through my hair, and I fold my arms around my chest, shivering as I walk. Apparently *LA cold* has a vastly different meaning than *Kansas cold*. This is going to take some getting used to.

It's the first week of January, but the trees and shops are still decked out in red, green, and yellow Christmas lights. A woman pushes past me with her young daughter, muttering something about bringing a scarf next time, and an attractive couple holds hands as they wait to cross the street. There's nothing sad in these people's eyes, nothing but signs of contentment, and it brings a slight smile to my lips. It might be silly, but I imagine a young Grams walking beneath the colorful lights, wearing that same expression on her youthful face. Maybe holding Mom's small hand as they walked through the neighborhood.

After dropping off the postcard, I notice a library to my right and decide on a whim to step inside. This is the longest I've gone without a phone, thanks to Tuttle Creek Lake. I figure I should at least check my email in case the realtor has news on Grams's house.

Check-in at the front desk takes a while, but then I claim an open computer in the corner and log in to my Gmail account.

Two unread emails: one from the realtor and one from Bobby.

I start with the realtor, hoping against hope there's good news, even if it has only been a week since I listed the place. It's a short email, informing me that he's just sending an update and there haven't been any hits yet. I groan. The sooner I get this over with, the sooner I can put it behind me and try to move forward. I type up a quick reply to let him know I'm without a cell phone but can be reached at the Ashwick Inn or by email.

I know I could get a new phone, but I don't want to just yet. I kind of like being disconnected right now. Jamie won't be affected by it. We were nine years old when we met through the pen pal program at our separate public schools—mine in LA, hers in Simi Valley—and communicating through good old-fashioned letters is a tradition we've proudly stuck with since.

I return my attention to the computer and open Bobby's email.

Baby, I get it, alright? But you don't have to ignore my calls and texts. Just wanna make sure you're okay, see where you ended up. Look, I know it's been rough but you don't have to deal with this shit on your own. You know you can always come back to me. I know how to take care of you. Come on, just hit me up.

I let out a long sigh. He rarely calls me 'baby' in person anymore, not since we broke up, but he likes to sneak it into texts and emails. It's only been four days since I left. Just how many times has he tried calling and texting me?

Sure, it only took one day for me to drive into a lake and practically die, but he doesn't know that.

Maybe I shouldn't be so hard on him. After all, he and Jamie are the only people left to check up on me now. There's something that gets under my skin about the way he does it though, like I can't be out on my own. And, *I know how to take care of you*, really? Yes, Bobby, for a long while there, you did know how to take care of me. But over these last couple of years . . . I think we both know what that line really means: I know how to take care of *him*.

I sit up straight and pull my shoulders back like I have something to prove. I don't know where it comes from, but the words just come popping into my brain, rolling down my arm and out of my fingers until I have a fabulous load of crap typed up on the screen in front of me.

Bobby,

I'm doing well. Found the perfect town in Kansas for me to clear my head. Think I'm going to settle in for a bit, get comfortable. Get a job. Thanks for your concern, but I'm doing great on my own. No need to wait up.

Lou

I hit *send* with a smug smile on my face, but it's wiped away by the time I exit the library and step back into the fresh winter air. I'm not doing great on my own, unless being a great liar counts.

Claire is still standing behind the front desk when I get back to the inn, and she smiles and waves when she spots me. "Miss Adaire!" she calls, as if we hadn't seen each other only twenty minutes ago.

"Just Lou," I remind her.

"Right, sorry. How was your walk?"

I settle somewhere in between the truth and a lie when I answer, "It was nice, thanks."

"Gorgeous in the winter, right? It's my favorite season." I nod in agreement, surprised that we have something in common. "The holiday cheer, winter festivals, family bonding—it's just so magical, so full of hope and love." She stares out the window dreamily, blue eyes sparkling, and suddenly we are back on different wavelengths.

"Something like that, yeah," I reply, amused by her pink and fluffy cotton candy take on things, and begin to turn toward the stairwell.

"Miss—uh, Lou?"

I look over my shoulder. "Yes?"

"If you want some company or something while you're visiting, you can always come down here." There are hints of concern in her bright eyes, and I realize now how it must have looked to her, me staying locked in my room for two days. I wonder if she knew about my accident too, with the town being so small. "Just, you know, if you want . . ."

It takes me a minute to respond, but I give her a genuine smile when I do. "Thank you."

I feel her eyes on my back as I proceed up the stairs. I expected to be annoyed at the sympathy like I usually would be, but I can't deny it's kind of comforting. My new key slides right into the keyhole and the door eases open. I lock it behind me and head into the bathroom, resting my palms on the sink rim as I gaze at my reflection.

"You're fine. You're good." I've never actually tried this whole 'talk to your reflection' thing, but it's something I used to overhear Grams doing. Worth a shot, right? Hell, why stop there? "You're wonderful. The bee's knees. Bodacious. Supernacular."

I snort and face-palm myself. Oh god. I don't even know how I turned British in the middle there, but this has to be a new low.

My sweater chafes my shoulder blade, and I wince as it irritates the raw, tender skin. I hadn't thought much about the injury since leaving the hospital, having had other things to focus on—or focus on *avoiding*—but now the memory resurfaces in my mind: rain smacking against the windshield, trees and darkness spinning around me, the booming *crack* of my window breaking, and shards of glass flying at me.

I pull my sweater off. Eyes closed, I reach an arm across my chest and over my shoulder, tracing the tips of my fingers along the thick, three-inch cut that hasn't quite scarred yet. It's smooth beneath the stitches. Too smooth, and it feels foreign; a piece of my body I don't recognize. I've always thought scars were meant to represent strength; all this one does is remind me that I shouldn't be alive right now.

That I'm lost.

Drifting.

My eyelids flutter open, and my breath catches at the sudden touch of strong, warm fingers moving over my own. A slow, gentle stroke glides over the wound, but it's not from me. It can't be. My hand is stuck, frozen in place over my shoulder blade as though not daring to move. The mirror before me proves I'm alone in the bathroom, and yet, I feel it again, the same presence I felt several nights ago. Heat radiates behind my body as though someone is standing right there.

Another stroke caresses the wound, and it's even lighter this time, like a feather brushing over me. The feeling of skin against skin is as real as anything. I can almost hear my heartbeat pounding within my chest. The fingers move past my wound, never breaking contact with my skin, and slowly trail upward, toward my neck. Though the texture feels strong and almost rough, the touch itself is impossibly gentle, treating me like something fragile.

No matter how loud my mind screams to fight it, my muscles are relaxing like jelly under the heavy sensation. My uplifted arm drops helplessly to my side. The warm touch strokes the side of my neck, wandering up further still until it's almost in my hair. It's light enough to send a shiver to my toes, and my eyelids start to close on their own, my head rolling slightly forward.

The presence behind me inches closer, and I hear breaths again. Just like the other night, they're deep and controlled, right by my ear.

I have no idea what's happening to me. Half of me is struck with a pang of fear, unease over the impossible experience. Yet the other half can't help but be soothed by the calming tingles running through the length of me. There's a trust I can't explain, like a gentle, unspoken lullaby, and I know I'm safe. The heat, the masculine touch, the warm breaths soft as a whisper that rise and fall at the nape of my neck. I don't want to think at all right now. I just want to *feel*.

The caress slides back down the right side of my neck, almost skimming along my collarbone, when it stops. Draws back. I hear a hitch in the breathing, a tremble for a fleeting moment, the smallest hint of the effort it takes to pull back. Then the touch returns, but only to my scar, traveling down the length of it with incredible slowness, taking its time. As though savoring every moment of contact with me, in a way I've never experienced. A sigh pours from my lips, and when my head falls back, it's caught by the solid warmth behind me. It's real enough that I could swear I'm pressed up against the presence right now, a presence that sure as hell feels like a man—tall, strong, sturdy. The feeling is so vivid I find myself thinking in terms of *him* instead of *it*.

A shake breaks his steady breathing again, another warm tremble in my ear, and I feel the tightness of his body rise and fall with each breath.

I'm letting myself go, relaxing every part of me until the only thing keeping me upright is his body, and as I do, the hard curves of muscle tense against my back.

Something in the air changes, and the presence behind me wavers. It's completely solid one moment, and in the next it's fluid, as though nothing more than a strong breeze props me up. Soon it's not even a breeze, just a puff of air, and I'm grabbing the edge of the counter with both hands to keep from tumbling backward.

My legs wobble, struggling to support the rest of me. When I catch sight of my reflection now, my face is flushed. I let out a loud exhale when I remember how to breathe and command myself to get a grip. I'm still feeling like a sloshy puddle when I slip my sweater back on over my head and drag myself to the front door of my room, unlocking it and yanking it open.

I need fresh air like a drug right now, and I can't stumble down the stairs fast enough. I hear Claire's bubbly greeting when I fly past the front desk, but I don't stop until I'm standing on the sidewalk, bending forward with my hands on my knees and soaking up the crisp winter breeze.

What the hell is happening? This can't just be in my head. I know I've been a little off since Grams's passing, but there's no way I'd be able to dream up something so freaking real.

It was here. *He* was here.

Whoever he is.

Chapter Five

"AH, LOU?" CLAIRE'S VOICE COMES from behind me, quiet and uncertain. "Are you all right?"

I take a second to try and pull it together, hoping I look collected by the time I turn around and give her a non-answer. "Just getting some air." She doesn't respond, so I shrug and steal her words from earlier. "You know, the magic of the winter season and all that."

Claire's frown tilts upward into a sweet smile, and her shoulders loosen a little. "It is pretty, isn't it?" She lifts her chin and gazes around wistfully.

"Sure is." I walk around her and slip through the inn's open door. I hear her close it behind us as I halt at the bottom of the staircase, unsure if I'm ready to go back up.

What if he comes back?

Nerves flutter through my stomach with the anticipation alone. It's almost enough to make me race up the steps, but for what? To demand answers? The sound of his steady breathing by my ear comes to the forefront of my mind, the heat of his body pressing into me. I can't move, still shaking from the shock and confusion of it.

"So . . ." Claire's already settled back behind the front desk. I hadn't noticed the Christmas-red clip pulling back the top layer of her blonde hair until now, and she's slipped a matching cardigan over her white top. "Got any plans for today?"

My feet are still cemented to the ground at the bottom of the steps. I forget to think before I answer with, "Lock myself in the bathroom. Cry. Loathe the world and make up imaginary friends."

Silence fills the room. I finally look over my shoulder and see her wide eyes and unhinged jaw.

Too much?

"Kidding," I say, silently reminding myself why it's easier to lie—polite questions like hers don't pair well with honesty.

Proving my words to be true, her entire body relaxes, and she lets out an uncomfortable laugh. "Yeah, of course." Her gaze shifts to the staircase I'm frozen in front of, and she tries again. "Well, um, Ashwick's really big on town events and stuff, and there are plenty of winter festivities coming up over the next couple weeks if you're, like, bored or looking for stuff to do while you're here. It's more fun than it sounds." Her eyes brighten up as a light bulb goes off in her head. "You can go with me! I participate every year."

Shocker. Her proud grin and the eagerness in her eyes beg me to accept. I know I won't go, but I don't have the heart to straight up decline either. "I'll think about it. Thanks."

I don't know what else to say, so I unglue my feet from the floor and am about to take the first step when the email I sent Bobby crosses my mind. *Think I'm going to settle in for a bit, get comfortable. Get a job.*

I don't know how long I'll end up staying, but I'm here now, and there's something that feels right about it. Maybe the small-town vibe's growing on me. Not to mention I'm stranded here without my truck. I'm sure I'll figure out a replacement vehicle with the insurance company eventually, but I'm not exactly in a hurry to get back behind the wheel anytime soon.

"Hey, Claire?"

She beams. "Yes?"

"You guys aren't hiring by chance, are you?"

"Oh Lord, do I wish we were! Could seriously use the company—I'm going out of my mind with how quiet this place is." She snorts between a bubbly chuckle, then glances at me and stops herself, clearing her throat. "Sorry. So you're thinking of staying?"

I shrug a shoulder. "For a little while."

"That's great! You're going to love it here, I just know it." Her enthusiasm is so genuine, the corners of my lips tip.

"Except, it's not the easiest place to find work. You know, more people than jobs and all that." She chews on her lip.

"It's okay," I say, already beginning to change my mind. "Don't worry about it; I'll think of something."

I resume the stairs and am halfway to the second floor when she calls my name. I pause to glance back.

"There is one opening I know of…" She looks away and drums her fingers on the desktop.

An unexpected spark of relief surges through me, and I cautiously come back down a few steps. A job. Something stable. Secure. And away from my room. Away from imaginary presences. "Yeah?"

"It's not exactly an *easy* job…"

"Okay . . ."

"And it might totally not even be your thing at all so—"

"Claire."

"Right. It's a caregiver position to an elderly gentleman."

I practically skip down the remaining steps to get back to the front desk. "That's definitely my thing. I wasn't getting paid for it, but for years I took care of my—" I gulp, not wanting to invite further questions by mentioning Grams aloud. "—of someone elderly."

"Great." Claire smiles, but she doesn't look entirely convinced. "It's just . . . it's not so much your experience they'd be interested in as your, um, ability to handle difficult people . . . ?"

A frown pulls at my lips.

"Mr. Blackwood, that's the gentleman's name," she continues, "he doesn't exactly like visitors, so he's not the most welcoming. What he does like is his liquor, if you know what I mean. No one's lasted more than a few weeks, and even that's a record because, these days, no one seems to make the cut to begin with. Hence, the ad goes out every month like clockwork."

I raise an eyebrow. "An alcoholic, too? Sounds like the job was made for me." Claire opens her mouth, but I continue, "Do you have the guy's info? A number?"

"Oh, you're not going to need that. He never answers his phone, so the best thing to do is just drop in."

I may be new to town, but showing up on an anti-social alcoholic's doorstep doesn't seem like the brightest idea to me. If Claire notices my hesitation, she doesn't let on. The second she resumes talking, not even a semi crashing through the front door could stop her.

"The house is at 3341 Miller Way, but you don't even need to remember that, trust me. You can't miss it. Just turn left out the door, take a right onto Main Street, and keep on going even when the houses disappear. It's the only residence on the hill up there. You really can't miss the thing. Want me to give you a ride when I get off here?"

Tempting. I hate walking, and Claire's been nothing but nice to me. But she's also bubbly and chatty, and being stuck in a car with her when I'm this moody would only drag her down and suffocate me. "It's all right, thanks. I can walk."

She tries to hide it, but her face falls slightly. "Okay. Well, let me know if you change your mind."

"I appreciate it." I smile and turn back toward the steps, ignoring the jitters forming in my stomach as I force my way to the top floor.

I step into my room, locking up behind me. My back is glued to the door as I scan the space with care. Looks empty. *Feels* empty. Such a different feeling than when I ran out of here earlier. When he was here, in my bathroom, his fingers running gently down my skin . . .

My body warms at the recollection, and I cross to the bathroom. It's just as empty as the bedroom, a lightness in the air, and I'm surprised to hear my disappointed sigh. I shouldn't be disappointed about this. Normal people would feel a weight's been lifted, relieved to know their mental health might still be salvageable, right?

Shoving the thoughts aside for now, I slink out of my clothes and get in the bath. I take my time shaving and exfoliating, the soap filling the bathroom with soft scents of vanilla. There's still nothing to indicate his return when I towel-dry and get dressed, and I'm not in the mood to deal with an angry alcoholic just yet. I end up spending the remainder of the day curled up in blankets watching TV reruns while devouring an entire box of pizza, until, eventually, I close my eyes and drift off.

A WARM BREEZE. DARK SKIES. WET grass beneath my bottom. And nothing but lightning bugs to cast a flickering, dim glow around us.

"What do you see?" I hear myself ask in that young, boyish voice. My skinny arm is outstretched before me, palm up, fist closed. I feel something small fluttering inside.

"Can't see nothin' if you ain't gonna show me," Tommy quips with a crooked grin. He tries to duck when my other hand comes up, but I'm too quick, giving a playful tug on his ear.

"You say anything, not nothin'. And it's are not, not ain't. Hear me?" I chide. "We're not like him, you and I. Not in speech or anything else. Got it?"

The younger boy nods slowly, then runs his fingers over a bruised cheek. "Got it," he mumbles.

"Now," I repeat, angling my head toward my outstretched fist. "I didn't ask what's inside my hand. I asked what you see."

The little boy's quiet for a moment, eying my fist like it's a trick question. "How am I gonna see if you ain—aren't—gonna show me?"

"Look closer."

And he does. He leans forward, eying the faint glow seeping through the tiny gaps between my fingers. "I see . . . light?" He glances up at me, then narrows his large, childish eyes. "Hey, you got a firefly in there, don't you!"

"Shush," I instruct, and I feel a smile tugging at the lips that aren't mine. "So, you see a light. That's good. And what else?"

"Um. Well. It's hard to see the light at all, with the way it's blocked in like that. Wait a minute," little Tommy says, flicking his gaze back at me, "you're not killin' it, are you? It's gotta be runnin' out of air."

My lips lift again. "No, this one's a fighter. Watch."

I open my fist, a twinkling glow illuminating the open palm of my hand as the beetle hovers above it. After a second, it must realize freedom is finally in its grasp, because it darts off into the distance, becoming nothing more than a speck in the sky.

"See, Tommy?" I say softly, the smile dropping as my eyes continue to gaze into the dark night. "He's not so different from us, that lightning bug. You can trap him. Try to shut out his glow. Try to block his light from ever being seen again. But not even the biggest fist, the darkest night, is strong enough to shut it out completely."

My head shifts, my gaze locking onto Tommy's.

"You understand what I'm telling you, Tommy? You have a light inside you, and the only person who gets to decide whether that light shines or not is you."

The boy nods, eyes twinkling up at me, clinging to every word I say. "I understand," he whispers.

I WAKE WITH WETNESS ON MY cheeks. Sitting up, I swipe the tears with the back of my hand. I don't know why I'm crying. It's only a dream, just like before. And just like before, I *felt* everything—the fierce love for his brother, the desperation in his heart, the hope that his words were true.

And it hurts. In the strangest way possible, it hurts. Why does it have to feel so real? Like I'm intruding on these boys' most private moments?

Except they aren't real boys, I remind myself. None of it is real. Just fictitious creations of my twisted mind. It really should come as no surprise that a mind capable of conjuring intimate moments between me and an imaginary being would also be capable of this. Why only mess with me during the day when there's so much fun to be had at night too, right?

That thought prompts me to consider something I hadn't thought of before. Both occurrences, the strange presence in my bathroom and the hauntingly realistic dreams, began around the same time.

After my accident.

Maybe I do need to see a specialist.

I don't let the revelation sit long before shoving it aside. No use letting it fester. I drag myself out of bed and get ready for the day before I can change my newly made up mind. I have too much time on my hands, that's what it is. Anyone would go crazy just sitting around all day without any aspirations, right?

Sounds like a reasonable explanation to me.

I'm staying in this town, at least for now, and I'm getting that job.

Chapter Six

"AFTERNOON, LOU," CLAIRE SINGS AS I stroll past her.

Does anyone else work here?

"Afternoon," I call back. My voice is friendly enough for her sake, but I'm outside before I'm forced to be conversational.

I turn right onto Main Street as instructed and tuck my red scarf beneath my sweater as I walk. The air is cold enough to produce white puffs with each breath, but I'm warming up little by little with every step. With my pace fast, it's not long before any sign of humanity fades into the distance. No more cute little houses to greet me now, just a deserted road surrounded by what looks like miles of red dirt and tree-littered fields. The flat road curves into an upward slope, and I'm feeling a bit leery now.

Massive iron gates ease into view at the top of the hill. Black birds watch me from the tree branches as I walk, and the sky is heavy above my head. The whole vibe feels like something out of a horror movie, and I'm about to be the poor dumb girl who ignores all the signs flashing *psycho* and finds herself hacked up for dinner. Okay, maybe that's a little dramatic, but it's at least at the level of *Goosebumps, Things That Go Bump in the Night*.

Once I arrive at the towering gate, I scan it for a latch,

a buzzer, or a camera—something to give me a clue on how to get past the thing. When I can't find anything obvious, I move forward and tug on the rusted metal. The gate swings open with a loud creak, and I pass through. A winding concrete path leads me to the front door, and I'm almost disappointed to see how normal looking the house is after all the creepy build up. No bats. No cobwebs to get tangled in my hands when I ring the doorbell. Just a nice, traditional, white house tucked beneath the trees.

A few moments pass with no response, so I ring again. Who is this old Mr. Blackwood, anyway? I realize a tad too late I probably should have gotten more info on this guy before up and waltzing myself over, unannounced.

It isn't the alcoholism that worries me so much. It's the kind of guy the stuff turns him into. *He likes his liquor* could mean a whole crap load of things. If he's just an unpleasant, bitter alcoholic, I can deal with it. Hell, Bobby's middle name was *Dick* whenever he drank too much. I'd had enough experience with that side of him over the span of our relationship that I should be able to add it to my resume. But Bobby was a quiet, lazy sort of dick, if that's a thing. His behavior was more out of ignorance than spite.

The fact that Claire said Mr. Blackwood couldn't keep a caretaker for more than a few weeks is what has me on edge. His previous employees would have been from this town, people who probably already knew the man's history, demeanor, and ticks before going in. If *they* couldn't even stick around, exactly what kind of person am I quite possibly about to be working for?

A few loud thumps and crashes sound from behind the door before it drifts open, but whoever unlatched it has already disappeared. I hesitate before I enter, stepping past the threshold and closing the door behind me as grim piano strokes from the classic Funeral March play in the back of my mind.

The man I presume is Mr. Blackwood stands in the middle of his living room—a good sized room with bland white walls, whose wooden coffee table and mocha-colored couches are strewn with crumpled pieces of paper and ink-filled notepads. I spot at least three empty glasses decorating the table, a mostly empty bottle of Three Ships Whisky serving as the centerpiece, and several plates of foul smelling food, which I suspect are not from today. Awesome. More whiskey. I don't know why, but it makes me think of one of those dreams. The smell in the air as that boy was being whipped. A shudder runs through me before I force it away. At least no cigar smoke wafts through the air this time.

His back is to me, greeting me with silence and a head of stringy grey hair brushing over hunched shoulders, as he lowers a new glass onto the table. Uncorking the whiskey, he takes his sweet time emptying the bottle down to the last drop. A cane rests dormant against the couch, and the glint of silver beside it catches my eye. It's coming from the man's right leg. Metallic grey peeks out from a small gap between the hemline of his pants and his black leather shoes. When he straightens himself to take a deep swig from the glass, his pants lower, covering it completely.

"So," he begins, his voice gruff and dripping with disdain, "who sent you this time, huh? Patty? Dr. Keirston?" He still doesn't turn to face me, just wanders over to the couch and picks up one of his notepads with his free hand. He lets out a bitter laugh and slurs, "I don't really give a shit, actually. Go home. You're wasting your time and mine."

I narrow my eyes, not yet decided on whether I should be falling for his I-hate-the-world act or not, and not sure if I care either way. Bushy, silvery facial hair hides most of his expression from view, making him difficult to read. One thing I can tell straight off the bat, though, is this man isn't the conversational type, and honestly, it's a relief.

"The hospital didn't send me," I say simply. "I was told

you need a caretaker, so I showed up for the job."

He grunts and ambles into the next room, which I assume from my partial view of the breakfast nook must be the kitchen. Cabinet doors open and slam as he searches for something. "Yeah, well they lied," he calls through the short wall dividing us. "Been taking care of myself for years."

I glance around at the messy, alcohol-stenched room and shake my head, muttering, "Clearly."

"Go. Home," he repeats, clipping the end of each word between drunken slurs.

I can tell he means to sound threatening, and it might have worked if he'd actually face me. Right now, he sounds like an old man who's about to pass out from one too many.

"Why do you keep putting an ad out if you don't want the help?" A small, disorganized stack of newspaper articles on the carpeted floor catch my eye, and I lean down to take a peek. The images are in black and white, and the edges are worn, frayed.

"Not that I owe you an explanation," he grunts, "but *I* don't keep doing anything. Some of the people in this town think they know me and what I need, and they won't stop with the bullshit ads. *Not lucid*, my ass." He mumbled the last line, but I heard it loud and clear.

"Look, Mr. Blackwood," I call, straightening and craning my neck to peek into the next room. "I'm not looking for a friend. I just need the work. I'll do what I'm being hired for, but otherwise . . . I keep to myself, you keep to yours."

He staggers back into the living room. He's got another bottle of whiskey now, but he doesn't bother to use a glass this time. Just takes a swig straight out of the bottle and walks toward me. "Well, isn't that consider—" He finally takes a second to look at me, his wrinkled forehead crinkling deeper and tired, hazel eyes narrowing as though he'd just caught me in a lie. "What'd you say your name was?"

"I didn't."

He shakes his head and quietly barks, "Dammit, what's your name, child?"

I cross my arms over my chest in reflex, as though the movement will somehow make me seem stronger. "Lou . . . Tallulah Adaire."

He watches me for another minute with skeptical eyes, then eventually rubs a hand over his untrimmed beard and swivels around. He's stumbling away again—this time, toward a set of stairs on the far-right corner—and I notice a limp in his step. He doesn't seem to mind, seeing as he's left his cane behind.

I roll my eyes. Well, it's been pleasant, but that must be my cue to leave. I spin on my heel and reach for the doorknob when I hear his garbled voice. "Housekeeping. Tomorrow, be here nine o'clock sharp for details. One slip and you're out."

When I turn back to question, he's already disappeared up the stairs. I'm not inclined to go after him for answers, so I step out into the brisk air and head toward the road, wondering what just happened.

Whatever his problem is, though, it doesn't bother me as much as I let on. Maybe it should. I know I'm selfish for this, but it's oddly comforting to find another person in this town who's got issues.

I swear something flickered in his eyes when he finally looked at me. Could he have known Grams?

The possibility alone makes my heart swell. I've seen enough pictures of her younger self to know how much we look alike: identical large brown eyes and fair skin, the same heart-shaped face, and we're both above average in height. The only major difference is our hair color, hers being almost black, while my lighter, honey-brown strands come from Dad's side of the family.

Still, even with our obvious resemblance, the chances of him having been close to Grams are slim. We had just celebrated her ninetieth birthday the month before her passing, and Mr. Blackwood only appears to be around seventy, possibly late sixties. That's a pretty big age gap.

Regardless, I didn't come here to pry into her past. I just wanted . . . Well, I suppose I didn't really know what I wanted, what I expected to gain out of moving here. Comfort, perhaps? Some sort of closure?

Maybe I just needed someplace to run to.

Chapter Seven

THE SKIES HAVE CAST A dark blanket over the town, and the temperature has dropped enough that my lips feel numb. A sharp breeze teases strands of my hair. This skinny road is nestled beneath a tower of trees on each side, their naked branches looming over me. I lift the scarf above my chin and pick up my pace toward the inn.

It's faint at first, the whisper of warmth that brushes over the back of my neck.

When my skin starts to tingle, the heat building up behind me, I slow my steps. Just a few seconds later and I can feel it completely, the presence I'm growing more familiar with, and I come to a halt. I'm shivering slightly in the cold, itching for the coziness of my room, but I can't seem to get my legs to take another step.

The heat behind me brushes closer until I can almost feel his body against mine. His build blocks most of the wind, and his warmth has my muscles relaxing from the frigid breeze. I want to melt into him so I can feel safe and sound, let the impossible heat he radiates relieve me of the evening's chill. But of course that's crazy. He's a stranger. A ghost. A . . . I have no idea what he is, and that might be what terrifies me most.

Slowly, I turn my head. Despite knowing I can't physically see him, I need to face him anyway. It's killing me, moving so slowly, but I'm afraid he might disappear again before I get any answers. Or am I afraid to discover he isn't real? I can already glimpse him from the corner of my eye, and the fact makes my breath catch in my throat. *Holy freaking fiddle sticks, I can see him.*

He's taller than I thought, maybe 6'4", with thick, slightly wild, dark brown hair. By the time I've unfrozen my legs and managed to turn the rest of my body around, my throat's gone dry and I can't take my eyes off him. With chiseled cheekbones, a prominent jaw, and nothing but taut, sculpted muscles beneath his fitted black T-shirt . . . he is *all* man. How he is not freezing in nothing but a T-shirt and jeans is beyond me. My gaze lazily wanders back up to his face. I swear my heart stops when I look right into his eyes, and I hear my own gasp.

Dark pools of grey and black fill the irises.

I've seen those eyes before. Except this time, there's no hint of the green I'd glimpsed then. No hint of color at all. Only darkness.

He stares downward, watching me just as intently as I'm watching him—perhaps even more so. His eyes are impossibly hard, a mixture of ice and steel, and I don't see how the hands that touched me so delicately before could belong to the same person.

At 5'8", every bit of a size seven in women's clothing, and with an athletic frame formed from twelve years of volleyball, I've never been considered a petite or fragile girl. But right now, standing beside his imposing build, I certainly feel like I'm both of those things.

I squint, trying to focus, but the outline of his frame begins to blur. *Am I seeing this right?* The edges of his shoulders, his hair, they're wavering, blending in with the shadows of the night. His eyes narrow as he watches me, then his gaze follows my own. The moment he notices his flickering form, his face twists into something fierce and, before I realize what's happening, he's gripping my arms and shoving me backward. Just when I think my back's about to slam into a tree, he controls his movements enough to gentle the impact into something I hardly notice at all.

I'm sandwiched between the sturdy frame of his body and the tree, with his arms on either side of me, blocking me in. My breaths are ragged, and my cheeks are burning hot with the adrenaline coursing through me. He's both tall and broad enough that the only thing in my line of sight is his chest.

The heavy, uneven sound of his breathing is coming from above my head. It quiets, like he's struggling to get it under control, and he doesn't move a muscle for what feels like an eternity. With his hands planted on the tree, he backs away from me, breaking contact between our clothes yet still close enough to feel his warmth, his invisible grip on me.

When I look up, my eyes skimming his shoulders and hair, he's not blending in with the background anymore. Just like the night of my accident, I find myself wondering . . . is he solid enough to touch?

Without thinking, I reach up and graze his wide shoulders, just above his collarbone. My fingers tremble against him. His body heat seeps through the fabric of his shirt like it's not even there, zipping through my fingertips and down my chest, until it warms the pit of my stomach like bourbon. Something white and rough on his skin catches my eye, poking out about half an inch from the top edge of his T-shirt. *A scar.* It looks so much like mine, reminding me of the other night, when he touched it. Touched me. It's just below his collarbone, and I lightly run my thumb across it.

His entire body stiffens, from his shoulders to his legs, and his Adam's apple bobs once in his throat.

It's not much, but it's the first real sign of vulnerability I've seen.

My hands look so small and delicate on him. I realize

I'm lingering a little longer than I'd intended, and I snap my fingers away. Eventually, I look back up into those steel eyes.

"Who . . . what are you?" I whisper.

He doesn't speak for a long while, and I wonder if he even can. He's never said a word to me before. Then again, I've never spoken to him until now either.

"I think you know." His voice is a low, quiet hum, but there's a rough, husky tone to it that leisurely travels down my spine.

I think I do, too, but it doesn't make sense. "I saw you . . . that night in the lake."

He says nothing, his eyes roaming over my face, but I know I'm right. It is him.

"Are you an . . ?" I want to say *angel*, it's at the tip of my tongue, but something about his eyes stops me. So cold. Empty.

As though reading my mind, he gives a small, steady shake of his head. "I'm no angel."

The way he says it, deep and slow . . . the hints of truth tinged with darkness behind his voice, it makes my breath shake. He's so quiet I can't tell if he's even breathing, but I can see the clench of his jaw, the tightening of his muscles rippling from his arms to the defined lines of his stomach.

An angel he certainly is not. I can't say where it comes from, but somehow, I know. I know what he is.

"Death." The word floats out of my mouth like a puff of air, drifting in the wind so softly I hardly hear it.

A quiver runs through the tightness of his chest as he watches me take it in, his heavy silence speaking louder than anything words could say. I'm trying to get my voice to work so I can ask what it means, what he wants from me, when the hard outlines of his body fade. This time, he drops his arms from either side of me.

That's all it takes for the icy wind to return, hitting my skin like daggers and serving as a harsh reminder of where

I am. I start to reach out to him, not sure why I'm missing his warmth, his touch, only that I am. He takes a step back, leaving me shivering.

The more he distances himself, the more he seems to fade. Until, suddenly, he's gone.

IT BURNS. IT CUTS. LIKE fangs, it bites into these wrists that are not mine.

But still, my hands tug relentlessly against the rope that binds them, yanking and writhing until warm blood trickles down my fingers.

The screams, they won't stop. The tortured sounds pierce through the hall, up the stairs, and into the shadows of this pitch-black closet, straight into my ears. Fear and rage consume me until any other sense of emotion runs numb. The fear is for little Tommy, but the rage . . . oh, the rage is for the monster.

Rip.

My hands break free. I don't stop to look at the bloody mess they've become; I can't even feel the pain anymore. I tear at the rope tying my ankles together then slam my body against the door, knocking it open on the second hit.

It's easy to follow the screams, even though they've become more like whimpers now. They lead me to the kitchen, where the monster has little Tommy tied to a chair, arms bound behind him, head hanging low. Even though Tommy's almost ten years old now, he looks so much smaller like this. Too small.

The monster has a knife. It's pressed against Tommy's right arm, slicing a shallow line through his skin. It's not the first cut tonight, either. Fresh slices line his left arm. Blood, red, so red, slides down his arms, drip drip, and onto the ground.

I don't pause to think before I reach down to untuck the pocket knife from my right boot. It's not there. Goddammit. The fucker must have snagged it after knocking me out earlier. I take advantage of being unnoticed as I scan the room, searching for a substitute weapon, and contemplate the most efficient form of attack.

"*What's the problem?*" *the monster sneers, grabbing ahold of Tommy's brown hair and yanking it back until their eyes are forced to lock. "Thought you'd like this. Ain't you boys attention whores like your mom?" He shoves Tommy's head before releasing it, then smirks. "Guess you can't help it, huh? It's in your DNA, built in from the smug Italian blood she gave you. Wonder what she's gonna think of your new tattoos."*

A fiery heat blazes behind my eyes at the sight. It boils and burns, flames coursing down my throat, past my chest, until scorching fire fuels every inch of me.

He. Will. Burn. For. This.

And I won't wait for the Devil to make sure of it.

BODY SHAKING, I GASP FOR air. Confusing images flood my mind, dreams clashing with reality, drowning me to the point I can't breathe. My hands claw at my throat.

Blood . . . red, red, so much red. The bathroom tiles, they swim in it. Dad. His body, so limp, so lifeless. The gun, it still touches his partially curled fingers. His heart, it's bleeding. *Really* bleeding, just like he always said it was. Those nights I'd find him shivering, when he'd stir and cry out in his sleep. He always said his heart had been cut open. He always said it bled raw without her. And now, right before my eyes, it did.

Daddy, no! My eight-year-old self couldn't comprehend it then, and my twenty-two-year-old self can't comprehend it now. *What did you do? What have you done, Daddy? Please, don't leave me. Please, come back for me . . .*

But he doesn't answer.

Of course he doesn't.

Because he's drowning in red.

Chapter Eight

I'M STILL IN BED WHEN the room's alarm clock blares in my ears. My skin's damp, eyes wide as I stare mindlessly at the white ceiling. I can still feel the fire running through my veins—hot, burning flames of rage mixed with despair. Rage toward the monster in my dreams; the devil I wanted to make suffer just as much as those boys did. And despair . . . despair from the unwelcome memories of Dad that came racing back without warning.

The temptation of sleep wove in and out throughout the night, trying to corner me in my own mind and lull me away. I couldn't do it, though. Couldn't close my eyes. What if I saw red again? What if that's all it takes to bring Dad's lifeless gaze back into view?

So I just lay here. Looking at the vast expanse of white above me. People think it's a bright and hopeful color, white. A promise of fulfillment. What they don't realize is it's a trick. A trap. It lures you in so effortlessly, and once it gets you, that's when you see the truth. It's just as empty as the rest of us.

Maybe that's why I usually prefer to bury myself beneath the blankets, surround myself in black. At least with black, you know what you're getting from the start.

I don't know when it happens, but eventually, my mind wanders away from last night until it finds its way back to *him.*

Death.

A shudder ripples through me, shooting from my fingers to my toes and making my heart rate pick up at just the thought of his steel eyes boring into mine. No matter how hard I try, I can't make sense of the reactions he pulls from me. It doesn't matter that he let me go that night in the lake, something still draws me to him, a subtle force tugging at my soul. It's not logical, not sound, yet it's there all the same.

Questions and theories burst through my mind, one after another, until it feels as if my head will explode. Of course the loudest voice of all is screaming, *You're losing your freaking mind, Lou!* but I prefer to ignore that one.

How could I see him yesterday, while other times I only heard or felt him? How does he just appear like that in the first place? And, more importantly, *why*? Also, that scar . . . I'd only glimpsed a small part of it, but how in the world would Death himself have a scar? I wouldn't have thought someone like him could be marked in such a way.

Then again, I'd never have thought someone like him could have existed in the first place.

I kick off the covers, rising from the bed in a zombie-like fashion. I'm eying the room suspiciously when I walk to the bathroom, as though maybe if I narrow my eyes enough I'll be able to see him. It doesn't matter that I know he's not here, that I can't feel the heat he radiates; I have to believe I have some sort of control in all this, even if it's from something dumb like squinting my eyes until I can hardly see.

I'm on autopilot while I freshen up for my first day with Mr. Blackwood. I slip on a pair of jeans and a loose sweatshirt, then tug my boots over my ankles and give my hair a quick brush through. My face looks like something out of *The Walking Dead* from such a rough night, but I don't care enough to try covering it up with makeup.

Claire's face is hidden by a curtain of blonde hair when I descend the steps. She's hunched forward, using a manicured finger to scroll through her pink-cased iPhone. It's because of her I'm on my way to work right now, and I figure the least I can do is be more considerate than I have been. Besides, the clock hanging on the wall behind her tells me I still have fifteen minutes to kill before I need to start walking.

I stop when I reach her, resting a hip against the desk's faded oak. I'm just about to greet her when I hear a sniff and she brings a tissue to her nose. If not for my own unfortunate bonding experiences with crying lately, I would've brushed it off as a cold.

"Claire?"

Her whole body jolts at the sound of my voice. "Lou!" Her face brightens when she spots me, but her nose is tinted pink and her eyes are swollen. "Good morning. I'm so sorry, I didn't see you there."

There's something wrong and unnatural about seeing innocent blue eyes gleam with repressed tears, and it makes my stomach drop. I want to ask what happened, but I don't. I won't pretend it's my business, force her to address it with me, or make her uncomfortable. Instead, I offer a small smile and keep my voice soft. "Don't worry about it. I haven't been here long."

Her lips curve, but the smile doesn't match her eyes. "It's great seeing you up and about so early."

"Thanks to you. Looks like I'm about to become a housekeeper."

Her brows furrow, and she tilts her chin to the side. "Housekeeper?"

"Yeah, it turns out Mr. Blackwood's not the one who's been putting the ads out for a caretaker. Seems to think he doesn't need one." I shrug a shoulder before adding, "Honestly, it didn't really look like he needed one to me either."

Claire's lips drop into a frown and the crease between her brows deepens. "Well of course *he'd* say that," she tells me between sniffs, "but my mom says he just doesn't know what's best for him."

This comment takes me aback. Her mom, too? It's no wonder the guy's so angry—everyone's shoving a huge slice of *I-know-what's-best-for-you* down his throat. No use in biting Claire's head off for it though, so I bite my tongue instead and change the subject. "When do you get off for the day?"

"If Paul gets here on time, six."

"Paul?"

"You haven't met him yet?"

I shake my head. I truly was starting to think Claire was the only employee working here.

She shrugs and says, "Probably because he's usually late, and he works the night shift most of the time anyway."

"Well, I ask because I'm thinking of checking out some of the restaurants around here and I'd rather not be the only total loser eating alone on a Friday night." I'm lying. Dinner out wasn't originally part of tonight's plan, and I couldn't care less about eating alone or what other people think of it. But it's obvious the girl could use some company, and I have to admit I could really use it, too. "Think you'd be up for it?"

She perks up, her smile finally beginning to reach her eyes. "Really?"

I nod in answer. She sets her phone down and looks upward in thought. "Okay, let's see. What do you like? If you're willing to venture outside Ashwick a bit, we can find Italian, Chinese, Thai, Mexican . . ."

I can't help but feel a bit better as I watch her bounce back to her sunny demeanor while she rattles off the various options. "I'm good with a burger and fries if you are."

"Done." She beams. "I'll text Paul to make sure he gets here on time."

Speaking of being on time, a quick glance at the clock reminds me to get going. I give her a smile and turn toward the door. "See you then."

"Have a good first day!" She waves a wide, bubbly goodbye.

I don't think I'll ever grow fond of walking, but it's not so bad today. Not so creepy at least, now that I've been inside the Blackwood house. It's kind of hard to be terrified of a man whose only weapons are a cane, stale food, and notepads, and it certainly wasn't what I'd expected to find when I stepped inside yesterday. I still don't know if I'll actually go through with accepting the job, though. Yes, I need the money, but my conversation with Mr. Blackwood seemed strange. One second he was telling me to get the hell out and the next he was hiring me as a housekeeper.

This time when I approach the heavy iron gates, I swing them open without pause and stroll down the winding path until I climb the few steps to his front door. I can hear the doorbell's high-pitched ring from the outside. It doesn't take long before the door swings open, and a familiar grunt sounds from inside.

I don't know what his thing is for abandoning the door before I can see him, but it definitely ups the creepy factor a notch.

I step into the living room, close the door behind me, and watch Mr. Blackwood settle onto the sofa. He doesn't bother to remove the crinkled sheets of newspaper littered over the cushions as he does so, and it makes for a loud and uncomfortable sight when he plops down, drink in hand. When he says nothing, I lower myself into the recliner before him, scooting a worn notepad aside before I crush it.

"Tallulah Adaire," he grumbles, almost to himself. His grey hair somehow manages to look even stringier today than it did yesterday, and his wool sweatshirt smells of whiskey.

"Lou," I remind him.

He ignores me and takes a swig. "Tell me something. *Lou.*" His wrinkled eyes are aimed downward, centered on the glass, his wrist rotating the drink so it sloshes around. "What year were you born?"

It's an odd way to ask how old I am, but I answer smoothly. "Nineteen ninety-five."

"Ninety-five . . . Christ, I'm old." He stays focused on his drink, but the distant look on his tired face tells me his thoughts are elsewhere. After a pause long enough to make me shift in my seat, he finally looks up and mutters, "Three days a week. I don't care which days you pick as long as you stay out of my way while I work."

I glance around the room again, wondering what the man actually does for a living. No one's mentioned it, but judging by the size of this property he's done well for himself. "What is it that you do?"

He lets out another grunt. "Research. Now how much do you need to make?"

"Oh." I wasn't prepared for the blunt question. When Dr. Gregorian hired me at the chiropractic office in LA, they set my salary, no questions asked. "I'm not sure what the standard rate for housekeeping is."

"That wasn't my question," he mutters before downing the remaining liquid and all but slamming the glass on the coffee table. "How much do you need to make?"

Why didn't I prepare for this? I don't know if he's being patient or if he's too wasted to care, but he doesn't pressure me while I calculate the costs in my head. It's a large property and a filthy one at that, so I'm assuming the days will be long. But I don't need much, and this town's dirt cheap. Mostly though, I don't want to charge an old man any more than I need to. "Um, seventy-five dollars per cleaning?"

"Six hundred bucks a week," he replies without hesitation.

"But that's—"

"You clean what you want, go where you need, but don't touch the damn papers." He looks me right in the eye, his stubby index finger pointed for emphasis and voice sharp as a knife. "Do not touch a single piece of paper in this house. Do you understand?"

I doubt my expression is doing much to hide the confusion I feel at the strange instructions, but I nod. When his aged eyes narrow in response, I add, "Okay. I won't touch any papers. But Mr. Blackwood . . ."

He doesn't wait for me to finish before pushing himself up from the sofa and heading into the kitchen. "Mr. Blackwood," I repeat. "Your offer. That's two-hundred dollars a day, just to clean."

"I know how to count," he slurs from the other side of the wall. "I'll draw up an agreement for you to sign by the end of the day. Otherwise, you're on the clock starting now."

Now? My back is stiff, hands clasping around my knees and fingers drumming anxiously. I shouldn't be so on edge; I'm not an anxious person. But I've never been hired to do housework before, and the fact that he's offering a novice like me more than double of what I'm fairly certain he should pay makes me uncomfortable. And what's up with the freaking papers? They're on the sofas, coffee table, and some are even on the carpet. I even spy a few white sheets wadded up on the dusty bookshelf across the room.

"I said *now*," he barks, coming into view with a fresh bottle of whiskey in hand, and I shoot to my feet.

"Yes, *sir*," I mumble under my breath. At least we're off to a great start. "Oh, and the cleaning suppl—"

"No one's going to hold your hand, child. You do your job, so I can do mine."

It isn't until six hours later, when my neck is cramped and my hands are blistered, that I realize just how sincerely he meant those two simple sentences.

I am on my own.

Chapter Nine

IT DIDN'T TAKE AS LONG as I expected to figure out which closet kept the cleaning products. Mr. Blackwood had no trouble at all ignoring me while I worked around him. He spent most of the day in the living room, his head buried behind books one minute and scribbling over old notepads the next. I felt like an intruder snooping around a stranger's house, walking on eggshells and going from room to room.

The Blackwood house is oddly fascinating. It's two stories, with five bedrooms situated on the second level, but most of the place looks entirely untouched. Three of the bedrooms aren't even furnished, with nothing but coarse, grey carpets, cobwebbed closets, and windows that look like they've never been cracked. But they looked ready to be shown in an open house by the time I was done with them.

What struck me most, though, was I didn't spot a single photograph in the house. And I was looking. No signs of the man's history or family were to be found.

Back home, Grams and I had framed photos everywhere—sitting on bookshelves, hanging on walls, topping dressers and nightstands, decorating hallways. I never met my mother, Talli, but it was those pictures that allowed me to see her dance as a teenager in our living room, smile shyly at the camera in her blue high school graduation cap and gown, and wrap her slim arms around her pregnant tummy with a gleam in her brown eyes that told me she loved me.

It was those eyes I ran to crying when Frankie Stuller lied and told everyone in school I let him feel me up beneath the bleachers, and it was to those eyes I boasted about socking Frankie Stuller the next day. Photographs might not be the real thing, but they still offered just enough truth to steady me when I was about to fall.

Now, as I lean into the living room closet and return the last of Mr. Blackwood's cleaning supplies, I find myself peeking at him with even more curiosity than I had when I'd first met him yesterday.

He's hunched over the coffee table with a pair of scissors, carefully cutting into a newspaper article, and I can't help but notice how frail he looks when he's not grunting, drinking, or barking. His bones are thin, poking out around the edges of his frame.

I didn't know it was possible, but he hasn't taken a single swig of liquor in six hours—ever since he dove into whatever he's been so focused on.

I shut the closet door with more force than necessary, hoping it'll get his attention. Of course, it doesn't. He didn't even speak to go over the new contract he'd typed out for me over an hour ago. Instead he set the papers on the corner of the table with a grunt and returned to his research as I read through it all and signed at the dotted line. I didn't mind it at the time, but now that my work for today is done, I don't know if I'm supposed to announce that I'm leaving or if he'd prefer not to be interrupted. Eventually I decide on the latter and tiptoe toward the front door, slipping it open with the care of a mother trying not to wake her sleeping newborn.

He doesn't look up before I close it behind me, and I don't say a word.

The second I step out from the shelter of his porch, I'm attacked by pouring rain. It's strong and mean, and I'm cursing myself for wearing such an ill-fitting sweatshirt. No hoodie, no umbrella.

So I hit the dirt running.

As I pass beneath a familiar line of trees, a part of me wonders if I'll see *him* again. Feel his warmth, hear his voice. But it's the same part of me that doesn't know if I even want to see him or not. Really, how great of an omen could it be if Death decides to follow you around?

My thighs are burning, but my hair and clothes are drenched, so I pick up the pace. It's times like these I wish I were a runner like Jamie. We did a 5K together once, one of those races to raise breast cancer awareness. She crossed the finish line with her head held high, part glistening goddess and part swimsuit model when she poured a light stream of water into her hair to cool down. I crossed the finish line with my skin red and blotchy, my knees wobbling, and my lungs convulsing, knocking people out of my goddamn way like a bulldozer so I could collapse in peace on the nearest bench.

I'm shivering and heaving when I arrive at the inn, leaving a trail of water with every step I take across the small lobby.

"Oh my gosh! Lou!" Claire's mouth drops open.

"Whoa . . ." The male voice behind me is drawn out and lazy, reminding me of Dexter Freiman—a likable kid, who also happened to be the biggest pothead in my high school. He strolls into view, a young guy with dirty blonde hair pulled back into a ponytail and a half-asleep look in his eyes. He closes his black umbrella as he takes me in with an expression of pure wonder. "You must really dig the rain, huh?"

"Yup," I answer through chattering teeth. "Decided to go for a run, dressed like this, because I love it so much."

He gives a slow and thoughtful nod, as if I've just stated

something profound. "Nice."

"Oh my gosh, Lou," Claire repeats, quieter this time. She jots something down on a rectangular sheet of paper that looks like a timecard and says, "You don't need to be catching a cold. Let's order in for tonight." She turns to the guy beside me. "Paul, would you hate me if I asked you to start your shift now?"

He gives another easy nod and ambles toward the desk. "Nah, that's why I'm here, right? You go ahead. I got this."

I'm already walking up the stairs, each step weighed down and uncomfortable with the soaked clothes sticking to my body, when Claire pops up beside me and matches my pace. "So," she whispers, as though she's got a secret, "I asked my mom about Mr. Blackwood today."

I glance at her, saying nothing. I can't deny I'm curious about what she has to say—the old man is like a puzzle, one from eBay that's missing half its pieces. But I also feel like I've invaded enough of his privacy for one day.

"Well," she continues, either not noticing my hesitation or choosing to ignore it, "she was pretty surprised he even hired you."

Yeah well, she's not the only one.

"How does she know him so well?" I ask.

"Oh, she doesn't. I don't think anyone really *knows* him. Not personally, anyway. But she's in all of Ashwick's social circles, and she runs the local paper." She shrugs. "A full time job in a town as small as this one."

"Hmm." I turn left when we reach the top level and jiggle my key in the door.

Claire continues, "He's more of a recluse than I thought." Her lips turn down in a frown, and her eyes drop toward the ground as she follows me into my room. "My mom says he moved to Ashwick over twenty years ago, but she's never seen anyone visit. No family, no friends."

That has my attention, but I'm struggling not to pry, so I just mumble an acknowledgement. If he only moved here twenty years ago, he couldn't have known Grams. She left this town long before then.

I grab a comfy pair of leggings and a long-sleeved top from the duffel bag I have yet to unpack and amble into the bathroom, closing the door behind me. As I peel the wet clothes off my body, I think her words over and feel a pang of sadness in my chest. I'm trying not to feel sympathetic because I know it's the last thing Mr. Blackwood would want. But when I think of how hard these past few weeks have been on me, how lonely I've felt—to imagine him feeling that way for years?

Whatever the reason he's so alone, it has to hurt.

"Do you, um, need help settling in?" Claire's voice calls from behind the door. She must be looking around the generic room, seeing nothing but a single duffel bag on a rocking chair to give away that a guest might be staying here, and wondering why I'm such a weirdo.

I hold back a chuckle when I answer, "I was going to unpack tomorrow, actually. Probably go pick up a few more things, too."

"Oh, good," Claire breathes. I can hear the relief in her voice. "That's good. Are you thinking you'll find an apartment or house to rent now that you're staying for a while?"

I shrug a shoulder even though she can't see me and adjust the leggings on my hips. "I don't know. I'm kind of liking it here."

"Yeah, lots of people stay long-term. Most of our guests are locals that rent it out like an apartment, since the nearest actual apartment complex is in the city. Helps that we're so cheap, too."

That it does. But that's not why I like it here. "Grams would have loved this place."

The second it slips, I regret it.

"Grams?" Claire presses.

Opening the bathroom door, I step out and offer a small smile. "Yeah, Grams. So where did Mr. Blackwood move here from?"

Thankfully, the question does enough to divert Claire's attention. "I don't know. Not too far from here, I don't think." Her eyebrows knit as she plops down on the love-seat. "I've always wondered what he does all day, never leaving his house."

"What do you mean? He works."

"Works? He was rich enough to retire ages ago." She withdraws her pink phone from her pocket and types something, her lips curving back into the friendly smile I'm growing used to. "So, I was thinking we could order a pizza? There aren't many places that deliver around here, sadly, but you can never go wrong with a good cheesy pizza, right?"

"Uh, yeah. Pizza's fine," I mutter, still thinking of Mr. Blackwood. If he retired so long ago, what has he been researching? "Do you know what he did? Before he retired?" So much for not butting in . . .

"He ran some investigative business. PI type stuff. But it's his books that made all his money."

"Books? He's an author?"

"Yup. They pretty much killed his credibility as a PI, but at least he made bank." I'm about to ask how his books could ruin his credibility when she continues, "He doesn't publish anymore, though. Not in years. He's kept to him-self ever since I've known him, and Mom says he totally lost it before he ever came out here. Like, to the point where people used to hear him talking to himself. Even out in public."

God, the poor man. The hard exterior, the barking and cursing, the endless whiskey.

Instead of digging deeper, like I want to, I force myself to drop it. I've already stepped too far into his business, and now I can't stop asking myself . . .

Who is Mr. Blackwood?

Chapter Ten

SUNDAY. WHAT USED TO BE my favorite day of the week has quickly turned into the monster under my bed—you can only ignore it for so long before it claws its way back into your mind.

It wasn't that Grams and I did anything particularly special on Sundays, but it was always just sort of 'our' day. It was a lounge-around-in-jammies, have-breakfast-for-dinner, watch-classics-till-we-pass-out kind of day. We'd argue over Carey Grant versus James Dean and throw popcorn across the sofa at each other like college roommates. Even when Bobby and I were together, he knew Sundays were reserved for Grams, and when I was younger, Jamie and I only ever did sleepovers on Friday nights, so they wouldn't interfere.

But all that went to crap when I woke up with a bad feeling four Sundays ago.

I had ignored it, of course—a talent of mine—but when she didn't come down to the kitchen for her usual breakfast tea, that bad feeling went from a dull ache in the back of my mind to a sharp twist in my gut. Sundays may have been her day to let loose, but that wasn't enough to make her lose sight of her morning routine. Not even a fire could stop her from showing up at the wooden breakfast nook, six o'clock sharp, ready for tea.

Literally.

I *may* have accidently started a small fire in the backyard when I was nine. Yet there was Grams sitting in our breakfast nook with her tea in hand, mere minutes after fixing my mess and while the place still smelled of smoke and ash.

But now, this day has evolved into something else entirely. Three weeks ago, I started this new routine of turning out the lights and pretending, just for a day, that that particular Sunday had turned out differently. That I'd heard the familiar sounds of Grams's walker scratching softly across the carpet, seen her small, wrinkled smile as she carefully lowered herself into the window seat, and listened to her voice, gentle and soothing, hum a slow tune.

The routine is an unhealthy one, and it only ends up making me cry, but I do it to myself anyway. Must be that mentally unstable half of my brain again.

I jolt and tug the comforter around me when a shrill noise sounds from my right. There's a standard, room-assigned phone sitting on the nightstand, vibrating with each ring. When it doesn't stop after the fifth time, I cave.

"Hello?"

"Hey, Lou! Good morning." Claire's been extra chirpy with me ever since our first 'girls' night'—her name for it, not mine—a week ago.

We've hung out three times since then, too, and I'm slowly beginning to admit even I've had a little pep in my step throughout the week, whether I was working for Mr. Blackwood or running errands. When I went to the shopping strip yesterday to pick up some more clothes and essentials, I caught myself humming the bubbly tune she has a habit of whistling. I immediately shut that crap down, but I can't deny it's been kind of nice hanging out with the queen of all things happy. I'm still concerned about whatever brought her to tears that morning last week, but I haven't asked, and she hasn't told.

I return my attention to the phone. "Morning, Claire.

What's up?"

"You have a visitor," she sings.

"I do?"

"Yup, one who's traveled a long way to see you."

Jamie. I practically dance out of bed. If there's anyone who might know how to pull me out of my Sunday funk, it's her. "Be right down!"

I brush my teeth in record time, throw my hair up in a pile on my head, and don't even bother to change out of my purple pajama shorts and thin T-shirt before racing down the stairs and skidding to a halt at the front desk.

My nose wrinkles. "Bobby?"

I'm not sure what surprises me more—the fact he's found me or the way he's cleaned himself up. The stubble on his face is gone, and he's dressed in a sky blue button down shirt paired with a decent pair of dark jeans. He's even styled his light brown hair. "What . . ."

"Lou," he says with that confident grin I haven't seen in a long, long time. He knows he cleans up good. "You look nice."

I glance from him to Claire, whose own grin is about to split her face as she stares unabashedly.

"Bobby," I repeat. "How'd you find me?"

He takes a few steps toward me, but when I retreat, he stops. There's only about five feet between us as it is, and I don't need him inching forward. "Jamie. When I went to shoot the shit with Daniel, I asked if she'd heard from you, and she showed me the postcard."

I roll my eyes toward the ceiling. Jamie's got a whole 'nother kind of letter coming to her. As good as Bobby looks, I don't let my guard down. Changing the person you've been for years takes a lot more than a razor blade and an ironing board.

"Baby—" I shoot him a warning glare, and he tries again. "Lou. I've missed you so much." His light blue eyes are so sincere, for a second I see the sweet boy he once was.

"Please . . ." He comes closer, and this time I let him. When his hand comes up to tuck a loose strand of hair behind my ear, his fingers brush my cheek.

Well, *hell*. My mind might be able to reason, but my body remembers his touch. Deep down, there will always be a part of me that longs for the comfort his familiarity provides. Not even I can deny that when it's staring me straight in the face.

I hear the sound of Claire shuffling away, but I don't turn to look. "Bobby." My voice comes out in a whisper, and I hate it. "What are you doing here?"

"Isn't it obvious?" he asks softly, his hand lingering. "I came for you. I'll always come for you."

I close my eyes. It's Sunday. *Sunday*. And Bobby is standing in front of me—cleaned up, with his hand in my hair. It's not even nine in the morning. I can't sort this out right now.

"Got any plans today?" he asks.

I shake my head.

"Let me take you out. Like I used to. Remember?"

My eyes fly open, and an eyebrow lifts. "Oh, I remember. Do you?"

He seems to doubt himself for a second, glancing away, and I know then that he doesn't.

"Last time you took me out was two years ago, Bobby. To Hooters, where you got so wasted, I had to have the guys at the next table help me carry you out to my truck."

This time he's the one to shut his eyes, squeezing them hard like it might wash the memory away. He shakes his head. "I've changed, Lou. I have. Somethin' happened the day you left." He lets his fingers slide down, skimming past my shoulder.

I don't know why, but I find myself thinking of someone else when he does this. Another, warmer, touch that stroked my skin. Rough fingers slowly trailing down the nape of my neck, the curve of my shoulders. What it felt like to have the heat of his firm body pressed against me. A low breath escapes through my lips.

Something flickers in Bobby's eyes as he watches my reaction, and it seems to make him bolder. He moves closer, leaning down so our faces are only inches apart. "When I saw you drive away from me, all your shit packed up and that For Sale sign in your yard, that was it. I swear to you, Lou, I haven't had a drink since."

It's not the first time he's told me he's sober. That he's changed for me. But it is the first time in a long while that I've smelled this fresh clean scent coming from him. Not even a hint of alcohol or cigarettes hits my nose.

"One more chance," he pleads, folding his hand over mine. "That's all I'm askin' for. I drove straight through the night to get this moment right here."

I chew on my lip, begging my brain to step up for once and pop out a logical answer for me.

"You don't want this." It comes out in a mumble because I'm still halfway biting down on my bottom lip, as though that'll get me to shut up. "If I agree, if I say yes, it won't be for the right reasons, Bobby." And it's the truth. What I don't elaborate on, though, is what those reasons would be: because it's Sunday, because I'm lonely, because I'm hurting more than I'll ever admit. And maybe, because I'm scared.

His fingers squeeze around my own. "I don't care. I'll take whatever I can get, Lou. Anything at all."

Voices trail down the stairwell as other guests make their way into the lobby, and I move back a step, pulling my hand from his grasp. "Okay." The word is hollow. "You can take me out."

Bobby looks almost as stunned as I feel. "Yeah? Today?" He pulls his hand through his hair and lets out a loud exhale he must've been holding in. "You won't regret it, bab—Lou. I promise, you won't."

"I better not," I warn, and his grin widens.

I can't remember the last time he's talked to me like this. Like I'm all he wants. Not for me to grab him another beer, to rub his back, to change the channel. Just . . . me. The corner of my lips lift a little.

I turn toward the stairwell and hear him call after me, "Wait, where you runnin' off to? I thought I was takin' you out."

"You are," I call back, glancing over my shoulder, "but I have things to do." *Lie, lie, lie.* "You can pick me up for dinner." He's got some groveling left to do, so I figure it's a win-win.

His cocky grin tells me he's up for the challenge. "All right. Pick you up at six then."

Chapter Eleven

IT TAKES ONLY A FEW hours of being alone in my room for the boredom to reach suffocation status. Maybe it's the anticipation for tonight, but nothing seems to be entertaining me. I spend some time organizing the items I purchased yesterday, then I flick through TV channels until my eyeballs hurt. I must be further gone than I realize, because a treadmill infomercial showcasing a Wonder Woman look-alike somehow convinces me to go for a run. I make it to the end of the block before remembering how much physical endurance sucks everything holy and turning around.

Now stiff and achy, I slide my clothes off and slip into a hot bath. *I can do this.* Take a nice, long bath, maybe even pamper myself a little before my . . . date? Is that what this is with Bobby? No, it can't be a date. The one thing drunk Bobby and sober Bobby have in common is they both have a way with words, with getting what they want when they set their mind to it. *Charm*, Grams called it. So tonight, I decide, is going to be about seeing if Bobby can walk the walk.

If there's anything I have to be thankful for, it's that his unexpected arrival has sufficiently distracted me from this particular day of the week.

I've just wrapped a white towel around my body when a

knock sounds at the door.

"Coming," I call out.

Please don't be Bobby, please don't be Bobby.

The second the *click* sounds from unlocking the bolt, the door's flying open, and Claire's blonde hair comes bouncing into my room. "Wow," she sighs, helping herself to the rocking chair and leaning back with a wistful look in her eye. "Why didn't you tell me you were hiding such a cute boyfriend? And his accent? Totally adorable."

I close the door and turn back to her with a smile. "Hello to you too."

She grins. "Oh, hi. But seriously . . ."

"Bobby's not my boyfriend."

"Really? Seemed like there's history there to me."

I shrug and stroll over to the dresser where I've finally stored my clothes like a grownup. "Ex-boyfriend."

"Ohh. I see." I don't miss the suggestive tone in her voice. "*Ex*-boyfriend. Well, he's really charming."

Snorting, I retreat to the bathroom to dress. "Yeah, that's Bobby," I call through the closed door. "He'll charm the pants right off you."

"So why aren't you two together again?" She asks the question like it's the most baffling thing in the universe, and it reminds me why I prefer to avoid revealing this stuff in the first place.

Claire sees the surface. The side of him that lures you, that hooks you and reels you in before you see how flimsy the fishing rod actually is—that it's about to snap, that he won't even notice when you begin to drown. It's not her fault; it's probably the same side of him that has me agreeing to this thing in the first place. "Like you said, there's a lot of history there. A lot of making up for him to do, too."

I step out of the bathroom to see Claire flipping through channels on the TV. "Aren't you supposed to be working?" I ask, realizing it's the middle of the day.

"Nope. I don't work Sundays. It's the one day shift Paul

has, but he wound up Lord knows where after a house party last night and asked me to cover for him till he got here. He just showed up a minute ago." She looks at me and smiles her smile. "Guess being the boss's son has its perks, eh? So, back to Ex-Boyfriend—"

"Bobby."

"Bobby. Was he a bad boyfriend?" Something about the way she asks, her tone softening and chin tilting, has me pausing to seriously consider my answer. I sit down beside the fireplace, and Claire waits quietly for me to speak.

"He didn't used to be," I say truthfully. "In fact, the way you saw him today is a lot like how he was when we met in high school. Confident grin, clean cut, determination in his eyes . . . warm."

"What happened?"

I frown, trying to recall the downward spiral, how it all began. But that's not how it works. There's no little calendar where all the answers are neatly filled in on the correct dates. In reality, the change happens so gradually you don't even hear the sirens when they pass by. "Life didn't go as planned, and he crumbled," I finally answer. "He replaced his dreams with alcohol and TV until he forgot he ever had anything else. *Anyone* else." Claire says nothing, and I give another shrug. "Eventually, I got tired of waiting around for him to remember."

After a brief pause, Claire lets out a heavy sigh. "It's all so romantic."

I gape at her. *Seriously?* What kind of romance novels has she been reading? "Romantic?"

She nods, staring wistfully out the window. "Yes, romantic. He's come back to prove his love. To be a better man for the woman who holds his heart."

Oh god. She's so wrapped up in the obvious fantasy playing out in her head that I don't have the heart to tell her just how far from reality it likely is. I've known Bobby long enough to not get my hopes up. And even if he really does have a handle on his sobriety now, even if he really is ready to make an effort again, I don't know if he's what I want anymore. But sweet Claire doesn't need to know that. *Come on, Lou, let the girl dream a little.*

"Okay," I concede. "We'll go with romantic."

She smiles again, turning back to me with a look that's surprisingly devious for such an angelic face. "Then what are we waiting for?"

The expression on my face must tell her I'm drawing a blank, because she says, "Let's show this guy Bobby just what he's been missing, and why he better not slip this time."

"Oh, no—"

"Yep." She's already out of her seat, yanking me up by the hand until I stumble after her. The girl is stronger than she looks. I may be taller, a little curvier, but she's got some muscles hiding beneath her slender frame.

"Claire—"

"Let's go."

"It's really not like that—"

"Uh huh."

My pleas are futile. Within half an hour I'm in a slinky black dress and my hair is blow dried, falling with silky smoothness down my back. The only part of the dress that isn't squeezing me for dear life is the waist, and that's only because it's busy with the curves of my chest and hips. Claire's rouged my fair cheeks, glossed my lips, and cat-eyed my eyelids. I'm staring at my reflection with my mouth agape, not sure if I want to hug her for making me feel sexy again or tie her down so I can escape and call this whole thing off.

Claire's standing beside me, pride and approval twinkling in her blue eyes. "Yup. He's done for."

"Claire . . ."

She pats my back, which happens to be bare, thanks to the deeply scooped drop at the rear of the dress. "You'll be fine."

Just then there's a knock at the door. I stare at Claire, who stares at me, then we stare through the bathroom's open doorway.

"What time is it?" I ask. Surely it can't be six already.

Claire hits the home button on her pink phone and says, "Four thirty."

Yeah, way too early. I'm still barefoot as my feet pad across the room, toward the door, where I carefully tug it open. There's no one there, but a splash of red from below catches my eye. I lower my gaze at the same time Claire lets out a gasp from over my shoulder. There, at my feet, sits a full bouquet of red roses fresh enough that I can smell their sweet scent. A glass vase holds them up in perfect form, and a squared, white note peeks out from between the stems. I retrieve the vase, a heavy thing, and turn back into the room to set it on my nightstand.

I stand back, distancing myself, and just stare at the gorgeous flowers for a minute. Do I want to read the note? Roses are a clear sign of romance, of a date. Silly or not, I'm afraid one look at that note might cross the line completely, locking me in, and I won't be able to turn back if I go through with dinner.

Why didn't I let him take me out this morning, when I saw him? Why did I have to pretend I was busy and suggest dinner instead? *Dinner*, of all things; of course he thinks it's a date. Or if he didn't before, one look at the way I'm dressed will certainly seal the deal.

"Well?" Claire breathes, about to burst. "Are you going to read the note?" When I don't respond, she waits a minute and asks softly, "Want me to read it for you?"

After another second, I nod. She plucks the note from the vase and reads aloud, "Thank you for giving me another chance."

That's all. Nice and simple. No 'baby' or 'love' mixed in there. No pressure. I let out an exhale and my shoulders relax.

"That's so sweet," Claire says, still staring at the note. And she's right. It is sweet. Bobby hasn't bought me flowers since my nineteenth birthday, and they were nowhere near as lovely as these. Could he be serious about this, after all? Could he have changed for me?

Do I want him to have changed for me?

That last question has me chewing my lip again. It's now been seven months since I first broke things off with him, and as horrible as it sounds, I haven't missed him. Not romantically, anyway. His friendship on the other hand . . . Then again, maybe if he hadn't injured his knee in the first place, if he'd never turned into the Bobby I walked away from, then maybe I *would* miss him romantically. Maybe I'd still want to be in a relationship with him.

The knot in my stomach suggests otherwise, but I shrug it off and nod at Claire. "Yes, it is sweet."

She looks pleased with my response, eyes lighting up and white teeth flashing. Claire the Matchmaker is sassier than Claire the Concierge. She walks over to the single closet and shuffles through my shoes. "No high heels?"

"I didn't exactly see this coming, so . . . nope. Just my old pair of sandals, two new pairs of boots, and the tennis shoes."

"But you bought that sexy dress you're wearing."

I shrug. She has a point there. But that's different; it isn't like I bought it with something special in mind. I'd been shopping for a warmer sweater when I spotted it yesterday, hanging just right on the mannequin, and well, what girl doesn't want a little black dress in her closet?

Thankfully, she doesn't make me explain and instead hands me my newest pair of boots, black with a slight heel. She smiles. "These are cute, and with legs like yours you can totally make it work." Her own legs start doing a little jig, and she says, "I have to pee. Would you mind if I used your restroom?"

"No, go ahead."

She disappears into the bathroom, closing the door behind her, and I sit on the end of my bed. Bending forward, I slide the first boot over my foot. Just as I begin to zip the second boot up, a familiar warmth brushes over my neck, my hair. I freeze, my fingers squeezing the zipper, and look around. My hair has fallen over my shoulders, blocking some of my view. I push it back with my free hand, still not seeing anyone.

But I know it's him.

I try to ignore the sudden thumping in my chest and slowly finish sliding the zipper up. When I straighten my back, propped against the bed for balance, I feel it again. The heat. It's coming from directly in front of me, like he's standing inches away, except he's not. Not visibly, anyway.

I wait a moment, unsure of what to do. When those rough fingertips I remember so well brush over my cheekbone, my back stiffens and my hands pull the comforter into a tight hold. His touch is like a feather stroking me as he carefully moves my hair away from my face. It's an innocent movement, revealing my eyes, and it shouldn't feel as intimate as it does, but I can't help it when my eyelids flutter closed.

How does he make such a simple gesture feel so damn sensual?

I don't realize I'm leaning into his touch until he pulls back, making me stumble forward. Before I can lose the rest of my footing, one firm hand curls around my waist, the other around the nape of my neck; both are strong and keeping me steady. I don't resist his hold. His warmth seeps through my dress and into my skin, and again, I find myself leaning into it. Into him.

Some part of my brain must have awakened, because it reprimands me with a hushed, *Pull yourself together*. The hypnotic lull coursing through my body urges me to ignore the voice of reason, but I know I probably shouldn't.

"It's okay." My whisper pours out into the empty room. "I can stand."

His grip on my waist loosens but doesn't fully let me go. The hold supporting my neck, though, disappears, and then what feels like a large thumb is gently pressing down on my lips. *Uh oh.* It would seem that my speaking has drawn his attention to my mouth. This can't be good for me. When he slowly, carefully, runs his thumb over the slope of my bottom lip, my mouth parts slightly and a small breath escapes me.

How does he do that? Does he even realize the sensations he's stirring in me? He certainly didn't try to touch me like this when I was able to see him the other day. In fact, he seemed flat-out distant then. I think about how, somehow, not being able to see him makes me feel less intimidated, and I wonder if it's the same way for him.

He stays like that, the tip of his thumb burning into my lips, and I forget how to breathe. How to move. There's something about the way he touches me—so careful, restrained. It doesn't feel cheap or like he's taking advantage, but rather . . . rather like he's touching a woman for the first time. Like he's trying to understand. Understand every curve, every sensation.

A noise sounds from behind the bathroom door, and his hand cuts away from me. In the same instant, his warmth begins to fade.

No, don't leave yet. There's so much to ask, so much to say.

Without thinking, I reach out toward where his heat seems to be centered in front of me. I don't know why, or what it is I intend to do, but it doesn't matter because I never get the chance. Just when my fingers connect with his heat, it disappears completely—and so does my hand. I gasp at the sight, my hand flickering in and out of solidity for a split second before it vanishes along with him. My arm is cut off at the wrist, and it's the most horrifying thing I've ever seen. Despite what my eyes tell me, I know my hand is not gone. Not entirely, anyway. I feel it connected to me in the same way the other one is. Except something's off. My fingers are growing numb, and there's a biting coldness wrapping around my entire hand like a glove. It's as if any blood has stopped circulating through that part of my body, leaving it feeling lifeless and out of my control.

A part of me and yet not. Not dead, nor alive.

"You ready?" Claire's peppy voice whips the moment away like a rug being pulled out from under my feet, and I hit the floor with a *thump*.

"Oh my god!" Claire's at my side in an instant, leaning down, eyebrows bunched together. "Are you okay?"

Completely at a loss for words, I stare down at the fingers pressing into the hard floor. *My* fingers. My hand. The same hand that was gone just a second ago, but now is so solid, right in front of me. Warm and full of life, moving at my command.

"Lou," she says softly.

Finally, I manage to shift my eyes, bringing them up to meet hers. Except I'm not looking at her at all. I'm trying to slow the beating in my chest and relearn how to prop myself up, but my arms won't stop shaking.

What. The. Fuck.

Chapter Twelve

W E'RE BOTH QUIET AS BOBBY pulls his truck out of Ashwick Inn's parking lot and onto the road. It's been over an hour since the incident with *him*, and I can't shake it. In fact, I can't stop shaking at all. I may look fine on the exterior, but inside my mind is racing.

Bobby makes a sharp turn that returns my attention to my surroundings. The leather seats beneath me, the evening skies outside our windows.

The quiet filling the air.

It's not a comfortable silence, and it makes me all too aware of the way the bottom of my little black dress hikes up with each of the truck's bumpy movements. I grab the hem and discreetly yank it back down. Claire didn't approve of my jacket selection for this outfit, so she lent me a coat of hers. It's smooth and black, and just barely longer than my dress. It doesn't do much to cover up my legs, but I pull it tighter around my body anyway.

What was I thinking? I should have changed outfits the minute Claire left. Well, except for maybe the little black clutch she lent me. It's pretty cute.

"Relax," Bobby says from beside me. I glance over at him and see the amused smile tugging at his lips. "It's just dinner."

I let out a small laugh, going for casual, but it ends up

sounding nervous. "Yeah. I know."

This is already awkward. Well, not so much *this* as *me*. Bobby seems fine, while I'm the one making it weirder than it needs to be. It would have been difficult enough trying to act as though this, the two of us going out for dinner, was normal on an ordinary day. But how exactly am I supposed to relax after what just happened in my room? All in a matter of minutes, I'd been sucked full-force into the sensual caress of a phantom being and then witnessed a piece of my body, my own flesh and bones, disappear with him.

Is that what it's like for him when he goes? When he fades away and leaves me, does he feel what I felt in that brief moment of time? The terrifying numbness? The sensation of coldness wrapping around you like a snake about to devour you whole?

Bobby reaches forward, snapping me away from my thoughts as he presses a button on the radio. "You still like The Lumineers?"

I clear my throat, finding my voice and forcing it to be steady. "Is the world still round?"

He grins. "Point taken."

The volume's soft, soothing, and I instantly begin to relax when the familiar music starts. It's just enough to remind me of where I am. Of the man beside me who seems to be making a genuine effort at repairing what happened between us. It's no secret The Lumineers are one of my favorites, but I'm still surprised Bobby went out of his way to put them on for me. He usually prefers listening to country or R&B.

Really, I owe it to both of us to try and be present for this. I shift in my seat a little, trying to look over at him without being too obvious. His light blue eyes are centered on the road ahead, his chestnut hair short and cropped. He's fairly tall, and his movements are masculine, but he'll forever have a baby face, especially without the facial hair.

Right now, he really does look like the Bobby I fell for. There's a pang in my chest at the recognition.

He glances at me, a goofy grin forming. *Dammit.* I look away, but it's too late. I'm waiting for him to call me out for staring, but he doesn't. Instead, he says, "You look real nice tonight, Lou." It's not sleazy or laced with sexual undertones. It's sincere, maybe even tinged with sadness.

I give him a soft smile. "Thanks, Bobby. So do you."

His eyes spark with something between desperation and appreciation when I say that, like he's holding onto every word, and I have to force myself to look away. *Jesus, I don't know if I'm ready for this.*

When he parks the car and I look up, I see the word *Steakhouse* and tense. It's too dark to tell how fancy the place is from the outside, so I won't know until we get through the front doors. Before I even finish unbuckling my seatbelt, a sharp breeze hits me as my door opens. Bobby stands there holding out his hand for me.

I grab my clutch and accept his hand but then glance back at him and say, "You really don't have to do all this, you know."

He smiles, raising an eyebrow, feigning innocence as he leads me around the building. "All what?"

I roll my eyes. "The flowers. The Lumineers. The door."

He doesn't respond as he opens the restaurant's front door, allowing me to enter before him. As we follow the hostess, I look around and let out an audible sigh of relief. The environment is laid back, casual, with wooden booths, small tables, and the buzzing sounds of overlapping conversations swirling around us.

Bobby sits first, leaving space for me beside him, but I slide into the empty booth across from him. He picks up his menu at the same time I pick up mine, and his eyes start slowly scanning it up and down. The expression on his face is relaxed enough, even confident, but his shoulders are stiff and I can tell his knee is bouncing beneath the table.

The sounds around us fade into the distance as our own silence drags on, until finally, what feels like an eternity later, a young guy dressed in a white and red uniform approaches our booth.

"Hello, my name's Dylan, and I'll be your server for tonight." The introduction comes off as an over-recited greeting, and the guy's busy eyeballing a blonde-haired waitress two tables down the entire time it spills from his mouth. I watch as the waitress catches him and winks before strutting away, swaying her hips as she does. It's not until she's disappeared behind the kitchen door that he looks over at us. "How you guys doing?"

"Doing good, man."

"All right, and what can I get for ya?" Dylan's holding a notepad and pen, tapping his foot on the ground, darting obvious glances back toward the kitchen.

"I'll have the Angus Ribeye with a water, and she'll have…" Bobby gestures to me with one hand, giving his menu to the server with his other.

I know he said he's sober, but it's still weird hearing him ask for a water. "Country Fried Steak for me, please. And an iced tea."

"Mhmm." Dylan jots it down and takes my menu, looking up at me for the first time. Something flashes in his brown eyes when he does, and I don't like the feel of it. "Anything else for you?" he asks me slowly, his attention wandering from my face to my, thankfully covered, chest.

"Nope." My voice is sharp, my eyes narrowed.

He rubs his hand through his blonde, buzzed hair. "Well, lemme know if you change your mind." He walks away with that, glancing back at me once with a smooth smile.

The disgust is still on my face when I turn my attention to Bobby, who's looking down at his cell phone, apparently texting someone. I'm assuming he missed the whole exchange, because when he finally sets the phone down, something's distant about him. He leans back against the bench, gazing at an empty spot on the table and chewing his lip.

"Hey," I say, "what just happened?"

He snaps out of it, glancing back over at me and shaking his head. "Nothin'. Why?"

"Don't tell me 'nothing' when it's something. What's up?"

This time when he shakes his head, he grins. "Shit, you know me well." I've always liked Bobby's smiles. They're full and genuine, a little goofy and always endearing.

I lift an eyebrow, nudging him.

"Really, it's no big deal," he says, but he's rubbing his chin in a way that says otherwise. "It's just that shithead Ryan. Sending me pics of him out with the guys, trying to get me back home."

He says *shithead* affectionately because he and Ryan have been best buds since elementary school, but the thing about Ryan is that he really *is* a shithead. He's the one who gave Bobby the idea that alcohol solves everything in the first place, and he somehow always managed to be behind our worst fights when we were together.

"Does he know you're sober?" I ask as an unfamiliar face sets our drinks down, smiles politely, and walks off.

"Yeah, he knows. He's just so used to me hangin' out with him all the time. He'll get over it."

I nod, but I'm not convinced. Ryan's the worst kind of influence for someone like Bobby, and unfortunately, I don't see him backing off so easily.

"Anyway," Bobby says with a sigh, "I didn't take you here to talk about that jackass." He winks. "I came here to be with you. To talk about you."

"What do you want to know?"

"How you're doin', what you're up to, if you're seein' anyone—"

"Bobby—"

"Kidding," he says, flashing me a grin that's surprisingly cute. "That's none of my business."

I laugh, and it's entirely natural this time. "Thank you."

"How've you been though? You get a job like you mentioned in your email?"

"Yeah, I just started a few days ago. Housekeeping."

His eyebrows shoot up. "Housekeeping?"

"Shut up." I cringe at how flirtatious those words sound and take another sip of tea to shut *myself* up.

He chuckles and shakes his head. "Hey, not judging. Just surprised. You always hated cleaning up after me." He winks again, and I roll my eyes. "Nah, really though. I'm happy for you. You're doin' better on your own than I thought you would."

"What, you didn't think I'd be okay?" It comes out more accusatory than I'd intended, my arms crossing over my chest.

"No, no, I didn't mean it like that." He leans forward, resting his elbows on the table. "I just—hell, I don't know. Been worried about you, that's all."

The server, Dylan, comes up with a tray of food, setting each plate down appropriately. I thank him but make a point not to look up at him this time. It seems to do the job, because he turns and leaves without lingering.

I clear my throat, speaking to Bobby again when I say, "Sorry. I don't know why I said it like that."

"I do. And it's okay, I deserved it."

When I look up at him, he's watching me. We stare at each other for a little too long, and I honestly don't know what's happening. His gaze is getting cloudy, and he bites down on his bottom lip in the way he used to right before . . . Okay, maybe I *do* know what's happening. And I'm nowhere near ready to go there.

"So . . ." I'm the first to break eye contact, grabbing my fork and using the food on my plate as the perfect excuse to look away. "How long are you staying out here?"

He follows my lead and cuts into his steak, taking a large bite. "No firm plans just yet," he says between chewing. "Got nothin' to tie me down back in LA while I'm still between jobs, so who knows . . ." He glances up at me, letting his words fade and leaving the rest of the sentence for me to fill in.

"Bobby, I don't want you going out of your way to—"

"It's not out of my way. Really. I wanted to see you, and the timing just fell into place."

I stay quiet for a minute, mulling over his words. Something about it doesn't sit right with me. I already know he's been in between jobs—again—and I'm not about to pretend I have any say in his choices. But he's basically telling me, without so many words, that his decisions are hanging on me. How long he stays, what he does next with his life, he's basing it on how things progress with us. If, *Lou, if things progress with us.*

That's a whole lot of pressure to add to an already rickety roof.

"What about Carol?" I finally ask. "Won't she miss you while you're away?" Carol, Bobby's mom, is half of the reason I stayed with him as long as I did.

"You kiddin'? You know how much my mom loves you. She threw my ass out the door when I told her I was gonna come see you."

I smile softly, because he's right. And I miss her. Her soothing words and the genuine southern charm she brought with her from Texas. Her warm hugs, fresh squeezed lemonade, sandy blonde hair that's always straying from her hair tie. Ugh, this dinner is stirring up more than I bargained for. Now I'm the one with my knee bouncing beneath the table. My eyes dart toward the back exit. It's only about fifteen feet from here to there. I bet if I wait for him to get distracted again, I can slip quietly from my seat and—

"Don't even think about it." Bobby's eyes are aimed

straight at me, squinted enough to suggest he saw every step of the silent plan playing out in my head.

"What?" I blink, chewing my steak.

"You know what. It's just dinner."

I try to relax again and give him a nod that I hope says, *Duh, I totally know that.*

"For now," he adds with a smirk.

I kick his foot lightly under the table, and he laughs.

The rest of dinner glides by, and by the time our check comes back for him to sign, I realize I'm feeling a little too at home with my ex. There's a twinkle in his blue eyes that oddly reminds me of Claire with their open hopefulness. It makes me shift in my seat, my uncertainty from earlier quickly returning.

"Here," I say, reaching into my clutch and withdrawing enough cash to cover my portion. I set the bills before him.

He glances down at the cash, then back at me. "You're not paying."

"Yes, I am."

"No."

"Yes."

He lets out an exasperated sigh. "Lou. I have years of fuck-ups to make up for here." He smiles and adds softly, "Just let me buy you some goddamn dinner." He's already sliding the cash across the table and finishing his signature when the server comes to collect. After a moment, I take it and stuff it back into my clutch.

We're quiet again when he leads me to his truck and opens the door for me. I slide in, buckle up, and keep my eyes on the passenger window as he starts the engine and backs out.

He presses a button by the radio, and this time Eden comes on. I sit back against the seat, relaxing my head on the cushioned headrest, trying to figure out how the hell I feel about tonight. About Bobby. Dinner went better than I expected, and I can't deny I had a good time. I even caught myself staring at his lips and remembering what it feels like to be kissed. To be held. To sleep in a bed warmed by a man's body.

And I hate it.

I hate that thoughts like this manage to make me feel even lonelier than I have been. I hate that Bobby is trying so hard, being so good, that I almost feel obligated to reciprocate. I hate that I can't tell if it's his touch I want or just a man's touch. I hate that when I think of a man's touch, I don't think of Bobby, but of *him*.

A man I don't even know.

A man that technically isn't even a man at all.

Chapter Thirteen

MY HANDS ARE ON MY lap, and Bobby's fingers briefly intertwine with mine, squeezing gently. His fingers are smooth, not rough like a certain other someone's. And his touch may be soft, but it's not careful or tender. His skin is warm, though it's not the kind of heat that makes my body tingle from contact alone. When I glance up at him, he looks over and smiles. It's innocent, friendly, yet there's something deeper in his eyes I know I can't match. I smile back but wiggle my hand out of his grasp, using my long hair as an excuse as I pull it back from my face, twisting it and wrapping it over my right shoulder.

I clear my throat, realizing we're entering Ashwick Inn's guest parking lot. "Thanks for dinner."

He nods, putting the truck into park and cutting the engine before turning his full attention to me. "I had a good time, Lou."

It takes me a minute to respond, but I'm sincere when I do. "Me too, Bobby."

The silence spreads, him staring at me and me itching to squirm in my seat again. I take a deep breath. I don't want to hurt him, especially not when he's sobering up and pulling himself together like this. Maybe a part of me doesn't want to completely lose him either. But I'm being selfish, and it'll hurt him more in the end if I don't set things straight. Just when I open my mouth to speak, he unlocks his door, stepping into the darkness and strolling around the truck.

I unbuckle and hop out before he reaches me, not needing another act of chivalry to feel guilty about. I know I shouldn't feel guilty, or like I owe him, for any of this evening—he was right when he said he has years to make up for. That doesn't make it any less weird for me, though.

This is a side of Bobby I haven't seen in a long, long time.

He pulls open the inn's front door for me, and neither of us speak as he leads me up the three flights of stairs. I stop when I get to my door, not wanting to unlock it yet in case he thinks I'm inviting him in. I can tell he wants to say something from the way he's looking down at me, but when he still doesn't speak, I start first.

"Look, Bobby—"

"Don't say it, Lou."

"But—"

He shakes his head, taking my hand in his. "We had a good time, right?"

I swallow, giving a small nod.

"Then let's leave it at that. It doesn't need to be complicated."

He says that, but at the same time, he's leaning in. It's such a slow, natural movement that I don't know if he's even aware he's doing it. I cut my eyes away, glancing at my door and clearing my throat. "Bobby . . ."

He keeps my right hand in his and brings his free hand up to my face, brushing back some strands of my hair. "I've missed you so much, Lou."

There's pain behind his voice, making it crack. I nod again and say softly, "I know."

After a long moment of silence, he drops both his hands and takes a step away. "Can I come back sometime? See you again?"

If I thought seeing him unkempt, zoned out, and reeking of beer was hard, it's got nothing on this. The mixture
of hope, hurt, and longing is written everywhere on his
face. He may not be my boyfriend anymore, but I still care
about him. His well-being, his sobriety.

Finally, I answer, "Of course you can."

He lets out a long, deep breath and takes another step
back. A small smile starts to spread. "See you later, then."

I smile back and nod.

"Well, all right." This time I get a full-blown, signature
Bobby grin, goofiness and all, just before he turns and
makes his way back toward the stairwell.

Alone in the quiet hall, I take a minute to pull myself
together. Confusion, longing, grief, loneliness—with all
the conflicted emotions bubbling inside me right now, I'm
feeling one small step away from fucked up. Half of me
wants to lock myself in my room with a bottle of vodka to
lose myself in, while the other half wants to yank Bobby
in there with me so I don't spend another Sunday night
alone.

Both halves sound like losers, so instead I open the door
and lock myself inside before I find myself at the liquor
store or back in Bobby's truck.

I strip out of the uncomfortable, barely-there dress and
change into jammies. After washing my face and brushing
my teeth, I numbly walk toward the oversized bed and slip
beneath the covers.

The tick-tock of a grandfather clock, the outside wind's
tug and pull rattling the window, the emptiness filling the
room.

I don't even know why I'm crying when the tears start
to fall, running down my cheeks and onto the white pillow beneath my head. Just like last Sunday, and the two
before that, I can't turn it off. Maybe allowing myself only
one day a week to cry isn't enough. It flows and flows like
endless rain, with nothing but the saltiness on my lips and

the quiet quivers of my body to remind me I'm feeling anything at all.

When that soothing warmth appears out of thin air, I stop. Glance around. I can't see him this time, but I know he's here.

It's the strangest thing, but he calms me in a way I don't think I've ever experienced. He shouldn't have such an effect on me, I know this. It goes against all of my instincts—the ones that tell me I should fear him. Especially after what happened earlier today. Whatever that was.

It doesn't matter what logic screams, I can't deny the connection I feel to him. It's deep in my chest, a soothing caress over the hole that usually aches there. His presence, it's not invasive, not demanding. There's no pressure, no expectations, no prompting. My breathing calms, my body stills. In and out, one breath at a time, until my stiff shoulders relax into the mattress.

I close my eyes and drift away.

THE SEARING PAIN IS WHAT hits me first. My eyes dart down toward a nasty gash above my chest. A thick piece of glass sticks out of my skin, but I tear my gaze away before I can get too caught up in it.

Damn, it hurts.

There's a small body in my arms, my bare feet trudging through slimy mud with each step I take across the farm. The body squirms against me until a familiar face angles upward to meet my eyes. I swallow hard, trying to ignore little Tommy's torn up clothes, the fresh burn marks on his stomach.

"You gotta put me down," he wheezes, cringing when his T-shirt rubs one of the wounds. "Put me down. I can probably walk better than you right now."

"Hush up, Tommy. I'm fine." I'm panting, but relief fills my mind when I catch a glimpse of the garden. "See, we're almost there now."

We sneak around the back of the garden, as always, and I pray the shed's unlocked when I reach for its handle. Thankfully it opens on the first try. I wince as I carefully lower Tommy onto the dusty cot, then turn to him with a questioning look. He nods, and I don't waste any time before stumbling back outside, picking a small handful of rosemary from the garden and setting it on the neighbor's window ledge as practiced.

We all know the drill. Now all he and I have to do is wait.

I head back to the shed, weakly collapsing beside my little brother. "See now?" I hear myself whisper, my eyes heavy as I rest my head against the hard wall. "We'll be good and fixed up in no time. Nothing at all to worry about."

I'M BREATHING HEAVILY WHEN I wake, clutching the blanket against me. Are they going to be okay? Is their neighbor someone who can help them? I squeeze my eyes closed, reminding myself to take a deep breath.

Stop it, Lou. It isn't real.

No one is hurt.

It's just a dream.

Go back to sleep.

Chapter Fourteen

THE FIRST THING I DO when I wake up is look for *him*. I don't know what it is exactly—it's not like I'm any braver today than I was before—but I need to speak to him. It's been a full three days since my hand seemed to vanish into thin air, so maybe having had a little time to let things sink in made a difference. I don't know. What I do know is that there are so many things in my life I have no control over. Too many things. Whether I'm asleep or awake, it's like I hardly know my own mind these days. And I'm tired of it. Literally. I'm exhausted.

Ready or not, it's time to ask questions. And hopefully get some answers.

But I feel no sign of him now. His heat is notably absent, and it makes me pull the covers around me tighter when I sit up in bed. Still, I look around a little, feeling silly for it but not knowing what else to do.

I clear my throat. "Hello?" My voice is quiet, shy, and I get no response. "Um . . . Death?"

Hearing those words come out of my mouth and drift into the empty bedroom makes it pretty damn hard not to stop and roll my eyes at myself. But I resist, sitting up a little straighter instead and trying to add backbone to my voice.

"If you can hear me, I'd like to . . . I don't know. I'd like to see you. To speak to you."

Silence.

"I—I have questions."

Still nothing.

Okay, this is ridiculous. He probably can't hear me; not that I know anything about him, how any of this works. If another person were to tell me they met Death himself and were having one-on-one conversations with him, I'd take their temp or give them a drug test.

Yet here I am.

After another long moment of silence, I shake my head and peel the covers off. The wooden floor is cold beneath my bare feet, and I pad to the restroom, where I brush my teeth and take a short bath. It's still early. I have no reason to rush before heading over to Mr. Blackwood's, but the time seems to be ticking slowly by, leaving me with over an hour to spare once I dress in dark jeans and a hooded sweatshirt. After pulling my hair into a ponytail, I turn on my heel and crash straight into a solid, warm figure.

"Wha—Jesus—" I look up to find those blackish grey eyes piercing into me and stumble back a step. The fact I just said *Jesus* to *Death* is not lost on me. His dark hair is just as disheveled as the last time I saw him, and he's wearing the exact same fitted, black T-shirt molded to the hard shape of him, with dark, worn jeans over sculpted thighs. "You can't just keep . . . sneaking up like that."

His jaw tightens, the only indication of a reaction. His eyes are closed off. Hard. Dark brows furrow, almost slight enough to miss the movement completely. He says nothing though, which only makes me more aware of the way he seems to take up my entire bathroom. He's practically pushing me out with his presence alone.

It's not the first time I've felt the all-consuming way he commands a room, but usually I can't see him. Somehow, this feels different. More intimate in some ways, letting me see every flicker in his eyes, every tick of his jaw, each curve of muscle. Less intimate in others, relying on words instead of touch.

I yank my eyes away from him and maneuver my way around his body until I'm standing in the large open space of my room. He turns his head over his shoulder, eyes tracing my movements. He exits the bathroom, taking two large strides until he's standing beside the unlit fireplace.

There's about ten feet of space between us, but it still doesn't feel like enough. I get the impression he wouldn't be able to simmer down his heat and intensity any more than the sun would.

Finally, he speaks; the roughness beneath the cultured tone of his voice makes my spine tingle. "Your questions."

Straight to the point. I wasn't prepared for that and don't really know where to start.

After a beat, I say, "So, you can hear me then."

"That's not a question."

"*Okay* . . . You can hear me then?" I make sure to emphasize the upward tilt at the end, exaggerating the—now—question.

"Apparently, yes."

"Apparently?"

"Are these your questions?" The way he asks, it's not like he's mocking me, but rather genuinely confused. His eyes narrow slightly, like he's trying to work out a puzzle.

"You were here a few nights ago," I mutter. When I realize that's another statement, I add, "Weren't you?"

A pause, then a firm nod. "In a way, yes."

I frown before recalling I wasn't able to see him that time. Is that what he means by *in a way*?

I'm about to ask when the hard edges of his body begin to blur, smooth shoulders fading enough that I catch glimpses of the brick wall behind them. It's not much, not like last time when he disappeared, but I realize he might be about to take off.

The next thing I say comes out of my mouth on its own,

in a hurry before I lose my chance. "You saved me."

His muscles tense, jaw ticking again and eyes somehow hardening even more. Scared he's going to leave before I can go any further, I force my legs to take a step forward, then another, until I'm close enough to have to lift my chin to see those eyes.

"Why?" I whisper. With the closeness, his warmth reaches me like a silky blanket teasing my skin, making me want to inch even closer. But I don't.

A moment of silence passes. "I can't answer that."

"Can't? Or won't?" My eyes drift briefly to his neck when I see him swallow, then flick back up to his face. "Please. Why did you save me?"

Finally, he just shakes his head, almost in defeat. Such a contrast to the stiffness of his body, the intimidating stance of his strong build. "I . . . don't exactly know."

The vulnerability of his answer hits me hard, for some reason. This man, so unyielding and centered, with enough strength to steal my soul with a single look. Yet in this moment, he seems so . . . uncertain? Cautious?

He takes one slow step back, away from me. "Next question." His back's almost pressed up against the wall now, nowhere else to go.

My eyebrows knit together, my eyes tracing the set of his jaw, the way his lips tighten as he watches me.

Wait, *am I making him uncomfortable?*

Just in case, I follow his lead and take a few steps back myself. His broad shoulders relax ever so slightly, just enough to confirm my suspicion. I keep my observation to myself and decide to take advantage of this time he's giving me.

I can't help it when my questions come tumbling out all together, rushed. "How do you do that? Just appear out of nowhere? And what happened to my hand the other day, when I reached out for you? How come sometimes, like now, I can see you, but other times I can . . . feel you? And why are you solid one minute, but then almost, like, fading away the next?"

He's shaking his head, fist clenching, clearly frustrated at something. At me? It doesn't reach his eyes, but that doesn't stop the tightening of my stomach. What he does next though almost makes my jaw drop, and I can't help but stare in fascination. He licks his lips, gently biting down on the bottom one, then rakes his fingers through those thick, wild strands of hair, like he's contemplating something.

I don't realize that watching him has me biting down on my own lip until it starts to hurt. I quickly release it and lift my chin, expression bold. It's my you-didn't-see-that pose.

When his dark gaze latches onto mine again, it's resolute. Some decision has been made.

"What?" I ask, still feeling thrown off and flustered.

"That's a lot of questions," he murmurs, a trace of irritation in his voice. He's still mostly guarded, though, unreadable through his eyes. "As far as the last one, it's simpler just to show you."

"Um . . ." What does that mean, exactly? Before I have time to respond, he's distanced himself by moving across the room, into the corner farthest from where I stand.

"I don't understand."

"Just wait."

A second goes by.

And another.

Then I notice it; how the wavering of his form increases, the way his chest and torso start to blur like the outline of his body. I open my mouth, not sure how this explains anything, and he catches my eye. He's focused entirely on me, his gaze like a penetrating thread connecting me to him, willing me to stay patient. With each second that passes, he fades a little more. I can make out the off-white colors of the wall behind him, flickering in and out of sight.

Without warning, he's crossing the room, taking long, steady strides until he's standing right in front of me.

"Touch me." His command is low, a rough timbre that sends a shiver down my body.

I'm frozen, willing the nerves that are suddenly fluttering in my stomach to settle. Slowly, I reach out and bring my fingers to his taut chest. The heat of his skin burns straight through his shirt and into me. A light stroke, a brush of his warmth beneath mine, and he's already becoming more solid. I gasp and my head tilts up so I can meet his eyes. I know what I see, the way his form solidifies when he's near me, but I still don't understand. How could that be? Why?

He's looking down at me, dark lashes casting half moons above his cheekbones. Unreadable.

I let both my gaze and hand wander. My fingers slide up his neck, taking their time. I stroke the hard edge of his jaw with my thumb, before drifting up and into his hair. It's softer than I thought it'd be, thicker too. Slowly, carefully, I smooth the strands falling messily over his forehead, bringing them over to the side, only for them to fall back disobediently. I've almost forgotten about the reason I'm doing this in the first place, and when I realize how this probably isn't what he meant, I drop my hand.

My throat's thick, and I clear it before returning my gaze to his. But what I find isn't the blackish grey I expect. There's a shimmering deep green at the edges of the iris, just like that first night in the lake.

"Your eyes," I breathe.

Some sort of recognition seems to spark in them, and he gives his head a small but firm shake. Just like that, the green is gone, leaving not even a trace to be found. He takes a slow step back, the sudden movement cracking the hypnotic trance he has over me. I let out a long breath.

Looking him over from head to toe, I notice he's now as solid as I am. Realization dawns. "That day on the sidewalk. That's why you blocked me in against that tree when you started to disappear. To close the distance between us, so you'd be able to . . . stay . . ."

He doesn't say anything, just watches me. His guard is up even more now. Eyes, mouth, and jaw hard. And I know that's all I'm going to get from him today. His patience with me has reached its limit.

"Can I ask just one more question before you go?"

His eyes narrow slightly, but he gives a barely noticeable nod.

"Have you ever done this before?" I pause for a second, working out how to phrase what I'm trying to say. "Saved a person? Or even . . . touched another person?"

He's so still, so quiet, I don't think he's going to answer. His lips press together, and I wonder if he's trying to decide whether he should. Within moments, the solid outline of his shoulders, his arms, begin to fade again, and I chew my lip. He's not going to tell me, is he?

But then, just when I'm about to give up altogether, he shakes his head. "No. I haven't."

He's gone before I can respond. I stand alone in my room, frozen in place for I don't know how long, replaying every second over and over.

No. I haven't.

That's the only part of our conversation that really makes sense to me. Not why he saved me—*me*, of all people—or what exactly happened with my hand the other night; I still wish I had the answers to those questions. But the fact that he's never done this before, that makes sense.

Never saved a life. Never touched a person. A woman.

This is just as new to him as it is to me. Perhaps newer to him in some ways; I've been surrounded by people on and off my entire life. I think back to that first time he felt me, skimming over my scar, my neck, in the bathroom. He was so gentle, so careful. Like I might break. And then the other night, when he traced his fingers along my lips . . . I remember thinking there was something so deliberate yet sensual about the way he did it, almost like it was his first time touching a woman's lips.

And it was.

The alarm clock on the nightstand blares, making me flinch as I snap back to reality. I let out a shaky breath and move my wobbly legs toward the clock, hitting the golden piece of metal at the top to make it stop.

Eight fifteen. Right.

Mr. Blackwood.

I have a job to get to.

Chapter Fifteen

CLAIRE'S NOT BEHIND THE FRONT desk when I descend the staircase. Instead I find her standing by the front door, dumping items into one of two large cardboard boxes. Her blonde hair is pulled back in a high, perky ponytail today, and when she sits beside the Christmas tree, dressed in brightly colored leggings and a sweater dress, she reminds me of a Christmas elf. I hold back a chuckle; does she not realize it's almost February now? It's not just her, either. The whole town seems to be the type to leave their Christmas lights on year-round.

"Morning." I stroll up beside her and peek into the boxes. One is partially filled with Christmas decorations, and the other carries a folded Happy New Year banner and other knick-knacks.

I'm half paying attention, half still reeling from my moment with *him* upstairs. It feels strange, almost unreal, being down here right now as though everything's normal, after . . . that.

"Morning, Lou!" Claire plucks four reindeer figurines off the window sill, then sheepishly glances from the boxes to me and back again. A scrunched up, embarrassed grin spreads across her face. "Better late than never, right?"

I smile back. "That's my motto."

"Right? Works wonders for me. I considered skipping

the New Year decorations altogether since it's so late, but how sad would that be? You can't just *skip* a holiday." Her eyes dart around once more. "You don't think it's a little over the top, though? I mean, a huge banner in a small place like this?"

"No way." Scanning the rest of the lobby, I see that most of the Christmas decorations have already been removed by now, other than the big things like the lights and tree. "Need a hand? I still have a minute before I need to head out."

"Really?" She sounds doubtful, but her blue eyes twinkle at me as she moves to a ladder and pulls it toward us.

I laugh. "Yeah, is it such a surprise?"

"No, it's just . . . I didn't think you'd be into this sort of thing, I guess."

I shrug a shoulder as I kneel down to retrieve the banner. "I love the New Year. It's my favorite holiday." It's the truth, even though my voice sounds small and sad when I say it. I can see Claire watching me silently, so I let myself continue. "Grams always said that a new year can mean a new beginning if you want it to." I chuckle dryly. "We had a lot of new beginnings."

I pause as I fumble with the banner, trying to stretch it out, and Claire grabs onto the other end. She climbs up the ladder with her end in hand and pins it easily above the doorway before climbing back down. I take my turn, adjusting the ladder a few feet to the right and making my way up its steps.

"Anyway," I continue as I pin the right side up, "with everything going on lately, I didn't get to celebrate like she and I usually would have. My first New Year ever that I didn't celebrate, actually. So I love that you're doing all this." I lower myself onto the ground, then step back to admire our work. "It's perfect."

Claire's mouth is hanging open, probably trying to process the talkative side of me. I can't blame her; even when we hang out after work, I haven't been the most open person. Things have been rough lately—not to mention more than a little odd—and she has no idea how much this small act has just helped me. I'm not even sure I know either just yet, but I already feel the way this space is soothing some of the ache in my chest.

Besides, it's about time for me to quit moping around and figure out how to live on my own.

"Well," she finally says, "I'm happy to help." Then she leans in, wraps her skinny arms around my own, and squeezes. After a second, I hug her back. It's kind of nice. "Oh!" Claire jumps back and skips—literally, she *skips*—toward the front desk. "I almost forgot, this came for you today."

She pulls open a drawer, grabs a small, rectangular card, then hands it to me. It's a postcard. I know who it's from before I even start reading the familiar cursive handwriting.

Hey, Bitch!

Sounds like a rad ass town! Other than the occasional farm, super nice people, and lack of anything resembling a mall, of course. But hey, that leaves you, which is reason enough for me to wish I was there! I miss you, lady. Been trying out this new lemon juice fad and without my bestie, I don't even have anyone to make fun of me over it. I tried using Daniel as a temporary Lou replacement, but you can imagine how that went over. He wouldn't even wear your signature perfume for me! Major party pooper, that one.

Speaking of parties and poop, I feel like I need to rub in your face that the kids and I partied hard without you for New Years. I'm talking breast milk shots, poopie diapers, and temper tantrums galore, so, yeah. Bet you're feeling pretty disappointed about your early midlife crisis now, aren't you?

P.S. You're beautiful. (I still hate you for leaving, though.)

xx

I can't help but laugh. God, I miss you, Jamie. Probably my one regret about moving. When I look up, Claire's tied up on a phone call. I tap the desk to get her attention, give her a wave, and head for the door.

Just as my hand reaches the handle, the door whips open, sending a blast of cold air over my face and through my hair. A guy walks in, pulling the door shut behind him as he glances between me and Claire, who still has the phone to her ear as she jots something down on a notepad. He returns his attention to me, a slow, deliberate smile lifting one side of his lips.

Wait, I know him. His blonde, buzzed hair, those light brown eyes that zero in on my curves. He's that waiter who flirted with another server on the night Bobby took me out. Dylan, I think.

I don't know if he recognizes me, but he doesn't refrain from letting his gaze rake me over. It feels sleazy, sinking into my skin. All the soap in Ashwick can't rid a girl of a look that dirty. I narrow my eyes, wishing looks could kill when he finally makes it back to my face.

"Dylan!" Claire's cheery voice snaps him out of it. She sounds both pleased and baffled. "What are you doing here?"

He strolls over to her. It's a lazy, arrogant walk. "Hey, baby."

Baby? He leans across the desk and presses his lips right onto Claire's. Perhaps *pressing* is too mild a word—this guy's practically eating her face. After a few seconds, she breaks away and shoves his shoulder playfully before glancing over at me, her face flushed.

Please don't tell me you're with that guy, Claire.

She clears her throat. "Lou, this is my boyfriend, Dylan." Her eyes warm as she gazes at him. "Dylan, this is Lou."

"Ah, the infamous Lou," he says with a smirk.

I'm grateful I'm still standing near the door, too far away to be expected to shake his hand. I do not want this guy's hand anywhere near me.

At my silence, he raises an eyebrow. "Not gonna ask how

you're infamous?"

"Nope." I glance back at Claire, whose eyes plead with me. *Give him a chance,* they say. *Please, for me.* The fact she even feels the need to plead with me this early upon introductions tells me that somewhere, hopefully not buried too deep down, she knows he's a douche.

My attention darts to the clock ticking away behind her. I need to leave. And I don't want to hurt Claire.

Finally, I turn back to Dylan. "Good to meet you," I offer, trying my best to sound sincere, "but I really need to get going."

"Hey, Lou," Claire shouts as I shove the door open. "Happy New Year!"

I smile over my shoulder. It's a genuine, full-hearted smile. "Thanks. Happy New Year to you, too."

I inhale the cold air as I walk, enjoying the quiet streets around me. I haven't quite sorted out my many conflicted emotions yet, and I get the feeling it may be a while before I do, but sometimes it helps to focus more on the things right in front of you.

Of course, there's still a hole in my heart; a gaping, burning void that had settled in uncomfortably the morning I found Grams's lifeless body. It's carved right in between the one I was born with from Mom being taken from this world, and the one Dad dug himself when he chose to follow her. But little by little, there's a new light building in there, too. A warmth that gives me hope. It's in the little things like Happy New Year wishes and a winter's breeze, and it's in the power of a friendly smile from Claire and a signature 'Hey, Bitch!' from Jamie.

I'm aware I've got a long way to go before I figure out my new normal, though—whatever that word means, anyway.

How can I even begin to scale 'normal', when I spent my morning conversing with a man who goes by Death?

Shaking my head, I listen to the gentle thump of my

boots hitting concrete as I walk. *Conversing* has to be the biggest understatement ever. I don't understand the way he makes me feel. How someone I don't even know could have such an effect on me. When he's near, it's like something else takes over entirely. It's a warm oil being slowly, lazily, drizzled down my neck, spine, and thighs before it's set on fire—a blazing, all-consuming, give-me-more kind of fire.

And I don't know what to do with it. Then again, I guess nothing *can* be done, so I should just stop thinking about him altogether until I know what's going on.

The iron gates creak behind me as I make my way toward Mr. Blackwood's front door—a door that's already partially opened, allowing me to hear his grunting before I even get up the porch steps. I poke my head inside. I don't immediately see anyone, but Mr. Blackwood's gruff voice is clashing against a sharp, feminine one. They're talking over each other like it's a competitive sport neither will quit until the trophy's in their hand.

Cautiously, I step inside, closing the door behind me. A second later, a plump woman exits the kitchen, her chest puffed out and agitation written all over her flushed face. "You hired me for the job, which means I'll use whichever methods I—"

"Bullshit methods produce bullshit products." Mr. Blackwood is right behind her, practically shoving her through the living room with his barking voice alone. "If I wanted candles and chants and whatever other nonsense you have up your sleeve, I would've called a goddamn reality show to get this crap on camera."

The woman *humphs* and *tsks* and shakes her head. "For seventeen years I've been doing this, Mr. Blackwood. I certainly know what I'm doing."

"Yeah, yeah, like I haven't heard that before." He yanks a leather wallet out of his pant pocket and shoves a wad of cash toward her. "Thank you for wasting my time. Now have a nice day." He extends a wrinkled hand toward the front door, not two feet away from where I stand.

The woman glances at me and flushes again. I offer a sympathetic smile, which earns me a glare from Mr. Blackwood. After a moment, the woman grabs the cash, lifts her chin, and gives Mr. Blackwood a pretty impressive do-your-damnedest look. "Fine. If this is how you do business then that's just fine. But when another year passes by and you still haven't made contact, just remember it was *you* who kicked me out before allowing me to finish the job."

With that, she turns on her heel, opens the door, and slams it behind her, the clicking sound of her shoes fading as she makes her way down the winding path. I glance over at Mr. Blackwood, trying to assess the situation.

I notice then that he looks different today. His long grey hair isn't stringy like usual, but smooth and freshly washed. He's dressed in a decent, if understated, grey suit—sans the tie—and his beard is neatly trimmed. Looking around the living room now, I see that there aren't any empty glass bottles either. I sniff the air, taking a few steps forward until I'm right in front of the old man, then sniff again.

The aged lines around his hazel eyes crinkle as he narrows them at me. "Quit it."

"Quit what?" I ask innocently, giving his suit another whiff.

"That . . . thing you're doing. It's weird."

"Is it?" I suppress a chuckle. "You smell nice today, Mr. Blackwood." My eyes wander around the room until they land on an opened water bottle at the breakfast nook. "Have you been drinking water?"

He ignores me, turning away and limping into the kitchen. I follow and watch him open a cabinet door, shuffle things around for a second until he retrieves a small bottle of whiskey. He turns around, looking me straight in the eye as he downs a large gulp and lets out a satisfied sigh. "Can't be reeking of liquor during a business meet-ing, can I?"

I quirk a skeptical eyebrow. Claire's already told me he doesn't work, so what kind of business meeting would he be having? I want to straight up ask him, but I don't want to overstep anymore. Not when he's given me a job—something I know he didn't have to do, wasn't even looking for. Plus, the man gets enough nosiness from the rest of the town as it is.

Instead, I ask, "Why'd you hire me?"

"What kinda question is that?" He slams the bottle on the counter and wipes his mouth with the back of his hand. He leans forward, eying me like I'm a child who doesn't know when to shut up. "Needed a job, didn't you?"

"Well yeah, but…"

"So?"

"So . . ." He's trying to intimidate me. I keep my voice nonchalant, my posture casual as I lean a hip against the wall, still lingering in the opening between the kitchen and the living room. "Why did *you* hire me? You were ready to throw me out the door when I showed up. In fact," I pause, narrowing my eyes as I recall the odd look that flashed upon his face when he finally looked at me that first day. "You didn't offer me the housekeeping job until you looked at me."

I've gone over the scenario in my head more than once, and despite knowing it may not be true, I can't fathom why else he would've reacted as he did after seeing my face that first time. Hearing my full first name.

I have to know. I have to say it aloud. I take in a deep breath, willing myself to just spit it out. *It's been over a month since she's been gone. You can talk about her without falling apart, Lou.*

"Did you know my Grams?" I finally ask. "Tallulah Mul-ligan?"

He brings the bottle back to his lips, taking several long

sips before pulling it away. He lets out a low hiss and shakes his head. "What, did no one ever tell you never to trust a loony alcoholic's memory?"

I roll my eyes for two reasons. One, he's avoiding the question. Two, a housekeeper collects more insight into their employer's life than a hired detective could. In just one week of employment, I've already begun to suspect Mr. Blackwood isn't as physically reliant on alcohol as he appears. Nor is he as—in his words—'loony' as he lets the town think. For these same reasons, I decide to ignore his question altogether and ask another of my own. "How well did you know her?"

Before the last word's even out of my mouth, Mr. Blackwood's setting down the whiskey bottle and striding toward the living room. Just as he's about to walk right past me, though, he pauses. "Well enough to recognize the spitting image of her with one glance."

He allows only a second for that to sink in before he's off again. I look over my shoulder to find him settling into a spot on the sofa and digging through a small pile of papers on the coffee table.

My feet are glued in place, a small smile playing on my lips. That may seem like an evasive answer, but really, what he just did was give me what I needed—confirmation that he knew Grams, and hope that he'll, one day, tell me more. And maybe . . . maybe he'll even get more comfortable having me around. Open up, wanna chat more, and we'll become almost friends, or—

"Hey," he grumbles from behind me, "am I paying you to stand there and stare at the wall?"

Yeah, too soon, Lou. Too soon.

Chapter Sixteen

I KEPT MY HEAD DOWN AND my hands busy all day, but really my mind was spinning with questions about Mr. Blackwood and Grams.

How exactly did he know her if he didn't move to town until twenty years ago? Then again, perhaps Claire's mom was wrong about that.

What would their relationship have been, though? Not going to lie—I even entertained the possibility of him being my grandfather, in spite of their huge age gap. *See, Grams?* I accuse silently. *Could've prevented all my wild notions if you were a little more open with me.* Sometimes refusing to talk about something is exactly what beckons the curiosity in others. Nosiness thrives on closed doors.

Dad called it 'filling the vacuum.' The expression had come up one day when I asked why he always seemed sad. Even on his happy days, the sadness never quite left his eyes. Just like all of my memories involving Dad, I remember the day as vividly as if it were yesterday.

"*Um . . . Daddy?*"

"*Yes, pumpkin?*"

"*Why . . . why are you so sad all the time?*"

He looked away from the open hood of his car, eyebrows furrowing as he fixed his gaze on me. "Now why would you think a thing like that, Lou? I'm not sad when I'm with you."

"Sometimes, I hear you at night. When you're having bad dreams. And I know you're sad, Daddy. I know it."

He squeezed his eyes shut, gripping the wrench in his hand a little tighter. After a moment, he opened them and smiled softly at me. Even his smiles were so, so sad. "I'll let you in on a little secret. Sometimes when you're sad, it just means your heart is so wonderfully full of happy moments. And mine, pumpkin? My heart is packed. Achingly so."

I smiled a little. That didn't sound like such a bad thing at all. "Can you tell me?" I asked, angling my head upward to see him better. Daddy was a tall man. "Can you tell me what kind of happy moments are making your heart ache?"

He opened his mouth, but the screen door swung open, and Grams quickly hushed him up, mumbling something about how wallowing in the past never helped anyone.

Dad turned to her and said, "And you think secrecy does? You think not talking about things means they never happened?" When she didn't respond, he shifted his attention back to me, kneeling down so we were eye-level. There was a serious look in his eyes then, a look that showed up often those days. "Never feel the need to close your eyes on the things that make you who you are. The good, the bad, and the ugly. You understand?"

I nodded eagerly, drinking his words down like chocolate milk despite having no concept of their meaning at the time. "Yes, Daddy. I understand."

"Good. That's good, pumpkin." Then he stood and walked over to Grams, raising an eyebrow. "And you," he said quietly, "the only thing you'll accomplish by constantly shutting down her questions is getting a girl who spends her time filling the vacuum, concocting wild stories in her mind to provide her own answers."

Grams took a step toward him, narrowed her eyes, and put a wrinkled hand on her hip. "Trust me, Steve. Sometimes even the wildest stories are better than learning the truth."

I shake my head, trying to push the memory away. I can never decide if reliving moments like that make me happier or sadder than I already am.

The more I thought the situation over while scrubbing down countertops today, the more I returned to the idea that Mr. Blackwood and Grams being romantically involved couldn't be right. I don't exactly know how old Mr. Blackwood is, but he must be around twenty years younger than she was. I've done the math, and he would have been only a child when my mother was born. There's no way.

Regardless, I found myself staring at him a little too much throughout the day.

He never once looked up from his papers, but I've suspected the man's more observant than he lets on. In an attempt to not seem so creepy, I tried to distract myself from disturbing images of him and Grams by filling a bucket with hot water and soap and working on all the baseboards in the house. I then occupied my mind by searching through his bookshelves under the guise of dusting. I was trying to glimpse his work, any of his published books, but I was disappointed to find none. Whenever I'd find my thoughts straying in the direction of Grams and Mr. Blackwood again, I'd force myself to think of other things.

Of course, that only led to one other thing. One certain individual, actually. By the time I'm saying goodbye to Mr. Blackwood and walking out the front door, all I can think about is *him*.

I wonder—or more accurately, obsess over—why he saved me, the mechanics behind how I can see him, talk to him, and who he really is beneath the morbid title. Where does he go when he disappears? I recall the ice-like sensation that consumed my hand when it trailed after him, and a shudder runs through me.

It doesn't help that all the questions racing through my head only bring to the surface the vivid image of him standing in my room. Right in front of me. The subtle roughness to his voice, the way his dark hair falls messily over his forehead, the green specks of color that sometimes seep into the otherwise blackish-grey of his eyes, and that tick of his strong jaw.

When I reach the inn's front door, I'm so lost in thought that it takes me a minute to notice the familiar black truck parked on the street just a few feet away. It isn't until the truck's door clicks shut that I snap out of my trance and fully look up. Bobby's walking around the vehicle, dressed casually in a pair of worn jeans and a grey pullover. He gives a slow, charming grin when he reaches me.

"I was hopin' to catch you," he says, pulling the door open for me.

"Really," I reply, returning his smile. I never thought I'd see the day where it's actually nice to run into my ex like this. At least, not during those last years of our relationship when all I ever saw was drunk Bobby. Sober Bobby, though, that's a different story. "And why's that?"

I nod at Claire, who's standing behind the front desk with a wide and suggestive grin as her pretty blue eyes dart between the pair of us. "Evening," she sings before he can answer my question.

Bobby turns his attention to her and smiles smoothly. "Hey, Claire."

A light blush creeps up Claire's cheeks. "H-hey."

I suppress a chuckle but let my eyes roll. It's a light-hearted gesture though, one that's been ingrained in me from so many years of being Bobby's girlfriend. Truthfully, I don't feel a lick of jealousy at the subtle interaction, not like a typical ex-girlfriend might anyway. Actually, I find Claire's reaction endearing. I don't know if that's a good thing or a bad thing, my lack of possessiveness toward Bobby . . . probably not so great for him, I realize with a frown.

After a painfully quiet moment of the three of us standing in place staring at each other, I decide to let Bobby come upstairs with me. My muscles are sore from a long day of crouching and scrubbing, and I want nothing more than to change out of my stiff jeans and collapse onto my mattress. Or the rocking chair . . . Nothing like sprawling out on your bed to send a guy the wrong message.

"Come on," I say, turning toward the stairwell. "I'm exhausted."

He offers Claire a small wave and trails up the steps until we reach the top level. I stick my key in the door before shoving it open. For half a second I'm busy looking down at my pocket as I tuck the key back inside, but when I finally bring my gaze up, I swear my heart leaps out of my body. My hand flies over my chest as though the gesture could keep it in place.

It's *him*. Death is standing—no, *pacing*—in the center of my room, stalking back and forth like a panther guarding its territory.

Chapter Seventeen

WITHOUT THINKING, I SNATCH THE knob and slam the door shut in my own face. My breathing is heavy, and I'm still staring at the door when I hear Bobby's voice right behind me.

"Hey," he says, making me jump. His voice is soft, but when I spin around to face him, he's looking all around like he's trying to figure out what in the hell he just missed. "You okay?"

"I—yeah, I'm fine," I manage, glancing back at my closed door. What in the world is he doing in my room? And while I was gone, too. My legs suddenly feel stiff, my chest tightening.

After a brief pause, Bobby shakes his head and grabs the knob. Before I realize what he's doing, he's pushing the door open and stepping inside. My jaw drops, the blood draining from my face as I wait for him to take in the man stalking my room. Except he doesn't. Instead, he walks right into the middle of the room, stops a mere two feet away from *him*, and turns back to face me, an easy smile forming on his face.

"All clear," he says, oblivious. He tugs at the bottom of his shirt, fanning it as he lets out a low whistle. "Feels like a fuckin' sauna though. You comin' in?"

Oh my god. Bobby can't see him. It's no wonder he can

feel him, though. His presence, his heat, warms the entire room more effectively than my damn fireplace would if it were lit. My feet apparently don't notice, though, because I'm pretty sure they've turned into blocks of ice—I can't seem to move them. I'm too busy gawking at the strange scene taking place before me.

While Bobby watches me, hands now in his pockets, eyebrows furrowed, and an amused smile tugging at his lips, Death has stopped moving completely. A good four or five inches taller than my ex, not to mention broader, he's eying Bobby like an annoying little bug that deserves to be squashed. He runs a large hand through his dark hair, lip lifting in a snarl, then shifts his attention to me.

It's not until then that I get a full look at the expression on his face, and it is not a friendly one. His eyes are furious, narrowed as though he might kill the first living thing that gets close enough, and his lips are set in a grim line.

"Lou?" Bobby asks, reminding me I still haven't moved from the doorway. He lifts an eyebrow. "I've known you since high school, and I don't think I've ever seen you wig out like this before. What's goin' on?"

"Um…" What am I supposed to say? *Well, so this one time, I died and met this guy who goes by Death, and he's kind of standing right next to you. Oh, and he looks like he might kill one of us. Or both. No big deal.* Yeah, not gonna work. So instead, I find myself spewing out random words in some form of verbal diarrhea. "Nothing. What? Nothing's going on. I just—I'm—cramps," I blurt, finally getting my legs to work and crossing the threshold into the room. Not even a five-year relationship with me could rid Bobby of his strong aversion of period-talk, and I'm taking full advantage of the fact right now. "You know, that time of the month."

I step closer, pleased to see I've managed to throw him off, and Death has returned to pacing. "I mean, we can talk about it more if you're so concerned—"

"Nope. No. I'm—nope. All good."

"You sure?" I ask innocently, forcing my posture to appear casual as I walk past both men and head toward my dresser. If either of them were really looking at me, they'd see my hands trembling against the golden knobs.

"Ah, yep."

I would chuckle at the way he's suddenly avoiding eye contact if I could relax enough to do so. Instead I shrug, pulling the middle drawer open. "Okay."

I'm so busy trying to keep discreet watch over the pair of them that I hardly pay attention to the mismatched pajama set I grab. I consider escaping into the bathroom to change, but leaving them alone out here seems like a very, very bad idea. After a moment's hesitation, I set the items on top of the dresser for later.

Bobby starts strolling around the room, taking his time as he soaks it all in. It hits me he's never been inside before.

"This place suits you," he eventually says, running a hand along the brick mantle above the fireplace. He glances at me over his shoulder, his expression softening. "So, why are you havin' so much trouble settling in?"

I frown. "I'm not. Why would you think that?"

"No pictures, none of those little trinkets Grams passed down to you, nothin' . . . *you*." He pauses, then takes a few steps toward me until our faces are no more than a foot apart. He leans down, lifts his hand to the loose hair hanging in my eyes, and gently twists it in his fingers. "I know you, Lou. And it looks to me like, for whatever reason, you aren't comfortable enough here to settle down yet. Something's holdin' you back."

I can understand why he's coming to that conclusion. He's referring to my stuff, the items he used to see almost every day for five years. Pieces of me, of my family. My life. He doesn't know my bland room wasn't a matter of choice, that Tuttle Creek Lake stole it all away.

I glance past Bobby, over his shoulder. Death has stopped

pacing again. He's watching our exchange, and I can feel the fire burning behind his dark gaze. It's licking at my skin, my neck, sending a shiver down my spine. He rakes his hands through his hair, before striding the short distance across the room and pressing his palms on the wall as if he's prepared to push the thing down to get out of here.

Why *is* he here? If he's so desperate to get out of my room, why doesn't he just do that fading act and disappear already?

Bobby pulls my attention back to him by giving my hair a tug, his blue eyes looking down at me with something new—hunger. Hope. Longing.

I need to say something. I make sure to look him right in the eye when I do. "Nothing's holding me back, Bobby. I know I made the right choice, coming here."

He swallows, looks away, and I know it isn't the answer he was looking for. I hate that I'm the cause of the broken expression on his face. But I'm not going to lie to him. If I still care for him at all, and I do, the best thing I can give him is my honesty.

After a moment, he releases my hair, dropping his hand. He takes a small, stiff, step back. "Okay," he finally mutters, giving a slight nod of his head. "Then you made the right choice."

I'm so surprised by the sincerity in his response, I'm sure it's written all over my face. He turns away before I can respond, continuing his slow, observant stroll around the room. When he reaches the restroom, he steps inside, grabbing the door handle and looking back at me briefly. "Be right out."

The bathroom door closes, effectively blocking him from the man whose eyes are burning into me like a laser and making me almost sigh in relief at Bobby's temporary departure. Not quite though; it's impossible to feel too much relief when boiling hot anger still licks at my skin. Still, I only have a few minutes, if that, before Bobby comes back out here. I need to find out what the hell is going on, and I need to do it now.

My heart beats sporadically in my chest, thumping like a hollow drum that can't settle on a rhythm. Slowly, I bring my gaze to *him*. He's still leaning against the wall, but his head is angled toward me, eyes locked on mine, making me shudder at the grip he always has over me. It's solid, tangible, as if his hands have a firm hold in place at the nape of my neck, ensuring I can't turn away even if I try.

I've seen frustration in him before. I've seen impatience. Conflict. Heat. But this, the fire bubbling inside him in a way that makes the muscles of his arms and shoulders contract as he digs his fingers into the wall, this is something entirely different.

"Why are you here?" I whisper.

He says nothing. Just watches me, drinking me in with his eyes like he's breathing in a long, deep drag.

"You need to leave," I try. The reality is if he's not gone by the time Bobby comes back, I have no idea how I'm supposed to act natural and ignore the fact that Death is in my bedroom with us. I don't have much time to figure out what he wants and somehow get him out of here.

Finally, he pushes off the wall with his hands, taking a step toward me that's filled with intention. This time, I do stumble back, straight into my dresser. A sharp corner of the cherry wood digs into my back, and I wince. He doesn't stop until he's standing close enough that the front of my shirt rubs lightly against his, creating an electric friction that bounces between our bodies and makes my breath hitch.

Oh, God. It hits me then that, somehow, I've gotten too comfortable with him. Assuming I can make demands and get away with it. It's true that he's only ever been gentle with me before, but I can tell from the everlasting coldness in his dark eyes that *gentle* is not likely a word that comes naturally to him. I have no idea what he's about to do.

What he *can* do. The true extent of what he's capable of.

"Please," I hear myself whisper, my voice shaky, my eyes on the only thing in my line of sight—his T-shirt covered chest. I don't know what I'm asking for, pleading for. For him to leave? Not to hurt me?

When I feel him press closer, his thighs rubbing against mine in the movement and his head leaning down until surprisingly soft lips brush my ear, every muscle in my body freezes. I'm a statue. I can't breathe. Can't think. All I can do is wait. Wait to see what he will do.

When he finally speaks, it's quieter than a whisper. A gentle caress of silk, his breath warm on my neck. "Do you think I *want* to be here?" There's a vibration from the low hum of his voice, and it sends a shiver through me. "That I sought you out?"

The questions catch me off guard. He's not here by choice?

"Believe me," he breathes—half whisper, half growl, "if I could leave right now, I would." I swallow, a lump forming in my dry, tight throat. There's a strange hint of torment lacing his voice. A quiet desperation. I want to look up at him, see his eyes when he speaks, but he's still got me caged against the dresser, his lips so close to my ear.

Without warning, the bathroom door swings open and Bobby steps out, looking like he just splashed water over his face and hair. He scrubs a hand over his eyes and jaw and gazes at me innocently. *Oh, Bobby*. He's entirely unaware that there's a 6'4" man trapping me where I stand, no more than four feet away from him.

As Death's body stiffens, hard muscle contracting against my chest, hips, and thighs, I try my best to relax my own body—no easy feat. But I know how strange it'll appear if I don't, standing against the dresser as though I'm . . . well, trapped here. I let out a low, uneven breath and try to pull off an easy smile when I glance at Bobby. He grins back, still clueless, and wanders past me, toward the loveseat at the foot of the bed.

I take the opportunity of his back being turned to hiss at Death and shove my hands against his chest.

I still don't know what he might do to me, and the fear over that hasn't completely diminished, but he has to know as well as I do how suspicious things will look to Bobby if he keeps me here like this. Does someone like Death care about arousing suspicion? I don't know. I guess I'm about to find out.

He takes the hint and backs off, but only enough to allow me some wiggle room. He lifts his arms until they're placed on either side of my own, gripping the dresser with his hands and thereby keeping me blocked in. Finally, I'm able to shift my position and lift my chin so I meet his gaze. But he's not looking at me. In fact, with the way his head's now angled toward the wall as he grinds his jaw, I'd even go so far as to say he's trying very hard to *avoid* looking at me.

"So," Bobby says, his voice so relaxed and carefree I could almost laugh. I turn my head to the right so I can see him, peering above the strong arm that locks me in place. "You got any plans tonight?"

"Um . . ." I don't know why, but I find myself glancing up at those cloudy, dark eyes before me, searching for an answer in them. Do I have plans? Will he be here all night, or will he be able to leave soon? Do I actually want him to leave just yet? I can never seem to place the conflicting sensations his presence sends rippling through me.

"Well?" Bobby's voice draws my gaze back to him.

"Sorry, yeah. I mean, no, but I'm exhausted from cleaning all day. I really wanna just stay in, relax."

"Hmm." Bobby looks thoughtful, glancing away for a second and brushing his thumb over his chin. "Yeah, wasn't sure if you'd be workin' today. Sorry about that, stopping by without notice."

I smile half-heartedly, finding it impossible to focus on

anything other than the large, unforgiving biceps caging me in, the steady rise and fall of the chest directly in front of my face. "No worries," I manage to mutter.

"You know, if you got a new phone I could just text you beforehand."

"Uh-huh." My voice is fainter than usual, and it sounds strange even to my own ears. "Think I—think I need—"

The arms caging me in suddenly drop as the man before me takes a step back. He lets out a ragged breath and rubs a hand behind his neck, then finally—reluctantly?—meets my gaze. "This would be better for everyone if the guy left. Right now," he says softly. There's no growl this time. No simmering anger. It comes out almost like a gentle suggestion.

"I really need to rest right now," I begin vaguely, my eyes still locked on clouds of black and grey, my palms pressing against the dresser behind me. "Those cramps . . ."

I hear Bobby let out a sigh, and the creak of the loveseat as he stands. "And that's my cue," he says, amusement in his tone. When he strolls toward me, I stiffen, unsure what to do. He walks right next to me, almost touching Death's arm in the process. "Better let you go for the night. Can I see you tomorrow?"

I nod without thinking, just needing him to leave. He reaches a hand up and tucks a strand of hair behind my ear. Once again, I can't breathe, watching him barely miss making contact with the other man before me. A man who suddenly looks ready to kill again, jaw locked and eyes hard. He doesn't move though, not in the least, as though daring Bobby to come closer.

I inhale a sharp breath and angle my head to see Bobby fully, hoping I sound sure and calm when I say, "Tomorrow. We'll have lunch." I even attempt a smile.

Bobby nods and lowers his hand. "Great. Lunch it is." He turns and walks toward the door. When his fingers squeeze the handle, he looks back with a parting smile.

Then he's gone.
And suddenly, it's just me . . . and Death.

Chapter Eighteen

ONE SECOND.
     Two seconds.
          Three.

The two of us are having the most intense staring contest of my life, as though winning is nothing less than a matter of survival. An invisible rope harnesses his gaze to mine, preventing me from pulling away. His arms may not be boxing me in any longer, but with less than two feet of space between us, they may as well be. The heat radiating off his body coats my skin in a light sweat. I don't want to be the first to look away, but I can't take this.

Whatever *this* is.

I need distance between us. I need to be able to think. To breathe.

Just when I open my mouth to say something—anything—he turns away and adds a few more feet of space between us, running a hand through his wild hair before bringing it back down to brush over his face. His warmth on my skin fades with the distance, cooling me slightly, and a rush of oxygen bursts through my lungs. With his back still facing me, I can feel the tension coursing through his body, see the defined lines of his shoulders and back tightening. There's so much turmoil boiling inside of him, I can't help but wonder what's racing through his mind right now.

I'm the first to speak. "How long have you been here? In my room?"

After a pause, he slowly turns. "Hours, possibly. I don't know." His cold, expressionless eyes are looking at me, his jaw hard. Whatever war was waging inside him when Bobby was here has been shoved down and locked away.

Hours. Hours of this man alone in my bedroom. Jesus.

"And you're . . . stuck here?"

He pushes out a rigid breath, yet his tone is under remarkable control, calm and collected. Such a contrast from just a few short moments ago. "It would seem that way."

"What are you going to do?"

The low, humorless chuckle that sounds from deep in his throat takes me by surprise. It doesn't reach those steel eyes. "Lou, is it?"

I try to ignore the foreign, tugging sensation stirring in my chest at hearing my name on his lips for the first time. Somehow, it feels both intimate and threatening coming from him. "Yes." I lift my chin, hoping I seem as sure of myself as he does himself. "That's my name."

"Where I'm from—it's not like this place." He inches toward me, but only slightly. Something about his movements feels reserved, like he's holding back. Still, it's enough to spike my heart rate again. "I don't know the rules here." He curses under his breath and swipes his hair back from his forehead. "I've never spent . . . time here. Not like this. This is all very new to me."

"Where you're from? Where is that, exactly?"

With eyes of black ice and a voice just as deadly, he answers, "You don't really want to know." After a beat he adds, "No one would."

Something about the intensity rattling through his tone sends another chill over me. It's laced with warning, and I find myself agreeing with him. He's right; I don't want to know.

"So you're just going to stay here then?" I ask, even though I'm pretty sure I already know the answer.

"Does it look like I have a choice?"

"Do *I* have a choice?"

"No."

"Are you always this easy to talk to?"

A second passes with him watching me closely, before he responds, "I wouldn't know."

"What do you mean? You don't know how you usually talk to others?"

"I *don't* talk to others."

"Not even where you're from?"

"Especially not where I'm from."

My eyebrows lift. "Is that by choice? Or by circumstance?"

"Circumstance."

Wow. Not a single person he can talk to? I hardly even notice when I take a step toward him, tilting my head to the side and softening my voice. "But . . . never?"

He tenses, almost like he's not sure how to react. For a moment I wonder what made him more uncomfortable— me inching closer or the gentle way I asked the question. Eventually, he replies, gentling his own voice in return. "No. No one other than you."

I've almost closed the gap between us now. He's barely breathing, his chest completely still before me. I hardly know him, this man with soulless eyes, yet somehow, a piece of my heart aches for him. I feel it, pulling at my chest, twisting deep. I thought I knew what it meant to be lonely. How long has it been since he's spoken to anyone but me? How much loneliness has he endured? My face falls, my own recent feelings of desolation so small in comparison.

I keep my gaze locked on his when I whisper, "I can't even imagine."

He doesn't respond. With his imposing height, taut muscles, and stone-like stature, he is a solid wall. Impenetrable. And yet, I don't miss the green shimmer that glints behind his eyes. It's only there for a second, almost fleeting enough for me to think it's a trick of the light. Except I've seen the color swirl there before, and there's no way I could mistake such a vibrant emerald blaze.

What *is* that? I almost ask him, but I quickly recall the last time I mentioned it, the way he'd retreated immediately. I don't know why, but right now, I don't want him to retreat. I want to keep him talking to me. I want to glimpse that emerald fire again.

"Do you have a name?"

His eyes narrow just a fraction, as though he's trying to comprehend why I'd ask such a question. Or perhaps it's the question itself that has him confused.

"Something I can call you, other than Death?"

"You don't need to be calling me anything." His response is commanding, a crisp slice through the air, but it doesn't deter me.

"But I do." I don't want to tell him *why* I do—that I find myself thinking of him so often I need something else to refer to him as. So instead I go with, "You know my name. It's only fair that I know yours."

He gives a slight, rigid shake of his head. "I have no name."

My focus wanders from his eyes down to the smooth curves of his lips when he pulls them into a tight line. Realizing how dry my own lips suddenly feel, I lick them without a thought. When I shift my gaze back up, he's honed in on my mouth. My stomach flutters before tightening at the intimacy of his stare, and it takes me a second to find my voice again. When I do, the shakiness betrays me. "I'm going to go get changed. Make yourself . . . comfortable . . . I guess."

I don't wait for a response. Turning my back to him floods

me with an odd and confusing mixture of relief, loss, and caution. I swipe the clothes off my dresser and step inside the bathroom, closing the door without looking back.

Just breathe, I tell myself, grasping the counter's ledge and inhaling slowly.

It's not the first time I've spoken to him. Been alone with him. I'm a grown woman, and I've faced more than many others my age have. *I can handle this.*

I force my body to move, pulling my top over my head before unzipping my jeans, sliding them to the ground. The bathroom's insulated cool air bounces off the tiles, skimming my bare skin. I'm all too aware of the fact I'm standing almost completely naked with nothing but a thin door separating me from him. I know he can't see me, but that doesn't prevent a cluster of tingles from chasing my spine. After slipping on the snug pair of pajama bottoms and the loose top, I grip the door handle, swallow hard, and twist.

He's standing before the window, his broad back toward me as he gazes down at the brightened shops below. The deafening silence only betrays each creak of the wooden floors, not to mention the loud thumping of my heart, so I walk quietly toward the nightstand and retrieve the TV remote. I flick the power on, paying no attention to the channel, and soften the volume until it fades to a hum filling the background of my room.

"Can you show me?" I ask.

He whips his head around at the sound of my voice, as if I've just yanked him away from some serious train of thought. "Show you what?"

"What happens when you try to leave."

"It's not that simple."

"So explain it to me." I desperately want to understand how all of this works. How this is happening. I *need* to understand. "Please."

A low breath escapes from his lips, and his jaw ticks.

He's hesitant. "What I can tell you," he finally says, "is that there's supposed to be a connection linking me to where I'm from. And right now, it's gone." He turns away, effectively ending the conversation.

I have more questions for him—so many questions. But it's clear he won't be answering them just yet. He needs space. Privacy. Time to work out whatever's going on in his head.

After tugging the silver throw from the foot of my bed, I settle onto the rocking chair. Really I want my bed, but that'd probably be too weird. His presence may have temporarily distracted me from my aching bones and sore muscles, but now that he's slunk away into his own private shell, the dull throbbing seems dead set on returning full force. Exhaustion consumes me. I groan as I adjust my position, crossing my ankles and draping the throw across myself.

His head shifts toward me at the sound, just enough to reveal the strong angle of his jaw, the straight line of his nose. His lashes cast downward. He doesn't say anything, though, and turns back to the window after a moment.

Flicking through the channels is nothing more than a means of appearing occupied. I don't want to reveal to him how much of my attention he really has, how my thoughts gravitate toward him like a magnet, even when I try to distract myself with other things.

The silence drones on, *tick tick tick*. Each second dragged out by the tall shadow he casts over my room, the heat emanating off of him, spilling into the air and filling every corner. *Thump thump thump*, my heart smacks against my chest. I'm not naïve, nor inexperienced. I may have only been fully intimate with one man in my life, but I've never been shy, not about my body. Not about my physical reactions to certain things. Certain men. As much as I wish it wasn't the case, I know exactly why he sends shivers through my body, warm vibrations across every inch of my skin.

"Why are you hurting?"

My stomach pulls tight at the hum of his voice, like I've been caught. *He can't read your mind, Lou.* The reminder helps my muscles unclench.

"What do you mean?"

He wheels around fully, so he's facing me, and gestures toward my body. "You're in pain. Why?"

"Oh." I swear my relief is tangible. "Long day at work." When his eyebrows draw together, two hard lines forming between them, I clarify, "Cleaning. A lot of scrubbing and kneeling. I'm fine, just still getting used to it."

His lips purse, but he says nothing. The way he's watching me, cautious yet almost fascinated, makes my throat thicken. I don't think he even knows he's lowered his guard enough to let me glimpse it, that look in his smoky, dark eyes.

I clear my throat. "You can sit down." His gaze follows my nod toward the loveseat just a few feet away from me. When he doesn't move, I add, "It'd make us both more comfortable."

I watch as he crosses the room and lowers himself into the seat, taking a ragged breath and leaning forward so his forearms are resting on his knees. His large frame makes the loveseat look like it was made for a child's doll.

I know I'm staring, but I can't help it. I'm beginning to realize just how much of an enigma this man is. A walking contradiction.

Everything about him—from his appearance to his voice to his mannerisms—is powerful, strong, filled with confidence and a foreboding sense of danger. Dark, mysterious, and deadly, in a way that will leave you breathless and unsure of what's to come. And yet, in moments like this, where it's just him and me, there's a vulnerability beneath it all that draws me to him like a moth to a flame. During the moments when there's lingering silence between us, I hear the shakiness behind his otherwise strong voice. Feel the quivering of corded muscles whenever our bodies brush up against each other. See the uncertainty flash through his hard eyes whenever he finds me looking at him.

In his world, whatever world that is, he is Death. In control and wielding all the power, he knows exactly who he is. What he's doing. What comes next. But here, in my bedroom, he's just a man. A man with an undercurrent of innocence that's at clashing odds with the rest of him.

His gaze, lowered toward the ground, slowly, leisurely drifts up until it slams into mine with the heavy force of steel against steel. The green is back, emerald flames dancing behind clouds of black and grey. And with just that single look, his head slightly dipped, I know . . . Here, right now, *I'm* the one with all the power.

Chapter Nineteen

SOMETHING ABOUT THAT KNOWLEDGE SENDS an electric spark through me. A part of me revels in it, knowing I have more control than even he might suspect, and yet another part of me is intimidated by it. I can stand and face the cold, commanding side of him, but I almost don't know how to respond to the glimpses of vulnerability I'm getting now.

"Tell me . . ." My voice comes out huskier than I intend. I'm not trying to seduce the man—*I don't think.* "Why did you save me, that night in the lake?"

He doesn't look away, doesn't try to avoid the question. A thousand unspoken thoughts deepen his gaze, darken his expression. It takes him a minute to respond, but I don't mind. I'll be patient. I know he's going to answer this time. Something about that green glimmer; it thaws the ice of his usually frigid stare. It adds warmth and fire, hinting at the kind of secrets I suddenly feel a burning ache to unravel.

"I needed to." It's a murmur, almost quiet enough to be a soothing whisper. "I recognized something about you. Your eyes, your soul. I don't—I don't know what it was. It felt like . . . I owed it to you."

"Owed me my life? W-why would you owe me anything?"

He lets out a deep sigh, like he's exhausted, and scrubs a hand over his face. "I've been asking myself the same damn thing."

Neither of us speak for a long, drawn-out minute. I don't know what to say. He recognized me? He owed me? How's that possible? Surprising me further is the knowledge that Death would even care about such a thing. Maybe I'm too judgmental, but even if it were true—if he did owe me somehow—I wouldn't have taken someone with his title or demeanor as the type to readily return favors.

He's still lost in thought when he leans back against the seat, stretching his long legs out before him. His shoes almost brush my bare feet. "I got myself into this mess," he mutters, though it's more like a groan. "Both of us. I crossed a line that night. Did something that isn't done—ever. Now the universe is confused, crossing more lines that aren't meant to be crossed. Blurring them altogether. Blurring you and me together."

His words hit me with surprising force. I never considered what that night might have resulted in for him. The consequences of such an act. How it's affecting him, his world, everything he knows. Everything he's a part of. It's like a thread that's come loose, slowly unraveling and taking everything he knows with it.

"And that . . . is that how this all started?" I whisper. "That first time in my bathroom, I heard you. The second time I felt you, when you touched me." He swallows at the mention of that moment, the act drawing my gaze to his throat. "And now, usually, I can see you."

There's a hard edge to his voice. "I didn't have enough control in the beginning to cross over fully. I was both here, in your world, and in mine."

"Your world," I say quickly, remembering what happened with my hand. "I think I felt it—"

"Where I come from," he growls, the strong reaction taking me by surprise, "is not someplace you will ever know. Do you understand?"

I swallow the lump in my throat. He looks impossibly threatening for someone lounging in a loveseat. "You're learning everything about me and my world firsthand. It only makes sense I'd want to know a little bit about yours. About the person who's stuck inside my room with me. I should get to know something about you, shouldn't I? What it's like being you?"

At that, he turns his gaze to the window, letting the silence build. When he responds, it's quiet. Low. Dangerous. "You shouldn't ask questions you don't really want the answers to."

"What makes you think you know what I do or don't want?"

His eyebrow arches, and he leans forward. Closer. And closer. There's something daunting about his movements, subtle as they are. Challenging. He doesn't stop until our faces are inches apart. His heat pours over me from head to toe at the close proximity. So much for me being the one in control.

"You want to know what it's like being me? What it's like to steal a person's soul?" he murmurs. The black in his eyes dances with the grey like wicked flames for a moment, until all that's left is a cold, dark void staring into me. When I don't respond, he continues, "To watch people die, every single second I'm in my world. See their fear when they look at me, when they feel my call. That moment they realize they will do anything, *anything*, I tell them to. Is that," he says slowly, "what you want from me?"

My pulse is racing, my chest rising and falling. He's so close that our uneven breaths tangle together.

I'm struck silent for a beat, frozen in place by his words, by his stare, by his essence. "Yes," I finally whisper back, "that's what I want." His gaze drops to my lips, following each movement as I speak. "I want to know the person the universe has me so confused with. I want to know who's sitting in front of me. That means all of it, the good and the bad."

His eyes close, and he draws a long breath. When they open again, they're colder than ever. "And that's where you'd be disappointed, Lou. There is no good to be found in Death."

Slowly, he backs away from me, until he's pressed against the loveseat. He turns his head so he's facing the window to his left.

"Maybe not in death," I answer hesitantly, "but there is good to be found in you." He doesn't move, doesn't flinch. Doesn't indicate he's heard me at all. Still, I continue, "I know there is, because I've seen it. It takes good to save a person's life. And it takes selflessness to do it when you know you shouldn't. When you don't know what the outcome for you will be. That night . . . it was the scariest moment of my life. I really thought that was it, that I'd never wake up to see the sun again."

Finally, he shifts his head just enough to look at me. And I mean *really* look at me. His eyes roam freely, lingering on every part they touch. They burn into my eyes, warm my neck, pierce my lips. I can't tell what he's thinking, but I take strange comfort in seeing that the green glint is back again. "Anyway, I didn't realize what it might be costing you. Just—thank you."

His silence torments me in the oddest way. *Say something,* I inwardly beg. *Anything.*

"Are there more of you?" I ask. It's a desperate, scrambling attempt to fill the void, and it works—my voice snapping his eyes back to mine, holding his gaze there. Unfortunately, it takes the green with it, swirls of black-grey eating up any hint of warmth and replacing his stare with that deadly black ice.

"Yes." He stands so gracefully it doesn't make a sound and distances himself until he reaches the window. He doesn't turn his back to me this time. Instead, he leans the side of his frame casually against the wall, in a way that looks almost unnatural for his sturdy build.

"Are they like you?"

"Our paths never cross."

"So how do you know they exist?"

One dark eyebrow quirks. "Death is an endless game. It takes more than one individual to keep up with the demand."

A cold, hard chill slides down my spine. I think back to the night I died. The first time I saw him. So firmly ingrained into my mind, I can remember every detail like I'm still there. *Coming closer, floating, steadily closing the gap of blue-black water between us. The edges of his large frame are blurred, almost convincing enough to be a dream.*

"And what—what exactly do you do? When someone dies?"

If voices had colors, his would be ash—black, smoky remnants of all that's been lost. "I collect them."

I can feel my life wasting away with each second, disconnecting me from my frozen heart. Something's tugging at me, calling my name. A magnetic force trying to yank me away from my body.

My heart pounds against my chest, a dull thump ringing through my ears. "Do they always come with you?"

The closer he gets, the stronger the pull.

The way he's looking at me, it's like he sees the images playing out in my head. He's right there with me in that ice-cold lake, flashes of lightening striking down above the water.

He knows as well as I do what I felt that night—that I already know the answer to my question.

And I know I will follow him anywhere.

He answers anyway. "Always."

He's too strong; I'm a tiny puff of smoke going up against a wall of stone.

I'm barely whispering, barely breathing, when I say, "And then what? What happens to them?"

His stare stays latched onto mine, an empty void gripping me tight and sucking me dry. Words clear as day yet dark as night, he says, "That's not my concern."

I'm whipped out of the hypnotic memory like a cold bucket of water has been poured over my head. "What?"

"I unlock the door, summon them through. Take their present, their past. What happens beyond that—like I said, not my concern."

"Take their past?" Before he can respond to that, my brows furrow, spine straightening as I sit up in the rocking chair. Grams, Mom, Dad . . . their faces surface, haunting my mind whether I want them to or not. "Wait, aren't you at least curious? Don't you want to know where people end up, after everything? If they're going to be okay?"

"No."

"How . . . How could you not care?"

"Care?" It's so subtle, I might not have noticed the way his eyes narrowed if I weren't paying such close attention. But I am. I don't miss the clench of his jaw, either. "You forget who I am," he says quietly, a dangerous hum sailing from his lips to my ears.

"Don't ever forget who I am."

Chapter Twenty

*A*STING RIPS THROUGH MY CHEST, *making me wince. I open my heavy eyes, but it's all a blur. A fuzzy hand pops into view, fingers pressing something white onto my wound. I groan, then tilt my chin down to see the gash. The thick shard of glass has already been removed, skin sealed up with raw stitches. It's a grisly sight but better than I could have hoped for without proper hospital care.*

"There, there," a gentle voice coos. The tension in my body eases as I remember where I am. The shed. Our neighbor's land.

"Tommy," I murmur, my voice wrangled as I try to lift my head.

"Shh." The hand guides me back down. I manage to turn, just enough to see the boy lying beside me. Tommy's bare waist is wrapped in white cloth, his eyes closed, chest rising and falling in his deep sleep.

He's okay.

We're okay.

For now . . .

WHEN I BEGIN TO STIR, it takes me all of three seconds to remember I didn't fall asleep alone. My eyes pop open, body stiff even as I slowly realize he's not here. He can't be. His warmth has completely evaporated, the naked chill from outside sweeping in through the cracked window and blowing lightly through my hair. I bolt upright in the bed. I can't resist scanning the room, just in case I'm wrong. But of course, I'm not.

He's gone.

Not a single shred of evidence proves he was ever here in the first place.

And yet, I feel . . . different.

When I swing my legs off the edge of the bed and stand, blood rushes to my head in a single, hard-hitting wave. I sway, pressing a hand to the mattress for stability. My heart, it doesn't feel right. There are no solid and timed thumps. Instead it flutters, like the swift wings of a tiny humming-bird in my chest. I'm careful when I walk to the bathroom, trying to keep my body steady even as my mind sways.

Something is off.

I'm drained. Weak. I've never been on a boat before, but I imagine this is what seasickness feels like. Trying to balance on a ship that rocks beneath your feet.

I splash cold water on my face, my neck, then look up. My reflection tells me I look as horrible as I feel. Drained of color, skin clammy, eyes heavy-lidded, I look like a ghost. *Ugh*. I must be getting sick. I never get sick. Not since I was young, anyway.

A ringing sounds from the nightstand, prompting me to groan. Just the thought of walking back across the room in this condition makes me want to hurl. When the high-pitched noise doesn't relent, I force my legs to move, one step at a time.

"Hello?"

"Hey, it's me." With my head spinning the way it is, it takes me a moment to place the male voice.

"Bobby?"

"Yeah." There's a pause, then his tone softens. "You okay?"

"Yeah, I'm—" I reach up to rub my temples as another wave of dizziness hits. I can't suppress my moan. "I've been better. Wait—what time is it?"

"Ten to twelve."

Holy crap. I haven't slept in like this since the first week I'd arrived here. Of course, I'd also completely forgotten Bobby's taking me to lunch today. At just the thought of food my stomach punishes me, instantly twisting. "Shit. Bobby . . ."

"What do you need?" He asks without hesitation, and it takes me by surprise. *Now there's a question I haven't heard from him in a long time.* "Tylenol? My mom says a heating pad on her back always helps. I can run down to the local—"

"What? Oh . . ." Right, my supposed cramps from last night. I'm going to hell for all my lies. And I know just the guy to drag me there. "No, it's not that. Think I must have caught something. I probably just need to sleep it off."

"Listen, I'm downstairs in the lobby—"

My groan cuts him off. "I'm so sorry, Bobby. I should've called—"

"Jesus, will you stop interruptin' me for a second?" I hear the amusement in his voice and nod, even though he can't see me. "Thank you. Now get your ass back in bed. I'm gonna pick up some things for you, 'kay? I'll be up in about fifteen minutes."

My legs feel like they're about to give out. I plop onto the bed with a long sigh, phone still pressed to my ear. As wonderful as it sounds to be taken care of right now, having Bobby locked in my room with me is a bad idea for too many reasons to count. "No, you really don't have to do that. I'll be fine. Just give me a few hours to sleep and I'll call you later to reschedule."

A low, exasperated breath sounds from the other end of the phone, but Bobby's tone is gentle when he speaks. "You're sick, Lou, and I'm standin' in your lobby with an hour to kill. It's not a difficult choice, all right?"

I'm silent, my skin getting clammier by the second. My throat is parched, but the thought of getting up to grab a bottle of water is exhausting.

"Lou . . ." He's even quieter now, a waver in his voice that says he's desperate for me to understand. "How am I ever gonna make up for all my wrongs if you don't let me in when it counts?"

I take in a long, deep breath. It reminds me of the night he took me to dinner, when he'd stated something similar. He might still feel things for me that I've lost for him, but he's also just a guy trying to make things right and get his life together.

"Okay." It comes out like a whisper, partially because I don't know if it's the right choice and partially because I'm too drained to manage anything else.

BOBBY MADE GOOD ON HIS word, spending over half an hour at my bedside. A cool wet cloth on my forehead, a glass of fresh water to my lips, a thermometer in his hand, and the comforting scent of chicken noodle soup filling my nostrils. He even gives me a fever reducer when it's time for him to leave.

Lifting the washcloth to touch the palm of his hand to my forehead, he mumbles, "Damn, I really don't think I should leave you alone like this. If I didn't have to get to the city—"

"Sick people stay home alone all the time." I groan, not bothering to open my eyes.

"No, I know, just—" He lets out a low sigh. "Claire's downstairs. I'll fill her in before I leave, make sure she checks up on you."

I grunt out a weak, "Thank you," and feel his shadow loom over me as he stands, before cool lips softly touch my cheek. It's comfortable, friendly, and I'm already drifting to sleep as the door clicks shut behind him.

I DON'T KNOW HOW LONG IT'S been by the time I start stirring again, but I'm freaking freezing when I do. The covers aren't serving their purpose. Chills run up and down my body like a million ants made of ice. I squeeze the comforter, curling into it seeking heat.

But I feel none.

Out of the corner of my eye, blurred and foggy, I think I see someone sitting in a chair beside me. Dark hair, dark eyes. I feel him, the tease of a hot breeze floating just out of reach. He's warm, so warm. If I could just get a little closer. I reach toward him, but the second my skin leaves the shelter of blankets, another wave of shivers rolls through me, making me wince and pull back.

I just need to get closer, I tell myself as my eyes fade back into a cloud of darkness. His heat. His warmth. Just . . . a little . . . closer.

<hr />

MMM. I BURROW MY HEAD into the pocket of warmth beside me. God, it feels good. The chills haven't totally let go of me yet, and my mind is somewhere between weak and loopy, like I've been drugged. But the more I rub against the solid, soothing heat pressing into my side, the more relief I feel.

On one half of my body, anyway. I'm lying on the left side of my bed, flat on my stomach. My right arm, hip, and leg are directly touching the source of the heat. The opposite side of me has been left in the cold, prickly needles racing down my arm and leg. Ugh, it isn't enough.

I need more. Yes, if I can just get a little *more*.

Keeping my eyes closed, I lift my right arm, wrapping it around the solid warmth and scooting myself closer.

Closer.

And closer. Until I'm more than halfway on top of it.

Finally. My stomach, chest, and hip make full contact as I drape my right thigh across it, capturing the penetrating warmth. The solid form shifts beneath me. A breath exhales, low and ragged, but it feels distant, hazy, and I think I might be imagining it.

It's so solid, so hard. I nestle my head into it, relaxing every part of me. *Mmm*, this time the sound pours out of me as a moan. It's like my body is sighing, finally tasting the relief it needed. Eyes still closed, my right hand starts to roam, idly teasing the warmth. Ah, so good. The tips of my fingers touch upon a thin layer of cloth. A barrier. I inwardly growl.

No, I need to be *closer*.

The heat, give me more.

I'm rough when I tug at the fabric, ruthlessly breaking the barrier away as I slide my hand beneath it, not stopping until my palm lies flat against the source.

Much better.

Hard lines ripple beneath my touch, flooding me with a deep warmth that settles into my stomach. What *is* that? I press my body closer, practically rubbing against it until I feel the solid mass beneath me stiffen.

For a second I almost freeze up at the strange movement, then resume blindly feeling around. Searching for clues. It's smooth, hard, everywhere, slightly dipping and curving in spots like a sculpture. And then, is that . . . a line of hair? Um . . . My fingers wander lower, taking in a hard, V-like curve as they do.

Then lower—

A sharp intake of breath sounds from above my head, and large fingers clasp over my own. My hand is yanked out from beneath the fabric, then dropped like my skin could burn.

Oh, crap.

This time, I really do freeze. Every part of my body tightens, from my arms to my stomach to my thighs . . . the same thighs that are wrapped around *his*. This isn't good. The tightening of my muscles has me clenching his and, well, our thighs aren't the only body parts touching. We're almost perfectly aligned. *Too* aligned. The shiver that sears through me now no longer has anything to do with my illness.

My arm is wrapped stiffly around his chest, rising and falling with the heavy pattern of his breathing. Oh my god, I don't even want to know what's going through his mind right now. He must have lain beside me to provide warmth, an innocent act of kindness, and here I am mauling him, sensations far from innocent pooling between my thighs.

Crap, crap, crap.

I need to move, right? I don't know what to do. If I scurry away from him now, it'll be obvious that I've woken. That I figured out what I'm doing, which will just make things way too uncomfortable between us from here on out. But if I remain in place, his warm breaths teasing my hair, the curves of my breasts pressed up against his hard chest, my open thighs gripping him in a way that sends delicious sparks of fire *right there . . .*

Yeah. I know what I need to do.

Without opening my eyes, I murmur a groggy groan, hoping it sounds like I'm just starting to stir, then lazily roll off him so I fall onto my back. *Calm, steady breaths, Lou.* Just like any ordinary sleeping person would do.

With our bodies still so close, I hear the distinct sound of him swallow. Feel the movement of his arm lifting, the sound of him running a hand through his hair as he lets out a long, uneven breath.

He doesn't move from beside me, though, and I can't decide if I want him to. Having him this close to me now, when I know what he feels like, the way my curves fit against his muscles . . . it's torture in the most unexpected way. But my chills are already coming back, cold bursts of air tingling across my skin, and I don't want to lose the single source of warmth I have.

I don't know how long we lie like this, two electrical wavelengths attempting to keep the sparks of our currents from ever touching. Twice, I feel the bed shift beside me, hear it creak as though he's about to distance himself. And twice, he curses under his breath and lies back down. I try to quiet the sounds of my shivers, try to will the chills away so he won't feel obligated to stay. But my body won't listen.

Eventually, who knows how long after, my heart regains a steady pace. My pulse quiets, muscles relax. The enticing lull of sleep pulls me into its soothing rhythm.

And the last lucid thought in my mind is that he, the unfeeling wall that is Death, stayed. He stayed beside me. Offered his warmth to soothe me, when he thought I wouldn't know. Maybe he's not the icy, stone-like being those haunting, steel eyes would have me believe after all. No. Maybe he's the evergreen buried beneath them.

Chapter Twenty-One

MR. BLACKWOOD HAS BEEN ABSENT for most of the day. I was surprised when he asked to see me after only an hour since my arrival this morning. He never asks for me. Never speaks at all, in fact, unless prompted. He grumbled something about having someplace to be and said I'd be on my own for the rest of the day, and that was that. He was out the door before I'd even formed a response.

It's not until my last hour, when all that's left to do is a final round of dusting, that I find myself eying the crinkled pieces of paper cluttering the coffee table and bookshelves. After all the time spent inside his house, avoiding any physical contact with the wadded-up pages, my fingers itch to pry them open. This is the first day he's left me alone, and I know better than to break his trust, but the curiosity is practically burning. Begging me to take advantage of the moment.

What could possibly make him so adamant about keeping me from looking at those papers? They aren't even organized or well-cared-for. In fact, from the wrinkles etched into most of them, they appear almost neglected. That, or overused. I suppose if he were constantly adding more notes to the pages then wadding them up again, that could cause them to wrinkle like this.

Shaking my head, I shrug the urge away. *Don't be that person, Lou.* Let the man have his privacy.

Finally, the dusting is complete. I restore the remaining cleaning supplies to the living room closet and am just about to lock up, when I remember I left my jacket upstairs. I'm extra achy as I climb up the steps, pacing myself to avoid another wave of nausea. It's been two days since The Fever—yes, I thought it memorable enough to give it a title—has come and gone, but I'm still waiting for my body to snap back to normalcy.

Once in the guest room, I grab the jacket, looking around the space as I tuck each arm through the sleeves. I can't help but wonder why he even has a guest bedroom if he never gets any visitors. It's obvious the room hasn't been used in ages, if ever, and the decor isn't exactly set up to receive guests, either. I mean, there's a spare bed and a nightstand, sure, but that's it. The closet is barren, there are no accent pieces on the walls or surfaces, no blinds on the window. There's not even a pillow on the bed, just a single, thin, grey blanket.

Strange.

A soft thump sounds as what looks like the spare key he'd lent me this morning slips from the jacket's pocket, tumbling beneath the bed. I groan as I lower myself onto my knees, the soreness from today's work already catching up to me. *Where is it?* I straighten out my legs and wiggle my way under the bed like a snake when the back of my head thumps against the metallic frame above me. A surge of pain shoots through my scalp, and small pieces of paper suddenly fall from over my head like rain sprinkling from the sky, before settling soundlessly onto the carpet.

"Shit. Shit, shit, shit."

I barely manage to wrap my fingers around the key before I scoot out and pull myself up into a sitting position. I rub a hand over the tender spot beneath my hair, flicking my gaze back toward the bed, where randomly sized paper cutouts are now scattered over the carpet. There aren't many of them, maybe five or six, but just the fact that there are any at all is odd. Where did they come from?

I duck my head back beneath the bed and scan the frame, until my eyes land on a manila folder that's been tucked into the springs, nestled against the mattress. Seriously, this man and his papers. Letting out a sigh, I begin to gather up the pages, intending on putting them back. When a scribbled word that reads *dead* catches my eye, I freeze. Lift the small, square-shaped paper. Narrow my eyes. It's a single sentence, all capital letters.

I AM NOT DEAD

My hand releases the sheet like it's made of poison. What. The. Hell. Slowly, I reach for it again, thinking maybe I read it wrong.

Nope.

The words are clear. Sloppy, but legible.

Cautiously, I pick up another one.

I CAN'T HOLD ON

Fingers now trembling, I reach for the next.

SAVE ME

The sharp sound of a car door slamming startles me and sends the pages drifting back to the floor. *Jesus.* He's back. I race to collect each sheet, then reach under the bed and stuff them back into the folder as quickly as possible. I'm already at the bottom of the stairwell when the front door opens. Thank god he doesn't even look at me, just barges inside and heads straight for the kitchen. To his beloved whiskey stash, no doubt.

Dropping the loaned key onto the coffee table as I scurry by, I exit the house without a word.

I hardly notice the cold, evening air that washes over me as I walk. The handwritten words are stapled to the forefront of my mind, forcing me to see them with each second that passes.

I AM NOT DEAD.

I CAN'T HOLD ON.
SAVE ME.

A shiver races down my spine.

Why would Mr. Blackwood be hiding notes like that? Why would anyone, for that matter?

I wonder for a second if he could have written them himself, but the missing logic in that assumption tells me it's more likely I'm just *hoping* that's the case—at least it would nix the chances of another party being involved, and I'd be able to figure out if I could help Mr. Blackwood. After a moment, it crosses my mind that the notes might not even be recent. In fact, with the worn edges, they might be fairly old. Something to do with his past? His secretive lifestyle, perhaps?

I really, *really* don't want to believe that Mr. Blackwood could be capable of endangering someone's life, but after seeing messages like that, and hidden away, no less . . . I'd have to be an idiot not to consider it.

A mixture of worry and plain curiosity grates at me with each step. I don't want to get involved. It's none of my business, and I'm not exactly the most stable person myself. But I can't quit the nagging in the back of my mind that begs the question, *What if someone's in trouble?*

Chapter Twenty-Two

BY THE TIME I REACH the inn, my bones scream for relief and my stomach demands food. After running a load of laundry through the wash, a good burger and a hot bath helped me settle somewhat. I'm still physically drained, but at least the dizzy spells have backed off. With my hair damp, dressed in a pair of leggings and a T-shirt, the second I exit the bathroom is the same moment a crash sounds from across the room. I look just in time to see *him* colliding full-on with my poor nightstand, sending the alarm clock flying to the ground. I say *poor* in reference to the piece of furniture and not the man who crashed into it, because it's obvious who took the beating here.

"Way to make an entrance," I murmur as I make my way to the closet. I haven't forgotten who he is, or the awkward situation I put him in while I was sick the other night, but sarcasm is a great go-to when you want to avoid real confrontation.

"Still working on it." The purr of his low voice is already gliding under my skin. I turn my head over my shoulder, taking him in.

Something's different about him tonight. He doesn't quite sound like the steely, foreboding Death I've come to expect. In fact, he even looks a little different. It's not his clothes, which are the same fitted T-shirt and worn jeans as always. It's not his hair, which still falls messily over his forehead. It's not in any one thing I can place, actually, but rather it's in a series of the tiniest things. His jaw isn't quite as hard as usual, and his lips are almost relaxed, rather than pulled into a tight line. But it's his eyes that are the center of my attention. Rich green swirls behind the black-grey; such a vivid and enchanting contrast, and I'm just as mesmerized by it as ever.

"The entrance," he elaborates, taking my silence for confusion. "I don't get much of a warning when it happens."

"That makes two of us." I tear my eyes away from the green to turn back to the closet. Glad for an excuse to stay occupied, I robotically go through the motions of placing shirts on hangers and setting them on the rail.

"Right," he mutters after a moment. My ears follow the sound of movement behind me until he comes into my peripheral as he settles in by the window, leaning half of his body against the wall. I watch him out of the corner of my eye. He takes a long, deep breath, gazing outward in silence. It's like we're both trying to pretend we accept this strange situation, being so out of control with our own lives.

He may not be up for chitchat, but I don't want to drown in silence this time. Grams always said that you learn the most about a person by looking in between the lines. Maybe if I can just get him talking . . .

"So what do you think so far?" I glance up at him, keeping my hands busy with the laundry.

"Of what?"

I clear my throat, ignoring the way his hypnotic voice pulls at me. "My world."

"It's . . ." His head shifts toward me, tilting. "Bright."

"Bright?" Turning away from him to sort my folded clothes into drawers, I smile slightly at that answer. "Wow, we've certainly made an impression."

He's quiet for a moment, and I have to resist the urge to

turn my head and look at him. "I've . . . not taken the time to really look around."

I snort, finding more amusement in this conversation than I probably should. Maybe it's because all the weird-ness in my life is finally taking its toll on me, and it turns out humor is a fantastic coping mechanism. Or maybe it's that starting the evening on a lighter, sarcastic note makes it hard to take anything afterward too seriously. Whatever the reason, my mood is shifting with each moment of our conversation, and I'm rolling with it.

"Well, since you're here," I place the last pair of jeans in my bottom drawer and turn to face him, "I may as well give you some more insight." His eyes narrow, like he's suspicious—as he should be. "I'm weeks behind on the rituals, so I guess that's a good place to start."

Whirling around, I head to the nightstand. I'm totally just winging this, which is not easy when someone like *him* is watching your every movement, every look. His gaze burns into my back as I pull the drawer open and withdraw a small box of playing cards supplied by the inn. I stroll to the loveseat and plop down, positioning myself into the nook on the right side and crisscrossing my legs. Glancing up at him, I raise an expectant eyebrow. "I'm going to need a hand for this. Rituals cannot be done alone."

His brows lift, and I feel a small pang of satisfaction at finally being the one to surprise him for a change. "I won't know what to do."

Ha, you and me both. "It's okay." I pat the empty space beside me. "I can show you."

He waits a beat, and though his face betrays nothing, I'm sure he's deliberating whether or not to agree to this.

"Who knows how long you'll be stuck here this time, and it *is* my room, so . . . please?" I don't know if it's the *please* that does it or what, but he seems to concede when he gives a small nod and walks toward me.

When he lowers himself beside me, it's an instant reminder of how drastically his large build dwarfs mine. His broad shoulders take up more than half of the petite loveseat, and though the width of his frame tapers off where his hips narrow, the way his legs are positioned, slightly spread out, counteracts that. He takes a breath and leans back, running a hand through his dark hair, then turns his head and looks straight into my eyes.

Holy hell, suddenly we are way too close to each other. I swear I'm burning up, his fiery heat brushing over every inch of my skin.

"Where do we begin?" he asks, and I take a deep breath. The low sound is even more hypnotic when it's coming from directly beside me.

"Okay." I pull my shoulders back, attempting to regain some of the composure he apparently melted right off me. "These," I hold up the playing cards, "are the key to any modern-day human ritual."

Once I see that the cards have his attention, I open the red and white box, then carefully pour them into one hand, as though I wouldn't fathom mistreating something so valuable. I split the deck in half, adopting a formal tone as I fake-explain my actions, shuffling the way Grams taught me years ago.

"I'll do this part myself, since it really depends on a balanced chi to be effective. This is what we call a *bridge shuffle*, and it's one of the more complex things our ancestors teach." I don't dare look up at him, knowing I'm about one step away from losing it. I really don't know how far I can take this. Once my subpar shuffle is complete, I fan out the cards in my fingers and extend them toward him. "Here is where you come in. Pick a card. Any card."

I don't know what I expect. For him to somehow realize I'm full of it? To lose his patience and stalk off?

Instead, he stares long and hard at the cards, eyebrows furrowed and lips pressed together, as though my fate is entirely dependent on his next move. "Any card?" he repeats quietly, not breaking his focus.

I shouldn't find it so captivating, even endearing, seeing him like this: out of his element yet so determined to get it right. "Yep. Memorize the front of the card once you do, and be sure not to show it to me."

He slowly leans forward, his thigh brushing across my knee as he picks a card. I swallow hard, breaking my gaze away and returning it to the cards remaining in my hands, while he lowers his own to his lap.

"That's good," I mumble, splitting them down the middle. With half the deck in one hand and half in the other, I rest my wrists on each crisscrossed thigh. "So, once you have it memorized, slide the card on top of either of these stacks."

His eyes drop to my thighs, leisurely traveling from one to the other, then back again, practically burning holes straight through my pants in the process. He shifts forward once more, slowly, carefully, sliding it onto the stack in my left hand. A vague vibration from the subtle movement strokes the palm of my hand. Without letting go, he returns his gaze to mine, and my breath catches in my throat. I've never seen so much green. It's like the emerald blaze has backed the black-ice into a corner, and all of the mesmerizing flames are now centered on me.

"Just like this?"

It's just a question. An ordinary, logical question. But there's a husky roughness in his tone and a look in those eyes that dares me to . . . to what, exactly?

I nod, my neck suddenly stiff, and my answer comes out as a whisper. "Just like that."

When he finally removes his hand and leans back against the seat, I release a breath I didn't realize I was holding. I force my brain to continue functioning, placing the right stack of cards on top of the left. After dividing the deck into four piles, one pile at a time, I spread them out in my fingers to reveal them. "Do you see your card in this stack?" I ask softly.

He only looks down for a second before flicking his eyes back to mine. "No."

"How about this one?"

"Yes."

I collect the other piles and realize I have no idea where to set them aside. The loveseat is already small and, with the way we're both positioned, there's not enough room on the cushions. "Mind holding these for the rest of the—" I almost blurt out *magic trick* but catch myself just in time, "um, ritual?"

Bringing my attention back to the last remaining pile before me, I mindlessly extend the extras toward him, setting them down on his warm lap. My grip hasn't quite released them yet when I hear him clear his throat, feel the friction of fabric moving beneath my fingers as his body shifts. I finally look in the direction of my hand and am instantly mortified.

My hand. Is on. His penis.

I mean, not really, but it's pretty damn close. Between the other night and tonight, it's like I'm hosting my own private show called *How Many Times Can Lou Touch Him Inappropriately.* Speaking of which, I should probably move right about now. I yank my fingers away so fast the cards almost spill from his lap to the ground, but he catches them with a quick move of his hand.

"Oh my god," I groan, reluctantly meeting his gaze. "I'm sorry. I swear that wasn't, like, me making a move or something." Does he even know what that means?

Apparently so. He presses his lips together in a tight line, jaw ticking. His eyes still burn a fierce green, but they don't give anything away. "Don't worry about it," he all but grinds out. "What's next?"

"Right." I glance back down at the remaining cards, ridiculously thankful he didn't drag that out like he definitely could have. I divide them again, then do all the separating and discarding Grams walked me through, and when I get to that last card, I pause. Regaining my formal tone, I say, "Now, everything hangs on this next part. If I get this wrong, my status in our, um, human rankings will be lowered."

His eyes narrow, and I wonder if I've pushed it too far. Maybe I'm being too obvious. But then his expression softens. "Go ahead."

Phew. I flip the card so it's face up, then lower my voice just enough to sound serious. "Was this your card?"

I watch as his face goes from hard, masked, to focused, then . . . surprised? Relieved? "Yes," he says with a satisfied nod. "That's the one." He brings his gaze back up to meet mine, a lightness dancing in his eyes that I've never seen before.

That's when I see it. It starts slow, the corner of his lips lifting. Then the other corner lifts to match it, and butterflies swirl in my stomach as I realize he's actually smiling at me. A definite, even sincere, smile. It's not what I'd expect; understated and almost shy, with a single dimple on his right cheek that manages to change his entire look. In a split second, he somehow went from intimidating and deadly to boyish and endearing.

"You did it," he murmurs, green gaze roaming my face.

I find myself grinning back, soaking up his smile like the first glimpse of sunlight after a long, rough winter.

Oh, boy. I'm in trouble.

Chapter Twenty-Three

WE SIT LIKE THAT FOR several beats, eyes locked together, bodies almost close enough to touch with the way we've both seemed to lean toward each other. His smile's already begun to drop, but the dimple hasn't fully disappeared yet and there's still a lightness in those eyes when they fall to my lips, tracing every curve.

I clear my throat and close my eyes, abruptly breaking the trance before it sucks me in further. "Okay," I whisper seriously, "now for the closing line." I can't justify my reasons for coming up with this next part, except that I want to test my theory that he can make anything teeter between sounding threatening and sensual. Without opening my eyes, I say, "Repeat after me: Leggo. My Eggo."

After a moment of silence passes, I keep one eye closed and squint through the other, trying to sneak a peek at him. Except he's looking right at me. And he does not look amused. Somehow, even though he can't possibly know the waffle reference, I think he's caught on—no thanks, I'm sure, to the way my face has twisted into a partial grimace, partial grin, as I try to hold back the laughter bubbling up my throat.

"Please?" I squeak out. It's childish, I know, but I *really* want to hear this.

After another brief second of taking in my expression,

he speaks. And it's almost like he knows exactly what he's doing when he does. "Leggo," he says it slowly, exaggerating each syllable, ensuring I feel the full effect of that low husk of his voice, "my Eggo."

My mouth opens to form an 'O' as I stare at him in shock—over the fact that he actually said it despite knowing it was bullshit and over confirmation that my theory is indeed correct. He totally pulled it off. I only hold the expression for a moment before finally letting out the bubble of laughter that's been itching to escape. It takes a second for my giggles to quiet, wiping a tear from the corner of my eye as they do. "I'm sorry," I murmur between one last snicker. "I'm not laughing at you, I promise. Well, not totally."

He lowers an eyebrow and tilts his head, apparently mulling something over. "Exactly how much of the ritual was real?"

"Um . . ."

He lets out a deep sigh, running a hand through his hair, and I start to worry that I've pissed him off. "None of it?"

I slowly shake my head in answer, then press my lips together, trying to bite back another laugh. *So not appropriate, Lou.*

His eyes narrow, lips tightening for a reason different from mine.

"It's called a joke," I explain gently, catching my bottom lip between my teeth before another smile escapes. "A sense of humor. Or in my case, a sad attempt to forget reality for a minute."

For a long moment, he doesn't move. Doesn't speak. And I wonder if this is what happens right before he decides to kill you, take your soul. Maybe he just freezes, time stands still, and then *wham bam, thank you ma'am,* he's got you.

Instead, he takes me by surprise again when he leans back against the seat and stretches out his legs. "A joke," he murmurs thoughtfully, running a thumb across his jaw. He shifts his head toward me, eyes blazing. "Okay, then. Tell me something real."

"Something real?"

He gives a nod, like it's the simplest request.

"How about . . ." I'm not sure if this'll work, but it's worth a shot. "I'll make you a deal." For some reason, the saying *never make a deal with the Devil* flashes through my mind. But he's not the Devil. Right? "I'll tell you several. But for everything I tell you, you tell me one back, about yourself."

He studies me in silence, tilting his head again in a way I'm getting familiar with. "Deal."

I grin, then extend my hand. His gaze flicks down, then he furrows his brow. Does he not know what a handshake is?

"You're supposed to take my hand and shake it," I explain, my own brow mirroring his. "Like this." I watch as the hand resting on his lap tenses in a moment of apprehension, fingers clenching to form a fist briefly before releasing. I ease my hand into his, swallowing as the bold heat of his skin connects with mine, and give it a light squeeze. Then he tightens his hold until he has a firm grip on me. "This," I whisper, still eying our touching hands, "is a handshake."

When I return my gaze to his, he's not looking at the contact at all. He's honed in on me, carefully scanning my face. Somehow, his expression has softened, like his guard is dropping little by little, and the gentle look does something to my stomach, my chest. It's like a soft squeeze, tugging me toward him. Making me want to inch closer. Instead, I withdraw my hand, wiping my palm on my pants.

"So, I'll start?" I glance away, trying to collect my thoughts and figure out where to begin. A part of me wants to stick with small, insignificant facts. Like my favorite color or a good band. But a larger part, the part of me that's suffocating from keeping everything bottled up inside, is screaming for me to break down my box and let it all out. Flood the room with confessions, emotions, and whatever mindless thoughts might manifest.

Eventually what comes out is, "I hate Sundays. It's the one day of the week I can't seem to stop myself from breaking down."

He's quiet for a second. "The night you were crying . . ."

I nod, feeling a strange sense of calm wash over me at revealing the simple, partial truth. He doesn't press me for more, and I'm relieved. This, I can do. "Your turn."

I hear the sharp inhale, see the rise and fall of his chest. The muscles in my stomach contract in anticipation as I realize he's really going to hold up his end of the deal. "You felt it once."

I blink. "Excuse me?"

"My world," he says slowly. "You felt it once, that night when I crossed back over. You reached out after me, and your hand got caught in my trail."

I let out a breath. "I knew it. I mean, I wondered if that's what that was." My gaze darts to my hands as I stretch out my very real, very solid fingers. "So that numbness, the weird, cold sensation that took over, that's what it's like for you? When you're there?"

He looks away for a second, his lips tightening into a fine line before relaxing again. "It's a small taste." Just a taste of what he experiences? Every second he's not here? I shudder at the thought. "You're next."

"Right," I mumble. "Um." I don't know why, but in this moment, I feel the need to be honest with him. To confess. I chew the corner of my lip, then, "I was awake." His gaze narrows, questioning. "When I was sick. Well, not at first, I wasn't. I felt your warmth, I wanted to get . . . closer. But when I felt you shift under me, I didn't want to let go. Then I was embarrassed, so I pretended I was still asleep."

I finally meet his eyes head on, to find them dead set on me. If I were the blushing type, I'm certain my skin would turn scarlet from that look alone. Burning, intense, filled to the brim with hidden meaning, and I wish, *God* do I wish, that I could see the thoughts igniting that flame. Another beat passes with no response, causing a silence-induced awkwardness to build. "Please say something," I breathe, surprised by how vulnerable the admission has made me feel.

Tearing his eyes from mine, he scrubs a hand down his face. "My turn." His voice is low when he murmurs, "I'm not built to . . . feel things."

I arch a brow. "What does that mean?"

"It means I witness emotions every day when I collect." I swallow at that word, *collect*, knowing he's referring to the moment he takes one's soul. "Everything from fear, to pain, grief, or relief. But I've never felt a single emotion myself. Not once." He leans forward, resting his forearms on his thighs, then those green eyes lock on mine, holding my gaze steady. "Never, until entering this world. Never, until you."

My eyes widen, my heart thumping in my chest. This is the first real thing he's told me about himself. Not of his world, but *himself*. Such a personal part of him, why he is the way he is. To go through life never having felt anything before, I can't even imagine. Thinking back now, it makes so much sense. How closed off he gets. The way he shuts down just when he starts opening up, starts allowing himself to *feel* anything.

God, what must this be like for him? Taking in all these emotions, all the new sensations suddenly running through him. I lean forward slightly, squinting as though it'll help me see into his mind, his heart.

"That first night you wound up here, when I walked in with—with a friend. You seemed so angry. Livid."

One corner of his mouth lifts, but it's a dry smile, his jaw clenching. "I was. I apologize for that. It was my first real experience with these emotions. I was . . . frustrated. I'm still trying to get used to this. To adjust."

My heart pulsates, his words sinking in.

I want so badly to press him for more. More answers, more anything. But his expression is already hardening again, and I don't want his guard to go back up. Not when I've just gotten it down. So I force myself to lean back against the seat, force my expression, my voice, to relax. And this time when I take my turn, I decide to let my guard down in the same way he's done for me.

"My turn," I whisper, locking my eyes with his. "Lately, I get these dreams. These boys, brothers—it's like I can feel everything they're feeling. And it's horrible. The way they're treated, it's disgusting." My throat constricts, and I swallow down the lump building there. "But they're so strong. So much stronger than me. And despite everything, their hearts are so full. Full of love for each other, and hope." Wetness pools at the corners of my eyes. I blink it away. "I know they're not real. I know it's just a dream. But in many ways, I look up to them. They're my role models."

After a quiet second, I shake my head, pushing the thought away and lightening my voice. "And . . . *go*," I nudge, trying to smile.

I watch as his hand slowly comes up, his chest rising and falling, then his thumb is just barely brushing over my lips. I can't tell if he's even touching me, or if the soft stroke I feel is purely from the heat of his skin moving against mine. Somehow we've leaned forward again, not a clue who's inching toward whom, but our lips are so close, our breaths tangle together. My exhales becoming his inhales. He traces the curve of my forced half-smile, like he's telling me he sees the truth. That I don't have to pretend. It's a small gesture, but it pierces straight through my chest.

Without warning, his heat starts to dissipate, and his form begins to blur. *No, not now. Stay*, I want to beg, even though I know he can't always control it. He keeps his thumb at my lips, the solid outline of his body fading all too quickly before my eyes, as he whispers, "Sometimes . . . I don't want to leave."

And then, before I can blink, he's gone.

Chapter Twenty-Four

I'M STILL SMILING WHEN I hear the door to the print shop close behind me, as I step out onto the quiet sidewalk. This is the perfect end to a day of running boring errands, including earlier this morning when I finally caved and picked up a new cell phone. Mundane, annoying tasks, but I'm really making an effort at adulting today. And this, my final trip to the little print shop, is my reward.

Feeling the plastic bag tap against my hip with each step I take is comforting, just knowing what it holds, and my heart feels fuller for it. I'm about to cross the street when a colorful gleam from a window to my left catches my eye. A jewelry shop? I scoot closer, squinting as I peer inside and scan the items on the store's display shelf. Huh. I'm not usually the jewelry kind of girl, but there's a particular little knick-knack perched atop the sale rack that I just can't resist. I smirk as I reach for the store's door handle, a fresh wave of flutters rushing through my stomach as I do.

Not even ten minutes later and I've arrived at the inn, pulling the door open to let another guest exit first.

"Lou!" Claire hollers from her desk as I step inside. She gives Dylan—*ugh*—a quick parting kiss and signals me over. As he passes by, he nods and his lips curve. Although I'd rather ignore him or flip him off, Claire's eyes are trained on our interaction, so I manage a tight-lipped smile for her sake.

"Hey, Claire." I reach her at the same time the front door closes behind Dylan, then set my bags on the desk.

Claire quirks an eyebrow and grins, an expression that has me wrinkling my nose in confusion. "What?"

"Oh, I don't know." Her grin widens. "Just that I happened to see a certain someone take you to breakfast this morning."

Oh, *that*. "Bobby didn't 'take me to breakfast.' We went out for a bite, because that's what friends do. There's a difference."

She narrows her eyes with the resemblance of a foxhound sniffing for clues, but doesn't press it. Instead, her expression softens as she pulls open her desk drawer and hands me a postcard. "Another one. Someone back in LA really misses you."

Oh no. I'm a terrible best friend. I've been so caught up with everything going on, I haven't even replied to her last one. Guilt consumes me as I grab the card and begin reading.

It's me again, Bitch!

I'm coming to visit you! Mom and Daniel are keeping the girls next weekend so we can have a sleepover like the good ol' days. I'm thinking we're long overdue for a girls' night! Hope you're free Saturday and Sunday. Otherwise, clear your schedule, slut, because there's no way in hell you're backing out of this.

P.S. I'm pumping enough milk to last baby Audrey a few days, so you better prepare yourself to get shit-faced with me.

P.P.S. You're still beautiful.

xx

It's only Sunday, and already next weekend can't get here soon enough. It hits me then that I'm grinning . . . on a Sunday. *Well this is new.* "Hey, you have plans Saturday night?" I ask Claire.

She pauses, eying the ceiling in thought, then says, "Nope, don't think so."

"Want to come over? My friend Jamie's going to be visiting, and we're gonna do another girls' night kinda thing."

Claire doesn't even hesitate. "Yes! I'm in!" She pauses, eyes dropping to the small plastic bags between us. "Did you go on a mini shopping spree?"

I shrug, remaining casual so she doesn't make too big a deal out of it. "Not really. Just picked up a few things for my room. Anyway, what's the story with you and Dylan?" It's a good way to change the subject, but it's also a question that's been eating at me.

"Story?" The notepad sitting in front of her must have suddenly become very interesting, because she picks it up, squints down, and flips through its pages.

"Yeah, like how'd you guys meet?"

She chuckles, tearing her eyes away from the pad to meet mine. "We're in Ashwick. Everyone knows everyone."

I arch a brow. "You know what I mean."

She sighs, leaning forward to rest her elbows on the desk. "He was my big high school crush," she explains. "Honestly, I think everyone knew I liked him. But the timing never worked out until after we graduated, and now . . . well, here we are." She's smiling when she looks back up at me, and unfortunately, I can see how much she likes him just by the dreamy look in her eyes.

"How long have you been together?"

"About nine months." Almost a year. Great. I really hope his whole sleazebag act is just that—an *act*, and that he's more loyal than he appears. "So," she says, flashing me pearly white teeth, "Dylan and I are participating in the winter festival, and I think you should come! We'll have our own booth and—"

Just as I'm about to interrupt with a made up excuse, the phone rings and saves the day. I really don't want to lie to her, but my desire to be stuck behind a booth as Dylan ogles over other girls when Claire's not looking is probably right up there with stabbing my eyeball.

Claire frowns. "Sorry, better get that."

"It's fine," I whisper, grabbing my bags as she puts the phone to her ear. "I'll talk to you later." She waves, and I head up the stairs.

I take my time with the photographs I'd just picked up, carefully pressing them into small frames and figuring out the right places to set them. There's one picture that's always been my favorite, and I decide to fix that one in the center of the fireplace mantle. It's the perfect spot; facing the bed when I wake in the morning and still visible when I enter my room. I play with the angle a little, then drop my hands and take a step back, admiring the image.

Grams sits on the front porch I know so well, perched on the top step and wearing her wistful smile, brown eyes wise and at peace. Mom is right beside her, grinning, legs crisscrossed and one arm draped over Grams's shoulders, the other arm hugging her perfectly round belly . . . hugging me. Dad's leaning over Mom, embracing her tightly and beaming in a way that's remarkably whole.

I wipe the corner of my eye before the tear can fall, then press a kiss to my fingers, and my fingers to the photograph. "I miss you guys," I whisper, wishing they could hear the words.

Straightening my spine, I take in a deep breath and lift my chin. I don't know when, or if, *he's* going to show up today, but if it's anything like the past few days, I'm guessing I have no more than an hour. I should probably take a bath sooner rather than later so it doesn't look like I'm making a move on him. Again.

My time in the bath is filled mostly with thoughts about the notes I found at Mr. Blackwood's place. I still don't know what to do about those, or if I should do anything at all. How could I ignore them though? Best case scenario, I ask the old man about it, and it turns out to be something really silly. He'll probably hate me for prying, maybe even put my job on the line, but at least I'd know no one's in trouble. Worst case scenario, the messages turn out to be even more serious than I'm willing to imagine. *Ugh.* I rub my temples, then lay back and rinse the rest of the conditioner from my hair. Any way I look at it, I know I can't ignore them. Even now, the letters flash like neon lights in my brain whenever there's nothing to distract me.

I AM NOT DEAD.
I CAN'T HOLD ON.
SAVE ME.

No, I won't ignore them. I've made my choice. At some point during this coming week, I'm confronting Mr. Blackwood about them. Satisfied with my decision, I pull myself from the water and towel dry, patting myself down before dressing in a comfy pair of shorts and an oversized top. I withdraw my new, black phone from its shopping bag and scroll through the apps.

Really, I should be emailing my realtor back. I have two notifications from him, both subject lines reading *Interested Buyer!* But those two words aren't pleasing me like I thought they would. What they do manage to do is close my throat up and tighten my chest. So instead, I happily ignore the emails and download a music app.

It's been way too long since I've blasted music, and the anticipation already has me feeling lighter. I hit play, smiling when Ed Sheeran's *Shape of You* blares through the speakers.

Closing my eyes, I let the beat run all the way through me. *God, I've missed you, music.* My head rolls forward, then side to side as I slowly soak it in. I inhale, feeling my muscles loosen as they respond to the lull, and start a smooth sway in my hips. Side to side, like my head, and then my feet are feeling it too.

I'm lost in the melody, consumed by the hypnotic spell only the magic of music can induce, the curves of my body moving without thought. Hips swaying, right, left, right, left, head falling back so my hair tumbles down my back.

My body gets warmer as I move, a fire burning through my veins. My teeth grab hold of my bottom lip, and I think my hands are in my hair, when I hear the low, raspy sound of a throat being cleared.

I jump, my hand snapping to my chest, until my now wide eyes land on him, and I relax. "Shit," I manage, breathless.

I honestly don't know what's knocked the breath out of me more—the dancing, or the way he's looking at me right now.

He's leaning against my dresser, his left forearm resting on the top and his head tilted just slightly, thick eyelashes shadowing specks of green as he watches me. His lips though, they send my pulse into overdrive. They're hooked up lazily at one corner, just enough to display that single dimple he let me glimpse last night. It's a simple look, but seeing it on him, and knowing it's aimed at me, it reminds me of the last words he spoke to me. *Sometimes . . . I don't want to leave.* My stomach flips, full somersault.

"Hi," he says, his voice both gentle and hypnotic.

I smile, already roped in and unable to look away. "Hi."

Chapter Twenty-Five

I REALIZE AFTER A SECOND I'M still frozen in place, so I stroll over to my phone and lower the volume until it fades into the background. I turn to him. "I didn't hear you."

He's still wearing that hint of a crooked smile. "Decided to give your furniture a break."

I quirk an eyebrow, my heart skipping a beat as I take in his words. "Did you just make a joke?"

His face stills for a moment, eyes flicking away, as though registering something, before settling back on me. "I guess I did."

I feel myself smile, take a step toward him. "I like it."

This time it's his brow that shoots up. "Yeah? I have more." His expression gets thoughtful again, eyes narrowing. "Your nightstand came on to me a little too strong last night. Think I'm going to have to break things off."

I snort out a laugh, a jolt coursing through me as I try to absorb this new side of him. "We'll have to work on it a little."

His smile widens just enough to let me know he's pleased by my reaction, and it squeezes my heart. I cock my head to one side, squinting as I inspect him closer. How does he even know what it means to *come on to someone*? To *break things off*?

"You seem different tonight." My voice is soft, still lost in my thoughts.

It's the same thing I'd noticed when he showed up last night, a distinct change in his demeanor. I still see it now, in the relaxed way his broad shoulders sit, the expressiveness of those vibrant eyes, the almost informal body language. Whatever it is, it was subtler yesterday; only obvious to someone looking close enough, as I had been. But now, it's enhanced tenfold somehow, and I don't know what to make of it.

He smoothly pushes his weight off the dresser with his hip, then shifts his gaze toward the unlit fireplace. As he nips at his bottom lip, he runs a hand through his tousled hair. "I feel different."

"How's that?" I settle into the rocking chair, tucking one foot beneath me.

"I don't know." He shrugs—another gesture I've never seen from him before—making his way to the loveseat and lowering himself down. It takes him a minute to answer, and I don't think I've ever seen him look so lost in thought before. Finally, he lets out a long, low sigh before turning his head to me. "In every sense of the word."

I want to ask what he means, but I get the impression he might not even understand it himself. "And what do you think? Does it scare you?"

"No. Not anymore. Now, it feels almost," he shakes his head, "familiar."

Our gazes stay locked, mine completely enthralled by the way the green blaze of his eyes so wholly overshadows the darkness now. He leans forward, resting his forearms on his thighs, his chin angled to the right as he watches me. We seem to do a lot of that, watching each other, and I always wonder if he feels it like I do, this pull. This tug between us, like a warm, soft line of thread linking me to him.

As usual, I'm the first to break our staring contest.

"So . . ." I stand and walk toward my nightstand, where the plastic bags sit. "I got you something."

I take a seat right beside him, close enough that our legs touch, and try to act casual—like I don't feel the heat of his body burning through his jeans, rubbing against the bare skin of my thigh. I ignore the way his body stiffens at my nearness, muscles pulling taut. I keep my eyes down, on the box in my hand, as I fumble to open it.

The lid finally pops up, revealing two rings. One is dainty, a silver band designed to appear like two vines twisting into one another, with a black, oval stone sitting in its center. The other is more masculine, a thick, stainless steel band with a simple, black design etched into the sides. That one has a dark rectangular stone at its center.

"These," I say, "are rings." I take the dainty one and am about to slip it onto my middle finger, when I pause, lifting my head to look at him.

He's not looking at the rings, but at me. His brows are drawn, but his eyes are tender, almost sad, and I can't place the expression at all. "You got me something," he says, as if to himself.

"I know it seems silly," I rush to elaborate, feeling the need to explain my gift choice, "but it's not just any ring. It's a mood ring."

"A what?"

I grin, my excitement growing at the thought of showing him what it does. "A mood ring. I figured with you being so new to emotions and all, this might be fun." With my free hand, I pluck the more masculine looking ring from the box and hand it to him. "I hope it fits."

Gently taking the ring from me, he holds it level with his eyes, rotating the item in his fingers for inspection. "What does it do, exactly?"

"Here, we'll start with mine. Watch the stone." I slide it down my finger, then hold up my hand in front of us, so we can both see it equally. We stare as the stone's black color turns cloudy. Specks of a bright, sky blue swirl in the middle of it until the blue takes over completely. Déjà vu? I can't help but be reminded of the way his eyes swirl from black to green.

"What does it mean?" he asks.

"I have no idea," I admit, chuckling softly. "I've never actually worn one of these things. Oh, it comes with a chart!" I sound way more excited than I probably should be, considering it's just a silly toy, but I can't help it. It's like his raw curiosity is contagious, sparking my own interest in the smallest things.

I untuck a small, folded paper from the bottom of the box and hold it up before us, scanning down the color schemes until I see an explanation for bright blue. I read it aloud. "Bright blue means you are doing something stimulating or something that makes you excited."

He shifts his head back toward me, a small smile playing at his lips. "And are you?" His voice is quiet, almost a whisper, yet every syllable of that freaking low hum seeps inside my body, loud and clear. "Stimulated, I mean?"

Oh, like he had to clarify.

Damn color chart. Suddenly flustered by being at the receiving end of his undivided attention, especially with the way our thighs still brush together from any slightest movement, I scoff and roll my eyes.

"It's not *real*," I explain. "The store clerk told me this whole thing is based on your body temperature. Apparently, the average person's body temp will turn the ring green. It gets into the blues the hotter the body is. Obviously, my body heats up around you because you're so hot." Did I seriously just say that? "Not like, *hot*, hot. I mean, not that you *aren't* that kind of hot . . ."

Jesus. I glance away and bite down on my lip, scrambling for any way to seem less like I'm, once again, hitting on him. Then I realize maybe I'm safe; maybe he doesn't even know the double meaning of that particular word. I mean, he didn't even know what a handshake was, right? Wary, I slowly turn my head back toward him, lifting my chin. I'm really hoping to find a confused look on his face. Unfortunately, what I find is anything but.

He's definitely smiling now, the ridiculously cute dimple in full effect. The simple curve of his full lips is easy and honest, genuine. Bringing my gaze upward, I'm surprised when his eyes don't match such a pure smile. No, there's nothing pure about the dangerous, almost daring, spark dancing in the green flames. I don't know if it's my stubbornness, my desire to take on the unspoken challenge—whatever the hell that is—but I can't look away.

"Go on." The huskiness behind the gentle command slides down my skin like warm, thick honey. "You were telling me how hot I make you." The corner of his lips hooks up again, smooth and slow.

"What?" I murmur, dazed-like, until I snap myself out of his spell and shake my head. Dammit. He knows exactly what he's doing. "Stop that."

"Stop what?"

My eyes narrow. "You know what."

If I'm being honest with myself, I don't totally know why I'm complaining. It's not as though I don't like the reactions he causes in my body, the quickening of my pulse, the warm sensations spiking low in my stomach—amongst other places. But I've never seen him blatantly flirt with me either, and there are too many sides to him for me to make sense of. In fact, that wasn't just flirting. It was one step away from dirty-talk territory.

How exactly does one talk dirty with Death, anyway?

Shaking it off before my imagination can run wild with that one, I clear my throat. "Your turn. Put it on," I urge, mindlessly tapping his knee with my hand. I know I just told him to shut up, but I can't resist when I casually say, "Let's see if you're as hot as I am."

His gaze lights up when it flicks to mine, but then he

goes serious as he focuses on the ring in his hand. He slides it over his middle finger, like mine, but it won't budge past the middle knuckle. His eyes are curious when he looks back at me, waiting for something to happen.

I nod toward his hand. "Keep your eyes on the ring. The stone."

He obliges, and I have to lean closer to see the change this time. It's so subtle as the black in his stone becomes the darkest possible shade of blue. He presses his lips together. "Do I want to know?"

I laugh softly, then glance down at the color chart to read it aloud. "Dark blue indicates romance or passion. Something electric is in the air if you see dark blue."

Chapter Twenty-Six

I'M CHEWING MY LIP AGAIN when I lower the chart and turn back to him. Note to self: never buy a mood ring again. "Like I said, it doesn't actually mean anything. Your ring turned dark blue because you're impossibly ho . . ."—Nope, not making that mistake again—"Thermogenic."

I grin, full and proud. *That's right. Good luck dirty-talking that one, mister.*

A low, guttural sound bubbles up through his throat, past a smile that shows off a row of perfectly straight, white teeth that I've never seen on display before, his shoulders and chest shaking. *Oh my god.* He's laughing. And it's the sexiest sound I've ever heard him make—that's saying something. It's a deep rumble, soft yet intoxicating, and it caresses everything from my ears to my neck, right through my chest, my stomach, until it hits the tips of my toes, literally making them curl.

After a beat, it quiets, his shoulders still shaking gently as he lets out a sigh. But it's not a frustrated sigh, or even pensive, like the ones he's given me before. It's as close to carefree as I've ever seen from him. He runs a large hand through those thick strands of hair, then relaxes deeper into the seat, a hint of a smile still tugging at the corner of his mouth when he looks at me.

It takes me a moment to find my voice. "You should do that more."

"What?"

"Laugh. It suits you."

His expression turns thoughtful. "I don't think I've ever done it before."

"Never?"

He shakes his head, sticking one hand into the pocket of his jeans as he spreads his legs.

"Wow." I don't like seeing the way verbalizing that realization makes his face fall, so I let myself smile coyly, trying to lighten the mood. "So I'm the first girl to ever make you laugh, hmm?"

He angles his head toward me, looking at me long and hard. There's nothing 'light' about the way he slowly says, "You're the first girl to make me do a lot of things."

A shiver runs down my back, and I'm pretty sure my heart actually skips a beat. There are so many things I can say to that, but I have no idea what direction to take this in.

The knock at the door makes me jump, before quickly filling me with relief. I'm off the hook. For now. "Just a second." I push myself up from the loveseat and cross the room, already missing his warmth when I reach the door and pull it open.

Claire's big, blue eyes meet my gaze, and I know something's off. Even her smile can't hide the broken look behind her expression. "Hey," she says softly, "mind if I hang out here for a little bit before heading home?"

Shoot. I glance over my shoulder to see him watching us. He squints, rubs his chin, then motions to let her in. I arch a brow, and I mouth, *You sure?* After what happened last time I had a guest while he was present, I don't know if this is such a good idea. But the corner of his lips tip up, eyes glimmering with something—amusement?—when he mouths back, *You won't even realize I'm here.*

I snort aloud and roll my eyes, knowing just how unlikely

that is, and his mouth curves deeper until his dimple shows. There's something wolfish in that crooked smile, giving me the urge to swallow.

"Lou?" Claire's gentle voice pulls my attention back to her, and she peeks around me, trying to get a better look at my apparently empty room. "Sorry, did I interrupt? Do you already have company?"

"Oh—no, sorry. Of course you can hang out here." I step aside to let her enter, then lock the door behind her. *Just a crazy person laughing at an empty room, that's me.*

I turn back to face her, trying my best to avoid looking over at the 6'4" man lounging on my loveseat. Not easy to do when, out of the corner of my eye, I can still see him observing me, sitting back comfortably like he's at a drive-in and I'm his entertainment for the evening.

"Mmm, it's nice and cozy in here," Claire murmurs, already unbuttoning her coat.

"Yeah, just turned off the fireplace," I lie, before narrowing my eyes accusingly at him. *Won't even realize I'm here,* my ass. Not that he can do anything about that, I suppose.

He just smirks, stretching his legs out further.

Claire drapes her coat over the rocking chair, then closes her eyes and heaves a deep breath. A second later, she opens them again and curves her pink-glossed lips upward, but it's forced. "Thanks. I should've called first, I know—"

"Hey, you can always drop by. Okay?"

Her entire posture relaxes, and she gives me the first genuine smile since she showed up. "Thank you."

I step toward her, my brows furrowing. "You all right?"

"Of course I am." Her eyes dart to the ground before coming back up. "Just, Dylan's been so busy. He just took on an extra job, and . . . anyway, he's a hard worker and I totally support him, I do." She pauses, chewing on the inside of her cheek and shuffling her feet. "But this is the third time he's cancelled on me this week and, well, obviously I'm the kind of girl that does better around company, huh? Hello, I'm Little Miss Chatterbox over here."

She chuckles weakly at that, and I hate it. I hate how that jerk's actions are making her talk about herself as though some of the best parts of who she is might actually be faults. I want to tell her that, too. That she deserves better, and Dylan doesn't deserve to feel the warmth of her constant sunshine. He's a leech, and leeches suck you dry until there's nothing left to give. But something about the way her kind eyes are wide and vulnerable, it makes me think maybe the quieter side of friendship will be better for her soul right now.

"Loners like me need people like you in the world, Claire. Otherwise we'd spend all day talking to our invisible friends, never leaving our room."

She laughs, a full-hearted belly laugh that makes me smile.

I glance over at my own personal invisible friend and quirk my head at the soft expression that's taken over his face. His eyes are still observant, but they're also warm, gentle, and his lips tilt up when our eyes connect. A flock of butterflies take flight in my stomach at such a sweet look, and I give him a little smile back before returning my attention to Claire. "So what's it going to be? Dance party or sing off?"

Her mouth opens, and she shakes her head. "Uh-uh, no way. I'm actually a terrible dancer, and I only sing in the shower."

"Hey, you're the one who knocked on my door, and it just so happens I'm in a dancing mood now that I finally got my music back. You're welcome to sit and watch but . . . that might get a little awkward."

She lets out another laugh. "Okay, fine. Can I borrow some of your clothes, though? These jeans are way too tight to dance in."

"Yup, right over here." I take her to my dresser and let her pick out a pair of shorts and a top, then lead her into the bathroom.

When I turn back around, Death is standing. One hand rests in his pocket, the other rubs the side of his sharp jaw. "It was good seeing you, Lou."

My heart flutters at the simple words. For a second, it sounds like he's a normal guy, just hanging out with a girl. For a second, it feels like whatever this is between us could be real. For a second, I even believe it. I have to close my eyes briefly to shake the thought away. When I open them again, he's taking a careful step toward me.

"Can I see you again? Would you . . ." His gaze flicks down, then slowly rises back up. "Would that be okay with you?"

My chest. It's about to burst. I nod for a moment as I try to find my voice, tension thickening the air around us. When I finally respond, my sarcasm coping mechanism kicks in before I can stop it, "Anytime, Grim."

"Grim?"

I glance up at him and bat my lashes innocently. "Yeah. You know, as in the Grim Reaper."

A look of confusion crosses over his handsome face. "Who?"

"Seriously?" I feel my shoulders relax, almost forgetting the tension as my mouth falls open. "Death himself doesn't know who the Grim Reaper is?"

His eyes narrow, brows pucker. "Should I?"

I chuckle softly. "I guess not. It feels weird calling you Death, though, so I thought I'd try it out. You don't like it?"

The crease in his brows deepens, and he looks like he's genuinely considering it. "I don't know."

"No, you're right. It's still way too morbid. How about if I drop the 'rim' and just call you G?" His nose crinkles. "Ghost boy?" He shakes his head, a smile toying with the corner of his lips. "Gumdrop?"

"Goodnight, Lou." His dimple flashes, head still shaking

as he fades.

It's quicker this time, the way it starts, a translucent shimmer of color until there's nothing at all, and his sudden absence hurts me in a way I've never experienced before. I feel the light in my eyes die down, the pounding strum in my chest quiets, the air around me returns to its natural cool chill, and I just want him to come back.

I want him to stay.

It's not until the bathroom door clicks and Claire steps out that it hits me: Tonight, he had a choice. He was able to leave at will. He wasn't here because he had to be.

A rush of air pours out of me at the realization, like my lungs are being released from a hold I didn't even know they were trapped in.

He was here, with me, because he wanted to be.

Chapter Twenty-Seven

SOMETIMES ALL IT TAKES ARE the little details to make us step back for a second, look around, and realize ... *Hey, I'm okay*. For me, it started with the way I dressed this morning. Not what I wore, but how I went about selecting the outfit. While I'd usually just throw something together based on the weather or practicality, today I took my time flipping through my jeans and tops, even stopping to check their fit in the mirror. Next was my hair. Instead of just a quick brush and dash, I did a full blow dry. I glossed my lips and added mascara, just for the hell of it. It didn't matter that it's a cleaning day, I did it for me, and damn if it didn't feel good.

The nightly visits with my Death might have a little something to do with it. Or a lot. *Wait, what? Whoa there, Lou*—not *my* Death. Just Death. The Death of the people. Nothing to see but equal Death opportunity rights here.

I'm smiling as I stroll up Main Street, unable to push him out of my mind, and not wanting to either. I haven't commented on the fact that he's coming over on his own accord now, but he has to know I've figured it out. It's not as though he's trying to hide it. It's Wednesday and he hasn't missed a single night.

There are a lot of things we haven't discussed yet, and I realize I should use his visits to ask important questions;

I even plan on doing that very thing every day before he shows up.

But then . . . well, he shows up. With those smoky eyes fixed on me, and that elusive dimple making an appearance here and there.

I can't suppress another smile when I think of the few laughs I've pulled out of him, each one mentally recorded as the clearest and most addictive reel in my mind. I'm still the more talkative one, but I don't mind. Not when I see the way he hangs onto every little thing I say. His expression reveals more these days than it ever has before. The way one corner of his lips slowly curves up when he quietly watches me, or the way he presses them together when he's trying not to laugh at something ridiculous I've said.

But sometimes, at random intervals when we're talking, I see these fleeting moments where his expression goes serious. He'll get quiet, face falling and eyes darkening, and I know he's thinking about the stark reality of our situation.

I know this because it hits me in spurts like that, too. The fact this shouldn't be possible. That we both know nothing good can come of it. That we come from entirely different universes and shouldn't fit together as well as we do. And that something must be terribly wrong in order for any of this to even be occurring. My throat thickens at the thought, a wave of nerves rolling through me.

But just when I think he's going to be the first one between us to voice these thoughts aloud, he seems to do the same thing I do—shove it away into the furthest corner of his mind.

Just until tomorrow.

It's always just until tomorrow.

Mr. Blackwood isn't home when I arrive at his place, which seems to be a bit of a theme for him lately. The moment I step past the front door, I notice he's actually organized his papers for once. There are still a few scattered notes here and there, but there's also a new accordion filing system tucked right beneath his coffee table.

I get right to work, and it takes extra effort today for me to avoid the guest room. I decide to skip that room again and instead focus my time on cleaning the main living areas. It's not because I don't want to dig around that particular bedroom some more, but because I do. I want to yank that manila folder from the bedsprings, pour out all of its contents, and find out what the rest of the messages say. Then I want to unclasp the accordion filing system sitting not ten feet away from me and flip through every piece of paper tucked inside. But, I won't. I won't because I need to give Mr. Blackwood a chance to clear this up with me himself. I won't because I don't want to put a dent in our already paper-thin relationship.

But he better get back soon because the curiosity is scratching at my back and I can't take much more.

Just then, the sound of keys jingling pulls my attention to the front of the room, the door swings open, and in walks Mr. Blackwood. Well, not so much *walks* as *stumbles*. And I'm not talking about his usual limp either; this is a full on drunken stupor type of stumble. A loud clank fills my ears as he tumbles right into the coffee table, grunts, and wobbles in place for a second as he tries to get his bearings. I've dropped the rag and spray bottle and am already rushing his way, reaching him just in time to pull his arm over my shoulders for support before he loses his balance completely.

"You stink," I mutter, carefully setting him onto the sofa. I'm used to the faint scent of whiskey lingering on him, but today he smells like he dumped a full bottle over his head and then rolled around in the dirt.

"Good morning to you, too," he slurs, "you ray of sunshine, you."

I snort and place a hand on my hip. "What would you know about rays of sunshine, Mr. Doom and Gloom?"

"I know more . . . I know more than . . . hey, where's my drink?" He shoves his right hand inside his coat, digging around the inner pockets, but I beat him to it and snag his hidden flask before he even knows what's happening. His white brows furrow, his thin body swaying as he takes a moment to center his eyes on me. "Give it back," he grumbles. "I'm thirsty."

"Oh? Would you like me to get you a glass of water?"

He scoffs. It's loud and exaggerated, and I've never seen him in quite this state. Not only is he far more inebriated than usual, but his brows seem glued downward, his eyes distant and bitter. I go into the kitchen and pour a glass of water anyway, setting it in front of him when I return.

"Mr. Blackwood," I begin, keeping my eyes trained on his as I settle into the recliner beside him, "where have you been going lately? You taking a break on your research?"

The look he throws my way is hard and cold. "None o' your business."

So that's how we're playing this.

"Okay." I keep my voice nonchalant. "You don't wanna tell me where you disappear to, that's fine." I press my lips together. "But I do want some answers."

His eyes narrow. "Answers to what." He barks it out like a statement, not a question.

"That's up to you. You can either tell me how you knew Grams . . ." I pause, looking for a reaction from him, but he doesn't give me one, "or, you can tell me why there's a hidden folder in your guest room with messages that say 'Save me.'"

His face goes slack for only a second before his jaw, buried beneath a scraggly beard, shifts from side to side as he grinds his teeth. I fold my legs beneath me, curling into the cushion, and let out a loud sigh that tells him I'm not going anywhere until he dishes.

"And how in the hell would you know anything about what's hidden in a house that is not yours?" His words are tight, controlled, as though my comment alone was almost enough to sober him up.

"I wasn't snooping, Mr. Blackwood. I dropped something under the bed and bumped into the folder when I went to grab it. A few pages came tumbling out, but that's it, okay? That's all I saw."

For a minute, he just stares at me, eyes stone-cold and unmoving in a way I've never seen from him. But then, his gaze drops to the ground. One wrinkled hand scrubs down his face. He leans back against the padded pillows and eyes the flask still in my hand. "If we're gonna do this, I need that back."

I have to force my jaw not to drop. He's really going to talk to me about this? He's going to answer my questions for once?

"The damn whiskey, child," he snaps. "Give it here."

"Oh. Right." I lean forward, hand him the bottle, then settle back into the recliner. I realize I probably shouldn't just hand the drink over to him when he's already so wasted, but if that's what it's going to take to get him to talk, so be it.

Several seconds pass while he twists the thing open, gulps it down, and seals it back up with a satisfied sigh. After tucking it securely back into his pocket, he pushes up from the sofa with his fists, knees shaking for a moment before he steadies himself into a standing position.

"Mr. Blackwood, what are you doing?"

Ignoring me entirely, he takes a few short steps toward the cane resting against the armrest—the one that's always there even though he never uses it, ever—and grabs its brown handle. He leans onto it, adjusting his weight, then turns around, limps his way past me, opens the front door, and walks right out. Not a word. Not a glance in my direction. He just shuts the door behind him, leaving me dumbfounded on the recliner.

Dammit. I should have known it wasn't going to be so

easy.

Chapter Twenty-Eight

WHERE'S HE GOING ANYWAY? I pop up from the seat and dash toward the front window, shoving the curtain aside just enough to peer out. Mr. Blackwood is stumbling down the winding pathway, inching toward the enormous iron gates. *Huh.* At least he didn't try to drive in his condition. Still, he can't expect me to just let him walk away on his own like this, can he? There's a steep dip just on the other side of those gates, and I don't know if a cane is going to be enough to keep him steady through it.

Without another thought, I push past the front door and jog after him. "Wait! Mr. Blackwood, wait!" He slows but doesn't stop or turn around to face me. "At least let me help you down the hill. Please."

He pauses just as I reach him, but he keeps his chin toward the gates. "What ever happened to 'I keep to myself, you keep to yours?'" He quotes my words from the first day we met, and guilt surges through me.

"Look . . . I just want to make sure you get to the bottom safely, okay? I'll keep my mouth shut."

He turns then, full circle, so he faces me head on. "Listen, Lou, and listen good. I hired you for Tallulah. You got that?"

My eyes widen at the unexpected mention of Grams, but I keep my mouth shut as promised and give a simple nod.

"The least I can do is give her granddaughter some work." His expression hardens, and such a look reminds me of someone, but I can't place the familiarity. "But I'm no one's charity case. I'm not a project to figure out. I'm not some ridiculous, superficial means of getting closer to Tallulah. And we, you and I, are not friends. I'm your employer. Now, if what you stumbled upon in my house bothers you so much, by all means quit. Won't make a damn difference to me." He quiets, letting those words sink in before adding, "Otherwise, I'm paying you to clean my crappy house, meaning what you will do while you are here is clean my crappy house. Nothing more, nothing less. Do I make myself clear?"

I can't pretend his words don't sting, no matter how much I know they shouldn't. What did I think, that we were going to chat about Grams over some tea and scones? That the company of another person might fill the void in his heart enough for him to set aside the liquor for a few hours? *Silly, naïve Lou.*

My jaw is tight when I respond through clenched teeth, "Perfectly."

"Good," he grunts, like he's relieved to be rid of me. "Now I'd appreciate some silence while I continue my escape." He whirls around, steadies himself on the cane, and takes another uneven step toward the gate before muttering, "Takes a shitload of concentration to avoid falling on my ass."

A smile tugs on my lips even as I roll my eyes. Just in case a miracle happens and he suddenly sees through his pride enough to ask for a helping hand, I stay rooted in place until he passes through the gates and disappears from view. Then I return to the house and get to work. That's something I got from Grams, keeping my hands busy whenever my mind feels overwhelmed. *Nothing like a good distraction to give one's mind a little clarity,* she'd say.

The thought of Grams makes Mr. Blackwood's words replay in my head. *The least I can do is give her granddaughter some work.* What could she have done for him? What could have made such a lasting impression on someone like him?

Five hours later, the mounds of questions eating at me are actually causing my head to ache. I'm light-headed as I finish up with the vacuum, and for the first time since working here, I need to take a five-minute rest break. Shit, I hope I'm not getting sick again. That'd have to be some kind of record, right?

But why won't he answer a single question? Just one? He and Grams have that in common, the desire to keep a tight lid on their pasts, and it's driving me freaking crazy. The creepy messages, all the drinking, his supposed research, his lack of family or friends, his mysterious relationship with Grams . . . it doesn't paint a very comforting picture.

It's one thing for someone to end up so alone out of pure spite, but something deep in my gut tells me there's more to Mr. Blackwood's story. That his loneliness has been shaped by circumstance, rather than carved by his own hand. Maybe it's the moments of sadness that pass through his eyes, or maybe it's my own somber past that has me seeking out similarities in his. I don't know. For whatever reason, I can't stand to see him suffer like this. He's downright killing himself.

Nope, no more. I decide right here and now that I'm a grown ass woman, and if I want answers, I'm going to get them myself. I slowly rise to my feet, taking a deep breath until I'm certain I'm not going to pass out from the nausea that's been creeping up on me, and move my gaze to the filing system stowed beneath the coffee table. I bet there are plenty of answers crammed into that little container. If Mr. Blackwood refuses to talk to me, I've got to explore other options, right?

Just one peek. One teeny, tiny peek.

I take a step toward it. Then another. I reach forward,

my hand only inches away—*ah, hell.* Who am I kidding? I can't do it. Can't cross that line. Clearly, I need to grow some balls.

In the meantime, there is another option that comes to mind.

The walk home is longer than usual, thanks to my increasing fatigue. I get a text from Bobby on the way that makes me laugh, though, which is nice. A few days ago, he accidentally sent me a random picture of his shoe, so I sent him a picture of a doorknob. And so a tradition was born. Yesterday our theme was windows, and today it's apparently sidewalks. I smile and slip the phone back into my pocket, making a mental note to text him later.

My legs are shaking by the time I pull open the inn's front door.

"Oh my gosh, Lou. Are you okay?"

Judging by Claire's greeting, I look fantastic right now.

"Yeah, I'm fine. It's not as bad as it looks," I lie, leaning onto her desk for support. "I was wondering . . . your mom knows everything about everything around here, right?"

She laughs. "That's what she likes to tell us, yes. Why? What's up?"

"I was hoping I could talk to her? It's about Mr. Blackwood."

"Oh, no." Her face falls in an instant, blonde brows knitting together. "I'd heard the rumors, but I try not to listen to them. He's really as bad as they say?"

"No, no, it's not that. He's fine. I just—I have a few questions."

"Sure. Well, you called it—my mom's the best person for the job. In fact, she's probably home right now if you want to . . ." Her words trail off as her nose scrunches up. "Um, well, maybe you should wait till tomorrow? After you rest some?"

I groan, becoming more nauseous with each passing second. "Yeah, probably a good idea. Where will I be able to find her tomorrow?"

"She's helping with setups for the weekend festival. It's right on Clark Street."

"Great. Thanks, Claire."

"Yup, anytime. Hope you feel better soon." She flashes me a warm smile.

"So do I."

Just as I start up the stairs, I hear her voice call from behind me, "And be sure to call the front desk if you need anything! Maybe Paul will share some of his . . . medicinal herbs . . . with you."

I can't help but laugh at that, and I can hear her own giggle fade behind me as I slowly progress up the steps. By the time I reach my level at the top, I swear the hall-way is spinning. The floor moves below my feet, and I'm impressed I've made it this far as I fumble with my key. I barely manage to close the door behind me before I head straight for the bed, so ready to collapse. Except I can't stop swaying. Or the room won't quit moving, it's one of those. Almost there. Just a few more steps now.

Crap, it's hot in here. Or is it cold? Am I even walking anymore? My vision is closing in on me, the shape of my bed gradually losing form. No, no, it's definitely warm. I know this heat. His warmth. It's here. Behind me. No, in front of me? My eyes squint, trying to latch onto some-thing solid, but it's all blending together . . . the bed, the loveseat, the nightstand. I can't make them stop spinning.

"H-hello?" I stutter. My voice sounds like someone else's. A far off, muffled noise. "Are you here?"

Seconds later, another wave of heat pours over me from head to toe. A heavy blanket settling over my body. He's here. He must be. I *feel* him. Right?

Jesus, I don't know what's real or what's in my head any-more.

My neck, scalp, shoulders, toes—that heat, it's every-where, hot breaths brushing over every inch of me. But something, something's wrong. I can't pinpoint it. Every second of contact he has with me is also a moment of absence, every stroke of heat mixed with ice. It's like the warm blanket wrapped around me has been punctured, and sharp icicles stab through its holes until I finally start to break down and shiver.

The clouded blur of my vision deepens, swirls of darkness taking over, and my bones ache beyond belief. I'm losing strength by the second, losing any part of myself that feels solid. My knees buckle, giving out from beneath me. I should be collapsing, but I can't tell if I am. I don't feel any muscles holding me up, even my neck has turned to mush, and by now all I see is pitch black.

Somehow, I know I'm no longer standing in my room.

What's happening to me?

My body, I'm drifting. Floating in a black void.

I've never heard a silence like this before. It's not like the night of my car accident, when the lightning filled my eardrums with a resounding echo. No, at least that kind of silence offered me something to hold onto. Something to fill the void. This here, it's not even a shell. No walls exist to catch an echo, no air brushes my skin, and I don't need to see to know it's deserted in the most literal form of the word.

I can't hear my heartbeat or my breaths. Don't know if I'm alive or dead. The single feeling I'm left with is an impossible sense of abandonment. It's a cold sensation. So numbingly cold. Not the kind that makes you shiver. The kind of cold that completely bypasses your flesh, reaching into your core and ripping your very soul open with a single slice, until it's raw and naked.

And it's the scariest moment of my life.

A sudden hot spark ignites in my fingertips, making me gasp, and a large hand wraps around my own through the darkness.

It's *him*.

I reach out with my free hand, grasping desperately for any part of him I can get. Anything but this. *Please, please make it stop.*

There's no way to spot him in the sea of black, and I'm grappling blindly with empty air until the hand holding mine squeezes and tugs me forward. I collide straight into his solid warmth. One strong arm wraps around my waist while the other comes up around my shoulders, fingers in my hair. He's holding me so tightly I don't even realize I'm crying until my body starts to tremble against his.

Piece by piece, his warmth sews me back together. My heartbeat finds its rhythm, air flows through my lungs, colors float into view as the darkness dissipates. The round rug, the rocking chair, the fireplace . . . I'm back in my room.

I don't know how much time passes before his grip loosens. Hair matted to my cheeks from my silent stream of tears, I finally look up to face him. Those steely grey-black eyes pierce into mine, unreadable and daunting. His jaw is locked, lips pressed in a tight line.

He's angry.

I don't remember doing it, but my arms are wrapped around his neck, my fingers tangled in his thick hair. I drop my arms quickly, but he's the one who pulls away. It's not much, but it's enough to leave me feeling strange and unsteady, knees weak. His eyes are locked on mine. Or maybe it's the other way around. For a moment, no one speaks. The tension building between us is like a tangible force, a heavy current emitting from him and ricocheting off me.

It's going to be a long night.

Chapter Twenty-Nine

IT TAKES ME A MINUTE to find my voice, and I'm still breathless when I do. "Is that where you . . ." How do I even ask this question? *Live* just doesn't seem like the right word here, so I finish with, "Stay?"

As though the sound of my voice triggers something inside him, all at once his rigid stance diminishes and he's whirling around so his back is to me. He rakes both hands through his hair, then clasps them behind his neck as he inhales a long, uneven breath. He waits a full three seconds before letting his arms drop and turning to face me.

His eyes are different now, the green gleaming through. There's a rough edge to his voice, like a bomb trying to contain itself before it goes off. "Are you okay?"

"I'm—yes. I think so—"

"You should lie down. You need rest." He's scooped me up before I can process what's happening, then takes steady, measured steps toward the bed. I would protest but it'd only be a waste of breath; we both know how weak I still am.

The blankets puff up around me as he sets me down, my head falling lightly on a pillow. He releases me and even though I still feel the soft strokes of his heat, I can't suppress a shiver at the loss of his touch. He reaches toward the foot of the bed to retrieve the silky throw, laying it delicately over my body. Then he plucks up the rocking chair as though it weighs nothing, places it beside the bed, and sinks heavily down.

He avoids meeting my gaze, but I'm watching closely as he leans forward, eyes flashing brightly, jaw clenching. There's so much emotion bottled up inside him, waiting to burst, that I can't seem to single out any one more than the others.

"Hey." I keep my voice gentle. "It's okay. I'm okay now, thanks to you."

He closes his eyes at my words, his lips pressing together in a hard line. "You were pulled in there, thanks to me."

"What?" I sit up, adjusting myself so my back rests against the headboard. "You can't seriously think that what happened tonight is your fault."

His eyes flash open, centering on me. "It is my fault, Lou. You should never have been able to cross over while your heart still beats. It could have . . . it could have killed you. Or worse."

I frown. "I can't think of anything worse than if it'd killed me."

He shakes his head, another quick tick of his jaw. "And let's keep it that way. Tell me how it happened."

"I—I don't really know," I murmur, my frown deepening. "One minute I was feeling sick, and the next I was . . . there."

His brow raises. "You were sick again?"

"Well, not totally. It was just starting, I think. It hit me hard, all at once." I pause, mentally reviewing this past week. "Actually, ever since that last fever I've been feeling a little off—"

"How so?"

I shrug. "Dizzy spells. Fatigue. Not all the time, but enough for it to be annoying."

"And your heart?"

"My heart?"

"Yes," he growls impatiently. Then he pauses, eyes falling closed as he pinches the bridge of his nose. His tone is strained when he calmly clarifies, "Have you noticed any differences with your heart?"

"I don't know. Maybe." I have to stop again to think about it, but it doesn't take long to remember the way my heart started fluttering the first day I'd been ill. "Yeah, when I had that fever. My heartbeat felt different. It wasn't steady like usual, but more like a flutter. It was fast and light and just strange. Almost like it wasn't really . . . like it wasn't fully beating." Oh, shit. Suddenly that sounds really, really bad.

He lets out a deep breath, then hangs his head low to his chest for a few seconds before bringing his now heavy gaze back up to mine. "Of course," he mutters, leaning back against the seat and pursing his lips.

"'Of course' what? Did I miss something?"

He shakes his head, his fingers rubbing his jaw. "No. I did." He bites the words out. "I should have known this could happen."

"What could happen?"

"Your body, it's . . . adjusting. Acclimating itself to my world."

My eyes just about pop out of their sockets. "Excuse me?" I'm not adding anything useful to this conversation, but I can't seem to assimilate anything properly right now.

"In order for you to fully cross into my world, your body would have to be . . . well, less *body*, and more *soul*."

I blink. "Except, I'm definitely body." I flip the throw off of me in demonstration and run my hands up and down my waist, my hips. "All body. See?"

His eyelids lower, gaze clinging to each spot my hands touch. A thick swallow passes through his throat, and I realize I should probably stop groping myself in front of him. "Yes," he all but groans, "I do see."

"Sorry," I mumble as I scrunch my face, pulling the

throw back over me. Such a tease.

He rips his eyes away, scrubbing a hand down his face as though to clear his mind. "Do you remember what I told you before about the universe being confused? Blurring us together?"

I nod. I get the feeling I'm not going to like where this is going.

He pushes himself up from the chair, taking the single step toward my bed until he's close enough to touch. He doesn't sit though, just hovers over me, his heat tickling my skin and his blazing eyes devouring mine. "Lou." It's just my name, but his voice is smooth, low, and caresses parts of me I didn't know a voice could reach. "Give me your hand."

I comply without thinking. His own large hand wraps fully around mine, shooting a ripple of warmth straight up my arm, down my chest, and pooling low in my stomach. He raises my hand until it rests palm-down on his chest. Now it's my turn to swallow. My gaze flickers from his face to his chest, unsure of where to land.

"Do you feel it?" he murmurs.

I pause, focusing my attention on the hard lines pressed up against the palm of my hand. I'm just about to ask what he's referring to, when a soft thump beats beneath my touch. And then another. And another. It's faint, barely noticeable in fact, but it's there. I lift my chin to see his face, my voice almost a whisper when I say, "I feel it."

His lips curve up, just on one side and not enough to show his dimple. The natural brightness of his eyes seems to have dimmed somehow, and I realize there's some-thing broken about this smile. "I'm not supposed to have a heartbeat." With my hand still against his chest, the soft rumble of his voice vibrates through my body. "See, my body started adjusting too, Lou. For your world, for you. I couldn't fully be here, all of me, until my heart began to beat."

I don't like the sadness coloring his tone, the foreboding look in his eyes. I smile up at him, eyelashes batting. "Are you saying that your heart literally beats for me, Gumdrop?"

His dimple flashes then, his eyes brightening gorgeously for a moment before quieting back down. "I think I'm saying that and more, Lou."

My smile falters as I try to process his words. There's no trace of humor in them, like there had been in mine. The way my heart squeezes at his response makes me seriously hope I'm not reading more into it than he intended. Before I have the chance to overthink it any further, he removes my hand from his chest and takes a step back, quietly lowering himself back into the rocking chair.

The sudden silence surrounding us makes me realize how tired I am, physically and mentally. I'm an aching mess from my head to my toes, and my heart is filling with a worry I don't quite understand. "What's going to happen to me? To both of us?"

He eyes me carefully for a second, a crease forming between his brows that tells me he can see the worry etched into my face. His hand comes up, and his fingers run gently through the long strands of my hair. Once, twice, that's it before he pulls back, but I'm already sighing.

"You?" He leans closer, elbows resting on his thighs, and looks me dead on. I always love when his eyes get overtaken by the green like this. For some reason, it makes me feel like it's not just Death talking to me, but *him*. The soul inside. "You're going to rest right here in your warm, comfortable bed. You'll wake up tomorrow ready for a new day. You'll slip on your fancy mood ring—" He pauses, glancing down at my bare fingers with a cocked brow, and I slink deeper into the bed. Why does it feel like I'm being chastised for not wearing the ring? And why do I like it? "And you'll go on with your life, just as you have been."

"But my heart—"

"Don't worry about that. Leave it to me."

"Don't worry? But—"

"Look at me, Lou." I lift my chin, just now noticing that I've already curled fully into the blankets, my eyelids growing heavy with the need to sleep. I hold them open to peer up at him, his face looming over mine. He's looking at me in a way I'm sure no one else has done before, because I'd recognize the wild rush it sends pulsing through my veins. "I don't have all the answers right now," he continues, his voice a smooth lullaby, "but I'm not going to let anything happen to you. Okay?"

I feel my head nod up and down, my eyes already closing. "Okay," I whisper into the darkness.

The chair creaks beneath his body as he leans back against it, the sound filling me with comfort. That sound means he's not leaving yet. It means he's still here, with me. As the gentle silence drones on, my mind drifts away with it. I should still be scared after a night like this. I should be freaking out. But my chest, it's somehow so full, and I can't help but feel a certain sense of peace. Even if I know the feeling won't last. Even if I know it's just for a little while, as he sits here beside me. I'll take what I can get.

"Gumdrop?" I whisper dazedly, just before my mind can shut down fully.

"Yes, Lou."

"I think my heart beats for you, too."

Chapter Thirty

LIQUOR, PUKE, AND BLOOD.
    The scents blend together to form a disgusting sea of filth in the air around us.

I shift my gaze to my right, attempting to lock eyes with the boy who sits tied up in a chair beside me. He's shaking, his entire twelve-year-old frame quivering as he stares down at his clothes, wide eyed.

"Look at me, Tommy," I hear myself command, my voice a firm whisper. I glance quickly at the monster, ensuring his back is still turned as he digs through the kitchen cabinets, then return my attention to the petrified boy. "You'll look at me right now, you hear me?"

Finally his head shifts toward me, his movements stiff. It's then that I see the way his teeth are chattering.

"What do you see?"

"I-I-I see you. I see you."

"Uh-huh. And who am I?"

"M-my brother."

"That's right. And is there any mess we haven't gotten out of together, little brother?"

He swallows, then shakes his head.

"Damn straight."

Tommy's gaze drops to my clothes, then raises back up to meet mine. "Y-you're going to be okay. He didn't soak you in the liquor like he did me."

I feel the snap of my jaw as my teeth grind together. My hands tug and yank behind me, still fumbling hard with the old rope I've gotten to know so well. "That's because he's a twisted fuck," I answer. "Not because he's feeling generous. He wants me to watch you suffer before he moves on to me."

"Goddamn bastard! He tell you that?" Tommy shrieks, and we both swing our heads toward the monster. He doesn't seem to have heard us though, so we turn back to face each other.

A grin stretches across my face despite the morbid clusterfuck we're in. "So all it took was knowing your big bro's life is at stake, too, for you to remember you've got a big ol' pair of balls in there? Well, shit, I should have said something sooner."

Just when Tommy starts to grin back, a loud roar rips through the kitchen. "Where is it!" The monster whirls around to face us then stomps over, his eyes narrowing right at me, index finger shoving against my chest. "You. I know you did this. Where are all the matches? Where are they!"

"What, so I can help you light your kid on fire? You sick son of a bitch."

The monster's face twists into something ugly as he sneers down at me, taking a step closer. His nose is red, pupils dilated, and I glimpse white residue around his nostrils. "Nah, boy. Think you got me confused with yourself. You're the real son of a bitch, ain't you? Your mom's mistaken if she thinks she can run off with another man without you two havin' to pay." I cry out as he digs his finger into an open gash on my thigh, crippling pain shooting all the way to my chest. "I ain't gonna kill you boys. Just teach her another lesson is all."

A snarl sounds from my right, taking us both by surprise. Little Tommy's got the fiery look in his eyes I usually only see in my own reflection. "She doesn't give a damn about your so-called 'lessons,' Pops! Stop using her as a shit excuse to take out your demented rage on us!"

The man before us stops, angles himself toward Tommy, and stares at him almost as though seeing him for the first time.

"What'd you say to me?"

Shit. My eyes close briefly as I shake my head, my hands fighting harder than ever to get freed. I almost smile when I feel the blood start to trickle down my wrists. So close now. "Forget him," *I mutter.* "You were talking to me, remember?"

"You shut your mouth. I believe Tommy, on the other hand, has somethin' to say. Anything else you'd like to add to that, little boy?" He inches closer, until the toes of his boots slam against Tommy's.

Tommy's eyes go wide, losing all of their spark as he watches the monster reach into his back pocket. "Uh, n-no. That was it."

"You sure about that?" A large, silver pocket knife appears in his hand, and he runs the blade smoothly across his fingers.

Tommy's swallow could be heard from where I sit. "Y-yes."

"Yes, what?"

"Yes, sir."

"Very good. Now you know it pains me to do this," he says with a soft chuckle, "but I still gotta teach you a lesson for that attitude of yours. I swear your mom gave you boys her worst qualities. Hmm, been awhile since I gave you a tattoo, hasn't it?" He bends forward, eyes scanning over Tommy's small torso. "Now where would you like it? I'll even let you choose."

I don't know if there's a name for the sensation that suddenly swells inside me, flooding my lungs with hot fumes, but I do know it's filled with red. Scorching flames of red, setting my veins on fire until I can't see clearly, can't think. There is one, single thought that rings through with utter clarity, though. Right here, right now, is where this ends.

And I'm going to be the one to end it.

⟨ℚ⟩

I WAKE UP TO THE RACING pulse I'm beginning to get a little too familiar with. *Dammit.* I wasn't supposed to wake up yet. I need to fall back asleep. I'm overcome with an urgent, desperate need to know that the brothers got out of there alive, that they're okay. That they're safe. Did he end it like he'd intended? Where is the closure for these poor boys? When will enough be enough?

My hand comes up to my chest, expecting to find a frantic rhythm beating within, but for a moment, I don't feel anything at all. And it scares the living hell out me. I freeze, palm still pressed against me, until finally I feel a vague thump. Then another. A breath of relief pours out of me, and I squeeze my eyes shut.

Calm down. You're okay.

He said I'd be fine, and I am.

I remember then that he was still here when I'd fallen asleep, and I quickly scan the room. I don't know why I'm so hopeful even though it's clear he's no longer here. The absence of his warmth surrounds me like an actual entity, each cold breeze seeping in through the window reminding me I'm alone again.

It seems he has a habit of disappearing on me while I sleep. I wonder what it'd be like to actually wake up to him. I bet I'd feel him against my skin before I even opened my eyes, the same way soft sun warms your skin in the middle of spring. Would he stroke my hair, like he did so briefly last night? Would he stay in the chair beside me, watching while I sleep, or would he sneak into my bed and let me curl into him? I smile at the thought, stretching my arms out over my head before making my way into the bathroom.

My smile immediately turns upside down when my gaze meets the mirror and drops to my chest. I press my fingers over my heart, rubbing the area in a soothing, circular motion. I don't want to worry, or be scared, because I know from experience that never gets you anywhere. But standing before my reflection reminds me I'm only human. I need to feel a solid drum within me to know I'm going to be okay. And right now, that beat is slowly slipping away. My eyes close, already begging for a break in reality. I can't do this. Can I? How do you figure out how to fix something you don't even understand?

For a moment I consider summoning Death back here to keep me from losing it completely, but then I remember I have somewhere to be. Still, I wish I could feel that safety net I had when he was here beside me, his hypnotic voice telling me not to worry. I wish he'd stay with me just a while longer. Does that make me weak?

Yes.

No.

Maybe . . .

It's funny, just a month ago I would have answered that question with a resounding yes. But now? Now I wonder if maybe allowing another person to give you strength takes a certain kind of strength in itself. To be able to lean all your weight on someone else with confidence in the knowledge they won't drop you. How often does a person really find that kind of trust in another?

My mind drifts back to the feelings that took over when I was with him last night, and I begin to wonder if maybe, just maybe, there's a chance I may have found it.

I groan aloud. *Just my luck.* Who else would find comfort in the Grim Reaper? And just when I might be about to drop dead, too. I frown and look up, past the ceiling and toward the sky, right as I feel another hitch in the rhythm of my heartbeat.

"You've got a sick sense of humor, buddy."

Chapter Thirty-One

CLARK STREET ISN'T LARGE. IT isn't super busy, either, and it's been closed off to vehicles for festival setups. One would think all these factors would make it easy to spot a Claire look-alike in the small crowd, yet I've been scanning the street for ten minutes without any luck. I even stopped by Claire's desk before heading here to make sure Lydia, her mom, would be here.

I decide to do another quick survey of the area before texting Claire. There's a pair of burly men to my right, unloading equipment from a truck. A trio of girls around my age chattering as they hang up banners and the likes. Several other people are setting up booths. Directly across from me, on the opposite sidewalk, stands a tall, African-American woman with a clipboard attached to her arm. She's the one everyone goes to with questions, and she also seems to be the most friendly of the group. Her smile is big and bright, and her eyes are warm.

If I don't end up finding Lydia on my own, and if Claire keeps refusing to help me, then maybe that woman is someone I can approach. Surely the person running the show would know everyone helping to put on the event, right?

I pull out my phone and start texting.

Me: You sure she's here?

Claire: Positive!

Me: Been standing here for ten minutes, and I don't see her.

Claire: Look harder ;)

Me: Can't you just send me her number so I can call her?

Claire: Oh, but this is so much more fun.

Me: Careful, your evil side is showing.

Claire: Hahaha, think you'll live!

I laugh as I slide the phone into my back pocket. All right, time to get this over with. I'm not exactly looking forward to digging around for info on Mr. Blackwood, but it has to be better than doing nothing and discovering too late that he needs help of some kind. I wait a second while the woman with the clipboard finishes wrapping up a conversation, then stroll toward her.

"Excuse me," I call, before someone else can steal her from me. "Sorry to bother you. I was just wondering if by chance you've seen a Lydia Birch around here?"

Her painted lips curve up warmly as she extends her free hand toward me. "That would be me. And you must be Claire's friend, Lou."

"Oh! I'm—yes, I'm Lou."

Lydia chuckles as we release hands. "Honey, it's okay. Claire's adopted, but she's been a part of our family since before she was born. She told me to expect you this morning, but with all the set ups and such I didn't notice you standing there. Have you been here long?"

"No, no," I lie. "Well, not really."

Seeing right through me, she wrinkles her nose. "Sorry. There's not much in the way of entertainment around here, so I allow myself to get caught up in all this." She waves a hand in the air, gesturing to the set ups, then wraps an arm around my shoulders and steers me across the street, away from the watchful eyes surrounding us. "Anyhow, Claire said you wanted to see me in regards to Mr. Blackwood?"

I nod, not quite sure how to begin. "I just . . . I don't know. I don't want to overstep, but I'm a little worried about him."

"Here, honey. Take a seat." We've reached a small outdoor seating area, and we're both silent as we get settled across the table from each other. "Mr. Blackwood . . . well, he certainly is a private man."

"Is he? I hadn't noticed."

She laughs. "I can see why Claire likes you. You two must get along pretty well."

"She's easy to get along with."

"That she is." Her smile widens, and my heart swells.

They're such simple, general words, but the way she says them . . . it's impossible not to feel the love she holds for her daughter. The woman is so motherly in this moment that the constant longing I have for my own mother bubbles back up to the surface.

"Lucky for you," Lydia continues, returning to the topic of Mr. Blackwood, "I just so happen to have a knack for learning about the residents in my town. Unlucky for both of us, however, that man is about as hardheaded as a mule, so I'm afraid I haven't discovered much."

"Yeah, that's what I was afraid of." I chew on the inside of my lip, my already minimal hope deflating. "Anything could be helpful, though, if it sheds more light on who he is. How I might be able to connect with him better."

She nods as though she understands, and I think she really does. I remember that, back when I first got the job, Claire said something to suggest her mother was one of the town folk urging Mr. Blackwood to get a caretaker. "Right," Lydia says, crossing one leg over the other as she leans back against the seat. "Well, you're aware he's an author?"

"Yes, but I haven't seen any of his work."

"Oh, you should. It's perhaps a bit far-fetched for some, but remarkable work regardless."

"Far-fetched? How's that?"

"We carry them in our library. You should check them out and see for yourself."

The library. Of course. Why hadn't I thought of that? "I think I will. Thanks."

"Other than that, I know he moved here about twenty years ago from Colorado. He's been the same way he is now ever since I've known him—closed off, and a little too friendly with his liquor."

"And his leg? Do you know what happened to him?" I ask, thinking back to the steel I've glimpsed multiple times now.

"Ah, yes. His leg. Some kind of car accident, I believe. It happened before he moved here."

I frown. Going through any accident like that is traumatic enough, but to have no one you love to lean on afterward? To have no support to get you through the inevitable rough times? Poor Mr. Blackwood. "No kids? Siblings? Any visitors at all?"

She shakes her head, a sad expression washing over her elegant features. "I wish I could say yes. For years when he'd first arrived, many of the locals tried involving him in activities, clubs . . . anything, really. But he wasn't having any of it. Always said he was busy working on his research. That was a little while before his latest book was ever published, though, and I really thought he'd become more available after that. As far as I know, he has no plans on publishing anything else, so I can't imagine that he's still spending all his time cooped up in his house over some research."

I almost snort aloud. The man rarely does anything *but* research.

"Well, I'm afraid that's all I know," she continues. "As I'm sure you've come to notice, he doesn't make many appearances in town."

I chuckle, trying to picture Mr. Blackwood standing in the middle of the winter festival as happy families surround him, his flask in one hand and the bird in the other. "Yeah, I have."

A moment of silence passes between us, my chest becoming heavy as I realize I truly might not be able to do much for this man. Lydia's gentle voice eventually interrupts my thoughts. "You know, it's been awhile since I've really tried reaching out to the gentleman. In fact, I've hardly spoken to him at all lately." She glances down briefly in guilt, pressing her lips together. "I can see how much you care about him, Lou. I'd be happy to try speaking to him again, to see if maybe—"

"Oh, no. Please." Now it's my turn to look away, to feel the guilt rise. "I shouldn't even be butting into his life like this. He wouldn't appreciate it. And I'm sure he wouldn't want anyone feeling sorry for him either, so I should . . . I should probably go." I stand, the metal chair scraping against the sidewalk as I do. "Thanks so much for taking the time to talk to me, Mrs. Birch. Really, it was so nice to meet you."

She smiles as she rises from her seat. "It was no trouble, honey. Hopefully I'll get to see more of you soon."

"Yeah, definitely." I'm about to give her an awkward wave when she reaches her arms around me in a tight embrace. It reminds me of the way Claire hugged me after putting up the New Year banner, and I instantly lean into it. Everyone could use a good hug in their life.

Just as I turn to walk away, I hear Lydia's voice behind me.

"Hey, Lou?"

"Yes?"

"The Hawkins family."

My eyebrows pucker together. "Sorry?"

"The Hawkins Family," she repeats, taking a step toward me. "They used to live here a while back. Ended in tragedy,

I'm afraid. But I know that Mr. Blackwood had some sort of connection with them. Not sure if it helps, but it's the only other thing I know about him."

Chapter Thirty-Two

I HEAD BACK TO THE INN, deciding to save the trip to the library for another day since I start work in less than an hour and still have to get ready. Should be more than enough time to squeeze in an internet search on the Hawkins family, though.

Claire's on the phone when I step inside. She catches my eye and grins wide. I give her a fake applaud as I pass by that says, *Yeah, yeah. You got me,* and she snickers.

Once in my room, I get comfortable on the bed and retrieve my phone, immediately starting a Google search. I don't even have to scroll through the search engine results, because right there at the top of the page reads: "Hawkins Family of Three, Burned to Death in Their Own Home."

My stomach twists at the words, eyes squeezing shut before I force myself to continue reading. There's a picture of the house—or what's left of it, but it's the wild flames that take over the image, swirling between dark clouds of smoke. I squint, focusing on the background scenery, and notice that the property is on some kind of small farm.

Ashwick, KS—Single father and two sons pronounced dead following a house fire apparently sparked by gasoline and a match.

About 2:30 p.m. on Tuesday, July 6, 1958,

**Kansas State Police troopers responded to
a medical call at 2139 Deer Lane. As they
neared the scene, they spotted smoke coming from the house, said Chief of Police
Wayne Mulligan—**

My fingers tighten around the phone as I carefully reread that last name. *Mulligan.* I know that name. I know it, because it was Grams's last name. Tallulah Mulligan. The Chief of Police, though? My mind immediately begins forming assumption after assumption, and I have to give my head a little shake. *Don't get ahead of yourself.* Mulligan is a fairly common last name, right? Still, I store the piece of information away for later.

I redirect my attention back to the article in front of me.

**Firefighters arrived and battled the blaze.
Once it was controlled, responders entered
the structure, which was left mostly in
ruins. They found resident and father of two
Sherman Hawkins lying on the living room
floor.**

**Hawkins was removed from the house
and paramedics pronounced him deceased,
Mulligan said.**

**An initial investigation showed the kitchen
floor had been doused in gasoline before
a match was lit to it. The physical state of
Hawkins's body suggests foul play, with a
severe injury to the back of his head having occurred just prior to the fire being
set. Additionally, blood residuals recovered
on Hawkins has since been matched to the
DNA of both his sons.**

**The investigator says at this time all evi-
dence suggests the fire was intentionally lit
by one of the Hawkins boys.**

While the bodies of the Hawkins boys—

seventeen-year-old Enzo Hawkins and twelve-year-old Thomas Hawkins—were never recovered due to the poor condition of the property's remains, further forensic evidence has since confirmed their deaths.

At present, Mulligan, who was also close friends with the now deceased Sherman Hawkins, says the case is currently closed.

Holy crap. My jaw aches from clenching it so hard, and my hand cramps around the phone I'm holding in a death grip.

It can't be them.

Can it?

My heart's racing as I release the phone and snap upright, my mind involuntarily darting back to my dreams.

Thomas. Twelve years old. An older brother. Evidence of foul play. Fire, the kitchen.

It all lines up. In fact, it could easily have been where my latest dream was headed if I hadn't woken in the middle of it. But really, how could that even be possible? They're *dreams*. I pause, reviewing all the impossible things that have already happened in my life lately. Dying, being saved by Death, him getting trapped in my room, me crossing over to the other side, my body attempting to adjust to life over there. Maybe it's not so unbelievable after all.

Even so, what are the odds that the people in my dreams would exist right here, in this very town? Or that they *did*, anyway. My eyes shut at that last thought, my insides churning so intensely it makes my head pound.

It can't be true. It can't end like that for them. God, I was there. Right there with them. I know what that monster did to them. Felt from a place deep within me the way that raw, blood-thick, brotherly love constantly burned between the boys. I *knew* them. I *was* them. I bled with them. And now it feels as though a part of me burned with them.

Tears roll down my cheeks, but I don't bother to wipe them. What's the point, when I know they'll just keep on coming?

There has to be more to their stories, right? They were so young, had so much more life to live. And after all they'd gone through, all the suffering, all the pain. Where's the justice? Where's their silver lining? It just doesn't seem right for that to be the ending to their story, when it should have been the beginning.

I grab my phone again, this time doing a search under the boys' names. I figure with an incident as big as this one happening in such a small town, there might be something more on them.

Nothing.

All that pops up is that same article. I try searching under the father's name instead. *Bingo.* It's just one photograph, but it's all the confirmation I need. A sickening feeling takes ahold of me as I instantly recognize the monster from my dreams. He sits on a chair in the grass, one leg kicked out and a pipe in his mouth, like he hasn't a care in the world. The woman beside him is gorgeous. There's a flashy, almost seductive smile on her face, one eyebrow arched daringly at the camera. Her hair is a silky black, perfectly coiffed in a way that makes her look out of place in the middle of a farm as they are. So this is the mother who was never there. The woman who cared more about her next fling than her own children.

My thumb clears the screen as I swallow down the urge to vomit. I have all the proof I need. It is them. Enzo and Thomas Hawkins. The brave brothers with hearts spun from gold. Survivors. Angels. And everything good and strong in between.

I can't take the heartache, still feeling the reality of this revelation sink into my mind, my soul.

Why? Why am I having dreams about these two people who existed decades ago? I may not have trouble believing in the impossible anymore, but I still want to understand it. Is there some connection I should be making here? Something I'm meant to do in relation to these boys?

It's on that heavy thought that the alarm goes off beside me. Ugh. I have to go. I can't imagine spending the day cleaning when I should be trying to figure out what's going on with me. With all of this. But I have to go. If I'm going to get anywhere with Mr. Blackwood, if I have any chance of getting answers from him about the Hawkins brothers, I need to repair the trust I broke with him first. Show him he won't scare me away. That he can yell, he can bark, he can push and shove all he wants, but I'm not going anywhere.

⁂

AS EXPECTED, MR. BLACKWOOD IGNORED me for most of the day. I was happy to find him already home when I arrived this time, rather than stumbling drunkenly through the door later on. He even seemed to be back at it with his research again.

I made a point to give him some space after our last little episode. It wasn't easy. I almost caved several times, my jaw about to snap from how hard I forced my mouth shut all day. It was difficult enough trying to stay out of his business before, but now that I know he has ties to the Hawkins boys, it's near impossible.

When it came time for me to leave, I gave him my usual goodbye and he gave me his usual grunt. He didn't toss me out on my ass mid-day or drink himself to death, so, yeah, I'd say the day was a success.

I almost stopped at the library on my way home, but the more I thought about it, the more I concluded I would rather he reach a point where he's willing to show me his work than have to go snooping around even more. As of now, the library is my Plan B.

After my bath once I'm back home, I mentally go over

exactly what Death and I need to focus on when he comes over tonight: how to get ourselves out of this mess before it gets any worse. That is what we need to discuss, and that is *all* we need to discuss.

I'm certainly *not* obsessing over my sleepy confession last night, which is also *not* replaying in my head like a broken record as I realize I'm about to face him for the first time since then. I'm not taking the time to blow dry my hair or put on my favorite lip gloss. And I'm especially not sliding my legs into the kind of jeans that highlight my curves in all the right ways.

But if I were . . . I might wonder what he'd think at seeing this look on me. I might wonder if he'd comment on it, or inch closer and slowly brush the hair from my face. I might wish for just one last moment to pretend we aren't from different worlds, we don't have an expiration date, and that I'm just a girl and he's just a boy.

I shift my head and eye the clock. At least I can always count on him being on time.

Which means I have exactly forty-five seconds.

Forty-five seconds to get my head together and stay focused on the reality of our situations. Thirty-nine seconds to remind myself why I can't get all girly on him now and need to concentrate on the issues with my *actual* heart, not my metaphorical heart. Twenty-two seconds to become a full-blown adult who knows how to get shit done.

Fifteen seconds.

Ten.

Five.

And . . .

I turn my head. Look around. Clear my throat. "Um, hello?"

Nothing. Strange.

I continue to wait, chewing my lip and allowing my mind to wander. I toy with the ring on my middle finger, the one I'd made sure to slip on after my bath. Then I continue to wait as I return to the bathroom to check my hair, adjust my top. And I flick through the channels as I wait some more. It's not until over an hour later as I lie restless on my bed that I finally get it.

He's not coming.

Chapter Thrity-Three

TILTING MY HEAD, I SQUINT and shift the phone. "So . . . is this what I think it is?"

"Well that depends." Jamie peeks over my shoulder, her jasmine scented perfume saturating my room. It's Saturday, and she arrived from LA over an hour ago, insisting through a thick, clogged voice that she is not coming down with anything and that she is here to have a crazy weekend of fun with her bestie. Apparently that involves staring at weird pictures. "Are you thinking it's the udder of a cow?" she asks.

"Yup."

"Then yes!"

"And are you, um, milking it?"

"Ew. Don't remind me." She sniffles, her nose pink from all of the sneezing she's been doing, and reaches over to pluck her cell phone from my hands. She cringes as she inspects the picture on the screen one last time. "I swear, the things I do for that man."

"Oh god," I groan. "Please don't tell me this is some kinky thing Daniel's into."

"What?" Her jaw drops dramatically, and she shoves my shoulder as I chuckle. "Not even. Well, kind of. The kinkiest thing we've ever done, though, involved a butt plug, a ladder, and one of those furry—"

"Nope." The palm of my hand shoots up between us. "Stop right there. I can't believe I'm about to say this, but can we get back to the cow udders, please?"

"Oh, right. I drove past quite a few farms to get here and," she shrugs, wandering toward the fireplace and picking up one of my framed photographs, "well, Daniel's always had this fantasy about cowgirls. I tried to tell him awhile back that real cowgirls aren't like they are in those porn videos—"

"Didn't need to know that—"

"But he wasn't having it. So anyway, this is just me making good on his fantasy." She turns back to me and winks.

I snort and shake my head as she lets out another little sneeze. "Ugh," she moans. "Be right back." She disappears into the bathroom.

After fixing the family photos she unwittingly rearranged, I step back and glance down at my mood ring, twisting it around my finger. He never came that night, or the next night either. Not when I made sure to be here at our usual time, just in case, and not when I tried calling out his name. All that answered was silence and an empty room.

A part of me worries. After all, I'm not the only one whose body is trying to acclimate. What if something happened to him? What if he's stuck somewhere? Or what if something went wrong and he wound up in some other girl's room somewhere across the globe? What if he's lost control of things again and can no longer come at will? Or what if his heart decided not to beat for me after all, and without a beating heart, he's unable to cross back over? The possibilities are endless, and my pulse rate picks up just thinking about them.

Another part of me, though, the part that's nestled deep down in my core, knows that this is intentional. For whatever reason, he's choosing not to see me anymore. Choosing to stay away.

I press my fingers to my chest, searching for that beat again, as I have been doing every morning when I wake up. The rhythm is still there, pounding gently beneath my touch, but it's even fainter now than it was a few days ago. Fear sneaks its way to the forefront of my mind, and I try to block it out. But it's stronger than me. I'm scared, and without him I have no one to talk to about it. No one to lean on. No one to turn to. It's a lonely place to be.

The bathroom door clicks open with Jamie stepping out, a tissue pressed firmly to her button nose, and I try to smile. I know I'm lucky to at least have friends here with me, even if I can't talk to them about these things. "Got any tape?" she murmurs, clearly annoyed. Her voice sounds even more nasally now that she's got her nose all plugged up. "I gotta stop the stupid leaking somehow if we're going out."

"Jamie . . ." My brows knit together. "You sure you want to be out and about when you're feeling like this?"

"Psh." She shoves my arm then pulls me in for a tight hug with her free hand, sniffling all over me. "You kidding? Like I'm going to let a little hiccup interfere with our plans. A-a-a—" I duck out of her grasp just in time. "CHOO!"

Well, this should be interesting.

∘ ∞ ∘

BY THE TIME EVENING ROLLS around, Jamie's tucked into my bed like a tall, skinny burrito. Her naturally tan face is tinted with rosy splotches, and used tissues are littered all around her. Claire's scooting the rocking chair and rug aside, making space for the air mattress she brought over for our sleepover.

"Seriously, you guys," Jamie mutters for the millionth time this hour. "You do not need to stay in just because I'm a wreck. Go out, have fun. Get drunk for me."

"We're not going anywhere," I repeat, also for the millionth time. "Staying in with you and Claire beats going out and getting drunk any day."

"Liar."

"Yes." I smirk, and she snickers.

A loud noise hits our eardrums as the mattress begins filling up, and Claire shouts to be heard. "I'm not old enough to buy alcohol!"

"Use your fake ID!" Jamie shouts back.

Claire scrunches her nose. "I don't have a fake ID."

"What?" Jamie's eyes go wide, but she quickly replaces the shocked expression with an excited one. "Lou can go out and buy some, and you guys can party here! Then I'll get to watch you two embarrass yourselves, and I can make fun of you in the morning while you're puking over the toilet seat. See? It's a win–win for everyone."

Claire laughs. "Clearly."

"No one's getting drunk tonight," I holler. "We're taking care of your sick butt and watching the classics."

The blaring noise around us finally simmers down as Claire unhooks the air pump. She turns to us then, an eyebrow quirked. "The classics? Um, I'm not really one for old movies—"

Jamie chuckles, shaking her head. "No, sweetie. *Our* classics." She flicks a finger between me and herself. "Clueless, Ten Things I Hate About You, and Mean Girls."

THE FAMILIAR TUNE SEEPS INTO my ears, distant and hazy. What the hell is that? I groan and roll over, my arm falling on Claire's, causing her to stir. Then it starts again, that high-pitched rhythm I'm slowly becoming able to place.

My phone. Great.

I climb off the air mattress, careful not to disturb Claire this time, and grab the object lighting up a few feet from me. I don't even look at the number before I answer the call and slip into the bathroom. I gently close the door behind me.

"Hello?" I whisper groggily.

"Yeah, is this Lou?" It's some guy's voice I don't recognize, and there's loud music in the background.

"Um, yes?"

"Listen, I'm sorry to disturb you at this hour but . . ." He pauses, his reluctance obvious. "Uh, well, your boyfriend is passed out on my bar's floor, and we closed over ten minutes ago."

What? I finally pause to glance down at my screen. It's Bobby's number. I return the phone to my ear, and the man is already speaking again.

"I really don't wanna have security kick him out. I like the dude. But he can't stay here all night."

It takes a minute for his words to really sink in. Bobby is on the floor. Passed out. At a bar. *Sober* Bobby is passed out in a bar. Oh, no.

"Um, yeah. Yeah, of course. I'll be right there. Can you text me the address?"

"Yup, sending it now."

"Thanks."

We hang up, and I quietly exit the bathroom. Claire is still asleep on the air mattress, and Jamie looks like she's in a full-on coma under my covers. I consider waking Claire for a minute since I really don't want to pick up my ex alone at some bar at two in the morning, but I'd rather not get her involved in this. It's not the first time I've received this kind of phone call regarding Bobby, and I've learned you never know what you'll find when you pick him up.

Instead, I grab a long, heavy winter coat from the closet and drape it over my pajamas, then snag Jamie's car keys from her purse, slide my feet into warm boots, and tiptoe out of there.

It takes a little while to get to the place because it's not in town, but the second I see the *Curly's Bar* sign I put the car in park and hop out. There are people lingering on the sidewalk, some puking and others making out. I ignore them as I make my way inside. True to form, Bobby is lying passed out in the middle of the room. I bend down beside him and lean closer.

"Bobby."

He grunts.

Could be worse. At least he's semi-responsive this time. "Bobby, we gotta go."

His eyelids start to open, slow and heavy, and he just stares up at me for a minute, eyes squinting. "Lou? Is that you?"

I smile softly, an unexpected wave of guilt flooding through me at seeing him like this. He was doing so well. Or at least, I thought he was. I should have been paying better attention. I should have been a better friend. "Yes, it's me, Bobby. Listen. I'm going to need your help, okay?"

Pause. Blink. "Okay."

"I'm going to slip my arm under your neck, but I'll need your help pushing off the ground, okay? I can't hold all of you on my own."

Another pause. A glance around. "Okay."

I do as I said I would, reaching down and curling one arm around his neck and shoulders, the other around his torso. "Now, Bobby. Push up now."

He shifts beneath me, groans, then hooks one of his arms around me and grabs on, using my body as partial leverage to pull himself up. It's not easy, but I've done it countless times before, so I know just how to hold my stance, just how to steady him once he's on his feet, and just how to walk while he's leaning half his weight on me.

"Lou," he whispers, once he stops swaying. He angles his head at me, and guilt is written all over his tired face. "I'm so sorry. I'm so sorry." It's all a slur, each word running into the next.

"Shh, shh. You're okay, Bobby. You're okay." I nod toward

the entrance. "See those doors? We're going to start walking toward them now. Can you take the first step?"

He knows what I'm really asking when I say that last part, because it's the same exact words he's heard hundreds of times before. He looks at me long and hard, probably remembering the same thing. Remembering our sad, useless tradition. And just like those times before, he slurs, "And the next. And the next."

A tear forms in the corner of my eye. How'd we get here again, Bobby? "That's right."

After a moment, he moves, his right foot slowly stepping forward, and I begin to move with him. The bartender's been watching us as he puts chairs up on tables, and I offer him a meaningful glance. I mouth a clear *thank you*, and he gives me a sad smile. How many times has he seen this before? Made calls like this? Sometimes I think being a bartender is the surest way to abstain from alcohol.

We're hit by a rush of wind, the cold breeze like a slap to my face, and the door slams behind us.

"Hey, look who it is! Little Miss Savior."

I close my eyes, wishing I didn't recognize the voice calling out to me. Of course he would be here. Who else would go out of his way to bring a good man like Bobby down when he's finally beginning to turn things around?

I don't look at him as I inch a barely conscious Bobby toward Jamie's car in front of us. I clumsily set him into the passenger seat and get him buckled up, watching as he closes his eyes. Then I close the door, take a deep breath, and turn to face Shithead Ryan.

There's a girl attached to his hip, and a small group of people cluttered around him, filling the sidewalk with the sounds of their lip-smacking and exaggerated laughter. I ignore them, centering my focus on Ryan.

"What the hell are you doing here?" I ask, gritting the words out.

"What, a guy can't come out to Bumfuck, Nowhere to

see his pal?" He kicks off the wall he's leaning on, and the girl squeals as she stumbles off him. He inches closer. He's not a tall guy, more short and stocky, but he likes to pretend he's big and bad. "How come you get to have visitors but Bobby can't?" I don't need to ask how he knows Jamie's in town because I'm sure Bobby told him. "Still the same old controlling Lou, I see. Trying to keep Bobby down, keep him from having a good time."

"Oh, is that what tonight was?" I gesture toward the vehicle behind me, where Bobby's curled up, two seconds away from passing out. "A good time?"

Ryan rolls his eyes. "If you were here a little earlier you'd have seen that *yes*, it was a hell of a good time. The guy finally let loose, remembered what it's like to just let go. But you never seem to wanna stick around for the fun stuff, do you?"

"Kind of like how you never seem to wanna stick around for the aftermath?" It's not until then that I catch a glimpse of a blonde buzz cut to my right. I shift my gaze, squinting. "Dylan?"

He separates his face from the petite girl wrapped in his arms, and I watch as recognition forms in his bloodshot eyes. His eyes widen, the alarm setting in immediately, but it quickly fades as he seems to realize it's useless. I've already seen more than I need to. "Well if it isn't Lou Adaire."

I let out an exasperated breath, shaking my head. "You've got to be kidding me."

Something darkens in Dylan's eyes, his face turning menacing in a quiet, subtle way that sends a shiver crawling down my spine. "You keep your mouth shut."

"Like hell I will."

You know what, screw this. I have a wasted friend in the car, it's almost three in the morning, and I'm fed up. I whirl away from the scene and begin making my way to the driver's side. "Have a nice life, Ryan," I call over my shoulder. "Just keep Bobby out of it."

"Oh, like you are?" His voice hikes up a notch as I unlock the door. "I see the way you lead him on, making him think if he changes he'll get you back. You think you're a better friend than I am, giving him false hope?"

I say nothing, hating the way his words slide past my eardrums and snake their way through my throat until it's constricted. I buckle up, sneaking a peek at the groaning man beside me. Is that what I'm doing? As though responding to my unspoken question, Bobby opens one eye, peers at me. A slow, sloppy smile appears on his face.

I try to swallow, but the lump in my throat is too thick. Refusing to meet the gazes of our audience on the sidewalk, I start the engine and take off.

There's too much truth in the way they're looking at me.

Chapter Thirty-Four

"SO WHERE AM I HEADED?" I ask, keeping my voice quiet so he doesn't hear the slight tremble in my tone.

Bobby slides his hand into his back pocket, clicks a few buttons on his phone, then hands it to me. "Right there." A map is pulled up on the screen, the automated voice already calling out directions.

We don't speak for the rest of the ride. I slow the car as we reach his driveway, taking a minute to look around while I park. It's a cute little house, actually. There's a small porch, a nice sized yard with a garden I'm sure would bloom beautifully in spring. "This is where you're staying?"

He shrugs, looking out the window with me. When he speaks, there's still a slur, but the time spent driving seems to have helped sober him up a little. "Hey, Lou . . . look, I, uh . . . I'm really sorry. I'm an asshole. I promised you this wouldn't happen again, and I'm just really so—"

"Stop it, Bobby."

"What?"

"Stop apologizing."

"But it was a dick move—"

"Yes, it was."

"So . . ."

"So, you apologized already back at the bar and that's

enough, okay? Now it's my turn."

That has his attention. He shifts in his seat to face me better, angling his head. "What would you need to apologize for?"

I look away, purse my lips. "For not being a better friend. For not paying more attention. For not being there for you when you need me, like you've been here for me."

He shakes his head. "Lou . . ." When he looks back up at me, his eyes are shiny, unshed tears gleaming through. "I—I don't know if I can do this sober thing. I mean, maybe Ryan's right. Maybe this is just who we are, and that's all we're supposed to be, people like us. Is this . . . is this who I'm supposed to be?"

"No." I reach forward and squeeze his hand. "Listen to me, Bobby. Shithead Ryan is a loser. You are not. Do you understand?" It takes him a minute, but he nods. "Would a loser look after his mom the way you do?" I wait for him to shake his head. "Would a loser check in on me just to make sure I'm doing okay? Would he take care of me when I'm sick, because he's trying to right his wrongs? Would he sit here, totally smashed in this car, and look me dead in the eye to ask if this is who he's supposed to be?"

Bobby doesn't respond that time, but it's okay, because I have the answer for him.

"No, Bobby. A true loser would accept the situation he's in without wondering if he should do better. Just the fact that you worry about who you should be in this life, what your role is, that is what separates you from the Shithead Ryans of the world." Something in his expression softens, and I know I'm getting through to him. To the Bobby I care for. I pause, suddenly recalling the wise words of a boy I met inside my dreams. A boy surrounded by fireflies. "You know, we all have a light inside of us. And the only person who gets to decide whether your light shines or not is you."

Bobby chuckles quietly, rubbing his chin. "Shit, Lou.

When'd you get so smart?"

"Please. I've always been smart." I grin mischievously. "But I may have stolen that last line."

We both laugh, then he sits back in his seat, taking in the dark skies. It's quiet, comfortable, but there's one more thing I need to say before I go.

"Hey, I'm proud of you, Bobby." His blue eyes twinkle as he turns them back to me. "You said you'd clean up, and you really did it."

He grunts. "Yeah. Till I went and messed it up tonight."

"Forget about tonight. Just listen, okay?"

"Okay."

I repeat my words slowly this time, ensuring they really soak in. "You said you'd clean up, and you really did. Do you know how many people say that and never actually do anything about it?" His lips press together. "A lot. But you, you actually did it. You've proven that you are strong. That you have what it takes. And you'll do it again. I'm not even worried, because I know you will. But can I ask you something?"

His brows furrow. "Of course."

"Will you promise me you'll do this for yourself? For you, and no one else?" He stares at me. "Not for your mom, and especially not for me."

"Why?"

"Because you're worth it, Bobby. *You* matter. The person you are when you're sober? Fight for that guy. I know I sure as hell will."

"I . . ." He blows out a deep breath and hangs his head. "Jesus, Lou. I don't think you know how much that means to me."

I give his hand another squeeze, and he holds mine tight for a long minute. It's a friendly gesture, two people leaning on each other, and I think we both need it.

He releases my grip, and I nod. "Friends?"

His eyes light up, a sweet, gentle smile forming on that

forever baby face. "Friends."

THIS SUNDAY SEEMS TO BE hitting me extra hard. I
don't know if it's having to say goodbye to Jamie, or
the way I'm seriously missing *him*, or the fear that consumes me every time I check if my heart's still beating, but
I ended up dedicating the day to cleaning at Mr. Blackwood's just to keep my mind occupied. I'm sick of sulking
and feeling sorry for myself, and by the time I walked out
of his house feeling stiff and sore from putting so much
into it, I was pretty happy with my choice.

Not only was it an effective distraction, but I made progress with Mr. Blackwood. He actually spoke to me today.
Like, real words, not just grunts. He even offered me a glass
of water. Of course, when he saw my surprise at the min-
iscule gesture, he said, "Get your damn jaw off the floor
and take the water before I change my mind," but still.
Progress.

I don't know if I've given him enough time to forgive
me yet, to rebuild the trust between us, but I don't think I
have a choice: next time, I'm asking him about the Hawkins brothers. He might try to walk out on me again, but
it turns out knowing your heart might stop at any second
can fill you with a crazy kind of determination.

This is it. He has to answer my questions next time
because, as morbid as it sounds, who knows how much
longer I have?

I've been thinking about it more lately, and if there is
some reason I've been dreaming about those boys, if there
is something I'm meant to do about it, maybe figuring out
that piece of the puzzle will help put the rest in place. If
anything, it's a starting point.

I've just stripped out of my clothes and am about to step
into a late-night bath when a knock sounds at the door.
I pause, take a few steps toward the bedroom. It sounds

again, louder this time. Impatient. Who could that be? It's almost ten at night, and Claire left hours ago, after a long day spent at the festival.

Bang, bang, bang.

"I'm coming, I'm coming." Jeez. I grab my silky robe and tie it shut, then head to the door, wishing it had a peephole. I've just begun twisting the handle when the thing's shoved open, and a blonde buzz cut strides into the room, closing the door behind him.

"Dylan? What are you doing in my room?"

He whirls around to face me, and I instantly notice the way his eyes are dilated. They're wide and red-rimmed, and I wonder what he's on. When he speaks, it comes out fast, almost manic. "Lou, I had to see you. I had to make sure we were good after last night. We're good, right?"

Is he serious right now? "No, Dylan. We're not good. Now can you leave?"

He shakes his head, then starts pacing. "I was thinking about it today, like all day long, and I just need you to promise you won't say anything to Claire. Okay?"

"Why would I promise that?"

"Because I love her." He stops in his tracks, looking at me with some kind of wild spark in his eyes. I've never seen him like this, and there's something deeply unsettling about it that causes my stomach muscles to clench.

"Dylan, I have nothing against you, okay?" Lie. "But if you really loved her, you would have been with her last night. Not making out with someone else."

"No, you don't understand." He takes a step toward me. I take a step back. "Claire . . . she's good. She's wholesome. She's perfect. She's the kind of girl I want to marry someday. But sometimes I just gotta take the edge off a little, and I can't do that with her. She—she wouldn't like that side of me. So I blow some steam with chicks who don't matter, who mean nothing to me. I swear, Lou . . . they are nothing to me."

I pause, clenching my jaw. "*They?*"

He closes his eyes, realizing his mistake, and when he opens them again, there's something dark dancing behind them. Such a quick shift from panic to anger, just like last night. And just like last night, there's a stillness, a calmness to his rage that has me taking another step back.

"I need you to leave, Dylan."

"And I will. Just as soon as you make me that promise."

"I'm not promising anything, so you may as well go now."

He's creeping toward me, hands balling into fists at his sides, the tendons in his neck bulging, and I realize he has me backed into a corner when my shoulders connect with the wall.

"I'm not going to tell you again. You need to leave."

"What?" He stops when there's just two feet of space between us, pausing for effect. "You afraid or something?"

I shake my head, hiding my quivering hands behind my back. "Not afraid, no. Just wondering . . ." I quiet, sniffing the air as I mentally prepare myself for my next move. "What kind of cologne you wear. Some kind of spice?"

A blank look crosses his face. I've thrown him off. And that's my cue. I feel the impact against my knee at the same time his yelp sounds, just before he folds over.

Holy crap. That really works.

"Fuck," he squeaks. "I wasn't even gonna touch you. But now—"

I rush to step around him but my head falls back as he grabs me by the hair. This time I yelp, a wave of pain running through my scalp, my neck. Before I can twist myself around to face him, the hold over my hair suddenly disappears, the unexpected release making me stumble to the floor. I look up, and it takes me a second to figure out what I'm seeing. My breathing all but stops once I do.

Dylan is frozen in place. With Death right behind him. One muscular arm is wrapped around Dylan's neck, locking him in place with ease. Dylan's chest rises and falls with quick, short movements. "Wh-who's there?"

Death doesn't hesitate, his low voice snaking around my body, hugging every curve it touches. "Who I am doesn't matter. It's who you are, and what you do after this moment, that does."

My eyes dart between the pair of them, one shaking as though he's about to pee himself, the other deadly calm. I had been assuming Dylan couldn't hear Death's voice, since no one other than me had before, but the way the guy's ears are perked up, his head angling toward where the sound's coming from, makes me think otherwise.

"You're going to walk out of here and never come back. You will never touch her, look at her, or even *breathe* in the same space as her again. Do you understand?"

"I-I-I—"

"I said"—the chokehold tightens, Dylan's reddening face the only giveaway—"do you understand?"

"Y-yes," he wheezes. "I under . . . stand."

The instant Dylan's released, he's grabbing at his throat with both hands, tripping over his feet to get to the door. I think I hear him mutter something like 'frickin mollies' as he ducks down the hall. I let out a breath, the relief at his absence instantaneous. After locking the door, I slowly turn to face the man whose mere presence has been sending heat waves across my skin.

Chapter Thirty-Five

HE'S STILL EYING THE CLOSED door, his face a stone-hard mask, eyes deadly. His shoulders are tight like he's braced to fight, and I know I need to snap him out of it somehow.

"Hey . . ." There's a slight tick of his jaw, but that's it. I try again. "Look at me."

After a moment, he closes his eyes. His stance relaxes just barely, and he eventually turns to face me. All at once, the mask melts away. His brows crease together, the sea of green in his eyes softening to an almost pained expression. It's a quiet look filled with unspoken thoughts, and it makes me take a step toward him. And another.

"You came for me."

Body rigid, his gaze drops to my lips. It's a quiet rasp when he says, "Of course I came for you."

God, just hearing that voice again, watching the way he looks at me as he speaks. I have the strangest desire to curl into his chest, wrap my arms around his neck, press my lips to his skin. I let out a breath, shaking the impulse away. "So that's what it takes to get your attention these days? A psycho in my room?"

I'm about to take another step closer when he swallows, shakes his head, steps back. "I'm not staying, Lou. I can't stay."

"What?" I stop and frown. "Why? You just got here."

His lips press together. He looks away, closes his eyes again. "It's good seeing you, Lou. Always is."

Then he turns so his back is to me, the ridges of his shoulders tensing as he rakes a hand through his hair, and he starts to fade. I've seen it so many times before. I've watched him leave, watched as he disappeared from my sight. From my grasp. Not this time.

I don't even think before I'm striding toward him. Just before he can vanish completely, I step into his space and grab his arm, my hand curling around the hard lines of his bicep. Something shifts around us, in the air, below our feet.

"What are you doing?" he quietly growls. "You need to let go. Now."

"No. You don't get to keep doing that, leaving whenever it suits you."

"Dammit, Lou—" There's a rumble beneath me, and I feel my knees go out in a way they have only once before. "I've already stepped through. I can't stop it."

"I . . ." I want to say something; I want to move, but I can't. My muscles aren't working properly, my throat is closing up.

The world's gone black and ice-cold quicker than I can blink, and I no longer know which way is up or down or in between. The warmth of his arm disappears, and that heavy feeling of abandonment consumes me—but it's different this time. Because this time, my body is shutting down. I can feel it; a stillness in my very being. Nothing is circulating within me.

My heart, it doesn't beat.

My veins are pure ice.

In fact, everything within me feels as though it's frozen. Yet there's something else, too. Something hot I've never known before. An outer layer of fire dancing just beneath the surface of my skin. So thin it only teases the boundaries of my organs, never quite reaching them. The heat, I can feel so clearly the way it counteracts the ice inside me. The key to my survival. Like a machine made of invisible flames, it's working every second I still breathe. The single thing that keeps me alive.

If you can even call this living.

My knees, they no longer wobble. A new, odd sort of strength fills me. One that tells me my bones are no longer jelly. They are now strong in this place. Yet still, I float. There's no ground beneath me to land on, no wall to grab onto for leverage. Not another soul to reach out to. I simply exist. A frozen body floating through an endless desert.

Darkness watches me from every angle. My only friend. From its own place within the silence, it speaks to me in a strange way. It whispers secrets in my ear, telling me this is where I'm meant to be. It's so certain, not a trace of doubt. And I think . . . I think it may be right.

"Lou . . ."

I hear my name, and I want to cringe. Though the sound is gentle, a deep voice in the shadows, my eardrums react like it's fingernails on a chalkboard.

"Stay with me, Lou . . ."

Shhh, I want to yell. *Make it stop.* My hands ball into tight fists.

"Be strong . . ."

It's quieter now. Fading more into the distance, and it's so much nicer this way. My fingers relax, unclenching. This is good. I need the quiet. Only quiet belongs in this void with me.

Only shadows.

Only silence.

Something grabs onto my waist, and I gasp. A hand, it wraps around both sides of me. *No!* Do not disturb this place. Not when I'm meant to stay here. I wiggle away, trying to fight my way out of their grasp, but the hands only hold on tighter. Fear hits me like an electric shot, my eyes darting blindly around the darkness. I am not supposed to feel this way. I am not supposed to feel at all. *Let me go!*

"Shhh."

It's that voice again. It threatens me. Threatens to take me from this place. The only place I know. The only place I've ever known. I can't go. I can't go.

"You're okay, you're okay."

I am not okay. You aren't listening! I grab onto the large hands and squeeze, struggling to uncurl the fingers that grip me, but it's useless. A strong arm snakes around my stomach until my back is pressed flat against a solid form. I squirm relentlessly against the tight embrace, refusing to leave the one place I know. Why aren't I stronger? Why won't it set me free?

My body lurches backward as the arms around me pull, and I shake against them as I start to cry. Please, I'm not meant to leave. I need the darkness. Another lurch, another tug, and every inch of separation from this world hurts my soul. I don't want the hurt, the pain. No.

The numbness . . . at least I can still sense the numbness.

Chapter Thirty-Six

LIGHT FLASHES IN MY EYES. I squeeze them shut in an effort to block it out. It's too much.

"Shhh." That voice. It's so soft, so gentle. How could a sound so sweet have hurt my ears before? "It's okay. You're okay."

Fingers stroke the side of my waist in slow, soothing motions. An arm is still curled around me, a warm body pushed up against my back. I start to breathe again, one inhale at a time. *It's okay. I'm okay.*

As though sensing my relief, the hold around me loosens, letting me go little by little. I let my eyes open. One by one, each piece of furniture comes into view. *My* furniture. My photographs above the mantle.

And then it clicks. Where I am, and who I'm with.

I whirl around, almost losing my balance if it weren't for his arm keeping me steady. It's him. Right in front of me. He's okay. I'm okay. That place . . . How did I lose myself like that? A visible shudder runs down my spine as it all sinks in. I never would have found my way out of the darkness, not with the all-consuming way it lured me in.

I could have been stranded there forever. An empty soul. A lost mind. A silent shadow.

Content with never speaking. Never feeling. Never loving. Never fighting. Never touching. Forever numb. Even now, the empty sensation crawls across my skin. How could I have thought I needed that?

All at once my fingers are in his hair, my face buried in the curve of his neck, standing on my tiptoes as I curl my arms around him and let silent tears run down my cheeks. His body stills in my hold, like he doesn't know how to react. But soon he pulls me in, warm arms wrapping tightly around me and enveloping me in his soothing heat.

I take in the scent of him, dizzyingly masculine. The texture of his hair, soft and full. The frame of his build, large and strong. The way his chest rises and falls, pressing against mine with each movement. The way his fingers twist my silk robe as though he can't get close enough, reminding me of just how thin the material is.

My breathing picks up, a bit faster, harder. My mouth is already so close to his neck . . . I inch closer, until my parted lips brush over his throat. It's such a subtle move, barely noticeable, yet the way his fingers dig into my skin in response tells me he's just as aware of our bodies as I am. My eyes close as I listen to his breathing quicken.

It's not quiet, the way it hits me—the deep-rooted need to feel him. To touch him. To have him touch me. Kiss, taste, explore. Take me as far away from the numbness as possible and just make me *feel* something. Make me feel *everything.*

My lips are pressed against his neck before I even register what I'm doing. They part a little more, until I'm kissing, tasting, exploring. A raw, guttural sound vibrates from his throat as I make my way up to his jaw, and for a moment he tightens his grip around me. But then he lifts his chin, pulling his lips away from my reach just before I can find them.

"Lou . . ." It's a plea, a desperate sort of groan.

Fine, if he won't let me have his lips, I'll take the parts of him I can reach. My mouth finds its way back to his neck, his collarbone, then my hand slips under his T-shirt, the fire of his skin coursing through me and making me feel *alive*. Exactly what I want. Exactly what I need.

His hands come down on my waist, planting me in place as he takes a step back. All that I'm left with is the grip on my waist and the heat I'm growing used to, and it's not enough. Every moment without feeling him is like another moment of being in the void, and I don't want it to take over. I can't let it take over.

"Lou . . . I can't."

"Why?" My exasperation is clear in my voice, my hand running through my hair. "Why can't you? Tell me."

He blows out a breath, his jaw clenching as he drops his head.

"Just tell me already. Please. Do you not want to be here with me? Do you not want to touch me?"

"I—dammit, Lou. Of course I want to be here with you. Of course I want to"—his hands come up and scrub down his face—"to touch you."

"Then why won't you? I'm throwing myself at you, and all you can do is push me away. What is it? Why won't you let me want you?"

"Because—" He squeezes his eyes shut, inhaling deeply. "Because it's not *real*, Lou. None of it is real."

"What?" I'm shaking my head. "What are you talking about?"

"Haven't you ever wondered why you're so drawn to someone like me?" He turns and takes a few steps away, fast and intimidating, with tense waves of anger rippling through each movement. "Why you weren't scared that first night in your bathroom, when you couldn't even see me?"

"I—I was scared. Kind of."

"No, you weren't. I see fear every day, Lou. And you, you weren't scared."

I don't reply, because he's right. That first night, and the next, I remember thinking I *should* have been scared. It would have been the logical reaction. But I wasn't. Instead I felt calm. I felt trust. And I wanted more.

"You felt connected to me immediately, didn't you?" He's taking a step toward me now, his voice quieting. "Just like that night in the lake. A pull to me, a call."

Still, I say nothing. What can I say that he doesn't already seem to know?

He comes closer. "It's not something I can shut off." And closer. "But you need to know, Lou. You need to know that what you think you feel for me? It's. Not. Real."

He whips away before I can respond, making his way to the far window and leaning forward, gripping its ledge. I stare at his back, unsure of what to say, what to feel. The trouble is, I'm not feeling much of anything right now. I suppose I should be experiencing a sense of shock, or anger, or unease. And I can sense it trying to stir within me, the appropriate reaction.

But all I can think about, all I can remember, is the darkness. The void. The numbness. The single moment I lost any semblance of who I was, including any will to find out. All in a matter of what? Minutes? Seconds? And I was calling that place my home. I blended into the pitch-black pit so completely I became it. Any memories before entering it were gone, wiped clean, any sense of purpose taken with them.

Is that what my life will be soon? Will my heart just stop, and then poof, I'll be a barren shadow of the void? An empty soul, unable to experience *anything*? A slave to the darkness, forever?

I can't suppress the way my lips tremble at the thought of it all, and I don't want to, either. I don't want to suppress any emotions at all, whether sad or happy. Right or wrong. Not tonight. Not after that glimpse of my future.

"I am scared," I finally whisper, gazing distantly at his back. "I'm scared that I won't wake up tomorrow. I'm scared my heart will freeze, and then when I open my eyes I'll be stuck *there*, in that horrible place. But mostly . . . mostly I'm terrified of the way I won't even fight to get free. The way I'll think I need it, the numbness that takes over."

He pushes off the ledge, slowly turning to face me.

"Do you know that I can still feel it lingering on me, even now?" I continue, taking a step in his direction. "Like this heavy, sticky, empty sensation I can't seem to shake. I just want to *feel* something." My voice breaks, betraying my desperation, but I don't care. I keep my steps slow and steady, one in front of the other. "I want a little bit. I want a lot. See, I don't care if what I feel for you is real or not, because it's sure as hell real enough to me. Just tell me one thing . . . is what *you* feel real?"

He rips his gaze away from me, shakes his head. "That doesn't matter, Lou. I'm not going to take advantage of the situation—"

"Answer the question. Is what you feel for me real?"

"Lou—"

"Yes. Or no. It's a simple question, really. Just—"

"Yes," he grits out, giving his head another shake and distancing himself. "Okay? Yes, the way I spend every damn second of every damn day thinking about you is real. Yes, the way I wish I could spend every Sunday with you so you'll never have to cry again is real. The way I wonder what it'd be like to be here when you wake up, to hold you when I want to, to kiss your lips, kiss your neck—yes, it's fucking real." He sweeps his hands across his eyes and pulls his hair. "Is that what you want to know?"

A fresh tear escapes, and I nod. Soak in the new feelings pouring into me. The shock over his confession. The way it almost makes me sadder, knowing I may never get the chance to hear those words from him again. May never again get to see that expression on his handsome face, both pained and longing as he stares deep into my eyes.

"So show me," I plead softly, taking a step forward. "Just

for tonight, show me what it's like to feel. To be kissed, to be held, to be wanted by you."

Chapter Thirty-Seven

"LOU ..." HIS voice quiets, a gentle whisper. "Please . . . I can't just—"

"Yes. You can." I inch toward him again, my voice shaking. "Make it go away. The fear. The emptiness. All of it. Just give me something more before I lose myself again. Give me *you*." My head drops when he doesn't respond, the desperation taking over, making my lips quiver. "Honestly, what do I have to do to get you to touch me? I mean, Jesus—"

The words are barely out before his hand is on my waist, the other cradling my neck, and his mouth crushes mine. My lips part, letting our tongues tangle together. His fingers dig into me, pulling me tighter against him. I let out a moan as relief and desire flood me. I've gone limp in his arms, letting him support my full weight, but he doesn't seem to mind. He shifts the angle of his head so he can go deeper, the movement sending a wild rush through me. My hands curl into his hair and tug, and he responds by trapping my bottom lip between his teeth and giving a firm tug of his own.

Holy hell, yes. The adrenaline spike is just what I need, and I want *more*.

My right hand releases his hair and finds its way to the grip he has over my waist. I pry his grasp free and guide his open palm around and down, until it's fixed on my behind. A growl sounds from somewhere deep in his throat as he presses my hips into him, allowing me to feel the full length of him. I swallow as he abandons my mouth for my neck, and my head falls back, giving him complete access.

Jesus.

His tongue. The bed. We need the bed.

But first . . . reluctantly, I pull my attention back to focus on his shirt, grappling for the material and shoving it up, up, until he has to break his lips away from me as I yank it over his arms, his head. It drops to the ground. My gaze flicks down, and I gasp.

The scar I'd glimpsed before by his collarbone is what catches my eye first, a severe roughness to it I hadn't noticed before, but it's the rest of him that has me speechless. I've never seen so many scars on one person. Marks of all shapes and sizes, on his chest, his torso, one etched over his ribcage. Most are so faded they almost blend in with his skin, but a few stand out enough for the pain to seep into my heart.

Oh, no. What happened to you? I lower myself slightly, using my fingertips to softly trace one that runs over his abs, and he takes in a sharp breath, every muscle tightening beneath my touch. I tilt my head to look up at him, and he swallows, staring down at me, heavy-lidded. My gaze wanders back to his body. Leaning forward, I slide the tip of my tongue higher, along another one of his scars. I hear that hitch in breathing again, then feel a groan as it vibrates from his chest to my tongue.

I pull away, straighten myself. My movements are sure and confident despite the butterflies swirling in my stomach; the nerves I revel in feeling, because it reminds me I *am* feeling. I inspect the man before me, the way his eyes dance with the most alluring combination of mesmerized wonder and pure hunger I've ever seen, and it sparks something raw inside me. I briefly think back to the fact he's never touched a woman. He sure as hell kisses like he knows what he's doing. There's something primal about his touches, almost instinctive. Intuitive. Fluid.

I want it, I want it all. Yet somehow, that doesn't seem to be enough. The emptiness takes advantage of our momentary silence, of our stillness, trying to lure me back into its sea of darkness. The constant reminder of my impending fate hangs over my head like a guillotine.

"Make me forget," I whisper.

He closes the gap between us and scoops me up. He eases me onto the bed, then hovers over my body, his weight resting on his forearms on either side of me. He's not touching me, but his heat wraps around me like a scarf, teasing my skin. His muscles are tight, shoulders tense and breathing ragged, revealing the control it takes to stay in place.

"Lou." His voice is strained, bringing out the roughness in his tone. "I'm going to ask you one more time. Are you sure this is what you want? Because," his eyes fall shut, a thick swallow passing through his throat, "because if I start touching you again I won't be able to stop."

He doesn't even know this is already working. Just the sound of his voice, his own need and restraint seeping through, it makes the adrenaline rush back like a fire igniting in my veins. "Trust me. I won't want you to stop."

Something darkens in his eyes for a split second, then his lips are back on mine, forcing them open with his tongue and making my fingers curl into the blanket beneath me. His body lowers onto me, and his hand slips between the folds of my thin robe, grazing my bare stomach. I groan, biting down on his lip, and he grunts, low and rough. His fingertips scorch my skin in the best possible way, and I lean into them. Into him.

He breaks away from my lips and trails open kisses along my jaw, down my neck, making sure I feel every taste, every lick, every nip. His hands don't stop either, sliding slowly, tauntingly, up my waist, my ribs. Just as his touch brushes along the bottom curve of my breast, he stops, centering his focus back on my neck and collarbone.

Now is not the time to be a gentleman.

I find his hand with mine, urging it higher until his heat cups my full breast, his thumb instantly caressing my hardened nipple. Something rough escapes his throat, and his teeth sink into my shoulder. The unexpected ripple of pain and pleasure sends a fresh shockwave through me. My eyelids flutter closed, and my head tilts back. The hand on my chest is firm, hot, and fervent in its strokes. I grip his shoulders and arch my hips, feeling the long, thick length of him rub against me between the fabric of our clothes. His breathing becomes heavier, faster, his own hips returning the movement as he presses himself into me.

More.

I reach down between us, fumbling with the buttons on his jeans and yanking down his zipper, my thumb brushing over the bulge in his underwear. His lips freeze, his head dropping until his forehead rests against my collarbone. A hot rush of breath pours from his mouth over my skin. I only falter for a second, letting the feel of his raw need sink in, then continue to tug the material down. He lifts his hips to help me, then uses his feet to kick them off the rest of the way.

He moves back to my mouth, reconnecting with my lips with a renewed sense of urgency. His hand comes down to pull at the string of my robe, then it falls open, revealing all of me. His lips remain on mine, his tongue continuing its caress. His hands, however, have a mind of their own, exploring everywhere from the shape of my breast to the flat of my stomach, the curve of my hips, to the slope of my thigh.

This time when I arch into him, my bare wetness rubs right against him, the sudden sensation taking us both by surprise and making the muscles in his back constrict beneath my hands. He goes still for a moment, his erection still pressed against me, but when I squirm impatiently, he sinks down further, the added pressure drawing a moan from my lips. A gentle roll of his hips and he's grinding. *Oh god.* The natural, fiery heat that radiates from his body hits my center just right with each roll. He's not even inside me yet, and the sensations are already teasing, building, rising, calling.

He tears himself away, making me whimper at the loss. His head pulls back, green eyes heavy and drugged when they lock onto mine. He just lingers there for a moment, like he's drinking in the sight of me beneath him, memorizing every part of my expression. I know my eyes are just as clouded as his, my lips still parted, probably red and swollen. Breathing hard. Wanting more.

As though reading the thoughts swirling within me, his hand finds a spot low on my stomach. He's still holding my gaze captive with his when his fingers travel downward, his warmth leaving a fiery trail on each part of skin he contacts.

He goes lower, and my breath hitches.

Just . . . a little . . . *lower.*

My fingernails scratch his back as he finds the area between my thighs. It's tentative at first, the way he reaches between me, sliding over me and just slightly inside. My hips buck in response, and his Adam's apple bobs up and down, his eyelids halfway shut, chest pounding. He moves up to the tender area just above, circling his fingers around it and watching intently as my head falls back, the blood inside me beginning to boil at his rhythmic touch. He keeps it going, the steady rhythm he's built, another stroke drawing another moan.

Eyes closed, hips moving against his fingers, I reach down between us and find his arousal, hard and thick, and degrees hotter than the rest of him. A primitive groan rumbles from his throat, his fingers faltering between my thighs, and my lips quirk. I wrap my hand around him as best as I can, my thumb circling the head of his length before exploring the expanse of him, up and down. Another rough vibration roars through him, and his mouth is suddenly back on my throat, sucking, licking, biting. Just as I start to speed up, his hand comes down on mine, holding it firmly in place. He pulls away from my neck, but just barely.

"I can't . . ." It's a husky whisper, hot breaths against my skin. "I need to . . ."

"I want you inside me. Now."

A low, guttural noise escapes him, and the fingers still pressed between my thighs slide into me as though by reflex, curling upward and making me cry out. "Goddamn, Lou," he breathes, ragged. "You don't even know what you do to me."

I'm panting now, unable to form a coherent thought while his fingers fill me up like this. "So . . . show . . . me."

All at once his hand is gone, the sudden loss taking me by surprise, but then the tip of his erection is gently, barely, pressing inside me. He lifts his head to meet my gaze, a desperate, almost pained look on his face as he struggles not to plunge in all at once.

But that's exactly what I need.

"You won't break me," I whisper, my eyes lowering to those lips that tease, taste, tantalize.

Slowly, I lift my hips, the slight movement bringing him inside just enough to give me a taste of his thickness, and it is his undoing. He drives his hips into mine, and my mouth falls open as the entire length of him pushes inside, stretching and filling me beyond anything I've ever felt. A strangled groan rips through him, his forehead softly connecting with mine as he squeezes his eyes shut. He holds himself like that, forearms propping up most of his weight, as my body tries to adjust to the size of him.

Then he's moving. Grinding. Rolling. It starts as a lazy sort of rhythm, slow and steady. Ensuring I feel the full effect of each shift, each stroke, within me. I close my eyes and moan into it, letting the deep caress overtake me, reaching places I didn't know existed. My hands are on his shoulders; the muscles tightening beneath my touch are like quiet ticks of a time bomb, his restraint about to cave in on itself.

I find the curve of his neck and press my lips to it, my tongue having a taste before I pull on his skin and gently suck. He draws in a shaky breath, his rhythm picking up, his strokes long and deep. Then his hand is on my breast as he rocks against me, squeezing and teasing and driving me insane.

Faster. Deeper. Harder.

Whatever thin thread was holding him together a moment ago snaps as he grabs my wrists and pins them against the headboard, my entire body trembling with pleasure in response.

He's sucking just above my collarbone when his free hand slides down, landing on the inside of my upper thigh and spreading me wide open. The shift somehow allows him to go even deeper, and my cry is silenced by his mouth over mine. The kiss becomes sloppy, rough, and desperate as he relentlessly drives into me, my own hips rising to meet each thrust. The bed creaks beneath us, fast and urgent, mixing with the sounds of our heavy panting. Then his strong fingers are right on my clit, rubbing, circling, stroking.

Oh god. Oh god. Oh god.

I turn my head and bite his shoulder, muffling my mewls. His growl is animalistic, his thrusts following suit, losing their tempo as he loses himself. He releases his grip on my wrists to take firm hold of my hips, pulling them up and grinding me into him. That's all it takes to set me over the edge. All the buildup, the pleasure, hitting me hard at my core and rising higher and higher, until I tense. My lips part, my back arches, my toes curl into the sheets, and I cry out as it finally consumes every inch of me.

I'm still riding the shocks when the grip of his fingers digs into me. He gives one last, hard pump, a mangled, masculine sound vibrating through his body as his muscles contract. A shudder ripples through him after he stills above me, then a few quieter ones follow. After a moment, he collapses, his head dropping into the curve of my neck.

Panting. Sweating. Sighing.

Hot breath caresses my throat as I hear a husky, "Fuck."

My lips curve. That's two times now I've heard him say that word, both of them tonight.

And I decide I really like it.

Chapter Thirty-Eight

THEY SAY IT'S BEST TO learn to accept the things you can't control. To conform your mind to all that surrounds you. Be thankful for those things you can control, and let the rest of the pieces fall where they may.

I say, fuck that.

At least that's the eloquent motto I woke up to this morning, when I opened my eyes to an empty bed, a cold room, and an absent heartbeat; not just faint, but absent. After the initial shock wore off, I was able to hold a trembling hand to my chest long enough to figure out that my heart *was*, in fact, still beating. However, only every ten seconds or so. Per Google—yes, I looked it up—that means a whopping twenty beats, give or take, during each interval are missing.

Gone.

Now, as I stand in place on the sidewalk, twisting my mood ring in the hope some comfort will magically rub off on me, I think back to Grams. She always said there's a die-hard fighter in all of us, ready to be awoken the moment you need it most. My question is: how do you summon said fighter? There should be some sort of code word, right? Seeing as my life's hourglass is down to the last few grains of sand, I'd really prefer the fierce version of myself to the scared one right now.

I take a deep breath and stare hard at the bland, unassuming view before me.

This is silly. They're just doors, I remind myself. Two white columns located on either side, old red bricks forming the walls around them. Of course, that huge *Ashwick Police Station* sign hanging above my head does add a slight edge to my nerves. There might be no relation to the man anyway, so I need to get this over with already. Without another thought, I grab the handle and yank the door open.

It's a small, quiet office, just as I expected for a town like this. There aren't many people here, but several personnel work away at their desks, another lingers around the coffee machine. All eyes turn to me when I enter, though, and I get the impression they don't receive many visitors.

I take the few, short steps to the front desk, where a heavyset woman with greying hair smiles kindly from below a pair of reading glasses.

"Well, hello," she greets, shuffling through a stack of envelopes. "How may we help you?"

"Hi." I glance around before scooting closer so I can lower my voice. "I have sort of an unusual question, actually."

"Not to worry, we get our fair share of those here," she says with a laugh. "Go ahead, hun."

"Um, is there a Wayne Mulligan still working here, by chance?"

"Oh lord, has it been awhile since I've heard that name." The woman removes her glasses and shakes her head, inspecting me closer. "You need him in particular, or just looking for whomever now holds the Chief of Police position?"

"Him, specifically."

"Hmm. I'm afraid that's going to be a bit on the tricky side of things, seeing as he's now six feet under and all." She chuckles awkwardly but seems to notice the way my face falls because she immediately quiets, straightening out her top. "Oh, I'm sorry, dear. I just meant that, well, he's no longer with us."

"Can you tell me how long ago he passed?"

"It's gotta be, what, seventeen years now? He was near seventy when he got hit by that last heart attack."

Near seventy. That would have put him around Grams's age at the time. I chew the inside of my cheek, that feeling in my gut deepening. "Did he have any family? Anyone I can speak to briefly just to ask a few questions?"

"Oh, well he did at one time, but, um . . ." The woman stops, clears her throat, then tosses a glance over her shoulder. "Hey, Pete!" She looks back at me and offers an apologetic smile. "One second, dear. Pete! You there?"

"Yeah, yeah, what is it?" A balding, uniformed man with a thinning mustache steps out from one of the back offices. His eyes dart from the woman to me, and he quirks an eyebrow as he approaches us. "Can I help you?"

"This nice young lady has a few questions about Wayne Mulligan," the woman explains. "Thought maybe you'd be the best one to help her, seeing as how you were with him the most toward the end there."

The officer nods thoughtfully. "Yeah, all right." He extends a hand toward me. "Deputy Mark Tallon."

"Lou Adaire. Nice to meet you."

"You as well." He releases his grip and gestures behind him, toward his office. "Why don't you follow me?"

After thanking the woman for her help, I follow Deputy Tallon inside a small room, where he closes the door and sits behind his desk. I take a seat across from him, trying to figure out how to even begin.

"So, how did you know Mulligan?" he asks, leaning back against his seat and taking a long sip of coffee.

I bite my lip. "Well, I didn't exactly know him." Deputy Tallon furrows his eyebrows, and I shake my head at the ridiculousness of this whole situation. "The thing is, I'm actually trying to figure out if maybe I'm related to him somehow?"

"You don't say." He sets his mug down and leans forward. "Why would you wonder a thing like that?"

"Just a few things that have me putting the pieces together."

He pauses, his fingers tapping on the desk. "What'd you say your last name was?"

"Adaire."

"Hmm." He shakes his head. "Doesn't ring a bell. Suppose that doesn't mean anything, though. Can you tell me more specifically what might lead you to believe there's some relationship there?"

"Well, for one, he and my grams were around the same age. And, for another, her last name was also Mulligan. I never knew my grandfather."

"And your grams, she left town, did she?"

"Yeah, a long time ago. She was probably only in her thirties at the time, and my mom would have been just a child."

That seems to have gotten his attention, but he stays quiet, pursing his lips together as though contemplating something. Contemplating what, exactly? Whether to talk to me? Whether to help me?

"Deputy, please." I sit up straighter, determined to get answers before I leave this building. "If there's anything you can tell me, anything that might help . . . I just need to know if he was who I think he might have been, before"—*before I lose my one chance to get answers, before I waste away*—"while I'm still here, in town."

He watches me carefully, the creases in his already wrinkled forehead deepening. "Listen, Miss Adaire," he finally says, his voice soft, concerned, "Mulligan was a fantastic chief. One of the best officers this town's seen, even to this day. He was well respected at the force, and I was honored to have gotten to work alongside him before he retired."

Then why doesn't your tone reflect your words? "But?"

"But, I'm afraid his family life was a bit of a different story. Now, I just want to make sure . . . I want to make sure you know what you're asking here. You can't rebury things like this once you've already dug them up."

I shift in my seat. I wasn't expecting a reaction like that. "Yes, I know what I'm asking, Deputy. I need to know."

Eventually, he lets out a breath, reaching his resolve. "All right. Well, Mulligan wasn't one to chitchat or divulge about his personal life. He lived and breathed the force, you understand? For a while there, it was this big mystery to the town, why his wife just up and left him one day, taking their only child with her."

He pauses, squinting as he peers over at me, like he's checking if I'm still okay. I don't know if I am. My stomach's tightening at his words, at the confirmation they bring. Clearly, I already have my answer. Wayne Mulligan was my grandfather. I give a small nod of my chin, urging him on.

"It wasn't until the end there, his last year in fact, that he actually told me anything about what had happened. He had recently retired and his life seemed to finally be catching up with him. But even then he didn't say much. I only got the gist of it, all right?"

Another nod. *Just tell me already.*

"Now, I know this may not make much of a difference, but for what it's worth, he did a lot of apologizing. Said he'd had many regrets, and he was sure he'd be paying for them soon enough." I swallow, suddenly nervous to hear the rest. This is just getting better and better. "He didn't exactly get into everything he was apologizing for—seemed to be a whole lotta water under that bridge—but one thing he mentioned was the way he'd treated his wife." He pauses, clearing his throat and adjusting his uniform collar. "Uh, physically. He didn't get into the details, and I didn't ask, but . . . uh, well, if it was enough to make her run, to make her fear for her daughter's safety . . ."

The color drains from my face, my throat constricting. This can't be right. Not another abuser, another monster. I know the other one was a man I'd only met in my dreams, but he certainly felt real enough. And now, my own flesh and blood. My own grams . . .

"Now, Miss Adaire," he starts, his voice becoming more and more distant as the blood rushes to my ears, "I realize this wasn't what you were hoping to find out, and especially after all this time you must have been wondering who your grandfather was, but . . . well, I've seen few women in my time as an officer actually free themselves from an abusive hand. And let me tell you, it takes a strong woman to get out of a situation like that." Strong. Yes. Of course she was strong. It's Grams, after all. The strongest woman I've ever known. I just never knew what had made her that way. "You and your mother are lucky to have had a woman like her in your life."

It takes a minute for me to realize it's my turn to say something, to respond. "Yes," I mumble, already scooting the chair back to stand. "Yes, we were. Thanks so much for your time, Deputy Tallon." I extend a shaky hand as he rises with me.

"Of course. I'm . . . I'm just really sorry I didn't have a different answer for you."

I offer a small smile as I pull my hand back, tug on my ring—a ring whose shade of blue seems to be getting darker and darker by the hour, as my body temperature spikes. It's not Deputy Tallon's fault my grandfather was an asshole. Scratch that, not my grandfather. As far as I'm concerned, he was just another ant in the dirt.

And moving on.

Chapter Thirty-Nine

MR. BLACKWOOD ISN'T EXPECTING ME today, because I rarely show up two consecutive days. I'm sure he won't be too pleased about the surprise, but he's going to have to deal with it. There won't be any running away this time.

The door's ajar when I arrive, which is more than a little odd. I peek inside cautiously, my eyes darting around the empty living room. Mr. Blackwood's keys sit forgotten on the floor, his cane appearing to have fallen near the sofa. I veer toward the kitchen, an uneasy feeling spiking in my stomach.

"Hello? Mr. Blackwood?"

Silence, and the kitchen is just as empty as the living room.

I turn then head for the stairs but stop when I hear a muffled gag to my right. It's coming from the bathroom, which I now happen to notice is shut. I inch closer. There's a thin stream of light gleaming below the door.

"Mr. Blackwood?" I give a gentle rap.

Another gag, some coughing, a choking sound, a flush.

What in the—

The door bursts open, barely missing me. Mr. Blackwood stands before me, one hand leaning on the doorframe, as he wipes his mouth with his shirt sleeve. "I see you're busy minding your own business again," he grumbles, before brushing past me and settling into his usual spot on the sofa.

I ignore the jab, mostly because I'm about to be doing a lot more 'minding my own business' in a minute, and pop into the kitchen to fill up a tall glass of water. I make my way back to the living room, setting the drink in front of him and taking a seat.

"Are you sick?" I ask.

"What does it sound like to you, brainiac?"

"Will you stop being difficult for five seconds?"

He only grunts, but I'm satisfied when he takes a sip of the water.

"What's going on with you?" I press.

"I'm an alcoholic, didn't you hear? Sometimes I overdo it and throw up. It's not the end of the world."

I narrow my eyes, looking him over. He was already frail when I'd met him, but I notice now that, despite his tall frame, he's practically swimming in his thin coat. The bones around his shoulders and knees protrude noticeably, and I wonder if he's always been so slight. "You promise you're okay?"

"What's it matter to—"

"Jesus, Mr. Blackwood, just answer the question."

He pauses, looking me over in much the same way I was just doing to him. "I'm fine, I'm fine."

I'm not sure how much I believe him, but I let out a breath and nod. All right. Now for the tough part. I straighten my spine, cross one leg over the other, and fold my hands over my knee. It's go-time. "So, I have a few questions for you."

"Not this again."

"I'm not leaving until you answer me this time."

"Looks like you're moving in, then, doesn't it?"

"If that's what it takes."

He squints, looks me up and down. Clearly trying to

determine if I'm bluffing. I arch an eyebrow that tells him just how serious I am. He gives me another signature grunt. He's really a man of few words.

I decide to come straight out with it. "It's about the Hawkins boys."

In a split second, a rush of tormented emotion crosses his face. And just as quickly, it disappears. "And what would you know about the Hawkins family?"

I haven't yet decided how much to reveal, worried if I tell him about the dreams it might scare him off and I'd never get any answers. For now, I'll test the waters. "The other day, I read an article about what happened to them, the year they died."

"You did, did you? You always spend your weekends reading about people dying?"

I don't bother to suppress my eye roll. "Yes, it's an uplifting hobby I decided to pursue."

"You're weird."

"You're weirder." Okay, we're getting off topic. "So what's your connection to them? Were you close?"

The rush of emotion I'd glimpsed earlier comes baring itself full force, wrinkles creasing and eyes flashing, and he's pushing himself off the seat. "I'm not doing this, not today—" His words are mumbled and angry and warbled as he stumbles toward his cane. "Don't need to talk about anything I don't want—" He's adjusting his weight on the cane, then aiming for the exit. "Goddamn nosy people everywhere I damn look—"

"Wait . . . Mr. Blackwood, stop." I shoot up from the recliner just before he reaches the door, the words out of my mouth before I can stop them. "I had a dream!" He pauses, his hand on the handle. "I—I met them, the boys. Well, not exactly, but . . . I saw them. Little Tommy, huddled up in the corner while Enzo was beaten. Their monster of a father, what he did with his knife. The—the disgusting so-called tattoos." Mr. Blackwood's face has gone sheet white beneath all his scruff, and he appears to be frozen in place as he stares at me. I take a step toward him.

"How . . ." His voice is so quiet I have to step closer to hear him. "How could you possibly know about any of that. You weren't even alive."

"I told you. I started having dreams. I don't know why, or how, or—"

"Don't lie to me, dammit!" He's trembling now, his skin turning red, and it has me backtracking my steps. "What else did she tell you?"

"What? Who?"

"Tallulah, of course! What else did she tell you?"

"What are you . . ." Wait. Grams? What did she have to do with any of this? Mr. Blackwood stumbles toward the sofa, sinking heavily into it, his eyes still fuming.

I'm slow, careful, as I make my way to him. I've never seen him like this before, and I certainly don't know how to react. I find myself passing over the recliner I'd usually choose, and instead easing into the open spot on the sofa, to his right. I'm quiet for a moment, waiting patiently as his skin returns to its normal shade, his eyes simmer down, his fingers stop trembling quite so much.

"I'm sorry," I whisper. "I didn't know it would upset you so much. But I swear Grams never said a thing. The dreams didn't even start until recently, after I moved here."

Whether he's ignoring me or soaking in my words, I can't tell, but he doesn't speak for a long minute. Eventually, he reaches forward and downs the rest of the water. I'm surprised he hasn't reached for his liquor yet, but I'm not going to be the one to mention it.

"I believe you," he finally says.

"You do?" My entire body relaxes, shoulders slumping forward. It's not until this very moment that I realize the power of hearing those words. It's as though another person believing me somehow confirms I'm not just going crazy.

To my surprise, Mr. Blackwood chuckles. It's tinged with bitterness, but still, it's a definite chuckle. "Yes, I do. You mustn't have read any of my books."

"Why do you say that?"

"Because maybe it takes a kook to believe a kook."

I'm too intrigued to be offended right now. I have to see these books I keep hearing about. "Can I see your work?"

"Really, Lou, it stings you haven't already bought a copy."

"Oh, sorry, I wasn't—" His expression stops me, the tiniest smirk lifting his lips, and I suppress another eye roll, shake my head. "Funny."

He shrugs. "I thought so." He starts to stand, but a wince takes over his face as he wobbles in place, one hand just barely holding him off the sofa.

"Stay there," I insist, already standing and gently nudging him back down. "Tell me what to get."

"I already told you I don't need a damn caretaker."

"Stop being so dramatic. I'm not a *damn caretaker*." I roll my eyes. "I'm a friend asking what you need." I know I snuck the 'f word' in there, but I kind of want to see how he'll take it. Maybe if I say it enough, he'll start to accept it as truth.

"Yeah, yeah," he grumbles, and I smile. He's so gonna be my friend. "Liquor cabinet. Two books."

"Um—"

"You heard me."

Okay. I make my way into the kitchen, pulling open the liquor cabinet for the first time ever. Sure enough, there are two books sitting on the lower shelf, far in the corner collecting dust. I grab them, wipe them off, and scan them over as I return to my spot beside Mr. Blackwood. "*A New Dimension*, and *Other Unsolved Mysteries*, by M. Blackwood," I read aloud. I glance up at him, brows knitting together. "What's the *M.* for?"

He grunts. "Matteo."

"Really?" He doesn't look like a Matteo. "I don't know,

that doesn't really fit."

"What are you, some kind of name expert? Do you want to open the books up or just talk nonsense all day?"

"Okay, okay." He's right, of course. I of all people should know how precious and limited time can be.

I begin with the first book, *A New Dimension*, setting it on my lap and peeling it open. The table of contents are first to greet me: *Quantum Mechanics (Behavior of Subatomic Particles), Eternal Inflation, Space-time Taking Shape, Mathematical Universes, Parallel Universes & Cosmic Patches.*

I glance up at Mr. Blackwood and playfully shove his knee. "Who knew you were the real brainiac here? Hiding in disguise."

He says nothing. Returning my attention to the pages, I flip straight to the chapter that's already caught my interest, *Parallel Universes & Cosmic Patches*. I scan through the lines, skimming over some since, who am I kidding, I don't know the first thing about this stuff.

To agree with the parallel universe theory, one would need to elaborate on the idea that space-time is flat. . . . With the number of cosmic patches being infinite, there must be a repeat of particle arrangements in them . . . I pause, my brows drawing together as I peek up at Mr. Blackwood once more. He's watching me, his attention focused, though giving nothing away in his expression. I carry on, jumping over a few more lines here and there. *This would mean there are infinite cosmic patches identical to ours. . . . Let me be clear that the multiverse concept cannot technically be classified as a theory when it, in fact, stems from current theories such as quantum mechanics and string theory.*

"Mr. Blackwood," I start, my index finger holding my spot. "What is this?"

When he doesn't reply, I skip several pages until I reach the closing section.

While the idea of an infinite number of parallel universes has long been considered a distinct scientific possibility, it will continue to be a matter of heated debate among physicists—as it should be. With our current proven concepts on the matter, room for inter-pretation is limitless, as is room for error. That being said, science and reality have long been on different wavelengths. If history has taught us anything, it is this: just because one theory has yet to be proven today, does not disqualify it from being an active truth—taking place before the very eyes we seek so desperately to prove them with.

I'm stunned into silence by the time I complete the next few pages, and I'm left wondering where all of this came about, and where he's going with it. After a moment, I'm able to close my mouth, and the book, and find my voice. "How exactly does one go from being a private investigator to researching work like . . . this?"

At that, Mr. Blackwood slowly rises to his feet. He eyes the door, and I instinctively tense up, bracing to tackle. "No way. You are not escaping again."

He rolls his eyes, an expression that looks particularly odd coming from him, and shakes his head. "Get up."

"Why?" I ask, even as I oblige.

"Because . . ." He grabs the book I haven't opened yet, then turns and wobbles toward the edge of the sofa, care-fully lowering himself as he retrieves his cane once more. "I believe it's time to explain those notes you found ear-lier."

Chapter Forty

A S MR. BLACKWOOD SITS AT the foot of the guest bed, the same manila folder I'd seen once before spread open in his hands, I find myself toying with my mood ring again as my thoughts wander back to *him*, the man I slept with last night. The man from another world, who, despite the steel-eyed ways he'd known before me, had somehow managed to make love with all the raw passion of someone from my own world. Someone human.

Mr. Blackwood's words float into mind, *just because one theory has yet to be proven today, does not disqualify it from being an active truth—taking place before the very eyes we seek so desperately to prove them with.* I can't help but connect them to my own situation; what's happening between me and Death. Crossing over to other worlds, the idea of the universe confusing us for one another, blending us together. What would Mr. Blackwood have to say about a thing like this? For a moment, I allow myself to contemplate revealing everything to him. To ponder over the possibility that there may be another person out there willing to try and understand.

"So," Mr. Blackwood's gruff voice calls me back into the guest room, to the manila folder he now extends to me. "You want answers?"

I take the file, opening it carefully. "Yes."

"Well, I do, too. Take another look at those notes."

And so I do. I remove them from the folder, fanning the small papers out. There are six all together. The ones that greet me first are the three I'd seen before.

I AM NOT DEAD.

I CAN'T HOLD ON.

SAVE ME.

The chill that came crawling up my back when I'd first set eyes on those words hits me again, chasing my spine with renewed purpose. I have to take a deep breath. Setting those behind the others, I read on.

I'M LOSING MYSELF.

THE DARKNESS CONSUMES ME.

PLEASE. I DON'T WANT TO FORGET.

The darkness. I'm losing myself. No. I know that feeling. I know that kind of darkness. But there's no way this is the same thing. My grip has tightened, the papers crinkling in my grasp, shaking as my fingers tremble. "Wh-what is this?"

The creases around Mr. Blackwood's eyes deepen as they narrow. "You look like you've seen a ghost."

"Mr. Blackwood, I'm serious. What is this?"

I don't know if it's the tone my voice has taken or if it's that he's just as tired of going in circles as I am, but he clears his throat, runs a hand through his scraggly grey beard, and gestures to an empty space beside him. Still trembling, I lower myself slowly onto the bed.

"You asked me before about the Hawkins boys," he begins.

"Yes," I breathe, barely a whisper.

"Well, I knew them once. We were . . . we were close." He stops, clears his throat, and it turns into a coughing fit. His face turns red, his eyes widening, and I jump from the bed to grab him more water. He reaches out to stop me with his hand. "I'm fine," he wheezes, the coughing fading and his coloring slowly returning to normal. "Sit yourself down."

"Are you sure?"

"Yes, dammit. Would I tell you so if I wasn't sure?"

I shrug, thinking *yes*, but keep my mouth shut and do as instructed.

"Anyway, what happened to them is what eventually drove me to become a PI. I specialized in domestic abuse. See, we didn't have CPS back then. If the cops didn't listen to you, you were screwed. So we worked the cases the cops couldn't be bothered with, and made sure families who were too scared to go to the authorities knew they could come to us."

"Is that how you met Grams? Did she hire you at some point?"

"Oh, no." He shakes his head. "Tallulah and I go way back, before my PI days. I wasn't the one who helped her—it was the other way around. But we're getting off track now, aren't we? Do you want to know about the Hawkins boys or not?"

After a beat, I nod. I desperately want to know his history with Grams, but figuring out my connection to those brothers is more important by a landslide right now.

"All right. Now, what I'm about to tell you is scientifically impossible. Do you understand? In fact, lately I've started to wonder if it ever really happened, or if it was in my head the whole time. I might really just be an old loon. Still up for it?"

Scientifically impossible? The man has no idea. "Trust me. I'm not going anywhere."

"You say that now . . ." He rubs his wrinkled hands together, lets out a grunt. "So, I was in my twenties when it happened. Just another ordinary day working cases. And I, uh, well . . ." He stops, shakes his head. "I started seeing things. Hearing things. Things that sure as shit were not normal."

"Like what sort of things?"

"Eh, you ever read ghost stories?"

"A little."

"Well, think ghosts. Spirits. Otherworldly and all that crap."

"So, you're saying you saw a ghost?"

He scoffs, looking at me like I'm the crazy one. "Don't be ridiculous. Of course I didn't see a damn ghost."

"I'm confused—"

"I *heard* one." He inhales, long and slow, his eyes glazing over like he's losing himself to the memory. "It started out at night, in my dreams. Sound familiar?" He doesn't wait for me to respond before he continues. "I'd feel this strange pull. Like, well, like something was calling to me. Tried ignoring it, taking sleeping pills, then it got worse. Eventually, I'd hear his voice when I went out. Didn't matter where I was, I'd hear him so much it nearly drove me mad. Not nearly, it *did* drive me mad."

"His voice?" My palms are beginning to sweat. "Whose voice?"

"Enzo's, dammit. Enzo Hawkins." My stomach does an odd flip, my mind trying to comprehend his words. A strange expression crosses over Mr. Blackwood's face, like a mixture of sadness and frustration, his hands clenching and unclenching.

"Enzo?" I repeat. "The older brother, the seventeen-year-old?"

"No, no, no." Mr. Blackwood gets up so quickly he nearly falls over. He grabs onto the bed to steady himself, then plucks up his cane. He just paces, wobbling and all. "He's not seventeen anymore. Well, he wasn't seventeen when he died, anyway."

"But I thought—"

"Just *listen*, child," he barks, instantly shutting me up. "Yes, Enzo was seventeen the day of the fire. But he didn't die that night. He—he needed to get away. He needed a life free of his past, where he could be his own person, move on. So, with the forced help of Chief Wayne Mulligan—" He pauses, stopping his frantic pacing to look me in the eye.

He doesn't need to worry though; he has my undivided attention.

"When Mulligan tried investigating the case further, he was able to get enough soft evidence to prove Thomas's death, but not Enzo's. And so he became determined to find the boy. Mulligan may have been a shit husband, a shit human being, but he was a decent cop with a reputation to uphold. Didn't hurt that he and the boys' father were long-time friends, either, but really it was his reputation on the line. Mulligan wanted Enzo found, so he was gonna find him. He quickly learned Enzo was the one who started the fire and was willing to set the boy up with a decent lawyer to prove it was self-defense. He didn't care so long as he was able to close the case."

Mr. Blackwood reaches a hand into his coat pocket, retrieving the flask I'm surprised he hasn't already chugged by now, and takes a long gulp. A sigh escapes him, and he squeezes the bottle like it's his lifeline. I begin to wonder how long it's been since he's spoken to anyone about this. Or if he's ever spoken about it at all.

"Anyway," he continues, wiping his mouth with his sleeve, "he wouldn't let it go. And Tallulah . . . well, Tallulah had left Mulligan that same year. He had a way of beating her into submission, threatening everyone she cared about if she ever talked, but after seeing what happened to those boys that night, that was it. She took her kid and got the hell out of there.

"She refused to have any contact with her husband at all, in fact, *except* when it came to this case. Eventually, she contacted him privately, blackmailed him to close the case. Said she'd stayed quiet about his abuse far too long. Now that she had gotten her daughter far enough away from him, she would do whatever it took to see that the boy, too, was free from that life. Let the report show Enzo Hawkins as being dead with the others, and allow him to live the new life he deserved. Otherwise he'd be spending who knows how long defending himself, and more than that, he'd always have his past tying him down in some way."

That's the second time he's mentioned Grams in relation to these boys. My mind feels like a cogwheel, turning and turning until it hurts, trying to keep working even as more info is dumped onto the cogs. "What did Grams have to do with the Hawkins family?"

Another scoff, another grunt. He shakes his head, taking a step closer to me. "Tallulah was those brothers' savior, child. They never could get to a hospital for their wounds, and with your grams being a nurse, she did the best she could for them. Stitching them up, about saving their lives every other week since their mom started taking off. Tallulah was practically their mother, for all terms and purposes. Even tried to report the abuse on several occasions but, well, you can imagine how that turned out with her husband as the chief."

It's then that a vivid image flashes in my mind. A piece of a dream. A piece of their memories.

We sneak around the back of the garden, as always, and I pray the shed's unlocked when I reach for its handle. Thankfully it opens on the first try. I wince as I carefully lower Tommy onto the dusty cot, then turn to him with a questioning look. He nods, and I don't waste any time before darting back outside, picking a small handful of rosemary from the garden and setting it on the neighbor's window ledge as practiced.

We all know the drill. Now all he and I have to do is wait.

I race back to the shed, weakly collapsing beside my little brother. "See now?" I hear myself whisper, my eyes heavy as I rest my head against the hard wall. "We'll be good and fixed up in no time. Nothing at all to worry about."

"Grams," I mutter, almost to myself. "She was their

neighbor, wasn't she?"

Mr. Blackwood only nods. My body feels heavy, the full weight of me sinking into the mattress as another piece of a dream dawns on me.

"There, there," a gentle voice coos. The tension in my body eases as I remember where I am. The shed. Our neighbor's land.

"Tommy," I murmur, my voice wrangled as I try to lift my head.

"Shh." The hand guides me back down. I manage to turn, just enough to see the boy lying beside me. Tommy's bare waist is wrapped in white cloth, his eyes closed, chest rising and falling in his deep sleep.

He's okay.

We're okay.

For now.

"As I was saying," Mr. Blackwood's voice yanks me back again, and I have to shake my head to snap out of it completely, "Enzo Hawkins was not seventeen when he died. He had moved out of state, started a life of his own, and he was a good and grown twenty-seven years old the day of his actual death."

Twenty-seven. I swallow, my throat suddenly painfully dry as I begin connecting more pieces together. "What . . . what happened to him? How did he die?"

The bed shifts as Mr. Blackwood lowers himself beside me. He's quiet for a long moment, and I'm almost about to repeat the question when I hear his voice, soft and distant. "It was a car accident. Would have been, oh, forty-five, fifty years ago now."

I turn my head at that, looking carefully at this man who sits beside me. This man with his cane, who lost his leg years ago in a car accident. "He was with you, wasn't he?"

He doesn't say anything right away, but he doesn't need to. I know the answer. Eventually, once the room is filled with the heaviness of his silence, he speaks. "He wasn't only *with* me, child. I was the one responsible for his death." He looks at me solemnly, nothing but guilt and sadness in his eyes, and I don't think I've ever seen so much torment written on a person's face before. It practically eats him alive right in front of me, making my own chest want to cry. "I'd been drinking—go figure—and he didn't know. Got behind the wheel thinking everything was just dandy, 'cause shit if I don't know how to handle my liquor, right?" He lets out a dark, sardonic chuckle. "But it gets worse."

My stomach twists, the anticipation hurting enough in itself. My throat's so dry that my voice is barely a croak when I ask, "What happened?"

"After the vehicle flipped, we were both in bad shape, but he—" He stops, swallows. "He was the worst. A piece of metal had lodged itself right in his chest and . . ." He closes his eyes, squeezes them hard like it could force the memory from getting too close. I've never seen the town's angry Mr. Blackwood so pained, so vulnerable. "We weren't as lucky with paramedics back then as your generation is now, but a passerby saw us and came to help. They tried to pull Enzo out first, but he wouldn't let them. Straight up refused, insisting they get me first. All I had was a goddamn torn leg, but the bastard insisted the guy pull me out first anyway. So he did."

He coughs as he takes another sip of whiskey, but he chugs right on through it. I don't know how much he manages to drink before he finally puts the flask down. "The guy barely got me settled onto the sidewalk when the whole thing blew to shreds." He pauses, shakes his head, his next words weak, broken. "It should've been me."

I can hardly breathe as I try to process all of this. Last night comes crawling back into view, images of *him*, his bare chest and torso, all of those scars. My dreams, it can't be a coincidence they'd begun just after he saved me in that lake. Just after the night my bond to him had been formed.

And in every dream, I'd felt everything the boy had felt. It's Enzo's mind I'd been inside. Enzo's memories.

If my heart wasn't quite literally broken right now, I'm certain it'd be in a frenzy, slamming against my chest and trying to beat its way out.

Chapter Forty-One

"TELL ME ABOUT THE NOTES," I demand. My lungs are losing oxygen as desperation for more answers consumes me.

"The notes, right." Mr. Blackwood rubs his face with his palms, exhaustion taking over his expression as he seems to gather his thoughts. "Like I said, I tried to ignore Enzo's calls to me. Even started seeing a therapist, convinced I was losing my mind. But one night, as I sat at my desk writing up a report on my latest case, the pen in my hand suddenly . . . well, it took on a life of its own." He shakes his head, mindlessly tracing over the folder with a finger. "That's the only way to explain it, really. My hands still held the pen, sure. But suddenly, I wasn't the one writing, controlling the motions. One after another, the notes wrote themselves. I about had a heart attack. There was no way for me to deny it at that point—not when I saw the damn words, clear as day, right in front of me."

His voice fades, silence creeping back into the room. I think he's done talking, that maybe I've burned him out, but then he speaks again. "Almost as soon as they started, though, the messages stopped. Everything stopped, in fact. As though it never even happened." His finger taps on the folder, *tap, tap, tap*. "Except I have these. No one else may believe me, but I know the truth, because I have the evidence right here."

My fingers are trembling again as I lift the folder. I reread each word, slowly, warily. Taking my time as though I might miss some hidden detail if I rush.

After a few more coughs, Mr. Blackwood continues. "And so begins the story of my downward spiral. As the locals would call it, anyway." I break my stare from the handwritten letters to glance up at the tired looking man. "I started researching. I was used to investigating already, so I knew how to do the initial footwork. Interviewed everyone from cosmologists to physicists to everything in between—anyone who would talk to me. Put together my own theories on it, some of which you read downstairs. None of them conclusive. All a bunch of hogwash and utter waste of time."

"So that's why you first moved here all those years ago? To try and get some answers?"

"Figured it was my best bet. Maybe he'd find his way home before anywhere else. And later, came this." He reaches behind him and picks up the other book, then hands it to me. It's the one I haven't yet seen: *Other Unsolved Mysteries.*

I set the book in my lap, flipping through it gingerly with one hand and pressing my fingers to my heart with the other, where a strange knot is forming. I try to soothe it with a circular motion. It doesn't take long to figure out what this book is about. *1908, boy claims to see deceased mother . . . 1922, family of six spends evenings speaking to the dead . . . 1949, woman wakes from coma claiming to have witnessed the other side . . .* Page after page, story after story.

Closing the book, I meet Mr. Blackwood's gaze once more. My voice is gentle when I speak, partially for his sake, and partially because the pressure in my chest only builds, the uncomfortable sensation taking over. "So much of your life, you've dedicated to trying to figure this out. Haven't you? Trying to work out what happened to him. What he was trying to tell you."

He grunts, hazel eyes turning bitter. "Lots of good it did me. Or him."

"Is that why that lady was here a while ago? I remember a woman coming by, talking about failing to make contact."

"Yeah, yeah. I've lost count of the money I've wasted on so-called clairvoyants or mediums, whatever you wanna call them."

A thought crosses my mind, but I need to take a second to steady my breathing before I speak. My fingers continue the circular motion over my heart, and I close my eyes for a moment, trying to block the discomfort out. "What if—what if he wasn't quite . . . on the other side, exactly?"

Mr. Blackwood's brows press together, a frown forming. "What are you talking about?"

I'm talking about the notes, I want to scream.

I'M LOSING MYSELF.

THE DARKNESS CONSUMES ME.

PLEASE. I DON'T WANT TO FORGET.

I've tasted what it's like to feel yourself slip away. To be consumed by the darkness, and to lose any sense of yourself. Who you were, who you are, who you're meant to be. And I was only there, in that place, for a matter of minutes. To be stuck for days, weeks, months . . . years. A shudder runs through me. I can't even imagine the type of strength it would take to try to hold onto yourself after all that time.

"I just mean, what if he never fully crossed over? If he's . . . I don't know. If he's somehow stuck somewhere? Couldn't that explain why none of the specialists you've hired have been able to reach him?"

"So could the fact they don't know what in the hell they're doing."

I shake my head, the pressure within me only increasing and my vision starting to blur. Something's not right. Slowly, I pull myself up. I don't know if it's the overload of information, or if it's something worse—far, far worse—

but something is definitely wrong. When I shift my feet, a wave of nausea hits me, and my entire body tenses. No. I know this feeling a little too well. Could it happen right here? Right now? I need to leave, to go home.

"I—I'm sorry, Mr. Blackwood. I'm not feeling so great. Can I come back another day?"

He pushes himself up, balancing with his cane, and eyes me carefully. "Yeah. You, uh, you need to stay here and rest awhile?"

I almost smile. I want to make a joke, tease him for sounding remarkably similar to how a friend might. But I can't seem to muster the energy. I need to get to where Death can find me. So I just shake my head.

I'm out the door and on the street in an instant, my thoughts as hazy as my vision. Not again, not again. Please don't be happening again. If I cross over now, I don't know that I'll ever find my way back.

I walk and I walk, one foot in front of the other, hardly feeling my legs as I do. The sky is a grey, dull blanket above me, the breeze a sharp whip to my desensitized skin. The streets are quiet other than the sparse vehicle here and there, nothing but the sound of the wind's push and pull whirling through my ears. Another step, and another, and soon I can't feel myself at all. Any sensations in my bones, my flesh, are fading away, becoming numb, until my body is nothing more than an empty shell of my soul; a part of me I'm not connected with and yet can't seem to separate from.

My surroundings swirl as I collapse on the sidewalk, but I don't feel the impact. I must be on my back because the sky looms over my face, spinning even as I lay still, trying hard not to blink.

Do.

Not.

Blink.

If I do, the darkness might take me. If I do, I may never

see the sky again.

"You're okay," a low, gentle voice soothes, then his face is looming over me. Dark lashes shadow those piercing green eyes, and windblown hair falls around his forehead. The firm line of his lips and hard clench of his jaw are such a contrast to the softness in his gaze. I see his arms wrap around me, but I can't feel them. I can't feel them at all, and it breaks my heart. I'm scared, so scared, and I need to feel his warmth, his touch, his comfort. "Shhh, you're okay." He's stroking my hair, and I must be crying because he keeps saying, *Shhh, shhh, you're okay*.

Colors blur around us as he walks, taking me away from the streets. As the sidewalk disappears, everything becomes green and deserted. We abandon civilization and press on, far into the meadow, until we're shadowed by long, barren branches as he leans back against a tree. He slides down to the ground, cradling me like a child.

I'm still shaky even as I realize I'm okay. I'm safe. I'm still here. "Y-you're here—"

"Shh, don't try to talk right now. Just rest."

"B-but I know . . . I know who you are . . ." My throat, it burns like matches scraping against a matchbox, too dry to catch a flame. I close my eyes, taking in the sensation. The burn. The pain. Because it means I can feel something again. It means the numbness is fading away.

"Rest," he murmurs, his fingers sliding through my hair, brushing over my neck. He pulls me in tighter, and I cuddle up against him, pleased to find that I can. That my body is listening to me again.

Fatigue floods me, and my eyes are still closed when I speak. "Do you know who you are? Who you *really* are?"

He's quiet for a moment, nothing but silence and darkness around me as my eyes rest. I wonder if I've fallen asleep, if the weight of my weariness has lulled me away. But then I feel the low rumble of his voice against me, making me curl into him even more. "I'm beginning to remember." His words are slow, almost careful. "Not all of it, but enough. Enough to know I can't . . ." He pauses, and the foreboding tone he's taken has my eyes fluttering open, my chin tilting up so I can look at him. His voice is hoarse when he says, "I can't keep coming back here, Lou. I can't—I can't see you again."

I sit up too fast, a dizzy wave rushing through my head, and I wince. His hands help steady me as I shift on his lap, so we're almost eye level. "Why would you say that? Of course you can see me again."

He shakes his head, a pained expression crossing over his face as he stares down at me. "It wasn't until last night, after my evening with you," his gaze drops to my mouth at the mention of last night, lingering, then his thumb slowly strokes my bottom lip, "that it started coming back to me. Images, memories. Most of it's in fragments, broken pieces, but the single moment I remember with full clarity is the day of my supposed death."

"*Supposed* death? But the accident."

He shakes his head again, his touch still holding me captive as he trails his fingers along my jaw, into my hair. "I was there, in the car, yes. And I was as good as dead. I knew I'd lost too much blood. There was no way I was making it out of there alive." His gaze goes distant, jaw clenching, and my heart breaks a little more. "I was already wasting away, drifting, losing consciousness. But I wasn't dead, not entirely, when that pull from the other side came for me. I still felt a shred of life running through me—hanging by a thread, but it was there." His eyes narrow, sparking with a quiet, simmering anger. The expression is almost intimidating enough to make me shrink back. "When the car blew, the world shifted below my feet. My surroundings changed, and then I was there. In the darkness."

I'm shaking my head, not wanting to believe it. What would it be like to go through something like that? It hits me now, as I really look at him, how exhausted he seems.

Like someone who's lost a week's worth of sleep. God, if he didn't start remembering any of this until last night, that means he's had less than twenty-four hours to process it. I can't even imagine coping with something like this, and all on your own, too.

"You see, Lou?" he says vaguely. "I wasn't dead, but I wasn't alive. I was something in between."

I hear myself swallow, my mind working a million miles per second and my eyes locked on his. *Something in between.* "That's . . . that's why you were stuck? Locked in the in between, unable to reach the other side?"

He nods slowly. "How do you cross over to the other side when you're more than just a soul, still connected to your body? And how do you return to reality when your heart can't remember how to function on its own? I was unfit for either world."

My eyes drop to the ground, taking it all in, and I find myself thinking back to the notes. His cries for help, his attempts to get his life back. "So you fought it. You some-how held on to who you were, and you tried reaching out through messages."

He lets out a breath, runs a hand through his hair, and leans back, his weight sinking further against the tree. "That part's a little hazier, but I remember fighting, yes. I remem-ber feeling that I was slipping away, forgetting everything I'd ever known. And I remember being desperate to get my life back." His lips press together tightly, letting me glimpse that anger again. "But you can only hold on for so long in a place like that. I don't even know how I became Death, exactly, except that over time, I'd evolved. Adjusted to my surroundings. Acclimated, until I was fully a part of that place. You stay there long enough, and you become it."

My stomach twists into knots, and I think I might be sick. The bile is coming up, and I have to force it back down. "So, does that mean . . . the others out there, in that place. You said before there's more than one Death." My eyes widen, the reality of what I'm about to say weighing heavily on me. "Does that mean they might be like you? Lost souls? Stuck, with no idea who they are?"

His gaze drops for a moment as he considers my question. "I'd say it's very possible."

I let out a loud whoosh of air, as if I'd been holding my breath for hours, and I shake my head. I don't know where it comes from, but fresh determination rises from somewhere deep within me. "Okay, well now we know. Now we know who you are, what's happened, and we can fix it. I can fix it. I'll go to Mr. Blackwood—"

"Who?" His brows are pulled together, eyes narrowed, and my face falls.

Could he really not remember Mr. Blackwood? The very man who's dedicated his life to helping him?

"Y-you don't remember who that is?"

I can see the focus on his face as he tries to recall, but he gets nothing.

"The man you sent your messages to. The person you contacted all those years ago."

Regret washes over his features, eyes closing briefly. "I'm sorry. I recall reaching out, but not to whom."

I stare dumbfounded for a moment, the realization of how that knowledge would affect Mr. Blackwood dawning over me. To dedicate your entire life to trying to help someone, to getting them back, and they don't even remember who you are? It would kill him. But then, I suppose he doesn't have to know.

I shake the thought away, pulling my shoulders back and returning to my new plan. The words come out rushed, almost desperate, but I can't help it. "Okay, that's okay. He's just someone who's done a lot of research on this sort of thing. So, between the three of us, we can figure something out. We'll put our heads together, and we can fix this. We can get you back."

The blood is coursing through me, adrenaline pumping

through my veins as I start to stand, but his hands come up around mine and gently tug me back down onto his lap.

"No."

I sit stunned, eyes widening. "What?"

"I said no." His voice is quiet but firm. Decisive. "Don't you understand, Lou?"

"No. No, I don't understand why you could possibly not want to fix something like this. You're not meant to be there. You're meant to be here, with me."

He shakes his head softly, his chin dipping toward his chest. "If it could happen to me, getting trapped in that place even while I was still alive, then it could happen to you. Dammit, Lou, it already *is* happening to you." His eyes squeeze shut. "Because of me. The more time I spend here in your world, the more it hurts you."

"What? No." I bring my hands up to his face, cupping his cheeks and gently lifting his head so he meets my gaze. "Death—" I shake my head, then correct myself. "*Enzo.*" His fingers come up over mine, and they tremble as I say his name. His *real* name. I lean in, planting a soft kiss on one cheek. "Enzo." The other cheek. "Enzo." And finally, his lips. "Enzo." His fingers dig into mine, his chest rising and falling.

"I won't." His words are tight, rough, the slightest quiver in his voice. "I won't let it happen to you, Lou. You're going to live a full life, here, where you belong. You'll get married, have a family if you want. Grow old, be free, always knowing who you are." He stops, giving his head a small, firm shake. "I won't let it take you."

I pull back slightly, my hands still locked on either side of his face by his own grip, and I watch as he swallows hard. "You can't blame yourself for what's happening to me. You saved my life, remember?" He says nothing, a sense of torment clouding his expression that tears me up inside. I lean forward again and press my forehead to his, my eyes falling closed at the same time his do.

"In so many ways, Enzo, you saved me."

Chapter Forty-Two

WE SIT LIKE THAT FOR a long while, tangled up in each other's arms, each other's warmth. Listening to the sounds of our rapid breathing. The crisp breeze pulls at the collar of my coat, the strands of my hair, intermingling with his fiery strokes of heat that slip beneath my clothes and caress every inch of me. When his eyes open, they're heavy-lidded, his gaze dropping to my mouth. My pulse picks up, my lips parting as I lick them. His Adam's apple bobs as his eyes cloud over.

Slowly, he lowers his head, and he presses his lips to mine in the softest kiss I've ever felt. It's feather light, a tender whisper, and a sigh pours out of my mouth and into his. My arms fall to my sides, my muscles melting beneath his touch. His hands come up to gently hold my face, fingers grazing my hair as he pulls me closer. When he slides his tongue into my mouth, it's slow and steady, deliberately so.

Almost like he's savoring the taste of me.

Almost like he's saying goodbye.

My chest tightens so painfully I'm sure it's about to burst, and I sink into him, spreading my legs enough to wrap them fully around his hips. I squeeze my thighs, making sure he feels the same pressure building in my chest, and a groan sounds from low within him. One hand glides leisurely down my back until it rests on my hips, then he's pulling me in with one swift motion. I connect with the full length of him between my thighs, hard and ready, and I grind, reminding him of how I feel, of what it's like to be inside me. A husky roar vibrates into my mouth, and I swallow it down with a moan of my own.

His other hand slips from my hair to grip my waist, and he's pulling me closer, using his strength to press me harder against him. I bite down on his lip in surprise at the way he hits me just right, his heat radiating straight through the fabric of my pants. Suddenly he's standing with my legs still wrapped around him, his hands propping me up. He turns us so my back's against the tree, and he presses his full weight into me in the most delicious way possible.

The position reminds me of that first night he showed himself to me, when he'd sandwiched me against a tree so he wouldn't be pulled away, and the thought sends a silent tear down my cheek, a quiet quiver through my body. He pulls his lips from mine, his gaze focusing on me, following the tear as it slides. Time stands still as he gently brushes the hair back from my face. He leans down and closes his eyes, sprinkling soft kisses over my skin, from the bottom of my jaw where the tear has landed, to the apple of my cheek.

When he pulls back, we lock eyes, green against brown. An electric wave bounces between us, a constant energy tugging us closer, closer. We don't say a word. We don't need to. His eyes glitter below his lashes, struggling not to overflow with all the emotions they hold back. Hard muscles contract beneath my grasp on his shoulders, his solid build shaking slightly as he lets out a ragged breath.

Watching him, taking in all the little details, only makes the tears come harder—he really is saying goodbye.

My fingers dig into his T-shirt as I pull him into me, lips parting and latching onto his. He groans, tilting his head down and exploring my mouth deeper as the grip supporting my weight squeezes. I slip my hand beneath his shirt and take in the hard contours of his body, from the ripple of his abs up to the smooth lines of his chest, then back down again until I'm teasing the hem of his jeans. His muscles tighten against my palm, and his erection grinds into me in response. He tears his mouth away from mine, moving down to the curve of my neck, right where I like it. I sigh into it, the feeling of his tongue on my skin, sucking and biting and riling me up.

I angle my head to make sure he can hear me when I whisper through uneven breaths, "Mark me, Enzo." His lips go still against my throat, his chest heaving against mine. "I don't ever want to belong to anyone but you."

A deep sound vibrates through his body, then he's unbuttoning my jeans and his lips are back in action. A strong, warm hand slides beneath my underwear, rubbing right against my wetness, and I cry out as my head falls back. Then it's gone, his hand and lips, and I bring my head back up, dazed eyes trying to focus. It's not until I feel the tug at my hips that I look down. He's on his knees, thumbs hooked into the loopholes of my jeans as he slides them down my thighs, and he's already working on my underwear before I've even stepped out of the pants or shoes.

I'm uncovered within seconds, wearing nothing but a top and my knee-length coat. I'm outside. Secluded, but outside. And I don't even care. Hell, I can't even think straight while he's still down there, eyes level with my nakedness and hot breaths brushing my thighs. My pulse is erratic, my breathing rough in anticipation. He spreads my thighs, then props them over his broad shoulders so my weight falls on him and the tree. I'm wide open to him now, and his fingertips dig into my hips as he takes in the sight.

"Fuck, Lou." It's a raw, almost agonized sound, and it sends sparks down to my toes.

Then he leans forward, and I suck in a breath.

When that first stroke of his tongue slides over me, my legs clench around him and my back arches. Then his whole mouth is on me, kissing and tasting. I can't suppress the mewls that pour out of me when he flicks his tongue again, up and down, around and around. When he sucks, I cry out, and he groans into me, the sound causing a deep vibration to ripple through my core. My hands are in his hair, pulling and tugging as I squirm against him, but he's relentless in his exploration, his grip on my hips holding me to his face.

"Oh god, oh god. I'm gonna . . . I'm gonna . . ." His fingers slip inside me, long and deep, adding to the pressure of his swirling tongue, and I can't hold back. I scream, my hips bucking against his face and his hands keeping me firmly planted in place. The aftershocks pour over me, my body shuddering against him. Finally, it simmers, and my head falls back against the tree. It takes me a second to get my breathing under control. "Holy shit."

I'm still on a cloud when he shifts beneath me, my bare feet touching the dirt as he stands. His lips are tilted up, a hint of a crooked smile, as he lowers his mouth to my ear. Warm breath teases my neck, strong hands slowly traveling down my waist, and my eyes flutter shut.

His voice is quiet and husky. "Are you tired, Lou?"

I swallow, my throat suddenly thick, and I feel my head shake side to side in answer.

"That's good." His tongue grazes my ear, then he pulls the lobe into his mouth and sucks. When his fingers slip under my shirt and softly stroke the thin lace over my breast, a shiver runs down my spine, a fresh ache forming between my legs. "Because I'm not done marking you yet."

I barely have time to register what he's said when he's flipping me over so my cheek is against the soft tree bark. His heat envelopes me as he inches closer from behind, my breath catching in my chest as I feel him approach. My wrists are pulled over my head as he pins them to the tree with one hand. His tongue is on my neck, his front pressing against my back, and my entire body sighs against him.

When I arch my back, grinding my butt against his hard length, a rough growl sounds by my ear and a hand wraps around my front, grabbing hold of my bare breast beneath my bra. I moan, my forehead resting against the tree.

"Is this what you want?" he growls softly. "To be mine?" His fingers trail down, down, down, until they slide just over my entrance, not quite slipping inside. I'm breathless when I answer, "Yes, that's what I want."

My mouth falls open when I'm quickly spun around, his chest pressing against mine as his lips come crashing down. The kiss starts out hard, rough, demanding, my eyes closing as he rolls his hips against mine. But soon, it slows, gentles, teases. I hear him swallow as he pulls back, rests his forehead against mine. When I open my eyes, his are closed, his chest rising and falling as he pants, struggling to calm his breathing. The hard ridges of his arms contract, his jaw tightens.

"What is it?" I breathe.

He lets out a deep breath, then slowly opens his eyes. The look he gives me twists my heart. From the tenderness in his eyes to the hard set of his jaw. From the thick swallow in his throat to the stock-still stance of his body, rigid and tense as he gently closes my coat, covering me up.

"Lou," he whispers, his voice hoarse, pained. "You will never be mine."

"What?" My face falls, an ache creeping into my chest and forming hundreds of tiny knots. "But I am—"

"No, you're not. If you were mine, I wouldn't fuck you against a tree in the middle of winter. I'd bring you to a warm bed and make love to you beside the fireplace. If you were mine, I'd wake up with you every morning and remind you how it feels to be loved by me. If you were mine, Lou . . . you wouldn't need me to mark you, because you'd know."

I've never been stunned speechless before. Never, until this moment. My breath hitches, chest swelling, as I stay frozen in place.

He takes a step back, away from me, and I already know where this is leading before his form starts to waver. He dips his head, glancing down at his feet before dragging those eyes back up to meet mine. He's gentle, quiet. "As for me, I've been yours since the day I met you." My heart stops, time freezing as I assimilate the words on his lips, devouring them whole. "You may never be mine, but I'll always be yours."

And then he's gone.

Nothing but a barren meadow and a shattered heart in his wake.

Chapter Forty-Three

B ACK WHEN I WAS YOUNG and hopped up on Disney fairytales, I had asked my dad if soulmates existed, and how I was supposed to know when I found mine.

He looked me in the eye and said, "Well I don't know if there are soulmates, but there sure as hell is your someone. It's easy to know once you've found them, though. Do you know why?"

I shook my head, thirsty for more. I wanted the Beast to my Beauty, and I was going to get him.

"Because with a single look, they can make you see the best parts of who you are. The purest version of yourself will be reflected in them. And when they walk away . . ." He paused, pinching the bridge of his nose as he gave a soft shake of his head. "When they walk away, they'll take a piece of you with them. Do you see, pumpkin? When you're with your someone, you can't help but feel it deep within your bones."

Try as I might, I never could figure out what he was talking about. Sometimes when I was with Bobby, I'd think back to Dad's words and wonder if maybe that's what I was experiencing. When Bobby's touch gave me butterflies, or when I'd feel let down after having to cancel plans with him. But that ache I expected to hit me when I broke things off with him never came. Then I began to think maybe it never would. Maybe what Dad and Mom had was so rare, no matter how hard we looked, it only ever happened to a few of us.

Now, as I stare at my reflection in the bathroom mirror, I see clearly what Dad was talking about. When Death—*Enzo* walked away from me today, I felt it. I heard the *snap* of my heart tearing in half. It wasn't a messy, dirty rip like I'd expected, but a smooth, clean line that knew just where to break to hurt me the most. The cracks spread through my heart, a piece crumbling in his wake.

This is what it feels like to have your heart break for someone. And I finally understand why Dad was never able to fix his without Mom. Because how do you make something whole again, when you're missing half of the pieces?

***

I'VE GOT ONE HAND AGAINST my chest, eyes closed as I lay beneath the blankets and concentrate. My stomach is tight with anticipation, my nerves electric livewires, ready to go off without warning at any moment. I think I might be about to break my twenty second record of no heartbeat.

Fifteen seconds. *Deep breath.* Sixteen. *Don't flinch.* Seventeen. *Come on, heart.* Eighteen. *Please.* Nineteen.

A sharp rap on the door whips my eyes open, and I release a loud exhale as I lose focus. When I decide to ignore it and return my attention to my faulty heart, the knocks come faster.

"Lou? Are you in there?"

Claire. I grumble and roll off the bed, padding toward the door.

Her eyes are puffed up and shiny. For the first time since I've met her, her hair is not perfectly styled. Instead, it sits in a messy pile on top of her head, and her outfit's not even color-coordinated today. I frown, wondering if Dylan has anything to do with this, and open the door wider to step aside.

"Hey," I say softly, locking up behind her. "You okay?"

"Yeah, I'm fine. I'm fine." She plops down at the foot of my bed, her hands fidgeting as she glances back at the rumpled blankets. "Oh. Sorry, did I wake you?"

I shake my head as I make my way to the bed, sitting beside her. "No, I couldn't sleep much last night. Been up for a while."

She nods, looks down, bites her lip.

"Claire?"

"No. No, I'm not okay." Tears are sliding down her cheeks when she looks back up at me. She shakes her head, rolling her eyes toward the ceiling. "I'm so stupid. So, so stupid."

I don't need to ask what she's talking about because I already know, so I just wrap my arms around her and pull her in tight. "Trust me. You're not the stupid one, Claire."

"I—I should have known, right? I mean, what kind of boyfriend cancels on you three times in one week?"

"The stupid kind."

"And what kind of girlfriend doesn't see right through it?"

"The trusting kind. The loving kind. The good kind."

She only shakes against me, squeezing tighter. "I don't know, Lou. Sometimes I wonder if I need to toughen up, stop being so naïve. Maybe then I wouldn't find myself in messes like this one."

"What?" I pull back, keeping my hands firmly on her shoulders as I look into her eyes. "Because you chose to trust in something, that means you're not tough?"

She gestures at herself, her nose wrinkling in distaste. "I think that's pretty obvious right about now, don't you?"

I shake my head. "No, I don't think that's obvious at all. You want to know the truth?" She says nothing, gaze latched on mine. "Sometimes I think people like you are the strongest of us all. The kind of person who can find beauty in anything. Who chooses to believe in love before hate. Who doesn't just hope for happy endings, but has what it takes to *create* the happy ending. It's so easy to be angry, to hate, to see the worst in a situation. But to actively choose to see the best? That's where all the courage is."

As I say the words, the truth they hold rings back at me with total clarity, my mind eager to grasp onto any straws of hope it can find. I find myself looking at Claire in a new light as I think back to my situation with Enzo. Maybe I can stand to learn a few things from her.

She's quiet for a long moment, so long in fact that I wonder if I've said the wrong thing. But then her lips start to quiver, and she yanks me toward her in the tightest hug I've ever received in my life. My eyes go wide, but I pull myself together and squeeze her back. I should seriously consider taking up writing Hallmark cards.

A ding from her pocket makes us pull apart. She wipes her eyes and chuckles, embarrassed. "What a thing to wake up to, huh? Bet you weren't expecting to start your day this way."

I shrug, thinking of the way I've had to start my days lately—with a hand on my heart to check if it's still working. "Could be worse."

She frowns, then opens her mouth as though to say something when her phone dings again. A grimace appears on her face as she reads the text. "Uh oh."

"What is it?"

"Oh, just Paul. When he came in to grab his paycheck this morning, I snagged him so he could cover the desk while I ran up to see you. But, um, I think he might be just a teensy bit high. Like, even more than usual."

My brows draw together as I lean in for a peek at the screen. It's a picture. A selfie, actually. Paul is at the front desk, leaning over a dead fly. His long hair is down, falling around his face, and he's got tears in his dazed eyes as he points at the insect. Below the image reads: *I dunno what happened. We were just talking. I swear, Claire. We were just talking.*

I can't suppress a chuckle as I shake my head. "Poor guy."

Claire snickers with me. "Yeah, I guess I better go help him before things get weirder down there."

"Good plan."

She flashes a quick grin as she gives me one last hug, then bounces off the bed, toward the door. As she turns the knob, she glances back at me. "Hey, Lou?"

"Yeah?"

"You're that kind of person, too, you know. The kind who has what it takes to create her own happy ending."

I smile vaguely, mulling those words over as the door closes behind her. Placing one hand over my heart, I listen to the silence that answers. A heavy anchor of fear wells in the pit of my stomach at the stillness beneath my palm.

I may not be able to have my own happy ending in this life. But I think I might be able to create one for someone else. Someone who deserves as fair a shot at happiness, at *life*, as the rest of us.

Chapter Forty-Four

A GE: 16
    Name: Jason Koryn
    Case #67 - Missing Child
    In the fall of 1986, sixteen-year-old Jason Koryn fell into a coma of unknown causes. Cared for by the Westlake Pediatric Center, he survived on life support for three weeks until being officially pronounced brain dead. Less than twenty-four hours from that point, he was reported missing by both the hospital staff and his parents. Jason's case was under investigation for several months before being left unresolved. Making Jason's case even more curious is that his is one of six known instances in United States hospitals in which the patients (all in near-fatal condition) have disappeared from their rooms.

I glance up from the book on my lap, chewing the inside of my cheek. How could a kid in a coma just disappear from a hospital? Despite having spent the last three hours reading and rereading Mr. Blackwood's *Other Unsolved Mysteries*, this is one of the few cases I keep gravitating back to.

Something about it reminds me of what Enzo was describing. The way he'd been on the brink of death, yet still technically alive, when he felt the pull come for him. Could that be what happened to this boy? Am I just reading too much into these stories, trying to find a connection that isn't there?

The only other cases that have caught my attention as much as this one are the four Sudden Unexplained Deaths recorded here. Four individuals, all different ages and all in different parts of the world—Houston, Montreal, Kiev, and Kampala. Each of them went to sleep perfectly healthy, and never woke up the next day.

What are we not seeing here? Why doesn't anyone have solid answers? I shake my head, running a hand through the strands of my hair as the frustration builds inside me. Case after case, page after page, all I'm left with are more questions. Of all the subjects philosophers, scientists, religions, and the like have tackled, the question of what exactly happens to us after life remains the biggest and most contradicting of all. If not even Death himself understands it, how can I expect to make any progress?

I set the book down, placing it beside *A New Dimension*—the other book I've been racking my brain over all day—and push myself up from the sofa. I pace in Mr. Blackwood's living room, back and forth, back and forth. *Think, think, think.*

Okay, well, clearly Mr. Blackwood's on the right track, vague as it still is. With his research and my own recent experiences combined, I'm convinced of his dimension theory; that other dimensions exist right on top of ours. There are a few kinks I haven't smoothed out, but still. I've seen it, felt it, the way I can step right into the dark void no matter where I seem to be, and at any given time. It's like an invisible world existing right where we stand, with the beating of our hearts and the pumping of our blood being the only thing separating us from it.

So my question is, if a person can be dragged into that world while they're still technically alive, can they be brought back into this one and survive it? I need to talk to Mr. Blackwood about this. I need to tell him everything. Where the hell is he? Why wasn't he home when I arrived today?

Shaking the thought away, I think back to Death—*Enzo, Lou. It's Enzo*—and the way his heart has started to beat again. That has to count for something, right? I'm not an idiot; I've noticed that his heartbeat, his presence here, only seems to get stronger as mine fades away. I've put the pieces together—what I can find, anyway—and I know he seems to believe if he stops coming here, to this world, it will somehow save me.

Yes, maybe that could have worked at one point, before we spent so much time together. Before he became such a solid part of this world. But now? Now the blood's already beginning to run through him again. He's already gained a stable heartbeat, far more stable than mine, and isn't it only a matter of time before he finds himself needing to sleep, to eat? Needing warmth, a home.

I know the truth now . . . that I'm too far gone. I feel the way my chest rings only of silence regardless of whether he's here or not. The way I become more and more a part of that world and less a part of this one with every moment that passes. I've seen how that place can get through to me, to my mind, within seconds of existing there. And how are his memories staying intact now, even as he continues to return to that dark place? Spending as much time there as he is? There's only one explanation I can come up with—because he's now more a part of this world than he is of that one. The darkness wouldn't have the same control over him it once did, would it?

Not in the way it now controls me.

Enslaves me.

I pull in a shaky breath, the fear seeping in more and more as reality sets in, overtaking the frustration. I don't even know when I started biting my nails, but my thumbnail is suddenly between my teeth, so apparently it's a new habit of mine.

I don't want to go back there. I can't go back to that.

What will it be like? Eternal numbness? Eternal darkness? What would happen to me? Would I evolve there like he did, acclimating enough to somehow survive it forever? Or would it break me, sucking my soul and mind dry until there's nothing left?

My muscles tense, palms sweating as I rub them together. Turns out the idea of eternal enslavement gives me anxiety. Shit, shit, shit. I can't do it. I'm not brave by nature. Do I even have a choice? Am I being ridiculous by focusing what are likely my final moments on trying to save someone else, when I could be focusing on trying to save myself? On trying to survive? Should I listen to Enzo without a second thought, let him go back to that place and stay locked away so I have a chance?

What about Enzo? What about his chance?

I try to imagine what it must have been like for him when the darkness first took over. He didn't have a warning, or the time to mentally prepare himself. He had a piece of metal lodged inside him, an explosion just waiting to take him, and on top of that, a lifetime of pain, suffering, and loss he'd already endured just to meet such an end. The one person he'd loved with all of himself, who'd loved him back unconditionally, had been killed before they'd even reached adulthood.

I wipe the tear from my eye, only to have more fall in its place. I haven't had the best life. Haven't had my family with me as much as I wanted. Haven't done half the things I've always thought of one day doing. Haven't done anything memorable, really. Anything to make a difference here, to make my mark, or give me a sense of pride.

But I've had the choice. I've been given a life, and with it the free will to make my own path. I've been loved. By a mother who gave her heart to me before she'd even met me. By a father who'd held on for eight long years just for me, after he'd already crumbled inside. By a grandmother who'd risked everything, given everything, to give my mother and I a chance at a good life. By Jamie, by Bobby, by Claire.

I've been *loved*.

I've been *free*.

I've been *me*.

I've had everything Enzo hasn't, and what have I done with it? Am I really so selfish I'd allow him, someone who's already been through more pain than I could imagine, to stay in that horrible, soul-sucking place for . . . for how long exactly? An eternity? Someone who's strong and good and so selfless that he'd sacrifice the one chance he may ever have at a real life, for me?

And then what? Say it works, his plan, and I get my life back. What kind of life would it be, knowing what I'd done? I'm not so blind to think I'm not in love with him. Not after the way my heart tore when he walked away. If Grams, Mom, and Dad taught me anything, it's the way love makes you strong and selfless in ways nothing else can.

No. When the backs of my hands are too damp from wiping the constant stream of tears, I switch to my sleeve. No, I won't let him do it. How could I? Maybe this is what I'm meant to do. Maybe this is my mark, the difference I'm supposed to make. Fate. I snort aloud, shaking my head. I'm probably just stuffing lies in my brain as a form of comfort, but I'll take what I can.

Letting out a long, uneven breath, I return to the sofa and snatch up *A New Dimension* again, flipping straight to the epilogue and scanning over its contents with revitalized determination.

Third paragraph down:

So yes, in short, what I'm getting at could be summed up in one, tiny, six-lettered word: glitch. A wrinkle in the afterlife, a kink in the system—call it what you will, it all boils down to the same thing. Not everything is the clean line we think it up to be. Even in the afterlife, mistakes are made, and I'm just one of countless individuals to have witnessed proof to this very fact.

The question remains: is there a solution? Is there a means of solving such an enormous and vaguely understood issue? The answer lies in the very definition of the word. Glitch: a sudden malfunction or irregularity. How does one get something to function properly that, scientifically speaking, doesn't even exist in the first place? Simple—you don't. You've got to get a grasp on it first.

I pause, my finger going back to the six-letter word. Glitch. Well that's a polite way to say we're fucked, isn't it?

Chapter Forty-Five

LOU ADAIRE, IF THERE'S ONE thing I can teach you right now it's this: never spring into action without a foolproof plan.

Oh, Grams. You'd be so disappointed right now.

This is probably as far from being planned out as it could get. In my defense, I doubt even she would be able to come up with a decent course of action for this sort of thing.

I step into my room and lock the door behind me, then take a deep breath. I don't know why I'm suddenly feeling nervous about this. Maybe it's because he already made it clear he was saying goodbye. That he never intends to see me again. Did he really expect me to be all right with that, though? Doesn't he know I need him to be okay in order for me to be okay?

I clear my throat, going for strong and confident. "De— Enzo?" No answer, but that was to be expected. "Enzo, I know you can hear me." Silence. *At least I hope you can.* I walk a few steps further into my room, scanning it for any signs of him. "I just want to talk, okay?"

I close my eyes, picturing him listening somewhere. Picturing his face, those green eyes, those lips I've kissed and want so badly to kiss again. Just once more.

"Please." The strong façade falters as quickly as I'd slipped it on. My voice breaks when I speak, betraying me. "I–I've been reading Mr. Blackwood's books again, you know. He's really onto something. I mean, I don't have enough to know exactly how to fix this yet, but I think . . . I think we can figure it out. Together. And I'm—I'm scared of running out of time to do it." I wander toward the bed, lowering myself slightly so I'm resting partially against it. I fidget with the ring around my finger. "I do have an idea, but I need to tell you in person."

I don't think the 'we should just let the switch happen, swap places' card will go over very well any way I play it, but I feel like something like that should at least be said face to face. Maybe if he sees how much I mean it, how desperate I am to see him get the life he deserves, then maybe I'll have a better shot at convincing him.

Not going to lie, a part of me still hopes if we really put our heads together, we can find some way for us both to stay here, in this world. Some way to be together. But that's also the part of me that believes in fairytales, so I'm not putting all my eggs in that basket.

"Enzo, please."

Nothing.

"Just hear me out."

Silence.

I take another breath, this time out of frustration. He can't go on ignoring me forever. Or can he? I frown. When I glance down at my ring, an idea crosses my mind. It's not a foolproof way to reel him in—sorry, Grams—but it's pretty close.

"Okay," I murmur, nonchalant, as I pull away from the bed. "I'm just going to come find you, then. Looking for an entrance to your world as we speak."

I don't know the first thing about finding an entrance. I wouldn't even know if such a thing is possible, since I've only ever wound up there by accident in the past. In reality, I'm walking aimlessly around the room, trying to appear like I know what I'm talking about on the off chance he can see me.

"Hmm, this feels like a good spot." I stop before the fireplace, miming in the air and looking like an idiot. "Yup, I can glimpse it now. Okay, stepping on through. See you soon."

Still no response.

Apparently I'm not the most convincing liar.

Giving up, I let out an exasperated noise and throw my hands in the air. "Are you really just going to ignore me forever? Is that what we do now?"

And nothing. This is getting ridiculous.

Why did I think he'd come? Of course he's not going to show up just because I ask him to. Not when he thinks it'll only hurt me. I shake my head, shoulders slumping in defeat. If he won't talk to me, the only other option I have is tracking Mr. Blackwood down. He'll have a far better shot at figuring this out than I do on my own.

Whirling around toward the door, my breath catches in my chest when I'm hit by a wall of black. There's no warning this time. No blurring of colors. No furniture fading from view. In the blink of an eye, I'm no longer in my room. The darkness snakes around my boots, sliding inside them and slowly up my legs. A clammy coldness forms over my skin. Then under my skin. A sickening feeling stirs in the pit of my stomach as the realization of what I've just done slaps me across the cheek with the force of a speeding train.

This wasn't supposed to happen. It wasn't even supposed to be possible. Just goes to show how far gone I really am if I can summon that world as easily as Enzo can.

The thoughts are washed away when my veins begin to freeze over and that thin layer of fire sparks beneath my skin. The transition happens so fast I hardly feel it this time. Just as my mind starts to connect with that strong magnetic pull within the darkness, two hands are around my waist and I'm yanked back.

My mouth falls open as fresh oxygen floods my lungs. Then I'm on my back, something soft and padded beneath me, and I'm staring wide-eyed at a flat, white ceiling. I lay stunned in place for a few moments, feeling the air rush in and out of me. Waiting for my mind to stop spinning. Finally, I carefully sit up.

The first thing I take notice of is the bed beneath me. My bed. My room. The next thing, is *him*.

His back is to me as he rests both palms against the wall, across the room. His head hangs down, the muscles in his shoulders and back rippling with tension. Even from here, with the slight angle of his face I can see, it's obvious the way his jaw clenches and his chest heaves.

"Enzo . . ."

Slowly, he turns. And I don't think I've ever seen him so livid. His body is the definition of rigid as he reins in his anger, and I'm afraid he's going to burn my room down with the heat radiating off of him.

"I-I'm sorry. I didn't know that was going to happen, I swear."

He says nothing, lips pressed into a thin line.

"I was just trying to get your attention." As soon as I say the words, I wish I could swallow them back down. I want to cringe at how pathetic they sound.

"You think this is a game?" He inches closer, just barely, and my pulse spikes. "You think your fate, your life, is something to mess with just to get my attention?"

My gaze follows the tightening of his fists, before he scrubs a hand down his face.

"No." I shake my head. "No, but you wouldn't answer me, and we're running out of time—"

"Time for what?" I see it begin to snap, the tension coursing through him. His hand rakes through his hair and his voice is rough. "For what, goddammit? To fix me? To save me? You can't fix me, Lou." He takes another step closer, looks me dead in the eye. "You. Can't. Fix. Me."

Everything about him in this moment makes me want to shrink back and cower. But I see what he's trying to do, and I refuse to be scared away. I force myself to sit up straighter, my voice rising with his. "That's just it. I've been reading more about it, and it's a glitch. That's all it is. Meaning you aren't meant to be there, Enzo. You really are meant to be here, just like I said before. And if you'd just calm down and talk to me about it for five minutes then maybe I can get you to understand."

He closes his eyes, takes a deep breath, like he's trying to calm himself. "What is it you think I need to understand?"

My lips part to speak, but I don't know how to form the words. How can I put this in a way that won't run him off again?

He moves closer, watching me struggle to get a grasp on my thoughts, until he's looming over me. "You want me to understand that me staying here with you is worth the risk. You want to see if this can work. If we'll defy the odds. You want us to be together, here, like normal people. Is that what you want to say?"

I swallow, my voice small when I answer, "Yup. Pretty much sums it up."

Something softens in his eyes as he gazes down at me, but the tension never leaves his body. The taut lines of muscle. The restraint in his posture. He's close to me now. So close I feel his breath when he speaks, and every bone in my body aches to reach out and touch him.

"We are not normal people, Lou. *I* am not normal. Every minute I'm here ties me closer to this world and pushes you further away. Every minute I'm here is a death sentence to you."

I shudder, his alarming words resounding a little too harshly in my ears.

He seems to notice, because he's leaning in. His hand comes up, fingers about to brush the hair from my face when he stops midair. Balls his hand into a fist and drops his arm to his side. "This is your life we're talking about."

"Exactly. *My* life." I tuck my hands beneath my thighs to hide their trembling. He needs to see my confidence in this decision, not my fear. "My choice."

"No." He shakes his head, taking a step away from me as his expression hardens, and the shift leaves me longing for him to come back. *Come closer.* "I'm not giving you the choice, Lou. You're not thinking clearly."

I narrow my eyes. "Like hell I'm not."

"You're not," he growls quietly, working his jaw. "You're only wanting this because of who I am as Death. Because of the pull I carry with me from the other world. You wouldn't be saying these things if I was just me, as Enzo. If you weren't connected to me through this . . ." He pauses, running a hand through his hair before gritting the next words out. "This damn *thing* forcing you to feel this way. It's making you blind."

My budding fear dissipates at that, certainty taking its place, strengthening me. I push off the bed and stand, my face inches from his, my voice ringing with conviction. "It may seem irrational. And yeah, maybe I am making a stupid decision. But I am not blind. I know exactly why I want this, and I want it because of *you*. That's never going to change."

The hard mask he's wearing falters, letting me glimpse the flurry of emotion that hits him at my words. Pain. Grief. Joy. Every tiny detail in this moment calls to me. The way he's leaning forward, eyes dropping to my lips. The ridges of his arms as his muscles tighten. But then, he pulls back again, taking an extra long step away from me.

So I take an extra long step toward him.

He stiffens. Swallows.

I press on. "So you could fight it. Pretend it's something less than it is. Push me away. But I'm not going anywhere. I'm going to find a way to get you out of there. To get you here, where you belong. Where you can live the life you deserve to live. Because you do deserve it, Enzo." My voice quivers, eyes watering as I try to keep the tears from spilling. To stay strong for him. "You deserve so, so much. So much more than me."

There's a glimmer in his gaze, a glint from the emotion he struggles to keep hidden. When his hand comes up, his thumb brushing over my bottom lip in that tender way only he can manage, I breathe out a sigh and my eyes flutter closed. *God, I need you, Enzo. If only you knew how much I need you.*

He's quiet, gentle, when he responds, the smoothness pouring into my chest like creamy, melted chocolate. "There are so many things I could stand here and tell you. So much I want to say, but I won't. I won't tell you how much I wish I could kiss you right now. How I just want to hold you and never let go. I won't tell you how you make me fucking crazy. How you're the only thing I know now, the only thing I ever want to know. And I definitely won't tell you I *want* the darkness to take me back, make me forget again, so it won't kill me so much to be away from you."

I don't know when my fingers wrapped themselves around the hand grazing my lips, but I feel it when they tremble against his. The tremble continues down my spine, making my body shake as tears pour over.

His eyes follow the stream, dropping to my lips as they do, and he wipes it away with a soft, slow swipe of his thumb. "But I will tell you this isn't something for you to fix. That your life, your *real* life, begins now. I'm walking away tonight, Lou." There's no shred of doubt on his face. Nothing but a calm, solid certainty that I know cannot be breeched. "And this time . . . this time I won't be coming back. So don't try to find me."

He pulls back, taking what's left of my heart with him. With each step he takes away from me, he fades a little more. With each step he takes away from me, an empty echo reverberates in my chest.

Reminding me of what I've lost.

Chapter Forty-Six

THE COLD WATER I SPLASH on my face does nothing to clear my mind. I look up, hardly recognizing the girl in my reflection. She stares at me with dazed brown eyes, dark circles shadowing them. Her lips are pale, just like her skin, and her hair falls wild and thick down her back. She's tired and broken in ways she never knew she could be.

I didn't sleep last night. Didn't even try. But I did spend every second of every hour thinking of ways to get through to him. To get him to come back to me. Yet here I stand, almost fourteen hours later, still achingly aware that nothing will change his mind. Nothing will bring him back to me.

With shaky fingers, I button the coat I've slipped on. I'm going to Mr. Blackwood. I'm going to tell him everything and get him to help me. To help Enzo. Yes, I realize it's probably useless. Yes, I realize that if Mr. Blackwood couldn't figure it out over the past twenty plus years, he won't figure it out over the next few days. Or even weeks. Or maybe ever. But I can't give up. I can't let go.

I won't.

I head into the hall, my body almost numb as I make my way down the stairs. I'm almost to the main floor when a familiar, bubbly giggle hits my ears. The sound has me tensing, making me all too aware of how disconnected I feel from reality right now.

The first thing I see is Claire's blonde hair, straight and sleek as usual. She's in a purple cardigan, with a color-coordinated ribbon around her ponytail and matching purple flats. She looks like she's doing a little better. I almost find it in me to smile.

Almost.

"Lou! Morning, sleepyhead." She nudges my elbow then gestures to the person on the other side of the desk.

Bobby's standing there, a soft smile on his face as his eyes linger on her. He tears his gaze away to turn to me, then lets out a low whistle as he looks me up and down. "You know I love you, but you look like hell."

"Thanks."

Claire's mouth twists into a frown as she observes the same thing as Bobby. "Hey, you okay?"

"No. How about you?"

She smiles softly, but I can see the sadness hasn't totally left her eyes. "I'll get there." I take her hand and give it a little squeeze. At least that makes one of us. "So Bobby came by to see you."

I shoot him a look that says I'm not up for chitchat, and he holds his hands up in mock surrender. "Whoa there, obviously not the best time. Just lettin' you know I'm going home in two weeks."

"You are?" The words take me by surprise, and an unexpected wave of uneasiness hits me. I know it's selfish, but I was just getting used to having him here with me. Being my friend again, like he was all those years ago. I don't know if I can lose another person in my life right now. "Why two weeks?"

He shrugs. "Gotta wrap up the contract on the temp job I picked up in the city. Otherwise that'd be plain irresponsible, and you know it's against my nature to be irresponsible."

My lips twitch up, and a grin stretches across his face as he points an accusing finger. "Ha! Gotcha."

I roll my eyes, ignoring Claire's matching grin. "Shut up."

"Nah, seriously though. What's going on with you?"

"I don't want to talk about it. In fact," I stop and gesture toward the clock hanging behind the desk, "I gotta go."

Claire grabs my hand just as I take the first step. "Come see me later. When you're ready to talk about it. Okay?"

I don't answer for a minute, because I don't know what to say. That I'll never be able to tell her? That there's no way she'd understand what's going on with me? The realization alone deepens the ache in my barren chest, but eventually I nod. "Okay."

I turn away, and I'm halfway out the door when I stop and look back. "Hey, Bobby."

He arches a brow.

"You can stay, you know. I mean, just if you want. It's not so bad having you around."

His mouth tilts up, blue eyes twinkling. "Thanks. Not so bad hangin' around, either."

We stare at each other for a second, a peaceful sort of understanding filling the gap between us, then I give them both a wave and step outside. Turns out a lack of sleep doesn't make walking harder. In fact, it's almost easier when you're in a foggy daze, never quite feeling the impact of your footsteps.

Mr. Blackwood's door is locked when I arrive, which is strange since I know he's home. Not only is his car parked out front, but another vehicle I don't recognize sits beside his. A guest? Another clairvoyant, maybe? That thought sparks an eagerness within me, reigniting what little determination I have left, and I give the door a quick rap. I wait a moment, expecting to hear the thump of his steps moving toward the foyer as I usually would, but I get nothing. I knock again, harder this time. After a minute, I hear it. *Thump, thump, thump.*

I take in a breath and place one hand on the handle, ready to get to work. Except the door doesn't open. Instead, Mr. Blackwood's voice booms through from the other side, grumpy as ever. "You're relieved from duty."

I frown, certain I misheard him. "What?"

"I said you're relieved! Go home. Celebrate. Get drunk."

"Mr. Blackwood, I'm not leaving."

"Well then I hope you brought an umbrella. I hear it's about to rain."

I look up at the clouds. Sure enough, they're grey and murky. Just my luck. "Let me in. I have to talk to you."

"No can do. I'm no longer in need of your services."

I let out a growl and bang once on the door. What the hell? "I'm serious. It's about Enzo."

There's a long pause. So long I wonder if he's walked away. But when he speaks again, his voice is somehow closer. Like he's standing right on the other side of the door. "Drop it, Lou. I am, and you need to, too."

"What? You can't drop it!" I don't care that I'm shouting, and the anger spiking my adrenaline sure doesn't either. I inch closer, ensuring he can hear every word I say next. "You don't understand. I *know* Enzo. I've seen him. I know where to find him."

He goes silent again, and I try to imagine what must be going through his mind. Does he even believe me?

When whole minutes pass and he still says nothing, the anger only soars again. "You're so close!"

To my surprise, he answers to that. "No, I'm not. Not by a long shot. It's over, all right? Now I need you to leave."

I scoff, pounding my fist again. "Oh, is that what you need? Well I need you to open up this stupid door and get to work with me. I need . . . I need you to have faith." I squeeze my eyes shut because, god, I don't want to cry again. Soon there won't be anything left. "*He* needs you. Y-you can't just give up on him."

He doesn't respond, but his silence answers me just as

well. He's not about to open the door. "Fine! I'll sit here all day if I have to, you know."

Still nothing. I know he's still standing there, though. His thumps would've given him away otherwise. I take a step back, lowering myself down and leaning my back against the wall.

He wants to be stubborn? Well, two can play that game.

I'M DRENCHED. THIS ISN'T JUST a light drizzle, but a full on raging downpour. It whips its way in every direction, teaming up with the wind to get to me despite the partial covering above my head. I'm shivering so hard my teeth chatter, but I'm not about to budge. If Enzo can put up with a dark void sucking the very life out of him as I sit here, on this porch, I can deal with a little rain.

I don't know how long I stay like that before the door creaks open, and a plate and sleeping bag are slipped out. All I can focus on is that slight opening, allowing me to see into the living room. And I lunge. The door slams shut, just before it can take my hand with it. I growl. Again. Like a dog being banned from going inside with the rest of the family. I almost chuckle at that thought, but then I realize the lack of sleep and food is making me delirious. I stare at the plate. A slice of pizza stares at me. We stare at each other.

I won't eat it, though, no matter how hard it taunts me. I'm on motherfuckin' strike.

Chapter Forty-Seven

IT'S BEEN SEVEN DAYS.
    Seven days since I've seen or heard from Enzo.

Seven days of camping out on Mr. Blackwood's porch.

Well, not technically camping out. I never actually use the sleeping bag he insists on giving me, allowing myself the one leniency of spending nights in my warm bed instead. But my days are spent on his porch, and today is no different. I finish off with my bath and dress, then head downstairs.

I'm surprised to see Bobby at the front desk again. This is the fourth time I've caught him here this week. The first two times he said he wanted to catch up with me, but I'm convinced that was an excuse. Because he doesn't bother to lie about it anymore. He grins and nods his head when he sees me, then goes right back to chatting with Claire.

I'm almost to the door when I hear her voice. "Lou, wait!"

I turn back to find her shuffling through some papers on her desk. "I almost forgot to give this to you. Someone was distracting me." She wiggles her eyebrows at Bobby, a playful look passing between the two of them, and I almost barf. Then I remember I love both of them and it's actually kind of sweet.

"Mr. Blackwood left a message with Paul last night." She

lifts the note, proceeding to read it aloud in a professional tone. "It's been fun, but it's time you quit. One more time and I'm—" She pauses, darting a curious glance at me before continuing. "I'm calling the cops."

My jaw drops. "Seriously?"

"Um, I guess." Her eyes flick to Bobby's, a silent question in them. Apparently they've already reached that stage of having private conversations with their eyes. "Why would he call the cops if you're just cleaning his house?"

"Because I'm stalking him. I gotta go."

I leave before either of them can respond, hightailing it to the Blackwood residence. I raise my fist, but before it connects with the door I hear a shout from the upstairs window. "You're trespassing on private property! That's a real crime, you know. With laws against it and everything."

I scoff—something I seem to be doing a lot around him lately—and puff up my chest, not ready to lose this battle. "Yeah? Well, you're—you're being ignorant, and selfish, and a whole bunch of other things!"

"Well, the cops will be here in ten, so feel free to file a report when you see them." He stops, and a coughing fit takes over. When he starts talking again, he's wheezing. "I'm sure they'll have the cuffs on me in no time for a claim like that."

My stomach drops, any last semblance of hope I had crashing with it. "You can't be serious!"

I pace back and forth, trying to calm myself before I break down the door and strangle him. It's not helping. "You don't realize what you're doing. You can't give up like this. You can't just leave him there. Please." I stop, my head thumping back against the door as a final, desperate plea pours out of me. "Please. I–I'm begging you, Mr. Blackwood."

There's no answer this time.

I close my eyes, squeezing them hard, the only real sign of my inner turmoil being the curled fists at my sides, the sharp dig of fingernails cutting into my palms. "Please . . ."

It doesn't matter how many times I try, he no longer responds.

"Please."

This is really it.

This can't be it.

He's done with me.

Please.

He's done with Enzo.

No . . .

THE DAYS HAVE BEGUN TO run together, blending in with the weeks. Seconds become minutes and minutes become hours, but I'm not counting. The only thing I am counting, is my heartbeat. Lying in bed, I stare wide-eyed at the ceiling's misleading white sea. Just like yesterday morning, and the one before that, and the weeks before that, one hand rests palm down on my chest.

One second. Two seconds. Three. Four.

Thump.

My eyes fall shut. Four seconds. Every day, the beats grow closer. Every day, my heart grows stronger. Just like he said it would without him here.

Then why does it feel like my heart's only breaking more and more with each day we're apart? I don't know how it happens, but every night I fall asleep with shattered pieces in my chest. Then every morning I feel the fresh *snap* as it breaks all over again. The pain, the deep ache crushing me until I can't breathe, it never leaves me alone. The crazy thing is, I don't think I want it to. At least it reminds me of what I had. And sometimes I think if he's suffering right now, maybe it's only fair I do, too.

Heartache is my constant companion, and we're perfect for one another. Two co-dependent peas in a pod. My past and my future.

I ignore my cell phone when it rings, opting to wallow in misery instead. *It gets me.* Then I ignore the inn's room phone, and the ding of a text coming through. I even ignore the knock at the door when it comes, but then I hear the jingle of a key and the turn of a knob.

When Claire walks in, her face is solemn. It's a strange and unnatural sight on her. She's slow with her footsteps, gentle as she lowers herself onto the bed. "Hey."

I glance at her. "Hi."

We haven't spoken over the last few days or so. I tried for a while. Tried acting like things were normal. Even stopped by her place to hang out with her and Bobby a few times last week—the same Bobby who was supposedly moving back to LA weeks ago. It's not just her though; I haven't spoken to anyone. I sent Jamie another postcard last week, and that seems to be keeping her happy.

"I, um, I've been trying to reach you."

"I'm sorry, Claire. I'm really not the best company right now."

"No, it's okay." She bites her lip. "It's okay. Listen, I wouldn't have come except . . ." She looks down. Closes her eyes. "Lou. It's Mr. Blackwood. He's in the hospital."

There's a hitch in my chest, even with my irregular heartbeat. I say nothing.

"He's had a stroke. And, well, it's pretty bad. I just—I thought you should know."

I shift my attention back to the ceiling, staring into the blinding whiteness. Staring and staring. Then staring some more, refusing to accept her words. A stroke. That's ridiculous is what it is. Mr. Blackwood couldn't have had a stroke, because he's a stubborn hard ass. Too much so for something like a little stroke to knock him down.

The bed shifts as she stands. She hovers beside me for a minute, and I watch out of the corner of my eye when she turns and walks away.

"Claire."

She whirls around so quickly I think she might fall. She doesn't, though. "Yes?"

"Can you take me to see him? Would you mind?"

"Of course I'll take you."

Chapter Forty-Eight

CLAIRE DROPPED ME OFF AT the hospital's entrance. She asked if I wanted her to come inside with me, but I insisted I'd be fine. Not that I am. But it's better this way. I pull back my shoulders, lift my chin, and reach for the handle.

It's not the first time I've been to this hospital, but it may as well be. The last time I woke up as a patient, and now I walk in as a visitor. The man at the front desk asks me to wait while he pages the doctor, so I do. Moments later, I'm greeted by a middle-aged brunette woman in a white coat. She's kind, I can tell, but her serious demeanor warns me off the bat. This can't be good.

"I've heard a lot about you, Lou," she says.

The comment has me hopeful. "You have? So he's up and talking?"

"Oh." Her gaze darts down, her solemn expression deepening when she looks back up at me. "Um, no. I'm afraid not. I was referring to his earlier visits. He mentioned you quite a bit, you know."

"Earlier visits?"

A crease forms between her brows, her head tilting. "Yes, that's right." I open my mouth to ask for clarification when she continues, taking off down the hall and gesturing for me to follow. "He told me what an excellent caretaker you've been, and that's high praise coming from Mr. Blackwood." *Um, what?* "Here we are."

She stops before one of the rooms, then nods toward its window. I step closer to peer inside. The color drains from my face as soon as I do, and I forget all about my confusion over her words. Mr. Blackwood lies in the hospital bed, eyes closed and skin ghostly. I've never seen him without many layers on, and the thin patient gown and blanket do nothing to hide the sharp points of his bones. I almost can't believe how frail he is.

"Lou," she mutters, voice gentle, "as I'm sure you're already aware, these recent weeks have been particularly rough on him. Unfortunately, it's not uncommon for cancer patients to experience a stroke"—I blink, certain I've misheard her—"especially considering the sudden way it recently spread from his lungs. That, combined with his age, and the condition his health was already in prior to the diagnosis . . ." She glances toward him, a sad look crossing her face. "Again, I'm very sorry."

"Wh-what are you saying?"

"I'm saying, we don't expect him to wake. I'm afraid he doesn't have very long, so I encourage you to see him soon if you'd like a moment to say goodbye."

If there's a way for all the air to leave your body at once without managing to kill you, I'm certain that's what's happening to me now. My throat's suddenly too tight to take in the oxygen. *Cancer?* How long has he been hiding this from me?

"Lou?"

"Yes." It's a whisper, a distant sound even to me.

"Would you like to see him now?"

I nod, my neck stiff, and she opens the door for me. I don't look back at her as I numbly walk toward him, but when the door clicks behind me, the distant sound feels too final. There's a chair beside the bed. I sit, my gaze wandering everywhere in the room except toward him. I don't think I can do it yet, being this close to him.

Then it would become real, and I don't want it to be real. Instead, I clear my throat, stare at the wall above his head. I pretend I can breathe, for his sake. Pretend I'm not about to break. Pretend I'm not wondering how a person can be expected to go on when they keep losing one person after another.

Because this isn't about me. This is about Mr. Blackwood, and only Mr. Blackwood.

"You know," I croak through the lump in my throat, "I knew you wanted to be rid of me . . ." I have to pause, feeling a fresh wave of tears. Refusing to let them fall. "But this seems a little over the top, even for you."

My laugh comes out choked and forced, and I can't talk anymore or I won't be able to hold the river back. So I continue to sit, this time in silence. I lean forward, resting my head in my hands, and I stay like that for a long while. I hear the door open once, twice, but I don't flinch. It's not until a ding sounds from my pocket that I move.

Bobby: Claire told me about Blackwood. I'm real sorry, Lou. Let us know if you need anything.

I decide to text him back. Anything to prolong me having to look at Mr. Blackwood directly.

Me: Thanks. Tell Claire I won't be coming back today. Going to stay here with him for a little while.
Bobby: Yeah, of course. We'll be here when you need us.

I manage a faint smile, rereading his texts. *We. Us.* At least that's two people I love who I don't have to worry about. They'll be okay, Bobby and Claire. I know they will, and the knowledge relieves some of the ache within me.

I take a deep, shaky breath. *Just get it over with.* Rip off the Band-Aid all at once, and all that. I wipe my palms on my thighs then finally look up. There he lies. So still. So calm. I frown, looking closer. He looks almost peaceful, actually. Like maybe he's just sleeping. Taking a nap on a lazy, weekend afternoon. I reach out and gently fold my hand over his bony one, through the blanket. A single tear slips down my cheek.

"So this is why you shut me out, huh?" I whisper, thinking back to our last conversations. "You could have just told me. I could have been there for you." I pause, closing my eyes. "God, you're so stubborn. And rude. And obnoxious. And stubborn." I peek over at him again before adding, "And weird. You know you're weird, right? Only a weirdo could hide their smart and sweet as well as you do."

When the silence begins to stretch, I lean forward, resting my forehead on his arm and closing my eyes.

"I know you don't want me to, but I'm going to stay here with you until you're ready to go. Because we're friends. And that's what friends do."

<hr />

I T WASN'T UNTIL MIDNIGHT THAT I finally left his side, and that was only to grab a cup of coffee. I'm sore from sitting in that chair all day, my legs stiff as I make my way down the hall, focused on keeping the hot to-go cup in my hands from spilling. When I reach for the doorknob, a sudden movement beyond the room's window catches my eye. I scoot closer. The windows are tinted, making them dark while the lights are dim, and I have to squint to peer through the glass.

As my vision adjusts, I'm slowly able to make out a dark figure, tall and broad. The coffee cup slips from my hands, crashing to the floor.

He's here. Enzo's here. Standing right beside Mr. Blackwood. The air is sucked from my lungs, catching in my throat. It's really him. I reach out, pressing the open palm of my hand against the glass.

The longer I stare, the more I notice there's something off about the way he looks. His body. It's not solid, but wavering. There's something dreamlike about it, dark and inky as he blends into the surroundings, looming over the hospital bed like some sort of shadowed god. I furrow my brows. He looks an awful lot like he did that night in the lake.

The night he came to take my soul.

My eyes widen. I'm just about to lunge for the door again when something stops me.

He's reaching forward, slow and hesitant, pulling down the hospital blanket. I frown, squinting again. He gently takes one of Mr. Blackwood's arms, inspecting it with care.

I don't understand. *What are you doing, Enzo?*

His fingers trace over the bony arm, then he lowers himself so he's kneeling beside the bed. His head drops, hanging down, and his eyes close. Then his body starts gently shaking, eyes still squeezed shut and Mr. Blackwood's arm still in his hands. And my heart breaks all over again, a sharp snap twisting my chest. *Oh, Enzo. Why are you crying?*

I tilt my head for a better view, shifting my attention back to the frail arm. It's not until then, when I really focus on Mr. Blackwood, that I see them.

The scars.

So. Many. Scars.

I gasp, my hand flying to my chest. I know those scars. I know them, because I watched as the monster carved them into his arm right in front of me. My knees go out, and I have to push a hand against the wall to keep upright.

Oh my god. I watch Enzo as he continues to sit there, continues to silently cry, alone in his agony. My trembling hands raise to my lips, trying to stop their quivering as my own body shakes. I turn away from them, not wanting to invade such a moment any more than I already have. My back hits the wall, and I slide down to the ground. I can't stop shaking. Crying. Can't release a single breath. Slowly, the pieces start falling into place.

All this time. All this time, he was right here. Alive. Searching for his big brother.

They both made it out of the fire that day, all those years ago. They stayed together, made a life in Colorado helping families like them. Then came the car accident. At the hands of Mr. Blackwood. My eyes shut, pain for these brothers hitting me like daggers. Seeping into my heart and tearing it apart. Oh god. It's no wonder Enzo made sure Mr. Blackwood—no, *Tommy*—Tommy Hawkins made it out of that car before him. He'd spent his entire life protecting his little brother. He wasn't about to stop then.

Tears race down my cheeks, my heart drowning in them. I hurt. For Enzo and Tommy Hawkins. For the life they ran from, then the life they lost. If it hurts me this much, what must Enzo be feeling? Seeing his brother for the first time after all these years. And only when it's time to take him away. It must be killing him.

Enzo. I scramble to my feet, shoving the door open. My ears are hit by the steady beep only a flat-line could produce. Enzo's back is to me. He's hardly more than a shadow now as he slowly fades away. Just before he disappears forever, he turns his head over his shoulder, eyes locking right onto mine. My heart slams against my chest so forcefully it reverberates throughout my body.

I part my lips, but no words come out. I want to cry. Want to beg. Want to scream. But mostly, I want to hold him until I know he's going to be okay. Then I want him to hold me until I'm okay, too.

Instead, I'm frozen in place, and he's already tearing his eyes from me. Turning away. *No.* Don't leave again. "Enzo, wait!"

I unfreeze my legs and rush toward him, my hands reaching out when all that's left is a smoky fog in his trail. My skin connects with the black smoke, just before it vanishes completely, and I'm struck by an icy sting zinging through my fingertips. I gasp and snatch my hand back, hugging it to my chest as I stumble backward.

I'm heaving, body trembling. I collapse against the nearest wall.

What the hell was that?

I've never seen him collect before. A shiver snakes down my spine, my eyes darting to the now lifeless body before me. He's gone. Really gone. Only taken when his time was right. I close my eyes, and my breathing slows slightly. He'll make it through to the other side, meeting his brother face to face again as he does.

Finally, he can say what he needs to.

Finally, he can be at peace.

Chapter Forty-Nine

"I DON'T UNDERSTAND."
The chair is hard as stone beneath me, only adding to my discomfort as I try to comprehend the legal documents in my hand. It's been three weeks since he's been gone. Three weeks since that day at the hospital. Yet uneasiness still rolls over me at just the mention of his name, let alone seeing his handwriting. His signature.

The stranger before me removes his glasses, setting them aside as he centers his brown gaze on mine, adjusts his suit collar. "It's simple, really. Just as the papers state. Just as I've already explained. Mr. Thomas Matteo Blackwood has left everything to you."

"Everything. As in . . ."

"His property and all possessions within. His money. His vehicle."

"Everything," I repeat again, still unable to grasp it.

"Yes, ma'am. Once again, that's *everything*."

I swallow, my eyes glued to the letters right here in front of me. Clear as day. Holy shit. The cancer-hiding bastard left me everything.

I knew he was a big softie.

CLAIRE SMILES AT ME FROM across the boutique. I smile back, because that's what normal people do.

When Bobby and his mom follow suit, catching my gaze as he pays for his items, I plaster an identical grin on my face for their benefit as well. It seems to please everyone, because they all look away and continue their transaction.

A glint from Bobby's pants pocket drags my gaze downward, to the key ring that's half hanging out, revealing the latest AA chip he's earned. Claire's been taking him to weekly AA meetings, now that Dylan's out of the picture—thanks to last month, when he stormed into the inn without realizing Bobby was there. Big mistake. They ended up getting a restraining order on the dickhead, and we found out the next day he was fired from his job, too. Just the cherry on top. Claire's been worry free lately, back to her bubbly nature and encouraging Bobby every step of the way, and he hasn't had another slip up since that one night.

Although the sobriety mission has done nothing to take the heat off me. They've both been extra concerned about me ever since Mr. Blackwood's passing, offering to take me out almost daily. This is the first time I've agreed to it over these past two months, and only because Bobby's mom is in town and I never could resist her motherly charm. How could I say no to a universal mother? That'd be like turning down Mrs. Weasley. Exactly, it isn't done.

It hasn't been the worst thing, having such close tabs over me. It's forced me to adult, to take care of things I should've dealt with long ago. Starting with Grams's house. I called the realtor several weeks ago, and we accepted an offer. I smile vaguely, recalling the family I chose. I think Grams would be happy with them living in her home—a single mother with a young daughter.

The soft sound of Claire's laughter brings me back to the boutique, my gaze finding her and Bobby huddled close together as his mom takes her turn at the register. Bobby's leaning forward, wearing that goofy grin as he whispers something in her ear, and she giggles again, a rosy blush reddening her cheeks. I don't miss the way his fingers tenderly entwine around hers or the squeeze she gives his hand in return. The boutique is dimly lit, but the way they're positioned beside the shop's window casts a romantic glow over them.

The sight is both soothing and painful to the broken pieces of my soul.

Really, Bobby and Claire are a perfect fit. I don't know why I didn't see it sooner. She gives him the courage to stay strong, and he gives her the love she deserves.

My fingers dart to my ring, rubbing it like it has the power to grant me three wishes. I haven't told anyone about the dreams. The dreams that returned to me ever since my fingers grazed Enzo's smoky trail more than two months ago. They don't come every day, but even once a week is enough to hurt. Enough to remind me how much I miss him. How much I hope he's somehow okay.

I close my eyes, trying to block the thoughts from my mind. I can't think of him. Not out in public. Alone in my room, yes. I spend every waking second consumed by thoughts of him when I'm locked up behind the privacy of my own four walls, where I'm free to cry and suffer in peace. But not here. Not now.

"You ready?" Claire's chirpy voice calls me back to the shop again, and I nod.

"Ready."

The ride is longer than usual, since Mr. Blackwood's property is farther from the small shopping strip than the inn is. No one seemed to mind when Bobby offered to drop me off. I give them each a hug, Bobby's mom getting an extra long one, before hopping out of his truck, then wave until they're past the gate, away from view.

Slowly, I turn around to face the house. A wave of uneasiness runs through me, leaving my body heavy and clammy. It doesn't feel right, being here. It's too empty. Too quiet. I know he left the place to me, but this is my first time at his door since my strike. I'm not even sure why I had them drop me off here today. Maybe for closure. Maybe so I won't feel so alone. I shake my head, forcing my stiff fingers to untuck the key from my pocket and unlock the door.

Plates of stale food greet me when I walk in. Three empty glasses sit around the Three Ships Whiskey centerpiece on the coffee table. Papers are littered over the couch and bookshelf.

I have to lean one hand on the sofa for support as I take in the moment of déjà vu. It looks just like it did the first day I ever stepped inside. And just like that first day, I'm walking on eggshells.

I don't let myself stare for long before I'm up the stairs, not stopping until I'm standing in the doorway of his bedroom. His bed isn't made. The comforter is pulled back in one corner, and a coffee mug sits on the nightstand. It's like he just stepped away and is coming right back.

The whole feel of the room is drab and dark, no thanks to the thick curtains he always kept pulled shut. So gloomy and depressing. Where's the sunlight? Where's the sign of another day? Eyes on the curtains, I march across the room, determination in every step. I grab ahold of the material with both hands and shove it to the side until light pours inside. It's not sunny today, but the daylight casts a faint stream over the room, just right. Gives the place a little life. Much better.

I turn back to the window for a final glance, and a piece of land with dried up grass and wild weeds catches my eye. I recognize it immediately.

The house isn't there anymore, just a pile of logs and barren land, but still, somehow I know. Maybe it's from trudging along the same dirt when it became mud as I carried little Tommy to the neighboring shed. Maybe it's from the old photo of the monster sitting in a chair on that very dirt as he eyed the camera, not a care in the world.

Whatever the reason, I know.

That's the Hawkins land. And Mr. Blackwood's house, up on the lone hill, is the only one with a clear view of it.

I take a step back, but not before grabbing the curtains and yanking them shut again. So this is why he bought this place? A house too big for him, with rooms that went unused, and stairs he had to climb with his limp. I shake my head, trying to understand. Had he been reminiscing or punishing himself? The fact he'd made sure to keep the land out of sight, locked up tight behind these curtains, makes me willing to bet on the latter.

I whirl around, striding toward the hallway and closing the door firmly behind me. He may have been sardonic about it, but I'm not. I've only ever seen the place in my dreams, and even that's enough to keep me from ever wanting to see it again.

I make my way down the steps, and I'm about to rush out the front door when I stop. I flick my gaze to my right, where the crinkled pieces of paper rest. Before I can stop myself, I pluck one up and open it. It's a sketch of our little town, and lines and dots are blanketed over it with terms too brainy for me to understand. Then I grab another one, smoothing out the wrinkles. This one is a note.

Two lines.

Seven words.

I'm so sorry.

I'll never give up.

My hand comes up over my chest as I reread the scribbled letters, then glance at the freshly scattered papers around me. *He lied to me.* He never stopped trying. Never lost faith. Until the day he died, he fought for a way to save Enzo.

I carefully set the note down on the table, fingers already trembling again as the realization seeps into my bones. My heart. My soul.

No, he never gave up.

And I never will either.

HE KNIFE LOOMS OVER TOMMY'S stomach, just about to make its mark. Not today, you son of a bitch.

Hands still bound to the chair, I lean forward and spin around, then lunge backward until I feel the solid force of impact. The monster roars as one of the chair legs digs into him, and I'm frantic as I look back at Tommy. I don't know how much time I can buy for him.

"Run! Take the damn chair with you for all I care. Just RUN!"

Tommy's hazel eyes go wide, but after a shell-shocked pause, he mimics me, leaning forward until the chair bound to his arms lifts off the ground. He's wobbling toward the front door, quick as his legs will take him, but I don't get to see how far he makes it before I'm yanked back, crashing against the ground. I cry out with the snap of my shoulder popping out of place, the weight of the chair pulling against bone.

The monster leers at me, then makes for the exit. For Tommy.

I lunge again, this time knocking him down with the force of my head against his back, and we both go tumbling. Something else snaps, but the pain's taken over so much of my body that I can't pinpoint where the sound comes from this time. My hands get back to work behind me, tugging hard against the rope.

A grunt sounds from beside me. I turn to see the monster pulling himself back to his feet. "So that's how you wanna do this? You really think you can fight me and win?"

I'm still lying sideways on the floor, limbs twisted awkwardly around the chair. The taste of metal swirls in my mouth, around my teeth, and I spit out a mouthful of blood. Then I lift my chin to look him straight in the eyes. "Any day, Pops. Any fuckin' day."

His face twists, turning beet red.

He charges.

Boot-clad toes meet my ribcage, sucking the air from my lungs. My hands freeze at the wave of pain, but soon they're at it again.

Looser and looser the rope becomes, fueling me with the fire I need to take him down. Just as that second kick comes, I feel it. The rope drops to the floor. I'm free.

The next time that boot comes, it's in my grip, and I twist. He crashes to the ground, crying out. Takes him a second to level his gaze at me, but when he does, his eyes drop to my freed hands. Then they go wide, and he scoots back on his elbows as I push myself up. Pain licks at my ribs, my wrists, my mouth, my shoulder. Everywhere. I don't wince. I learned to block out the pain long ago. My eyes narrow in disgust as he cowers before me, his expression a silent plea for mercy. "Thought you wanted a fight."

Before he can respond, the creak of a screen door has me whipping my head over my shoulder.

Tommy stands in the doorway.

With our neighbor.

My eyes squeeze shut for the briefest second. Why'd you have to come back for me, Tommy? The damn stubborn idiot.

Fingers wrap around my ankle, and I hit the floor. Nausea washes over me as the brunt of the impact strikes my shoulder. I hear a scream, but it's not mine. Tommy's running, fists swinging. He's a lot smaller than I am, lanky too, and the monster knows it. He gives a single solid swing of his own, straight across Tommy's jaw, and the boy goes crashing down beside me with a thump.

A growl rips through me. Just as I begin to pick myself up, my gaze is locked straight down the barrel of a revolver.

The room stills, silence falling over us like the death sentence we all know this is. I didn't know there was a gun in this house. The monster's eyes are wild, manic. And afraid. There's a tremor in his fingers, causing the barrel to shake. "It's you or me, boy. You or me."

I hear a click. *The final nail to my coffin. But the bullet never comes. Because a hard* thunk *sounds behind him. His eyes roll back, and he collapses in a heap before me.*

Mrs. Mulligan stands above the three of us, a cast-iron frying pan in her tight grip. Her face is stoic as ever, eyes filled with determination as she stares down at him, but her chest heaves. Slowly, when he stays down, motionless, she lowers the instrument. Shifts her gaze to me and Tommy. And I somehow manage to breathe again. To relax a little.

I don't know how she does it with the close tabs Chief Mulligan keeps on her, and I don't know why she risks it, either. But the woman always comes through for us.

"Thank you," I whisper between pants, one arm wrapped around my tender ribs.

She doesn't say you're welcome. Hardly allows us to see the glint of fear in her eyes over the near-death experience we just had. She nods, turns to Tommy, and lowers herself down before him. She places a hand beneath his chin, tilting his head as she inspects his jaw. She looks satisfied when she turns back to me, her eyes roaming over my injuries.

"You boys will be all right. But we need to get out of here. Now."

"Not yet." I shake my head. "You need to leave, yes. But us, we'll never be able to run from him." We know this, because we've tried. She knows this, because she's the one who's had to clean our wounds whenever he caught us. And he always catches us.

Next time, he'll go for the kill. Next time, he'll go for Tommy alone. Next time . . . well, there won't be a next time.

When I turn to Tommy, his eyes narrow. There's that fire again, burning bright, and I know his mind is right there with mine when we shift our attention to the unconscious lump beside us. I feel the outline of the matchbox in my back pocket, red flames dancing in my eyes.

"There's just one more thing we need to do before we leave."

Chapter Fifty

THERE COMES A MOMENT IN everyone's life when you're hit with a pang of undeniable clarity. Sometimes it's about your career choice. Or your next love. Maybe it's finally finding the right major. The right house. The time to walk away, or the time to stay and fight for what you want. The chance to make a mistake you know will be worth it, or the choice to stay on your path.

Or, if you're me, it's the moment you choose your fate.

I could look at it like the end of the road. Like the morbid truth it may be. Instead, I decide to see it for the beginning it also is. The end of suffering for a brave and selfless soul and a chance at the peace they so deserve.

I'm gentle and fluid in my movements as I dress for today. A warm, soothing strength flows through my veins. The thin sweatshirt slips over my body like smooth silk, and I'm slow and calm as I brush my hair. I listen to the soft tap of my boots as I glide across the floor, feel the final click of my room's door wash over me as it closes.

Claire and Bobby catch my gaze, and I smile as I steadily pass them by. It's not a wide, cheerful smile, but soft and content. Bobby's brows furrow, but his lips quirk all the same. Claire waves, her eyes lingering on me with a quiet curiosity. Fresh, spring air fills my lungs as I step outside, and I breathe it in. Trees bloom with new life, strangers chatter as they breeze past them, not even noticing the beauty right in front of their eyes.

But I do. I notice everything. From the green leaves to the red dirt. From the blue skies above my head to the sidewalk below my feet. Each step forward is so easy, like this is what I'm meant to do, and I focus on the serenity that knowledge brings me. Not the fear bubbling beneath.

I don't stop until I reach it, the narrow road I recall so vividly. It looks different now than it did then, though. Then it was clouded and dark. Tree branches were barren, the cold air sharp enough to sting. Today, full-bodied trees shadow the sleepy road, shading it in a cloak of mystery and peace. I make my way to the tree. Our tree. The first one he ever pinned me against, and a crooked smile lifts my lips. I stroke the rough bark, then turn around and lean against it.

Just one more deep breath. One more rush of air before I go. I swallow it down, reveling in the sensation.

And then I'm ready.

Closing my eyes, I let my surroundings wash away. My heartbeat may be whole again, but my dreams tell me we are still connected, he and I. And if we're still tied together, then so am I to his world. There's no manual on how to do this sort of thing. No instructions laid out for me to follow. So I focus my energy on blocking out the things around me. The things that connect me to my own world.

With my eyes still closed, the blue skies turn black. The lively wind against my skin fades into a vague caress, and the bird calls become echoes in the distance. It's not long before I feel it. That pull. That tug, lulling me into its binding spell. The coldness rushes through me, and I don't fight it this time. I soak in the ice, the deadly silence that lies so still in wait.

With my heart back at full strength, this place doesn't have the full control over me it once did. And this time, it doesn't have the advantage of surprising me. Of frightening me with the unexpected, the unknown.

This time, I've come on my own determination.

This time, I've come prepared.

I open my eyes, coming face to face with the familiar sea of darkness.

"Enzo." I let his name pour out of my mouth in a whisper, knowing he'll hear me. Hoping he'll break his promise. Hoping he'll come for me. Hoping he's not already too far gone. That he'll remember. "Enzo, I need you."

When there's no answer, I try again. I have to try again. "Please. Come find me, Enzo. Come find me."

Within seconds, the fire builds behind me, his burning touch is on my waist, and my eyes widen. I let out a shaky breath. He's here. He came for me. His grip tightens around me, and I try to engrave the sensation into my brain as I let him pull me away. When we reach the brink, that fine line between his world and mine, I dig my feet into the ground, stopping him from going any farther. There's still nothing but endless darkness before me, but I know that behind me, where Enzo stands, is a different sight. The trees and the wind, the birds and the dirt.

We're walking the foggy line between life and death.

I spin around so I can see him, and my heart tightens in my chest, crushing me all over again. He looks down at me, gaze boring into mine, but the green has all but washed away. Black and grey clouds are fixed on me, his expression a stone wall. A stranger and yet not a stranger at all.

"Enzo," I whisper, reaching up and gently cupping his face with my hands. "My sweet, strong Enzo."

I slide my fingers over his jaw, until they're brushing back the hair on his forehead. A tremor runs through him beneath my touch, his eyes falling shut and his grip pulling me closer. My breathing picks up as my chest threatens to burst from within me.

He does remember. Maybe deep down, he'll always remember.

I lean forward, standing on my tiptoes and lifting my chin. "Kiss me."

His eyes are still closed when I softly press my lips to his. A shudder slides over him again, muscles rippling as he fights not to kiss me back. I close the small gap between us and wrap my arms around his neck, allowing the curves of my breasts to press against his hard chest, allowing the slight trembles of his body to shake my own. When I run the tip of my tongue over his lips, he breaks.

Strong arms pull me tight as his lips part for me, and he quickly takes over, a rough groan rumbling through him and making me moan in response. He tilts his head, his tongue sparring dangerously with mine, and he gives my lip a bite that tells me he's not pleased. But the way his fingers dig into my hips argue that, and soon his tongue is wandering to my neck and my head's falling back.

A small voice in the back of my mind orders me to stop. *This is not what you're here for,* she reminds me. *You're running out of time.*

I whimper at the thought, but I know what must be done.

My head snaps up, and I guide his lips back to mine. My eyes are wide as I watch him lose himself in devouring me, and a tear slowly slides down my cheek. Our tongues still tangled together, I latch onto the strong and steady sound of my heart's beat. The beat that belongs to him. Then I do it. I breathe. Straight into his mouth. I seal my lips to his, pouring my oxygen, my soul, the very life of me, into his lungs.

The way he once did for me.

His kiss softens, eyes drifting open. They're dazed and heavy, confusion taking over. I don't stop. I breathe and breathe, giving all of myself to him. I wonder if he feels it the way I did; a strong beat playing in his chest and a flutter running down his spine. Can he feel the life pouring through him?

As though in answer, something fierce flashes in his gaze, and he tears his lips away from mine, releasing me from his grip and stumbling back a step, toward the road that's blurred behind him. "What . . ." His breathing is hard, uneven as he takes a look around like he's seeing the world for the first time. "What did you do, Lou?" It's a growl, angry and confused all at once.

More tears spill as I realize it's working. It's really working. He'll finally have his life back. I try to smile, but I know it must look lost and strange.

Because that's how I feel as the darkness around me seeps into my skin in a whole new way. The ice is no longer ice, but prickling needles pounding into my skin, my soul, one after the other. I cough, the oxygen in my lungs evolving into something dry and scratchy, and this time it's me who takes a step back.

Closer to the darkness. Further from him.

"No." His hands are in his hair. His jaw is tight, body rigid, his eyes greener than I've ever seen them in my life. "No, no, no. Dammit, Lou! What the hell did you do!"

My voice is steady when I answer, no trace of regret because there is none to be found in my heart. "You saved me once, remember?" I whisper. "Now I've saved you."

His head is shaking. "You weren't meant to save me, Lou. You're meant to live your life. A full—" He stops, his face twisting for a second as his fingers come up to rub his chest. He tries again. "A full . . . a long—"

He cries out, dropping to his knees with a hand clutching his chest, and a pang of fear ripples through me.

"Enzo?" I rush forward, but the darkness only stretches before me. It's becoming a thick cloud of smoke, slowly inching up from the ground like it's building a wall between us. I try again, but I can't get through. The pull, the tug to the other world, it holds me back like firm hands planted on my shoulders.

Panic floods me, my mind spinning so fast it makes my

vision blur. I can't go to him. Can't help him. I'm officially a slave to the darkness, the growing haze before me the equivalent of steel bars, my prison. As I squint through the fog to find him heaving, the cold seed of fear in my stomach shoots through my nerves until my entire body is tight with it.

"Enzo!" *Talk to me.* I need to know what's happening. *I need you to be okay.* It isn't until he brings his gaze to mine, full of pain and anguish, that I see it.

The red.

So much red.

Seeping out from beneath the hand that squeezes his chest. Sliding over his fingers, clinging to his T-shirt. It's a gash. A hole. A wound. Just like the day of his car accident. The day he was on the brink of death.

Oh god. Enzo.

I did this to him. Singlehandedly.

And now, all I can do is watch him die.

Chapter Fifty-One

IT'S QUIET HERE. SO QUIET. Calm. Empty, like me. Like we're meant to be. I can hardly feel the fiery layer beneath my skin anymore. This is good. I'm not meant to feel.

Feel.

Feel.

What is it about that word, nagging at me. I slap it away with my mind, but it only swims back. *Feel something.* It's a small voice from deep within me, when all I want is silence.

Remember.

Remember.

I shake my head, blocking my ears with my hands. This isn't right. It isn't right. The sounds grate at me, scratching my brain relentlessly until I finally cave and let it in. And when I do, I stop hearing anything at all. Instead, I *see.* And all I see is red. No, no. Red doesn't belong here. Not in so much black. But it is here. So much red. It shakes. A tremble, a jolt. I come to realize there's more than just the red. There's the hand it oozes onto. The shirt it slowly soaks.

Something stirs in my gut, pulling against me. It's heavy and commanding and forces me to look deeper into my mind. So I do. What I find is a head of dark hair as a man stares down at the wound. He's on the ground, hunched over.

Should I know this person?

I concentrate harder, getting the image to look up, lift his head. Then I know. I know that face. Those eyes. The tick of that jaw.

The pain. Enzo. Enzo was in pain. He was in trouble. My hands drop from my ears, my head whipping side to side. Searching for a way out. It's all black, everywhere I turn. Up, down, left, right. Endless, eternal black.

No. I can't be here.

I need to go back.

I need to fight.

The numbness tries to soothe my heart, trick me into complacency, but I refuse. When it claws at my throat, I claw right back. When it snakes around my skin, I stand tall and think only of him. The man who makes me feel everything the numbness is against. I will not forget again. I cannot forget again. And so I do the only thing I can do. I command my legs to function.

And I run.

I run, then I yell. The sound roars deep from within my throat, tendons straining against my neck as I unleash the blistering rage and heartbreak boiling inside me. Determined to disrupt the delicate shell around me until it cracks. I don't know where it comes from, the wild urge to tear the silence to shreds. I pick it apart, daring it to shut me up. Screaming so hard my voice breaks.

"You can't have me!" There's no response, not even an echo. But the incredible fire coursing through me doesn't waver as I scream. As I cry. As I finally release the fury of pent up emotions banging against my chest. As I defy the very rules of this world. I'm overcome with a strength I've never known. "You will never have me," I whisper.

I will break all of its rules if I have to, because my strength is powered by the strongest combining forces of all. Love and fear.

I close my eyes, rejecting the darkness entirely. And I *remember*. I remember the shape of his lips. I remember the spark in his eyes when he looks at me. The dimple when he smiles. The deep symphony of his laugh. I remember how it feels, his lips on mine. I remember what it's like to breathe him in.

My knees buckle, and I hit the ground, letting out a yelp at the fresh scrape on my hand. What the hell? I look below me and see the dirt. Then I glance up and see the trees. The sky. Feel the air fill my lungs.

Tears sting my eyes. I made it. I'm here.

I shoot to my feet, steadying myself against a tree until I stop swaying. *Enzo*. I need to find him.

Chapter Fifty-Two

Four Days Later…

MY HANDS SHAKE, LEGS BOUNCING in my seat, teetering the steaming coffee I hold above my lap. Somehow, I'm still here. Somehow, I'm still alive. Somehow, my heart beats again.

Part of me wants to know why. How it's even possible. Learn the truth about what's happening to me, if only to ease the fear that consumes me every night before I fall asleep. The fear that reminds me I'm only part of a glitch. The fear that tells me I'm not supposed to be here, and I might not be when the sun rises.

But another, larger part takes comfort in not knowing. Maybe it's better this way. Maybe the answers to all my questions end in pain, death, or misery. Or somewhere in between. They say ignorance is bliss, and right now, I'm tempted to believe them.

I scan the waiting room, taking in the empty chairs. It's three in the morning, and I'm not allowed to be here. But this doctor happens to be the same as Mr. Blackwood's was, and she took pity on me. It's been four days since Enzo's surgery. Three days since he slipped into a coma. There's no way in hell I'm leaving this place until he wakes up.

And he has to wake up. He has to. Because we can't have

gone through all that we have just to wind up losing each other.

"Lou?" I jolt at the unexpected sound, almost knocking the coffee to the ground. Again. "Sorry, didn't mean to startle you."

I set the cup down and look up at the doctor, the faint lines around her eyes creased as she gazes down at me.

"You're still here," I murmur, my exhaustion making it extra challenging to speak in full sentences. "I mean, I thought you left hours ago."

She nods. "I did. Then I received an important call and decided to come see for myself."

A surge of hope bubbles up, but I quickly shove it back down. What if it's not what I think? What if it's worse? "Wh-what? What is it?"

A small smile lifts her lips, and that's it. That's all the answer I need. I'm out of my chair, breaking out in strange goosebumps as waves of anticipation stir in the pit of my stomach.

Her hand comes up around my arm. "Hold on, now. Yes, I'm very happy to inform you he's up. But there is something you should know."

I don't care. Enzo is here. With me. In my world. *Our* world. And now, he's awake. Whatever it is, we'll deal with it. We'll deal with it together. "Okay, but can I see him?"

Her lips purse. "You may, but—"

I'm already swinging around and taking a step toward his room when her grip stops me. "Lou, wait. Please. I need you to understand something before you go in there."

I turn back to her, taking in the serious lines of her expression. A frown pulls my lips down. "I'm listening."

She lets out a breath, then closes her eyes briefly before beginning. "A coma can really take its toll on a person, both mentally and physically. Combine that with severe trauma, and, well, it's a lot for someone to deal with. It can be difficult to adjust."

Yes, I'm aware. This is not groundbreaking stuff. "And?"

"And, in this case . . . in this case, dear, he may not remember much at all."

The way my stomach drops, I'm certain an anchor is in there, weighing it down. "You're talking about amnesia."

Another nod. "I am, yes. Now, we did try speaking to him and he was able to tell us some things. However . . ."

She continues talking, but I may as well be submerged in a tank of water. The sound of her voice drowns out in the distance, unclear and muddled as I shake my head. No. He remembers me. He has to. If he could hold onto me during all that time in the void, he can sure as hell hold onto me during a coma. Can't he? An uneasiness sits in my gut, forcing me to face the very real possibility that I will walk into that room, look him dead in the eye, and he'll have no idea who I am.

"Lou?"

Her voice comes back clearer as my mind gradually returns to the waiting room. "Sorry. Yes?"

"I asked if you think you're ready to see him now."

I wipe my hands on my jeans, suddenly not sure how to answer.

"Are you all right? We can always do this another time. There's no need to rush this sort of—"

"No, no. I'm ready." Of course I'm ready. I've been dreaming of this day for too long. The day we'd meet in this world with both our hearts beating. "Please. I-I'd like to see him now."

She hesitates, but turns and gestures for me to follow. I already know where his room is, of course, but I trail behind her anyway, stopping when she stops. She gives a light rap on the door, then pokes her head inside. I don't hear what she says, but the next thing I know, she's holding the door wide open and stepping aside, and I don't know how to breathe. Don't know how to move. How to think. How to feel.

"Lou, it's okay," she says gently. "You can go on in now."
I let out a quivering breath, and I nod.

It's time. It's finally time.

I don't even feel my legs move when I take the first step,
but then I'm in the room and the door clicks behind me.
And it's just me. And him.

I stay frozen in place by the door, my heart thumping
against my chest as I rake my eyes over his wounds, not yet
ready to meet his gaze. Not yet ready to discover the blank
stare as he fails to recognize me. The hospital blanket is
folded over, covering everything below his hips. His upper
half is bare, revealing the hard lines of his body I've memorized, the scars I've kissed, and a wide, white bandage
I've never seen that's wrapped around his chest. I watch it
rise and fall with his slow, measured breaths, and when the
steady beeps from the heart monitor make their way to
my ears, I squeeze my eyes shut and choke out a quiet sob.

He's really here. He's alive. Away from suffering, and able
to create a new life.

The knowledge ignites a gentle glow within my heart,
thawing the icy nerves and repairing them with the soothing balm of relief. I shake my head at myself, feeling the
pure joy and love warm my soul. I'm so happy for him it
hurts, the feeling expanding inside of me so thoroughly
I'm about to burst. The truth is, even if he doesn't remember me, even if he asks me to turn around and leave, I will
never regret any of it. Because he got his life back, and in
the process, he showed me what it means to love and be
loved in ways I never knew possible.

Finally, I open my mouth and suck in a lungful of air.
Then I pull back my tears, open my eyes, and place one
foot in front of the other. I keep my chin up as I reach the
bed, determined not to ruin this beautiful day for him.
Then I look him in the eye.

The first thing I take in is the sea of green. Not a hint
of grey, black, or any shades in between to muddle the

iris. Just the deepest hues of green I've ever laid eyes on, shadowed beneath thick, dark lashes, and for a moment, I can't look away. My gaze drops to his throat as he swallows, and I notice as the rise and fall of his chest becomes a little faster, a little harder. When his warm hand wraps around mine, I go still, breath catching and eyes closing as I realize what it means.

"Lou." Even as his voice breaks, strained, the sound is just as addictive as ever. Low and rough in all the right places, it glides over my skin like a warm glove.

"I–is this real?" I whisper, a fresh tear spilling over my sealed lashes.

"You tell me." He lifts my hand, slowly bringing it higher, and the soft brush of his lips against my skin sends a shiver straight to my toes. "Does this feel real?"

When he tugs me gently toward him, my eyes open and I'm suddenly in the bed right beside him. He grips my waist with one strong hand until my hips are rubbing against his, and another thick swallow passes through his throat at the contact. "How about this?"

My heart pounds so rapidly I'm certain it's going to break some sort of record. Then his fingers are curling around the nape of my neck, and he's slowly pulling my face closer to his. And closer, until our lips almost touch. When I exhale, he breathes it in. He's staring at my mouth, his eyes darkening with something hungry and tender all at once, and it sends my pulse into overdrive. "And this, Lou. Does this feel real?"

Finally, I whisper, "Yes," through another sob, and he closes his eyes tightly, a pained look crossing over his expression.

"Thank fucking god," he breathes, his breath ragged, "because I'm never walking away from you again."

I laugh out a strangled cry, unable to believe I'm actually hearing those words from him, and he closes the gap between us, crushing my lips with his. His mouth is demanding, exploring like he's tasting me for the very first time. Every movement of his tongue tangling with mine, every graze of teeth as he nips—he's claiming me in a way I've never experienced. Raw, hungry, and rippling with power, it shoots electric tingles down my back, snaking around my body and pooling between my thighs.

Lips still locked on mine, his fingers wrap around my own, holding them with the kind of tenderness that makes me squeeze my eyes tight. I'm scared that if I open them, I'll find it's all been a dream, and it will break me into a million pieces.

As if sensing my fear, his hands come up to cradle my face. He pulls me in closer, deepening the kiss, and as he does his movements slow into a lazy exploration of me. Every stroke of his tongue speaks straight to my soul. He tells me with his kiss that this is as real as our beating hearts, and I don't have to be afraid. He tells me to never let go, because now, we will never have to. That last thought echoes in my mind like the reflection of a thousand mirrors staring back at me.

I don't have to let go.

A fresh wave of desperation floods me, filling me with the urgent need to close any gap between us. I shift until I'm straddling him, careful to avoid touching his wound, and he groans into my mouth, his hands gripping my hair.

When I grind against him, he growls and places both hands on my hips, halting the movement completely. He's panting, trying to slow his breathing. "No."

I frown, my eyes dropping to the bulge beneath the thin blanket. "Why?" Clearly his mouth and his body need to get on the same page.

He chuckles softly as he notices where my gaze has strayed, the low sound vibrating through his chest and making my lips curve. *God, that laugh.* Still the best sound I've ever heard.

"Why?" His voice trails off, his hand stroking the side

of my face. "Because you're finally *mine*, Lou. And the first thing I'm going to do when I get out of here is show you exactly how it feels to be mine."

Epilogue

THERE ARE THINGS IN THIS world, and others, I may never come to understand. Unsolved mysteries of disappearing bodies, deaths without a cause, and being taken while a thread of life still survives within you. Then there are those things I wish I never came to understand quite so intimately. What it feels like to have the life sucked out of you, to know a darkness that whispers dangerous secrets in your ear, and to see innocent lives crushed at the hands of a little thing called a *glitch*.

I could choose to get lost in my endless questions, to devote myself to a quest for answers. But I've touched on that path before, reached the brink of obsession, and right now, I don't have plans to go back.

What I do have is my life. I have a heart that beats strong and steady every day and every night. I have choices. I have love. Friendship. Mistakes to make and lessons to learn. Sunlight on my back and a breeze in my hair. A fire running through my veins that reminds me who I am.

Right now, what I have, is the warm brush of a sigh against my neck. The soft graze of lips trailing kisses down my stomach. The feel of strong fingers gently digging into my hips. And the only whispers I'll ever want being poured into my ear.

When he pulls my hand up to his chest, allowing me to

feel the rapid thumping of his heart, he leans down, pressing his cheek to mine. "Do you feel what you do to me?"

My lips pull into the smile they never seem to stray far from these days, and I turn so my breath strokes his skin. "Are you saying your heart beats for me, Gumdrop?"

A shudder runs through his body, soaking in the question he's heard from me once before. His lashes tickle my cheek as he closes his eyes. "I'm saying that and more, Lou," he groans, before shifting his head and kissing my neck, deep and hard. "So much fucking more."

Acknowledgments

TO YOU, THE READER: SOMETIMES all we need is that one person willing to spend a little time in our minds, share a little piece of our hearts, and breathe a little life into our words. You single handedly have turned Lou's journey into something tangible, something colorful enough to dance in, and for every moment spent within these pages, you've made my heart that much fuller.

For that, I can't thank you enough.

To my husband, Michael: For every date-night you sacrificed so I could dedicate our rare kid-free evenings to writing another chapter. For each extra diaper you changed while I edited "just one more line." For every night you caught me writing at three in the morning while the kids were asleep, and you reminded me that moms need sleep, too . . . thank you. I'm so lucky to have you, and I love you.

To my three little munchkins: I know you're too young to understand this in its entirety right now, but you are my world, my life, my loves. Your smiles are my fuel. Your tiny arms wrapping around my waist is my caffeine. Your soft lips pressing against my cheek as you whisper silly secrets in my ear is the strongest force that keeps me going. As Lou and her love would say, my heart beats for you.

Endless thanks to my proofreaders, Grace Li and Katrina Teele Fair, as well as those who read my manuscript in its roughest forms and helped to make it shine. You were each so wonderful to work with, and I couldn't value your time or your feedback more.

Samantha Armstrong and Danielle Mathison—I never knew going into this that I'd find such amazing friends in the writing world. Not only are you both wonderful writers and inspirations to me in your craft alone, but your constant support, putting up with my millions of emails, and never failing to help me in a time of need is call for more thanks than I can ever give.

To my incredible and patient editor Sarah Collingwood, I'm beyond grateful I stumbled upon you so early in my writing journey. I'm sure you know you're stuck with me now. ;)

To my full-service team at The Killion Group, Inc., you guys are simply amazing to work with. The best. I'll never stop recommending your services.

Final note to readers: Please take a second to share your thoughts with a rating/review on Goodreads/Amazon! I make sure to read each review posted, and I'd love to see yours! Another way you could melt my heart and bring the biggest smile to my face is by sharing your thoughts/ pics of the book on your social media sites. <3

Thanks again, and happy reading. :)

T.L.

About the Author

T.L. Martin is an author of both young adult and new adult titles. The paranormal romance Touched by Death is her first published work for adults. She's presently branching out into new adult contemporary romance, and is loving every second of it!

Also a wife and stay-at-home mother to three young children, she spends her days tripping over Legos, pretending she can cook, and collecting food stains on her clothes. As glamorous a life it is, it's the wee hours of the night she dedicates to writing.

Connect with me!
Sign up for my newsletter to receive occasional updates
about new releases
Follow me on Instagram to see bookish posts, along
with pics of my cute kids ;)
Like my author page on Facebook
Or catch me on Twitter

Made in the USA
San Bernardino, CA
08 August 2017